Praise for
THE ROMAN MYSTERIES

'superb detective series set in ancient Rome, where four children from different backgrounds band together to solve mysteries and right wrongs . . . steeped in fantastically interesting and authentic historical detail.' *Daily Mail*

'instantly accessible adventure . . . which has trans-century appeal' *Guardian*

'The wonders of ancient Rome weren't quite so wonderful in my schooldays . . . but this is about to change all that . . . If they liked *Gladiator*, young readers will appreciate this too.'
Belfast Telegraph

To find out more about the Roman Mysteries, visit
www.romanmysteries.com

THE ROMAN MYSTERIES
by *Caroline Lawrence*

Also available

— A Roman Mystery —

THE ROMAN MYSTERIES OMNIBUS II

Caroline Lawrence

Orion
Children's Books

This omnibus edition first published in Great Britain in 2008
by Orion Children's Books
a division of the Orion Publishing Group Ltd
Orion House
5 Upper St Martin's Lane
London WC2H 9EA
An Hachette Livre UK Company

3 5 7 9 10 8 6 4

Originally published as three separate volumes:
The Assassins of Rome
First published in Great Britain in 2002 by Orion Children's Books
The Dolphins of Laurentum
First published in Great Britain in 2003 by Orion Children's Books
The Twelve Tasks of Flavia Gemina
First published in Great Britain in 2003 by Orion Children's Books

Text copyright © Caroline Lawrence 2002, 2003
Maps and plans by Richard Russell Lawrence
© Orion Children's Books 2002 and 2003

The right of Caroline Lawrence to be identified as the
author of this work has been asserted.

All rights reserved. No part of this publication may be
reproduced, stored in a retrieval system, or transmitted,
in any form or by any means, electronic, mechanical,
photocopying, recording or otherwise, without the prior
permission of Orion Children's Books.

The Orion Publishing Group's policy is to use papers that
are natural, renewable and recyclable products and made
from wood grown in sustainable forests. The logging and
manufacturing processes are expected to conform to the
environmental regulations of the country of origin.

A catalogue record for this book is
available from the British Library

ISBN 978 1 84255 674 0

Typeset at The Spartan Press Ltd,
Lymington, Hants

Printed and bound in Great Britain by
Clays Ltd, St Ives plc

www.orionbooks.co.uk

CONTENTS

These stories take place in Ancient Roman times, so a few of the words may look strange. If you don't know them, 'Aristo's Scroll' at the back of the book will tell you what they mean and how to pronounce them.

The Dolphins of Laurentum contains descriptions of 'free diving', a very dangerous activity which involves holding your breath underwater for as long as possible. Don't try this at home.

THE ASSASSINS OF ROME

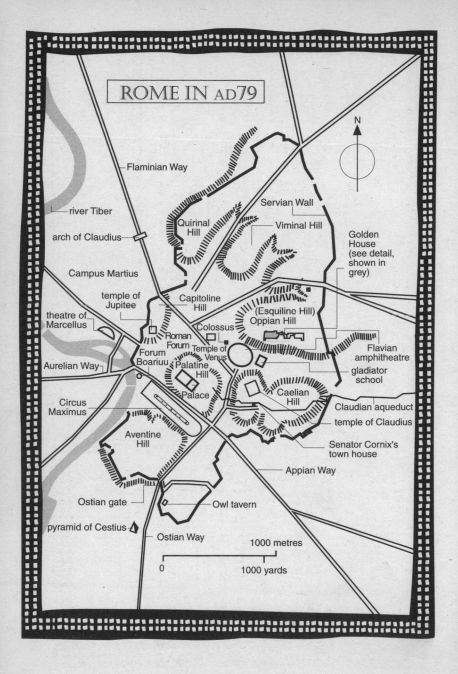

ROME IN AD79

- Flaminian Way
- river Tiber
- arch of Claudius
- Campus Martius
- temple of Jupitee
- theatre of Marcellus
- Aurelian Way
- Circus Maximus

Quirinal Hill

Capitoline Hill

Servian Wall

Viminal Hill

Golden House (see detail, shown in grey)

(Esquiline Hill) Oppian Hill

Colossus

Roman Forum

Temple of Venus

Forum Boariuu

Palatine Hill

Palace

Caelian Hill

Flavian amphitheatre

gladiator school

Claudian aqueduct

temple of Claudius

Senator Cornix's town house

Aventine Hill

Appian Way

- Ostian gate
- Owl tavern
- pyramid of Cestius
- Ostian Way

N

1000 metres

0

1000 yards

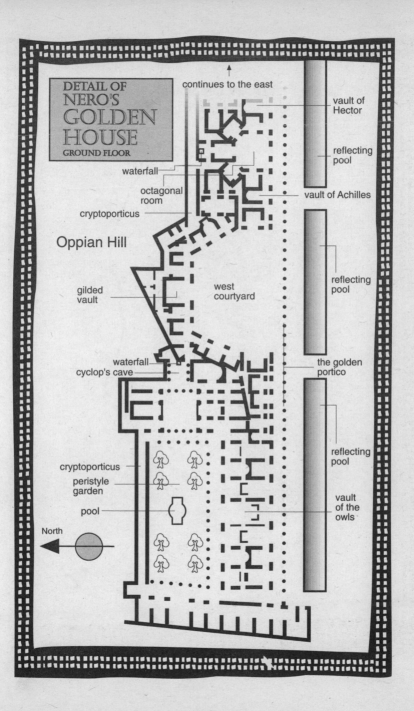

DETAIL OF
NERO'S
GOLDEN
HOUSE
GROUND FLOOR

continues to the east

vault of
Hector

reflecting
pool

waterfall

octagonal
room

vault of Achilles

cryptoporticus

Oppian Hill

gilded
vault

west
courtyard

reflecting
pool

waterfall

cyclop's cave

the golden
portico

cryptoporticus

peristyle
garden

reflecting
pool

pool

vault
of the
owls

North

To my son Simon,
the realist

SCROLL I

One hot morning in the Roman port of Ostia, two days after the Ides of September, a dark-eyed boy stared gloomily at four presents.

The boy and his three friends sat on cushions around a low octagonal table in a small triclinium. It was a pleasant room, with cinnabar red walls, a black and white mosaic floor and a view through columns into a green inner garden. A faint sea breeze rustled the leaves of the fig tree and they could hear the fountain splashing.

'I'm telling you,' said the boy. 'Something bad always happens on my birthday.'

'Jonathan,' sighed his friend Flavia Gemina. 'In the past month you've survived a volcanic eruption, a coma and capture by pirates. But now you're safe at home and it's a beautiful day. What could possibly happen? Don't be such a pessimist.'

'What is sessimisp?' asked a dark-skinned girl in a yellow tunic, taking a sip of pomegranate juice. Nubia was Flavia's former slave-girl. She had only been in Italia for a few months. Although Nubia was a quick learner, she was not yet fluent in Latin.

Flavia drank some of her own pomegranate juice. Then she held out the ceramic cup.

'Nubia,' she said. 'Would you say this cup was half empty or half full?'

Nubia studied the ruby red liquid and said, 'Half full.'

'Then you're an optimist. An optimist always looks on the bright side of things. What do *you* think, Jonathan? Is it half full or half empty?'

Jonathan glanced into Flavia's cup. 'Half empty. And it's not even very good pomegranate juice. It's too sour.'

Flavia grinned at Nubia. 'See? Jonathan's a pessimist. Someone who always expects the worst.'

'I'm not a pessimist,' said Jonathan. 'I'm a realist.'

Flavia laughed and handed the cup to the youngest of them, a boy in a sea-green tunic the same colour as his eyes.

'How about you, Lupus?' she asked. 'Would you say the cup is half full or half empty?'

'He can't say anything,' said Jonathan. 'He's got no tongue.'

'Shhh!' said Flavia. 'Well, Lupus? Half full or half empty?'

Lupus tipped the contents of the cup down his throat.

'Hey!' Flavia protested. But they all laughed when Lupus wrote on his wax tablet:

COMPLETELY EMPTY

Lupus grinned but did not look up. He was writing something else on his tablet, using a brass stylus to push back the yellow beeswax and expose the wood beneath. He showed it to Jonathan:

OPEN PRESENTS!

'All right, all right,' said Jonathan. 'I'll open yours first.'

He picked up a grubby linen handkerchief tied with an old piece of twine and weighed it in his hand. 'It's heavy. And knobbly. And . . .' Jonathan tipped the contents onto the octagonal table. '. . . it's rocks. You gave me rocks for my birthday.'

'They're not just *any* rocks,' said Flavia. 'Lupus searched a long time for those.'

Lupus nodded vigorously.

'They are smooth and round and perfect for your sling,' explained Nubia. She held one up. 'See? Now open my present.' She placed a twist of papyrus into Jonathan's hands.

Jonathan undid the papyrus and pulled out a leather strap. 'A dog collar?' he said with a frown. 'So you can take me for a walk without worrying that I might run off?'

'My present is for you *and* for Tigris,' said Nubia. 'Maybe more for Tigris.'

'Thanks, Nubia.' Jonathan gave her a wry smile and showed the collar to his puppy Tigris, who was gnawing a lamb bone beneath the table. 'And thank you, too,

Lupus. Rocks *and* a dog collar. This morning I got an abacus from Miriam and a new cloak from father. Useful presents all round.' He sighed.

'Well, I know you'll like *my* present,' said Flavia, handing Jonathan a blue linen bag. 'It's not useful at all.'

'Hmmn. A present from Flavia. I wonder what it could be? It's the same size and shape as a scroll. And surprise, surprise – it *is* a scroll. *The Love Poetry of Sextus Propertius*?' Jonathan raised an eyebrow at Flavia. 'Isn't that the scroll you told me *you* wanted?'

'Was it?' Flavia grinned sheepishly. 'No, but I think you'll really like it, Jonathan. There's a wonderful poem about a beautiful girl with yellow hair just like you-know-who.'

Jonathan made a sour face, put down the scroll and examined the blue bag it had been wrapped in.

'I do like this bag though,' he said, in a more cheerful tone of voice. 'I could use it to keep my nice sling stones in.'

'Oh, you can't have that,' said Flavia, unrolling Jonathan's new scroll. 'It's pater's. I just needed something to wrap it in.'

Jonathan sighed again. 'Who's this one from?' He reached for the last present, a small pouch of yellow silk.

Flavia looked up. 'That's from you-know-who,' she said. 'From Pulchra. And from Felix. Pulchra asked me when your birthday was, and they gave it to me before we left.'

'Now this . . .' said Jonathan. 'This is a nice present.'

In his hand he held a small jar with black glazed figures on apricot-coloured clay.

'Pulchra told me the vase is from Corinth,' said Flavia. 'It's called an alabastron. It's very old and fabulously expensive.'

'Everything in Pulchra's house is fabulously expensive,' said Jonathan dryly. But he looked pleased and showed it to the others.

'Look, Nubia,' said Flavia. 'It's a scene from the poem we were studying in lessons this morning. Odysseus and three of his companions. They're putting out the eye of the Cyclops with a sharpened stick.'

'Great Neptune's beard!' exclaimed Nubia. 'Why are they doing that?'

'Because he's a huge, ugly old giant who's planning to eat them,' said Jonathan as he started to pick the yellow wax away from the cork stopper.

Flavia nodded. 'Remember how Aristo told us it took Odysseus ten years to return from Troy? Polyphemus the Cyclops was one of the monsters Odysseus faced on his journey home.'

'I remember,' said Nubia. 'Odysseus is the hero whose wife is always weaving and unweaving.'

'That's right,' said Flavia. 'Everyone thought Odysseus was dead and all the men wanted to marry Queen Penelope so they could become king. But she was a faithful wife and never gave up hope. She said she would marry one of her suitors as soon as she finished

5

weaving a carpet. But every night she lit torches and undid what she had woven by day. She was sure that Odysseus would return.'

'Happy birthday, little brother!' Jonathan's beautiful sister Miriam came into the dining room and set a platter on the low table. 'I've baked your favourite sesame seed and honeycakes. But you can only have a few. Otherwise you'll spoil your appetite for later.'

'Thanks,' said Jonathan. He popped a cake into his mouth and offered the plate to the others.

'Miriam,' said Flavia, taking a bite of her sesame cake, 'is it true that something bad always happens on Jonathan's birthday?'

Miriam looked thoughtful. 'Now that you mention it . . . See this scar on my arm?' She pushed back the sleeve of her lavender tunic to show them a barely visible mark just above her left elbow. 'That's where Jonathan shot me with an arrow on his eighth birthday.'

'That was an accident,' said Jonathan with his mouth full. 'But remember how I fell out of the tree at our old house last year and was knocked unconscious and father made me stay in bed all afternoon?'

Miriam nodded. 'And on your birthday the year before, you ran outside to try out your new sling and stepped right on a bee.'

'It wasn't a bee.' Jonathan reached for a third honeycake. 'It was a wasp.'

Miriam gently slapped his hand and picked up the

platter. 'Jonathan's foot swelled up like a melon and he couldn't walk for three days,' she said over her shoulder as she took the cakes out of the room.

'Yes.' Jonathan sucked the honey from his fingers and reached for the alabastron again. 'Something bad always happens on my birthday. And it's usually my own . . . Oops!'

Suddenly the room was filled with a heady fragrance. The little jar lay in pieces on the black and white mosaic floor. Tigris sniffed at the pool of spreading oil.

'Oh, Jonathan,' said Nubia. 'You dropped the bottle of Pulchra.'

'And it was filled with scented oil,' said Flavia. 'Wonderful scented oil.'

Jonathan was silent. He stared miserably at the broken jar and the golden oil seeping into the spaces between the small black and white chips of marble.

'Quickly!' cried Flavia. 'Mop it up. Save it.' She pulled Jonathan's linen handkerchief from his belt and pressed it to the glistening oil. Then she used her own. Nubia did likewise. Lupus looked round and grabbed the handkerchief he'd wrapped the stones in. As he got down on his hands and knees to wipe up the last of the oil, Tigris licked his face.

'What *is* that scent?' Flavia closed her eyes and inhaled deeply. 'It's not balsam or myrrh or frankincense.'

'I know I've smelled it before,' said Jonathan. 'It makes me feel so sad.'

'How can it make you feel sad?' Flavia said. 'It's a wonderful scent. It makes me feel . . . excited.'

'It makes me feel freedom,' said Nubia solemnly.

Lupus took his wax tablet and wrote:

LEMON BLOSSOM

'Of course,' said Jonathan. 'It's the perfume they make from their citron tree at the Villa Limona.'

For a moment they were silent, as they recalled the beautiful villa on the Cape of Surrentum and the events of the previous month. Despite their encounters with pirates and slave-dealers, each one of them had special memories of the Villa Limona, its owner Pollius Felix, and his beautiful daughter Pulchra.

'Maybe we'll return there one day,' said Jonathan, staring out between the red and white columns of the peristyle into the leafy inner garden. The others nodded.

'Felix was so generous,' sighed Flavia. 'He gave me that Athenian drinking cup, and he gave you the bottle with scented oil and he gave Nubia a new flute.' She tipped her head to one side. 'Lupus, did Felix ever give you anything? He liked you best.'

Lupus patted out a beat in the air with the flattened palms of his hands.

'That's right,' said Flavia. 'He gave you a drum.'

Lupus stopped air-drumming and reached for his wax tablet. He smoothed over his previous words with the flat end of his stylus, then wrote a new message:

'For you? He's looking for something else to give you?' asked Flavia.

Lupus nodded.

'What?' asked Jonathan.

Lupus shrugged and looked down.

'Well,' said Flavia, pushing a strand of light brown hair behind her ear, 'Whatever it is he's looking for, I'm sure he'll find it. Felix is even more powerful than the Emperor.'

'I wouldn't repeat that statement,' came a voice from outside the dining room. 'Emperors have been known to kill people for saying such things!'

SCROLL II

'Doctor Mordecai!' cried Flavia.

Jonathan's father stood in the doorway of the triclinium. Dressed in a loose blue kaftan with a black sash and turban, he blocked some of the light from the garden.

'Peace be with you, Flavia and Nubia.' Mordecai bowed to the girls and as he stepped into the room it grew brighter again. 'It is not wise even to hint that someone might be as powerful as the Emperor,' he said gravely. 'Less than a year ago Titus killed a man who suggested he should not be Emperor. And I'm sure you would not want any harm to come to Publius Pollius Felix. He proved to be a most valuable friend – dear Lord.' Mordecai sat heavily beside the girls. 'That smell.'

'It's lemon blossom,' said Jonathan in a small voice. 'I broke a perfume bottle.'

'I have not smelled that scent in nearly ten years.'

'Where do you know the smell from?' Jonathan looked at his father.

Mordecai was silent for a moment. Flavia could see

where his beard had been singed by a hot wind from the eruption of Vesuvius.

'In Jerusalem,' said Mordecai at last, 'in the courtyard of your grandparents' house. A beautiful lemon tree grew there. Your mother loved that tree. The only scent she ever wore was lemon blossom.'

'Oh, Jonathan,' said Flavia. 'That's why the scent makes you sad. It makes you think of your mother.' She tried to swallow the lump in her throat.

'But I was only a baby when we were separated,' Jonathan said. 'How could I remember her perfume?'

'The sense of smell is the first and most primitive of all our senses,' said Mordecai. 'I doubt if you remember your mother's face, and yet you remember her scent. As do I,' he added quietly.

Flavia's eyes filled with tears. She couldn't remember her mother's face either. She had been three years old when her mother died giving birth to twin baby boys. Thinking about her mother reminded Flavia of her father, the sea captain Marcus Flavius Geminus. He had left on a voyage before the volcano erupted and there had been no news of him since. Flavia told herself he was fine and would soon be home, but a hot tear rolled down her cheek and she had to bite her lower lip to stop it trembling.

There was a sniff to her left and Flavia saw that Nubia's cheeks were also wet. Nubia's father had been killed by slave traders and the rest of her family led off in chains.

Lupus's eyes were dry, but red-rimmed. He seemed to stare through the garden and into the past.

'I never realised it before,' said Flavia. 'But we all have something in common: none of us have mothers.'

'That's right,' murmured Jonathan and glanced up at Mordecai. 'Father?'

'Yes, Jonathan?'

'Why did mother die?'

'I've told you before. She was killed during the siege of Jerusalem nine years ago.'

'I know *how* my mother died. But I want to know *why* she died. Why did she stay behind in Jerusalem when we got away? Why didn't she escape with us?'

Mordecai lowered his eyes. 'Your mother's father was a priest. He said it would be unseemly for his daughter to flee the city. She chose to obey her father rather than me.'

'But didn't she mind that you took Miriam and me with you? Didn't she love us?'

His father was silent.

'Father?'

Mordecai lifted his head but he did not meet Jonathan's gaze. 'Of course she loved you,' he said briskly. 'She loved you very much. But I insisted on taking you and Miriam with me. At least she obeyed me in that.'

Flavia looked sharply at Mordecai. She sensed he wasn't telling them everything. And she could see Jonathan was dissatisfied with his answer, too.

Suddenly Tigris barked and scampered out of the

dining room. The next instant Flavia heard pounding at the front door, followed by Miriam's voice, sounding worried. A moment later Miriam appeared in the doorway, her face even paler than usual.

'Soldiers,' she whispered, her violet eyes huge with alarm. 'Two soldiers and a magistrate are here to see you, father!'

Three men stood in the atrium of Jonathan's house: two burly soldiers and a short man in a white toga. Tigris had planted himself at their feet and was barking steadily up at them. Next door, in Flavia's house, Ferox, Scuto and Nipur had begun to bark in sympathy. Soon all the dogs in Ostia would be at it.

'Tigris! Be quiet!' Jonathan picked up his puppy and scratched him behind his ear. 'Good dog.'

'Peace be with you.' Mordecai gave the men a small bow. 'Every stranger is an uninvited guest. May I help you?'

'Doctor ben Ezra,' said the man in the toga. He was young, with thinning hair and light brown eyes. 'We meet again.'

'Bato!' cried Flavia. 'You're Marcus Artorius Bato, the magistrate. Remember me? You helped us catch a thief a few months ago.'

'Of course I remember. You're Flavia Gemina.' A half smile passed across his face and then he frowned at their tear-stained cheeks and red eyes. 'Has someone died?' he asked.

Jonathan nodded. 'Our mothers,' he said.

Bato's frown deepened as he studied their four very different faces. Then he gave his head a little shake, as if to clear his mind.

'Doctor,' he said, turning his pale eyes back to Mordecai. 'We have reason to believe that a dangerous criminal may be on his way here. Do you know a man called Simeon?'

'Simeon?' said Mordecai.

'Simeon ben Jonah.' Bato consulted his wax tablet. 'A ship from Greece docked this morning and the suspect was seen disembarking. Our informant recognised this man Simeon and followed him long enough to hear him ask where the Jewish doctor lived. As far as I know, you are the only Jewish doctor here in Ostia.'

Jonathan glanced at his father as Bato continued, 'Apparently this Simeon is extremely dangerous. We believe he's an assassin. Do you have any enemies, doctor? Anyone who would hire someone to kill you?'

'No. That is, I don't think so . . .' Mordecai's face was pale.

'Well, I suggest you bolt your door. And don't go out without a bodyguard. We have men out looking for him but if you like, I can assign a pair of soldiers to guard your house.'

'Er . . . no. No, thank you. That won't be necessary,' said Jonathan's father. 'We will be careful.'

'Another mystery,' exclaimed Flavia. 'How exciting!'

'It's not a game.' Bato frowned at her. 'This assassin is dangerous.'

'What is sassassin?' whispered Nubia.

'Someone hired to kill people,' replied Flavia under her breath.

'What does he look like?' asked Jonathan.

Bato flipped open his wax tablet again. 'Our informant says Simeon is about thirty years old. Tall, slim, and dark. Has a beard and long frizzy hair. Exceptionally long hair, which may be hidden by a turban.' He turned back to Mordecai. 'I'm sorry. My notes are brief. Obviously, if you see anyone of that description lurking about—'

'We will inform you at once,' said Mordecai.

'Has he killed many people?' said Flavia quickly, as the magistrate turned to go.

'Yes he has. According to my notes.' Bato hesitated. 'In fact, his name is on a list of known assassins whom we have orders to arrest on sight.'

The four friends glanced at each other in alarm.

'We'll be careful,' said Mordecai and held the door open for Bato and his soldiers.

As soon as they left, Jonathan turned to his friends. 'Wonderful,' he said. 'A deadly assassin on his way to murder us. No, nothing bad ever happens on my birthday!'

SCROLL III

'Nubia, how many days has pater been gone?' said Flavia.

The two girls had been to the baths and were resting in their garden until it was time to go next door to Jonathan's birthday dinner party.

Nubia was lying on her stomach underneath a bubbling fountain. 'We are sailing in the boat of your father to the farm of your uncle,' she said. 'Then two days after, we are carting to Pompeii to see your father sail away again. The night before, there is no moon.'

'That's right,' Flavia murmured. She was sitting on the marble bench in the shade of the fig tree, making marks on a wax tablet. 'Pater sailed from the harbour of Pompeii on the day of the new moon. And tonight's the new moon again.'

Nubia turned back to look at the dust at the base of the fountain's marble column. She was watching some black ants struggle to push a grain of barley up a small anthill. Nearby, under the jasmine bush, Ferox, Scuto and Nipur panted like three sphinxes in a row: one big, one medium and one little.

'That means pater's been gone exactly a month,' sighed Flavia, putting the tablet down on the shade-dappled bench. 'It seems like so much longer.'

'Many things happen,' said Nubia, keeping her eyes on the ants.

'I know,' said Flavia. 'The volcano, Jonathan almost dying, Miriam falling in love, the pirates . . . That's why I'm going to keep a journal. I don't want to forget anything that's happened. Maybe I'll ask Lupus to illustrate it.'

Nipur gave a gentle whining yawn and thumped his tail; he was getting bored. But Nubia was fascinated by the four ants who were still trying to manoeuvre the barley grain into their anthill. As the barley rolled away for the third time, Nubia decided to help.

Carefully, with the tip of her forefinger, she nudged the barley up the mound and left it poised at the very opening. Presently the ants found it and waved their feelers with excitement. Then they tipped the grain of barley into the cool depths of their ant-home and disappeared after it.

Nubia smiled and rolled over onto her back. Now the ants would have their banquet and sing tiny ant songs, never dreaming that a huge creature loomed above them and took an interest in their fate.

She sighed. The splashing of the fountain and the rhythmic buzz of the cicadas in the umbrella pines was making her drowsy. She closed her eyes.

Abruptly, she opened them again. Next door, Tigris was barking his alarm bark.

Jonathan walked downstairs very slowly, one step at a time. When they had moved to Green Fountain Street a few months earlier, one of the items he remembered unpacking was his mother's yellow jewellery box. His father had forbidden him to look inside.

As Jonathan reached the bottom of the stairs, he caught a whiff of the lemon perfume which still lingered in the triclinium. He paused for a moment, to make sure he hadn't been noticed. Tigris wasn't barking any more: Lupus was playing with him in their bedroom. His father was in the study with the gauzy curtain drawn, which meant he was studying Torah. Miriam was the one to worry about. He had to pass the kitchen, where she was preparing his birthday dinner.

Jonathan slipped off his sandals and left them at the bottom of the wooden stairs. He wished he could be more like Flavia: she never felt guilty when she disobeyed her father.

Jonathan took a deep breath and walked. Thankfully, Miriam had her back to him; she was kneading dough and singing in Hebrew.

With a sigh of relief, Jonathan slipped into the storeroom, leaving the door open just enough to admit a beam of dusty light.

Cautiously, he picked his way between the half-buried amphoras of wine, dried fruit and grain. In the dimmest corner of the storeroom were some wooden shelves. His mother's jewellery box was on one of these, up high. But he was tall enough to reach it.

The box was wooden, with a vaulted top and a flat bottom, painted in a glaze of clear yellow resin and decorated with red and blue dots in neat rows. Jonathan examined it for a moment in the bar of light from the doorway. At last he found the catch. What he had taken for the bottom was actually the lid. It slid open smoothly to reveal some jewellery and a small papyrus scroll tied with a yellow cord.

Jonathan's heart was pounding. He shouldn't be doing this, but he had to know why his mother hadn't escaped with them. He had a nagging suspicion that it had been his fault. That was why his father had never told him the real reason she stayed in Jerusalem.

Jonathan examined the jewellery first: a silver necklace with pendants of green jasper, some plain silver thumb bands, and what might have been a nose ring. There was also a signet ring.

The stone was sardonyx, the same colour and transparency as a nugget of dried apricot. It had a dove carved into it. Jonathan tried the ring for size and managed to squeeze it on the little finger of his left hand.

Still wearing the ring, he picked up the small scroll. It wasn't a continuous strip, but several sheets of papyrus rolled together. He was able to slip out the innermost sheet without undoing the knot in the cord.

The sheets were yellow with age. They must be at least ten years old. Maybe fifteen.

'How much more pleasing is your love to me than wine,' Jonathan read in Hebrew, 'and the fragrance of your perfume than any spice. With one glance of your eyes, Susannah, you have stolen my heart.'

The scraps weren't signed but Jonathan knew they must be love letters from his father to his mother. The handwriting looked like his father's, but it was stronger, bolder, more vigorous.

Jonathan felt his face grow hot. It was hard to imagine his father as a bold young man in love. Jonathan scanned the other sheets, but they were also love letters. Nothing there. Nothing to indicate why his mother hadn't come with them when they left Jerusalem. What had he expected to find? He tried to swallow, but disappointment filled his throat.

Carefully, he rolled up the sheets of papyrus and slipped them back into the knotted cord. Then he frowned, and sniffed the roll. Lemon. Faint but unmistakable.

'Mother,' he whispered. 'Why didn't you come with us? What did I do wrong?'

He was about to put the jewellery box back on the shelf when he remembered the ring on his little finger. He tried to pull it off, but in vain. The day was very hot and his hand was sticky. Never mind. He would hold his finger under the fountain for a few moments and put a drop of olive oil on it to help it slide off.

As Jonathan crept out of the storeroom and eased the door shut behind him he frowned. Why were men's voices coming from the study? Surely his father was alone?

He took a step closer. Now he could see his father's turbaned head through a gap in the gauzy curtain. Mordecai was sitting on the striped divan beneath the scroll shelves. His head was in his hands.

'Of course she's dead,' Jonathan heard his father say in Hebrew. 'And it's my fault. As her husband, I should have insisted she come with us.'

'No, no,' came a deep voice, as low as a lion's purr. 'She'd made up her mind to stay. Because of Jonathan. It wasn't your fault.'

Jonathan's heart pounded. 'Because of Jonathan.' He'd been right. It *was* his fault. But who was the man? Jonathan took another cautious step. As he moved forward, the man sitting next to his father came into view. In the garden a bee buzzed among the lavender and he could hear Miriam singing softly in the kitchen.

The man sitting next to his father had a dark beard and frizzy hair so long it fell over his shoulders.

Jonathan's blood went cold.

Simeon.

It could only be Simeon the assassin.

Jonathan opened his mouth and yelled.

SCROLL IV

'Help! Assassin!' Jonathan yanked aside the study curtain. The man leapt to his feet but before he could run away or pull out a weapon Jonathan head-butted him in the stomach.

'Ooof!' The tall man collapsed on the floor.

'Quick, father!' Jonathan looked around for something heavy. 'Hit him while he's confused!'

'It's all right, Jonathan!' Mordecai cried in Hebrew. 'He won't hurt us.'

The long-haired man lay gasping on the floor.

'Simeon! Are you all right?' Mordecai's prayer shawl slipped to the floor as he bent to help the man to his feet. The man groaned and lifted his big head. Jonathan found himself looking into a pair of amused blue eyes.

At that moment there was the sound of running feet and barking puppy. Lupus and Tigris raced into the study. Lupus was brandishing Mordecai's curved sword.

'Stop!' cried Mordecai in Latin. 'It's Jonathan's uncle!'

Lupus skidded to a halt.

Tigris, however, did not understand Latin. All he knew was that his master was in danger and there was only one possible threat. With a fierce growl, Jonathan's puppy leapt forward and sank his sharp teeth into the stranger's ankle.

'Simeon is your uncle?' Flavia stared at Jonathan as he dried his hands on a linen towel. Jonathan nodded. It was early evening and they had all gathered for his birthday dinner party.

'Why didn't you tell us?' asked Flavia.

'We didn't know ourselves,' said Miriam, pouring a stream of water over Nubia's hands. 'He arrived this morning while we were having lessons at your house. Apparently Simeon was upstairs asleep in father's room when the soldiers arrived. I didn't recognise the name Simeon; I always called him Uncle Simi.'

'And I was just a toddler, too young to remember him at all,' said Jonathan.

'Then your father lied to Bato?'

'He had a good reason. Uncle Simi is on an important mission. No one must know.'

Flavia's eyes opened wide. She lowered her voice: 'But Bato said Simeon was—'

'—an assassin?' A tall man with long dark hair followed Mordecai into the dining room. He had intense blue eyes above his dark beard.

Flavia swallowed and nodded.

'Flavia,' said Jonathan, 'this is my uncle Simeon. Simeon, these are my friends Flavia and Nubia.'

Simeon nodded at the girls and sat cross-legged beside Jonathan on an embroidered cushion. Instead of reclining on couches, Jonathan's family preferred to sit on the floor.

'Are you sassassin?' asked Nubia, her amber eyes wide.

'I am . . . a messenger,' said Simeon. 'With important information for the Emperor Titus.' Simeon leaned forward to hold his hands over the copper bowl while Miriam poured water on them.

'But you're Jewish like us,' said Jonathan. 'Don't you hate Titus for destroying Jerusalem? Because father said, I mean . . . Is it true you were in Jerusalem when Titus destroyed it?'

'Yes,' said Simeon quietly. 'I was there.'

'Will you tell us what happened?' asked Flavia.

'I was nineteen years old when Titus sacked Jerusalem,' began Simeon. The candles had been lit and Mordecai had pronounced the blessing. Now Miriam was passing round the first course – a tray of hard-boiled eggs – while Lupus filled the cups with well-watered wine.

Nubia frowned. 'How did Titus sack Jerusalem?'

'I think you mean "why",' said Mordecai. 'Jerusalem and Rome have long been enemies, mainly for religious reasons.'

'But how?' persisted Nubia. 'Titus is not a very big man.' Nubia had seen the Emperor a few weeks earlier at the refugee camp south of Stabia.

'He had four legions with him.' Simeon dipped his egg in the mixture of salt and chopped coriander, then sniffed it reverently before biting into it. 'Legions,' he repeated at Nubia's blank look. 'Five and a half thousand soldiers per legion plus as many auxiliaries. That makes nearly fifty thousand men.'

'Oh,' said Nubia, and nodded solemnly. 'But what did he do with the sack?'

Simeon almost smiled. 'To sack a city means to kill the defenders, carry off valuable objects and enslave the people who live there.'

'Oh,' said Nubia again. 'You must were afraid.'

'It was unspeakably awful. There was a famine. No food,' he explained quietly, lowering his eyes. He had thick eyelashes, and despite his long face there was something appealing about him. He reminded Nubia of a sad puppy and she had the sudden urge to pat him on the head.

Simeon continued: 'There should have been food enough to feed everyone for ten years, but some of our own people destroyed the grain stores. They thought it would force us to come out of the city and fight the Romans. But it didn't work. Within a few months the food was gone. Soon we began to eat horses, mules and dogs. Finally we resorted to sandals, belts, even rats.'

Nubia shuddered and Flavia put down her half-eaten egg.

'When Titus's legions finally broke through the walls and took the city, it was almost a mercy,' said Simeon. 'His soldiers killed the weak and the old and they enslaved the rest of us. Some were thrown to animals in the arenas. Others were taken to Rome for Titus's triumphal procession; to be paraded and then executed. I was one of those sent to Corinth to join thousands of other Jewish slaves working on Nero's isthmus.'

'What is ithamus?' asked Nubia.

'An isthmus is a deep ditch joining two seas so that ships can sail through. It cuts months off their journey time.'

'Pater sails through the Isthmus of Corinth all the time,' said Flavia to Nubia, and turned to Simeon: 'Our tutor Aristo comes from Corinth. Do you know him?'

'I doubt it,' said Simeon. 'We Jews have our own camp outside Corinth. Though it's more like a town now. We've been there many years.'

Miriam rose to her feet. 'I must get the stew before it gets cold,' she said. 'Lupus, can you bring the bread?'

Lupus nodded. He and Tigris followed Miriam out of the dining room. They were back a moment later: Miriam with a big ceramic bowl, Lupus holding a fat round loaf.

'It's venison, lentil and apricot stew,' said Miriam, setting the bowl on the low octagonal table. 'With cumin and honey. It's Jonathan's favourite. Get down,

Tigris! Or Jonathan will have to shut you in the storeroom.'

They tore pieces of bread from the loaf and used them to scoop up the sweet stew straight from the bowl.

'Wonderful!' Simeon closed his eyes. 'Ever since those terrible days of hunger in Jerusalem, I never take even a dry crust of bread for granted. But this! This is sublime.'

'It is delicious, Miriam,' said Flavia, and everyone else nodded.

Nubia noticed that Jonathan had hardly touched his food. 'Uncle Simeon,' he said slowly, with a glance at his father. 'Why did you stay in Jerusalem? Why didn't you escape when we did?'

'I was a Zealot, a freedom-fighter,' said Simeon. 'I was young and wanted to fight Romans. We called those who left cowards, but I wish now . . . You were right, Mordecai. In the terrible days that followed I often cursed myself for not listening to you.'

Mordecai nodded sadly.

Jonathan gave Tigris a piece of gravy-soaked bread. 'Simeon,' he said. 'Was my mother with you in Jerusalem?'

'Yes, of course,' said Simeon. 'Susannah was my younger sister.'

'What happened to her? After Titus sacked Jerusalem.'

'I don't know. I was telling your father earlier that

they separated the men and women. There was terrible confusion. It was the last time I saw her alive.'

'Do you know why she stayed? Did she ever tell you why she didn't—'

'Jonathan.' Mordecai's expression was grim. 'Please don't pursue this subject. I told you already why she didn't come with us.'

Nubia saw the injured expression on Jonathan's face. He hung his head and stroked Tigris. Suddenly the puppy stiffened and gave a single bark. A moment later they heard pounding on the front door.

'You must hide at once, Simeon,' hissed Mordecai, as Miriam ran to answer the door. 'It may be the magistrate again.'

SCROLL V

'It's not the magistrate, father. It's Gaius.' Miriam held the hand of a tall, fair-haired man.

Everyone breathed a sigh of relief and Mordecai turned to Lupus. 'You can give Simeon the signal to come out now.'

'Did you find a house, Uncle Gaius?' asked Flavia.

Her uncle shook his head. Despite a broken nose and a scar across one cheekbone, Flavia still thought him very handsome.

Gaius smiled down at Jonathan.

'I'm sorry I'm late for your dinner party, Jonathan. Happy birthday!' He extended a flat wooden object painted with red and blue stripes. 'It's just a wax tablet but I thought you might like the stripes.'

'I do,' said Jonathan reaching to take it. 'Thank you. It's very . . . useful.'

'Jonathan!' cried Flavia. 'You've hurt your finger!'

A strip of white linen was wrapped round the little finger of his left hand.

'It's nothing,' Jonathan flushed and put his hand under the table.

Mordecai gave his son a sharp look, but at that

moment Lupus and Simeon came back into the dining room.

'Gaius,' said Miriam, 'this is my Uncle Simeon.'

After the introductions had been made and Miriam had washed Gaius's hands, they tucked into the venison stew again.

'It looks lovely on you,' said Gaius.

'Thank you,' Miriam whispered, and blushed as everyone looked at her. 'My new tunic,' she explained. 'It's a present from Gaius.' The long tunic was white linen, edged with a narrow gold border.

Simeon looked at Miriam. 'It's been nearly ten years since I saw you last,' he said slowly. 'You have become a great beauty, like your mother.' He looked at Gaius. 'You are very blessed.'

'I know,' said Gaius, without taking his eyes from Miriam.

'Have you set a date for the wedding yet?' asked Simeon.

Gaius shook his head and dipped his bread in the stew. 'I won't set a date until I've found somewhere for us to live. And that reminds me . . .' He looked up at Flavia. 'Tomorrow I must go to Stabia. I have some unfinished business with Felix and I want to see whether it's possible to rebuild the farm.'

Flavia and Nubia glanced at each other. Soon after the eruption, they had looked down on the remains of Gaius's farm from a nearby mountain ridge. It had been almost completely buried by ash.

Suddenly Lupus grunted and held up his hand.

'What is it, Lupus?' asked Flavia.

Lupus put his finger to his lips and widened his eyes.

In the silence they all heard the noise: a distant moan coming from the direction of the sea. Then came several short blasts, followed by a long mournful note again.

'It makes the hair on the back of my neck all prickly,' said Flavia. 'What is it?'

'It is sounding like a horn,' said Nubia.

'It's the shofar,' said Miriam. 'A trumpet made from a ram's horn. And that means it's time for our last course.' On her way out of the dining room, Miriam glanced up at the darkening sky. 'Yes. I can see three stars. The first day of the new year has begun.' Flavia saw her give Gaius a radiant smile before she went out towards the kitchen.

The ram's horn trumpet sounded again, a long blast followed by nine staccato bursts and a final long note.

'It's coming from the synagogue, isn't it?' said Flavia.

Mordecai nodded. 'We celebrate our New Year today,' he said. 'We call it the Day of Trumpets.'

'But I thought you were Christians,' said Flavia with a frown.

'We are,' said Mordecai. 'We haven't abandoned our customs and festivals. We have merely added to them our belief in a Jewish prophet we call the Messiah.'

Miriam came back into the dining room with a platter.

'It's apple and honey. For the festival,' she said. 'Happy New Year, everyone!'

'Happy New Year!' they replied.

A warm breeze drifted in from the dusky garden, bringing with it the shofar's haunting call.

'Why do they blow it?' asked Flavia, crunching a piece of apple.

'To get our attention,' smiled Mordecai. 'To remind us that today we can make a fresh start. Have our sins wiped away.'

'What is arsons?' asked Nubia.

'Our sins,' said Mordecai. 'Things we've done wrong. We remember them over the next ten days, which are called the Days of Awe. Then on our most holy day, Yom Kippur, we fast and pray and say sorry to God and to our fellow man.'

Simeon looked around at them. 'I'm sorry I frightened you. Especially you, Jonathan. Will you forgive me?'

Jonathan shrugged, not even bothering to look at his uncle. Flavia realised he had hardly touched the stew.

Mordecai frowned at Jonathan's rudeness, and said to Simeon. 'Of course we forgive you.'

Simeon smiled, took a piece of apple, dipped it in the honey and ate it.

'Does anyone else want to say sorry?' said Mordecai. 'Perhaps you, Jonathan?'

'Why are you asking me?' Jonathan scowled and glanced around. 'What about Lupus? He has plenty to be sorry about.'

Lupus's head jerked up. He stared at Jonathan, then rose slowly to his feet and took out his wax tablet. His ears deepened from pink to bright red as he wrote on it. Finally, he threw it down onto the table with such force that it sent a wine cup flying. Then he ran out of the triclinium. A moment later they heard the sound of the back door slamming shut.

Miriam burst into tears. A pink wine stain was spreading across the front of her white tunic.

Abruptly Jonathan got up and ran out of the room. Flavia was surprised to hear his footsteps going upstairs instead of to the back door, so she got up, too, and hurried through the twilit garden.

'Lupus!' she called through the open door. 'Come back!' But the sky above the graveyard was such a deep blue that she could barely make out the tops of the umbrella pines. Flavia closed the door and ran back to the triclinium.

'It's too dark,' she said breathlessly. 'I couldn't see which way he went. Shall we light torches and go after him?'

Mordecai shook his head. 'You know Lupus often loses his temper and runs off like that. He'll come back when he's ready.'

Gaius was comforting Miriam while Nubia dabbed at the wine stain with her napkin. Simeon held the wax tablet that Lupus had thrown down.

'What does it say?' asked Flavia.

Jonathan's uncle silently handed her the tablet.

'Oh, no,' murmured Flavia, and read aloud what Lupus had written:

GOD SHOULD SAY SORRY FOR WHAT HE'S DONE TO ME!!

Lupus ran through the purple twilight. Angry tears blurred his vision as he plunged into the pine woods.

He was only wearing his linen dining slippers and the stones and sharp twigs hurt the soles of his feet. He was not as tough as he had been a few months earlier. Living in Jonathan's house had made him soft.

He could barely see now, for dusk was becoming night and the moon was the merest sliver. Black shapes of pine trunks loomed up suddenly like an advancing army of dark opponents. He veered left and right, silently daring them to catch him.

At last something did catch him. But it was not a tree.

Flavia scratched softly on the wall beside Jonathan's doorway. There was no reply, so she pushed the curtain aside and entered.

By the light of the oil lamp in her hand, she could see Jonathan lying on his bed. He had his back to her.

'Jonathan?' she whispered.

There was no reply.

'Jonathan, what's the matter?' said Flavia. 'You really upset Lupus, not to mention your father and Miriam. This isn't like you.'

'Yes, it is. I ruin everything.' His voice was muffled.

Flavia carefully set the oil lamp on a low table and perched on the edge of his bed. Tigris looked at her over Jonathan's shoulder and thumped his tail.

'It's my fault Lupus ran off,' Jonathan continued. 'It's my fault that Miriam's new tunic is ruined. I insulted our guest and I upset father.'

Flavia hugged her knees. 'Well, it's only partly your fault that Miriam's tunic has a wine stain on it and Lupus didn't *have* to storm off into the graveyard. Your father is upset, but you know he loves you.'

'No, he doesn't,' said Jonathan. 'Father hates me.'

'Of course he doesn't hate you. What are you talking about?'

Jonathan turned and looked up at her. In the dim light his brown eyes looked almost black. 'He hates me because it's my fault that mother died.'

Lupus swung gently in the darkness, his feet higher than his head, his right arm twisted awkwardly behind his back, the net tight around him.

He knew it was a trap for wild boar. When an animal stepped onto a certain rope the whole net rose up into the trees. This one was particularly well-made. It was designed to withstand the thrashings of a creature twice his weight and strength.

Lupus waited until his heart stopped pounding. Then he took several deep breaths and tried to ease his right arm into a less painful position.

In the Cyclops' cave, Odysseus's faithful wife Penelope sat at her loom. A waterfall splashed somewhere nearby. As Jonathan entered the cave, she turned and looked at him.

Though it was dim, he could see that she was very beautiful. She had pale skin and dark blue eyes and her straight black hair was as smooth as silk. When she smiled, she looked like his sister Miriam.

'I weave all day, and undo what I've woven at night,' she whispered to Jonathan. 'I wait for him every day.'

Jonathan took a step into the cave, terrified that the Cyclops might return. Penelope held out a handful of yellow wool. 'Do you want to smell it? It's my favourite.'

The scent of lemon blossom filled the cave.

'Mother?' said Jonathan, 'Is it you? Are you still alive?'

She smiled at him and nodded.

Then Jonathan woke up.

SCROLL VI

Jonathan was coming back up the stairs from the latrine when he noticed a light flickering in the guest bedroom.

'Lupus?' he whispered, looking in.

'No,' said his uncle Simeon. 'Just me.' He sat on the side of his bed. A flickering oil lamp on the low table made his shadow huge on the wall behind.

'What are you doing?' asked Jonathan wide-eyed. His uncle held a kitchen knife in one hand and a mass of frizzy hair in the other.

'I'm cutting off my hair,' said Simeon in his deep voice.

Jonathan stepped into the room.

'Uncle Simeon,' he said. 'Please tell me about my mother. I have to know.'

The blade gleamed in the dim lamplight as Simeon lifted the knife towards his head. Another long strand of dark hair fell onto the bed. 'They say long hair is a disgrace to a man,' he said. 'But when I was a Zealot, we always considered it a mark of bravery and courage.'

'Uncle Simeon. I just dreamt about my mother. I dreamt she was alive.'

His uncle's head snapped up.

'You what?' He slowly lowered the knife.

'I dreamt she was weaving in a cave. And in my dream she told me she was still alive.'

'Dear God,' whispered Simeon, and even in the dim lamplight Jonathan could see him grow pale.

'What? What is it?' asked Jonathan.

Simeon looked up at him. The lamp lit his face from beneath and made his face look like a mask. 'Jonathan. As you know, I'm on my way to Rome to see the Emperor. Even though my mission is urgent, I came via Ostia specifically to see your father and tell him something of great importance. He is not ready to hear. But perhaps . . .' Simeon laid the knife beside the oil-lamp, '. . . perhaps you are the one I was meant to tell. Jonathan. Are you prepared to believe something extraordinary?'

'Yes.' Jonathan sat on the bed next to his uncle. 'Tell me.'

The next day dawned hot and still. Nubia saw that the sky was a curious colour, a green so pale it was almost white.

She watched Flavia's uncle Gaius peer up at it, too, as he slung his travel bag over his shoulder.

'It's going to be very hot today,' he observed. 'As hot as the days of the Dog Star.' He unbolted the front door and stepped out into the early morning street.

'Aren't you going to say goodbye to Miriam?' Flavia stood beside Nubia.

He shook his head and glanced at the house next door. 'It's a special day for them today. Miriam and I said our goodbyes last night.' He turned back, kissed Flavia on the forehead, patted Nubia on the head, and set off towards the harbour with his faithful dog Ferox limping along beside him. Nubia knew he intended to sail to Puteoli and from there to Stabia.

The girls watched him out of sight, then went back in and carefully bolted the door behind them. Because the first day of the Jewish New Year was a day of rest for Jonathan and his family, there were no lessons that morning. Their tutor Aristo had taken the day off to go hunting with a friend.

Nubia spent most of the morning listening to Flavia read the *Odyssey* in Latin. They sat in the shadiest corner of the garden but even there the heat soon became almost unbearable. They had just reached the part about the return of Odysseus when the door-slave Caudex showed Miriam into the garden. Nubia immediately knew something was wrong. Miriam's eyes were red and she was hugging Tigris tightly in her arms.

'Jonathan's disappeared,' said Miriam. 'Simeon's gone, Lupus hasn't come back yet and . . . and father's been arrested.'

'Drink this barley water, Miriam,' said Flavia in her calmest voice. 'And tell us what happened.'

Miriam was sitting on the marble bench between Nubia and Flavia. Scuto and the puppies lay panting beneath the jasmine bush.

'Just before dawn,' said Miriam, 'father and I were called out to see a patient: a woman near the Laurentum Gate in the final stages of labour. We managed to save her, but the baby died.' Miriam took a sip of barley water and looked at Flavia. 'That always upsets me.'

'I know,' said Flavia gently. Nubia patted Miriam's shoulder.

'When we got back a short while ago, the house was empty. Jonathan and Uncle Simi were nowhere to be seen. And we haven't seen Lupus since he ran off last night.'

'Maybe Jonathan is seeking Lupus,' suggested Nubia.

'I don't think so,' said Miriam. 'If Jonathan had gone looking for Lupus, he would have taken Tigris.'

'Jonathan's been acting strangely,' said Flavia. 'Last night, he told me your father hates him. He thinks it's his fault your mother died.'

Miriam stared at Flavia. 'Of course it wasn't his fault. And father loves Jonathan terribly.'

'I know,' said Flavia. 'But that's not how he feels. Did anything else happen after we left last night? Anything at all?'

'There was something,' said Miriam slowly. 'Late last night something woke me. I think it was Jonathan crying out in his sleep. Then, just as I was dropping off again, I heard him talking to someone.'

'Who?'

'It wasn't father, so it must have been Uncle Simi.'

'Did you hear what they were saying?'

'No. Maybe I only dreamt it.'

Flavia fanned herself with her hand. 'Even if he is upset, it's not like Jonathan to run off. Lupus, yes; but Jonathan, no. You're sure he didn't leave a message?'

'He might have,' said Miriam. 'Father and I were just about to look for one when that magistrate Bato and his two big soldiers knocked on the door. This time they looked angry. They searched the house and they found . . .' She began to cry.

'What?' said Flavia, 'What did they find?'

'They found some strands of long hair in the kitchen. Uncle Simi must have cut it off and tried to burn it on the hearth. But he didn't burn it all, and Bato said it was evidence. Then he arrested father.'

'Oh Pollux!' muttered Flavia. She stood up and walked to the fountain. 'Maybe . . .' she said slowly, 'maybe Simeon and Jonathan saw the soldiers coming and went to hide somewhere. We'd better go next door to your house and look for clues.'

'We can't just look for clues!' There was a note of hysteria in Miriam's voice. 'They may be torturing father!'

'Don't worry,' said Flavia. 'I don't think they torture freeborn people, only slaves. There's no point any of us going to the basilica, anyway. They'd never listen to girls. Oh, I wish Uncle Gaius were here. He could talk to the magistrate.'

'Gaius won't be back for at least a week,' said Miriam.

'I know,' said Flavia, and then: 'What about Aristo? Miriam, you wait here in case Aristo gets back early from hunting. If he does, tell him what's happened. He can go to the forum and find out about your father. Meanwhile, Nubia and I will see if Jonathan left a message at your house.'

'I don't want to be on my own,' said Miriam in a small voice.

'Alma and Caudex are here. And the dogs,' said Flavia. 'Look! Here comes Alma now with more barley water. Alma, will you look after Miriam?'

'Of course,' said Flavia's former nursemaid, a cheerful, well-padded woman. 'Would you like to help me shell peas, Miriam?'

Miriam gave a small nod.

'Thanks, Alma,' said Flavia. 'Come on, Nubia. Let's look for clues.'

Flavia found Jonathan's wax tablet lying open on Mordecai's table in the study. She recognised the red and blue stripes on the edge. She lifted it carefully because the late morning sun pouring on to the desk had melted the soft beeswax. Only the top part of the message, still in the shade, was legible.

And that was in Hebrew.

'Yes, I can read it,' said Miriam a few minutes later. They had brought the tablet carefully back to Flavia's house. Miriam was sitting in the shady part of the peristyle shelling peas with Alma. Flavia slid the wax tablet onto the table.

'No! Don't touch it!' cried Flavia, as Miriam reached for the tablet. 'Jonathan left it open so your father would see it, but the sun melted the wax. If you tip it, the liquid wax will cover up the letters.'

'All right,' said Miriam. She leant forward, 'The message says: "Gone to Rome. Please . . ."' Miriam looked up at them, her violet eyes wide. 'That's all there is,' she said.

'Can't you make out anything else?' said Flavia. 'Is that a word there?'

Miriam bent her curly head over the tablet. 'It might be "Simeon",' she said after a moment. 'But I'm not positive.'

'That's strange,' said Flavia, pacing back and forth in the shade of the peristyle. 'Why would Jonathan suddenly go to Rome? And what does it have to do with Simeon?'

Then she stood as still as a statue. 'Maybe,' she said slowly, 'maybe Simeon really *is* an assassin and an enemy of your father's! What if he kidnapped Jonathan as revenge and forced him to write this message? Or somehow tricked him into going away with him?' Despite the intense heat, Flavia shivered. 'If Simeon is just a messenger as he told us, why does he need

Jonathan? Oh Pollux! This really is a mystery.' She left the shade of the columned peristyle and walked to the fountain.

'Too hot to think,' she muttered, and took a long drink from the cool jet of water. 'Plan, plan, need a plan . . .' She wiped her wet mouth with her hand, then splashed some water on her face and the back of her neck. 'We have to find Jonathan and help him.'

Abruptly she stopped, then slowly turned. 'Nubia,' she said, with a gleam in her eye, 'how would you like to visit the Eternal City?'

SCROLL VII

Just inside the arch of Ostia's Roman Gate was a long stone trough where the cart-drivers watered their mules. Several tall umbrella pines cast their cool shadows over the trough and the area around it. In this shady patch stood a small altar to Mercury, a folding table and several benches.

The cart-drivers had their own tavern and stables just behind the trough, and their own baths complex across the road, but after they had bathed and filled their stomachs, this was where they waited for their next fare to Rome.

It was almost noon, and only two drivers still sat at the table, playing knucklebones and watching the world pass by. Above them – in the high branches of the umbrella pines – the cicadas buzzed slowly. The heat was ferocious. Even in the shade, the men were sweating.

'I've never known it so hot after the Ides of September,' Flavia heard the bald man say to his friend.

'Blame the mountain,' said the other man, whose short tunic revealed the hairiest legs Flavia had ever seen. 'Ever since it erupted the weather's changed. Seen the sunsets?'

'Who hasn't?' Baldy reached for his wine cup. 'And this morning the sky was green. They say it's going to be a bad year for crops. There's talk of drought.'

'There's already a blight on the vines.' Hairy-legs tossed his knucklebones on the table and winced.

Baldy made a sour face, too, as he tasted his wine. 'The vintage can't be any worse than what we're drinking now,' he said, putting down his cup. 'This stuff tastes like donkey's—'

'Ahem!' Hairy-legs cleared his throat loudly and indicated the girls with his chin.

'Can I help you girls?' said Baldy.

'Yes, please,' said Flavia politely. She was wearing her coolest blue tunic and a wide brimmed straw travelling hat, but already rivulets of sweat were tickling her spine. 'We'd like a lift to Rome.'

The two men glanced at each other with amusement.

'I have the fare,' said Flavia, standing a little taller. 'I believe the standard rate is twenty sestercii.'

'That's right.' Hairy-legs picked up his knucklebones and tossed them again. 'Venus or nothing,' he muttered to Baldy, and to the girls: 'I suggest you come back tomorrow morning, girls. Best time is just after dawn.'

'But we have to go *today*.' Flavia tried to keep her voice low and confident.

Hairy-legs glanced up at her. 'You sometimes find drivers leaving a couple of hours before dusk,' he said. 'But those are mostly delivery carts.'

Flavia knew that if they waited till dusk she'd have to ask Aristo's permission. And he might not give it.

'We have to go as soon as possible,' she said, but her resolve was already beginning to falter. Maybe they shouldn't rush off to Rome, a tiny voice seemed to be saying. Lupus still wasn't back. Miriam was on her own. It was an extremely rash thing to do.

Baldy tutted. 'It's noon,' he said. 'The hottest time of the day on the hottest day of the year. Only a madman would set off for Rome in this heat.'

'Or someone with an urgent delivery for the Emperor,' said a voice behind them.

Flavia and Nubia both turned to see a young man in a brown cart-driver's tunic. He had round green eyes, a snub nose and short, spiky brown hair. He reminded Flavia of a cat.

'What are you talking about, Feles?' said Baldy, with a laugh. 'Since when are you delivering to the Palatine Hill?'

Feles ignored Baldy. 'I can see you're a girl of good birth,' he said to Flavia with a polite smile. 'I'm just off to Rome. Taking a load of exotic fruit that can't wait. It's not a big load and I've got some extra space. If you don't mind a rather cramped journey I'll take you for only ten sestercii.'

'Um . . . well . . .' began Flavia.

'Now she's changed her mind.' Baldy laughed and shook his head. 'Just like a female.'

Flavia glared at him and turned to Feles. 'Of course we'll accept your kind offer.'

'Good,' said Feles. 'It'll be nice to have some company. My cart's just there by the trough. If we – who's this?' he said, as Caudex lumbered up to them gripping a satchel in each hand.

'It's our bodyguard, of course,' said Flavia. 'You don't think we'd be foolish enough to go up to Rome on our own?'

'Been to Rome before?'

Flavia shook her head. She sat beside Feles at the front. Nubia and Caudex rode in the back of the cart, shaded by a canvas tarpaulin.

The carriage had rolled slowly out of Ostia down an oven-hot, deserted road. First they had passed between the tombs of the rich and then, as these thinned out, the salt flats on either side, thickly bordered with reeds and papyrus. Presently the road rose up on a sort of causeway. Beside it towered the red-brick aqueduct which brought water from the hills to Ostia. The road ran steadily alongside it and presently both road and aqueduct left the marshes behind and began to pass scattered farmsteads surrounded by melon and cabbage patches. Beneath the arches of the aqueduct were small vegetable allotments, as colourful as patchwork blankets.

Flavia glanced back at Nubia and Caudex. They were leaning against wooden crates and facing the open back of the cart. Flavia could just see Nubia's shoulder and arm. In the crates was a fruit Flavia had heard of but never seen. Oranges. Their colour was beautiful and their scent divine. Flavia had asked to try one, but Feles said they were worth their weight in gold.

'Twelve crates, each with forty oranges, that's 480 pieces of fruit. If even one's missing, I could feel the sting of the lash.'

Now Feles was asking her about Rome.

'Going for the *Ludi Romani*? Plan to watch a few chariot races? See a few plays?'

Flavia shook her head, and gripped the side of the cart as they rocked over a bump. 'No, we're visiting relatives.'

'Well, make sure you see a race, as it's your first time in Rome. And don't miss the new amphitheatre. Titus is trying to finish it in time for the Saturnalia, but I don't think he'll do it. Even with two thousand slaves working dawn till dusk.'

Feles uncorked a water gourd with his teeth and had a long drink. Then he offered it to Flavia. She took a drink of water from the gourd and handed it back. Feles shook his head. 'Let Nubia and the big guy finish it. There's a tavern and a fountain by that row of cypress trees up ahead. I can refill it there and we'll have a little rest.'

Flavia passed the gourd back to Nubia and squinted

against the sunlight. She could just make out dark, flame-shaped smudges floating above the shimmering waves of heat which rose up from the road.

'The trees look like they're up in the air,' she said.

'Trick of the heat. Like what you get in the desert. Right, Nubia?'

'Yes. Like desert.' A voice from the back of the cart, barely audible above the clipping of sixteen hooves on the stone-paved road.

'How did you know Nubia comes from the desert?' asked Flavia.

'It's obvious, isn't it?' Feles grinned. 'But I am a bit of a detective. I could tell you were high-born the moment I saw you. And I know the big guy used to be a gladiator by the way he stands.'

'That's right!' said Flavia. 'Feles, have you heard of a man called Simeon? Simeon ben Jonah?'

'Name sounds Jewish,' said Feles.

'It is.'

Feles laughed. 'Well,' he said, 'you'll have your work cut out for you if you're looking for a Jew in Rome. You know those two thousand slaves I mentioned?'

'Yes . . .'

'They're all Jewish. Titus captured them when he took Jerusalem a few years ago. No, wait. More like ten years now. Doesn't time fly?'

Flavia frowned. 'I thought Titus sent the Jewish slaves to Corinth.'

'Yes, some went to Corinth. But there were plenty to

go around. Titus brought the strongest and handsomest back here to Rome,' Feles chuckled to himself. 'And the prettiest . . .' he added.

'What do you mean?'

'Those Jewish women,' said Feles, shaking his head in admiration, 'are the most beautiful in the world.' He gave Flavia a sideways glance and added proudly. 'My girlfriend's one. She's lovely. Huldah's her name. She's a slave-girl in the Imperial Palace on the Palatine Hill.'

Flavia twisted her whole torso to face him. 'Then some of the women from Jerusalem are in the Imperial Palace?'

'About two hundred,' said Feles, 'all of them high-born.' He mopped his brow. 'This heat. Never known it so hot. How're you doing back there?' he called.

Caudex grunted and Nubia said, 'We are doing fine.'

'We'll stop for a break soon,' said Feles. 'Then you can change places.'

The cart rolled on and presently tall cypress trees on the left threw bands of delicious shadows across the white road. The mules quickened their pace. They smelled water and green shade up ahead.

'This tavern's roughly the halfway point to Rome,' said Feles. 'See the milestone? Seven miles. It'll take us about two more hours.'

Later, standing in the shade of cypress and pines, drinking cool water from the fountain, Flavia took Nubia aside.

'Nubia,' she whispered. 'Did you hear what Feles

told me? There are lots of female slaves from Jerusalem in Titus's Palace. One of them might know how Jonathan's mother died. And if I figured that out, so could Jonathan.'

SCROLL VIII

After their short stop at the tavern, Nubia took her turn beside Feles at the front, and Flavia joined Caudex in the back. The road was climbing more steeply now, and the line of the aqueduct guided Flavia's eye back down to Ostia and the red brick lighthouse – minuscule at this distance – with its dark plume of smoke rising straight into the dirty blue sky.

They passed through woods of poplar, ash and alder. Presently Ostia was hidden from view. On any other day the tree-shaded road would have been deliciously cool. But today Flavia's blue tunic was soaked with perspiration and clinging to her back.

'Caudex?' Flavia whispered because the big slave's eyes were closed.

He didn't reply and presently she too dozed fitfully, occasionally jolted out of sleep when the cart left the deep ruts in the stone road and rocked from side to side. The rumble of the cart was louder back here and she was glad the wheels weren't rimmed with iron, like some.

She dreamt briefly at one point. She was hunting

with Jonathan and Nubia among the tombs outside Ostia. In her dream she heard a voice calling her and looked up. A small, dark-haired girl in orange was running along the top of the town wall from the Laurentum Gate towards the Fountain Gate.

It was their friend Clio from Stabia. She had been trapped in Herculaneum when the volcano erupted and none of them knew whether she had survived. But now here she was in Flavia's dream, laughing as she ran. Lupus should be here, Flavia said to Nubia, still in her dream. Where is he?

Lupus hung in full sunlight, unable to brush away the flies which covered his mouth and nose. It had taken him all night to work his right arm from behind his back, but he still couldn't bring his hands to his face. Now it was after midday and he had been crying out regularly until his voice was almost gone. He was terrified that if he opened his tongueless mouth one of the big horseflies might crawl in and choke him, so he kept his lips firmly shut and tried to breathe through his nose.

It was no use crying out now, anyway. His voice had nearly gone. All he could do was curse his bad temper and pray that whoever had set the trap would check their nets soon.

Something woke Flavia and it took her a moment to realise what it was: the cart had stopped. She heard voices and rubbed her eyes. Her mouth was dry and the tops of her sandalled feet, which had been in the sunshine for the last few miles, were pink with sunburn.

'Here we are,' said Feles from the front. 'The great city of Rome. They won't let me in for an hour or two because I'm wheeled traffic. If you want to get to your relatives before dark you'd better continue on foot. You can hire a litter just inside the city gates.'

'Thanks,' said Flavia, and gratefully allowed Caudex to lift her off the back of the cart. She pulled her damp tunic away from her back, then stretched and looked around. The road was lined with tombs and umbrella pines, casting long shadows in the late afternoon sunlight. Already a queue of carts sat waiting for dusk, when they would be allowed into the city. Flavia could see a white, three-arched gate up ahead. Not far from it, among the other tombs along the road, was a white marble pyramid almost as high as the city walls.

Nubia came up, wearing Flavia's broad-brimmed sun-hat. She was smiling.

'Did you have a nice time at the front?' asked Flavia.

Nubia nodded and took off the hat. 'Feles lets me hold the reins. And he tells me the names of the mules: Pudes, Podagrosus, Barosus and Potiscus.'

'Do you know what their names mean?' asked Flavia.

'She does now,' said Feles with a grin, and leaned against the cart. 'Show us how Barosus walks.'

Nubia handed Flavia the sun-hat and then minced along the road in dainty little steps. Flavia laughed.

'And this is the Podagrosus,' said Nubia, coming back along the hot road with a heavy, exaggerated limp. 'And the Potiscus.' She staggered the last few steps as if she were tipsy.

Flavia turned laughing to Feles. 'Thank you very much for taking us. Here's twenty sestercii.'

Feles stepped forward and took the coins. 'I thought we agreed ten,' he said, his cat-like eyes round with surprise.

'That was before you knew Caudex was coming,' said Flavia. 'Fair's fair.'

'Thank you, Flavia Gemina,' said Feles. 'I won't forget it. If you ever need a cart-driver – or help of any kind – just ask for me. I usually stay at the Owl Tavern inside the city gates, near the tomb of Cestius, that big white pyramid over there.'

'Thank you,' said Flavia. 'Maybe we'll meet again one day.' She waved and started to lead Caudex and Nubia past the tombs and waiting carts towards the three-arched gate.

'Flavia Gemina!'

Flavia turned back. 'Yes?'

Feles tossed something like a ball. Flavia caught it and gasped when she saw what it was.

'An orange! But you said . . .'

'Don't worry.' Feles grinned. 'I'll tell them that one or two were rotten.'

'Where will we sleep tonight?' asked Nubia.

56

'I have relatives here in Rome,' said Flavia, looking around. 'We haven't seen them in ages but I'm sure they wouldn't turn away their own family.' She tried to make her voice sound confident. Inwardly, she was praying that they wouldn't be stranded with nowhere to stay.

Before them, a large marble fountain sputtered in the middle of a crowded square. Two main roads led from the other side of the square into Rome, no gleaming city of marble and gold, but a mass of red-roofed apartment blocks in peeling shades of putty, apricot, carrot and mustard. Although the tall buildings threw long violet shadows across the square, the heat still muffled Rome like a woollen blanket. The stench of donkey dung, human sewage and sweat was almost overpowering.

Flavia breathed through her mouth and looked around. To the right of the gate was a queue of litter-bearers, waiting to take people into the city. On the left – up against the high city wall – were three shrines: one to Mercury, for those hoping to make their fortune; one to Venus, for those who wanted to find love; and one to Fortuna, for general good luck.

Flavia looked at the orange in her hand, a rare and valuable fruit she had never tasted. She sighed.

'Wait here for a moment,' she said to Nubia and Caudex, and picked her way through donkey dung to one of the shrines. When she stood before it, she bowed her head.

'Dear Fortuna, goddess of success,' she whispered,

'please watch over us and help us find somewhere to sleep and not get lost or pickpocketed. And help us find our friend Jonathan.' Flavia laid the precious orange in the miniature temple, among the other offerings of flowers, copper coins and fruit.

Something tugged at the hem of her tunic. Flavia looked down and gasped.

A pile of old rags beside the shrine had lifted its head to reveal a gaunt face with terrible burns over one side.

'Please,' croaked the beggar, 'I lost everything when the mountain exploded. Please help . . .'

'Sorry.' Flavia backed away, feeling sick. She turned and pushed through a crowd of women who had suddenly gathered to present their offerings at the shrine of Venus.

'I hope we have enough money for a litter,' she muttered to Nubia and then turned to the door slave. 'Caudex, you don't mind walking beside us, do you?'

Caudex shook his head. 'Been sitting long enough,' he said. 'Good to give my legs a stretch.'

'I thought you had to see the Emperor urgently.' Jonathan tossed his shoulder bag onto a low cot.

'I do,' said Simeon, 'but I must proceed carefully.'

He looked round the room and grunted. 'This will do. You wait here. I'll be back as soon as I can.' He went out, closing the flimsy wooden door behind him.

Jonathan stood in the middle of a small room in a cheap tenement block, a room that managed to be both dark and hot at the same time. And noisy. Although they were five floors up, Jonathan could clearly hear the people on the street far below. He went to the window and pushed at the wooden shutters.

One of the shutters was rusted into a fixed position, but after a moment's struggle the other opened with a piercing squeal of hinges. The room was flooded with the sudden hot sunlight of late afternoon.

Jonathan squinted against the light and leaned out of the window. There was a street market down below, and most stalls seemed to be selling cloth of some kind. Jonathan could hear the cries of the stallholders, the low urgent bargaining voices, the spatter of water from a fountain onto the pavement, even the clink of coins.

It was as if the stone street and brick walls amplified and focused the sound, throwing it up to where he stood. Jonathan leaned further out, shading his eyes with his hand. He must be facing west because he could see the sun sinking above the red-tiled rooftops.

Far below he saw Simeon's head and shoulders emerge from the building and move slowly up the street. Occasionally Simeon stopped and spoke to a stallholder, then moved on. Jonathan watched his uncle until he was out of sight.

Then he closed the shutter and lay on one of the cots. It was lumpy and smelled of sour hay, but it was good to rest.

Jonathan stared up at the ceiling and cast his mind back over the day's events.

The night before, his uncle had told him something so astounding that he could still hardly believe it: his mother might still be alive! Jonathan had begged Simeon to take him to Rome. His uncle had refused, claiming it was too dangerous.

But Jonathan hadn't been able to sleep and when he heard his father and Miriam going out before dawn, he had quickly dressed and gone downstairs. Simeon had been powdering his roughly cut hair and beard with flour.

'Why are you doing that?'

'Makes my hair look grey.'

'Please let me come with you,' Jonathan begged. 'With me along, nobody will look twice at you.'

'No.'

'What about my dream? Simeon. I'm meant to go with you.'

His uncle hesitated.

'How old were you when you first risked your life fighting for the Zealots?' asked Jonathan.

'You could die.'

'I don't care. I'll follow you whether you take me or not,' said Jonathan. And he meant it.

Simeon sighed and nodded his head.

And so, pretending to be grandfather and grandson, they had found a lift to Rome on the back of a bread cart. Nobody gave them a second glance, including the soldiers guarding the gate.

Now he was in Rome. A mile, maybe two, from his

mother. His heart pounded when he thought about it. Could she really be alive? Jonathan took a deep breath and closed his eyes and tried to recall the face of the woman from his dream.

Something tickled his nose and he brushed at it. Then it came again. Jonathan opened his eyes and flinched as a trickle of fine plaster dust drifted into them.

He sat up, coughing and rubbing his eyes. The drift of fine dust was coming from a crack in the ceiling above his bed. He realised he had been hearing angry voices from up there for some time now. A man and a woman. He could hear them stomping about, too.

Jonathan felt a stab of panic. He had heard stories about poorly built tenement houses and how they could collapse without warning. He was in a strange city and only one person knew exactly where he was. If the block collapsed, no one would be able to identify his body. If they even found it.

'Pull yourself together!' Jonathan muttered to himself. 'Don't be such a pessimist.'

Nevertheless, he went to the darkest corner of the room and crouched there. Any moment he expected the arguing couple to come crashing through the roof onto his bed, bringing the whole insula down around them. Pulling out his handkerchief, Jonathan pressed it to his face. He closed his eyes, inhaled its lemon fragrance and prayed.

SCROLL IX

Nubia stretched out on the litter beside Flavia. It was like reclining on a floating couch. They had started out with the linen curtains closed, but it had been unbearably hot and the scent of cheap perfume from the previous occupant still clung to the fabric. As soon as they left the smelly area of the three-arched gate, Flavia had pulled back the curtains, and they had both sighed with relief at the cool evening breeze. Then they had settled back to watch Rome move past.

At first, the broad street they were travelling down was lined with noisy stalls. There were markets in the narrow side streets, too, though most stallholders were beginning to pack up. Some sold spices, some metal objects, some pottery. The warbling notes of a flute alerted Nubia to a side street selling nothing but musical instruments. But they were past it before she could see anything.

Presently, the stalls and shops seemed to sell higher quality goods and the pedestrians were better dressed. The stalls were replaced by shops built into the ground floor of the buildings, alternating with porches flanked by columns.

Then the litter turned so that the sun was behind them. From the angle of the couch and the puffing of the bearers' breath, Nubia could tell they were climbing a hill. Another litter passed them coming the opposite way, and Nubia turned her head in amazement. It was carried by four large Ethiopians, their skin as black as polished jet. The filmy red curtains of this litter were drawn but as it passed Nubia caught a whiff of a musky, exotic fragrance – patchouli.

There were trees here, ancient umbrella pines rising from behind walls, hinting at shaded gardens beyond. Now the shops had completely given way to porches with double doors set behind red and white columns. Sometimes the plaster was peeling, but Nubia knew this was no indication of what lay behind. Roman houses presented deceptively blank faces, with small, barred windows and heavy doors. But she knew that behind those doors were inner gardens, splashing fountains, mosaics, marble columns and rich, elegant men and women.

It occurred to Nubia that behind each door was a different story and that there were hundreds, maybe thousands of doors in this great, strange city. She lay back on the greasy cushion, overwhelmed.

'Are you all right, Nubia?'

Nubia nodded. She wanted to tell Flavia that some-times she felt as if everything that had happened to her in the last few months was a dream. Any moment she would wake up back in her tent in the desert, with her mother bringing her a foaming bowl of goat's milk and her little brothers squabbling on the carpets and her dog emerging from the covers, yawning and grinning. But she didn't have the words to express all that so she said simply, 'Sometimes I'm feeling in a dream.'

Flavia smiled and squeezed Nubia's hand. Then she turned her head away and rubbed her eye, as if to brush away a speck of dust.

The litter slowed and stopped before a porch with two simple white columns. Set back from these columns were sky-blue double doors, with big brass studs in them. They gave no hint at what lay beyond.

'Here we are,' said one of the litter-bearers. 'The house of the senator Aulus Caecilius Cornix.' He extended his hand to Flavia.

As soon as Flavia stepped onto the pavement her eye was drawn upwards. Running behind the umbrella pines was a tall aqueduct, its arches red-orange in the light of the setting sun.

Flavia turned back to the litter-bearer and said with all the confidence she could muster, 'Please don't go until I know if they're home.'

The man nodded and turned to help Nubia out of the litter.

Flavia took a deep breath, stepped forward and banged the knocker smartly. It was made of heavy brass, shaped like a woman's hand holding an apple. Flavia heard it echo inside, and presently the welcome sound of shuffling footsteps. The rectangular door of the peephole slid open and dark eyes regarded her suspiciously.

'Is the Lady Cynthia Caecilia in?' said Flavia in her most imperious voice.

'Who wants her?' growled the doorkeeper.

'Flavia Gemina, daughter of Marcus Flavius Geminus, sea captain,' said Flavia, and added, 'her niece.'

'They've gone away to Tuscany. Won't be back until the Kalends of October,' he said. 'Nobody told me about any guests. Come back in two weeks.'

'No! Wait!' begged Flavia, her poise evaporating. 'Please let us in. We've nowhere else to go and it will be dark soon!'

'Sorry.' The little door of the peephole slid emphatically shut.

A terrible panic squeezed Flavia's throat and she slowly turned to face Nubia and Caudex.

The litter-bearers glanced at each other and one of them stepped forward. 'I'm afraid you'll have to pay us, now, miss,' he said. 'That'll be forty sestercii.'

Flavia Gemina burst into tears.

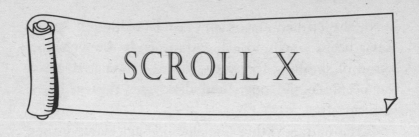

Lupus could hear a strange whimpering noise.

He opened his swollen eyelids to see what it was. But all he could see were the rough hemp ropes that formed his prison, dark against the red light of the setting sun. Presently he realised the whimpering noise was coming from his own throat.

At least the flies had left him. He opened his mouth and tried to cry out, but there was no moisture left.

He closed his eyes. Better just to die. Then his short, wretched life would finally be over. He had only two regrets. He would never know if Clio was still alive. And he would never avenge his parents' murder.

Voices were calling him. Voices from beyond. Lupus opened his eyes again.

He could just make out the god, young and beardless, with bronzed curly hair like Mercury, or the Shepherd. The young god was giving him water, pushing a skin of it through the ropes, and Lupus could feel it squirting over his swollen lips and running down his chin and then into his mouth and it was wonderful.

'Lupus! Can you hear me? How on earth did you get here? What are you playing at?' said the Shepherd, or Mercury. 'You're lucky we came along. I wanted to go home. It was Lysander here who saw a deer pass this way.'

Suddenly Lupus was swinging and falling and strong arms caught him and cut away the ropes and he felt cool water on his face and was finally able to fully open his eyes.

It wasn't a god. It was his tutor Aristo, ruddy from a day in the sun, with a brace of rabbits over his shoulder, speaking Greek to his short dark friend, then smiling at the expression on Lupus's face and now laughing with his white teeth as he carried Lupus home.

Flavia sat on the sun-warmed pavement with her feet in a Roman gutter and sobbed. Nubia crouched beside her and patted her back. Caudex, still holding their bags, looked stupidly at the litter-bearer.

'Forty sestercii,' repeated the bearer, with a glance at his friend.

Flavia looked up at him with red eyes. 'How can it be forty sestercii?' she said through her tears. 'That's twice as much as the fare from Ostia.'

'She's right,' said a voice behind Flavia. 'You'll take ten sestercii and no more. Or I'll have to mention it to Senator Cornix.' The voice was light and confident, with a Greek accent, like Aristo's.

Flavia looked over her shoulder. The sky-blue doors

of the house stood open and a smiling man in a lavender tunic stepped forward. He winked at Flavia as he handed the litter-bearer something. Flavia heard the clink of coins.

'Off you go now, boys,' said the man in lavender, flapping his hand dismissively. The bearers glanced at each other, nodded and took their empty litter back the way they had come.

The smiling man turned to Flavia and extended a hand. 'Up you get, Miss Flavia,' he said. 'I have to apologise for Bulbus. He's a good doorkeeper but he's as stupid as an onion. A very small onion.'

Flavia laughed through her tears and took his hand, which was covered in rings. He pulled her gently to her feet.

He was not much taller than she was, slim and dark, and his bright black eyes were lined with kohl. She liked him at once.

'My name is Sisyphus.' He bent his head politely. 'Your uncle's secretary. I am certain that Senator Cornix and the Lady Cynthia would want to extend the hospitality of their home to a relative, even in their absence. Do please come in.'

Aristo was furious.

Lupus had never seen him so angry.

'I leave them alone for a few hours and what happens?' he yelled at Miriam, who was bending over Lupus, spooning soup into his cracked mouth.

'This one runs off and gets himself caught in a boar trap, Jonathan disappears, apparently to Rome, and then Flavia and Nubia charge off after him! Do you realise Captain Geminus will hold me responsible if anything happens to them? He could take me to court, have me sent to the mines of Sicily. Or worse. Dear Apollo!'

Miriam looked up at him with tear-filled eyes.

'Oh, I'm sorry, Miriam,' said Aristo. He started to reach out a hand to pat her shoulder and then let it drop to his side. Lupus knew Aristo was still in love with Miriam, even though she was betrothed to Flavia's uncle.

'I didn't mean to make you cry,' said Aristo.

'It's not you,' said Miriam. 'It's father. I'm worried about him.'

'Don't worry,' said Aristo, and this time he did touch her very briefly on the shoulder. 'It's late now and the basilica will be closed, but I'll go first thing tomorrow morning and see how your father is doing.' Aristo turned and looked at Lupus, and his expression softened. 'And if you're feeling better tomorrow, Lupus, you can come with me.'

The squalid room was filled with the deep purple gloom of dusk by the time Simeon returned. He held a sputtering oil lamp in one hand and two flat circular loaves in another. He set the lamp on the window ledge and turned to look down at Jonathan.

'What are you doing cowering in the corner?' he asked in his deep voice.

'I'm sure that crack wasn't here when we arrived,' said Jonathan. 'I think the whole ceiling is going to come down on us.'

Simeon looked up and studied the ceiling. 'Very possibly,' he said. 'But if it does there's nothing we can do about it. Here. You may as well die on a full stomach.' He tossed Jonathan one of the loaves. Despite himself, Jonathan grinned.

'That's better,' said Simeon. He eased something off his shoulders and onto the bed. It was a long cloth case with a leather carrying strap.

'What's that?' said Jonathan, tearing a piece from his loaf as he moved out of the dark corner.

'It's a key. Our key to the Imperial Palace.' Simeon undid several ties on one side of the case and pulled out a wooden instrument with four strings. It looked like a lyre, but it was longer and thinner with a bulbous sound box. 'My real instrument is the psaltery,' said Simeon, 'but this will have to do.' He gave it an experimental strum. The notes were rich and very deep.

Simeon sat on the edge of his bed and tuned the strings for a moment. 'How's the bread?' he asked, as he twisted one of the wooden pegs.

'Not bad,' admitted Jonathan. 'It's rye and aniseed. Here.' He stood and broke off a piece and handed it to his uncle and sat down again on his own bed.

Simeon grunted his thanks and ate the bread as he strummed and tuned. Finally he kicked off his sandals and settled the bulb of the instrument between the soles of his bare feet. Then he began to play.

'You're Myrtilla's daughter, is that right?'

Flavia looked up from her bowl of cold, solidified black bean soup and nodded.

'Thought so,' said Sisyphus, and handed Flavia two small ceramic jars. 'Sprinkle some oil and vinegar on your soup; it makes it taste much better.'

Flavia did so and took another mouthful.

'I believe I met your mother once,' he said. 'Lady Cynthia's younger sister, the one who married a sea captain. Is that right?'

Flavia nodded.

'That's why I've never seen you here before,' said Sisyphus. 'My mistress Cynthia and your father fell out several years ago, didn't they?'

'Yes,' said Flavia, digging her spoon in again. 'I don't think my aunt likes pater very much.'

'Well,' said Sisyphus, 'I only met your mother the once, but I remember she was lovely. You have her nose and mouth, I think.'

'Thank you,' said Flavia. 'And thank you for taking us in. And for the bath and the room and this soup. It's delicious.'

'I told you the oil and vinegar would transform it.'

Flavia and Nubia had bathed in a small cold plunge

and put on fresh clothes. Now they were dining in a courtyard beneath a grape arbour. At the wooden table sat Sisyphus, Bulbus, Caudex and a silent female slave named Niobe who was the cook and housekeeper. It was dusk, and moths fluttered round a dozen oil-lamps hanging among the vine leaves.

'And you're Nubia? Flavia's slave girl?' asked Sisyphus.

Nubia nodded.

'She used to be my slave girl,' said Flavia, 'but last month I set her free. Now Nubia's my . . . friend.'

'I utterly approve,' said Sisyphus. 'I hope to earn my freedom one day, too.' He dabbed his mouth with a napkin and frowned at Caudex, who had already finished his soup and was wiping the clay bowl with a hunk of caraway seed bread. 'Tell me, Miss Flavia, why have you made this sudden trip to Rome?'

'Well, our friend Jonathan is Jewish and his mother Susannah died in the destruction of Jerusalem and he blames himself for some reason. But he might have found out that there are lots of Jewish women—'

'—in Titus's palace?' Sisyphus finished her sentence.

'Exactly!' cried Flavia. 'I think he wants to ask them about his mother.' Suddenly she frowned. 'How did you know there are Jewish slaves in the palace?'

Sisyphus shrugged. 'Everyone knows that Titus's palace is full of beautiful Jewish slaves. They were his gift to Berenice.'

'Who?'

'My dear girl.' Sisyphus put down his spoon and widened his kohl-rimmed eyes at her. 'Don't tell me you've never heard of Queen Berenice?'

SCROLL XI

In a dark room in a Roman apartment block, Jonathan's uncle Simeon thumbed the deepest string of the instrument.

It was a note so deep that Jonathan did not so much hear it as feel it reverberate on the bone above his heart. Simeon pulled the string again and again until it was a beat, low and steady. Presently his other hand began to pluck the thinner strings and a melody flowed above the beat.

Then his uncle began to sing.

Once, Jonathan had felt the thick brown pelt of a mink. Simeon's voice was as soft and rich as that pelt. He sang of a weeping willow tree and a river but Jonathan was scarcely aware of the words. He closed his eyes.

Everything was strange. The sounds outside his head, the feelings inside his heart, the smells and textures of Rome. But the music carried him away from all that. He felt that if he could learn to play this strange deep lyre it would heal his pain. Or at least bring some relief.

After a time the song ended, and Jonathan opened his eyes to find his uncle looking at him with raised eyebrows.

'What's that instrument called?' said Jonathan huskily.

'It's a bass lyre. Some people call it a barbiton. This is the Syrian model. Do you like it?'

Jonathan nodded. 'Will you teach me to play it?'

Simeon smiled and Jonathan realised he had never seen his uncle smile before. Some of Simeon's teeth were missing but the smile transformed his face so delightfully that Jonathan had to laugh.

Then Simeon laughed, too, and tossed him something jingly. It was a small tambourine.

'Let's see if you can keep a beat first,' he said, and began his next song.

'My dears, the story of Titus and Berenice is terribly romantic.' Sisyphus leant back in his chair and took a sip of wine. A lamp hanging among the vine leaves illuminated one side of his face dramatically and made his dark eyes liquid and mysterious.

'Berenice was a beautiful Jewish queen,' he began. 'She met Titus in Judaea, the year before he took Jerusalem. He was a handsome commander in his prime and she a beautiful widow. They were attracted to each other like . . . those moths to the flame. They fell passionately in love. Despite the fact that she was nearly forty and he was only twenty-eight. Despite the fact that she believed in one god and he in many. Despite the fact that she was a Jewish subject and he a Roman conqueror.'

Sisyphus closed his eyes.

'I saw her once here in Rome, about five years ago. She must have been at least forty-five but she was glorious! Sensuous lips, eyes like emeralds, and jet black tresses tied up with ropes of seed pearls. Her skin was silky smooth and honey-coloured.' He opened his eyes again. 'They say she kept it soft by bathing in milk and aloes, like Cleopatra.'

'Milk?' repeated Caudex thickly. He was listening as intently as the girls.

Sisyphus nodded. 'What banquets they had!' he sighed. 'Titus lived it up in his palace on the Palatine as if he were already Emperor and Berenice his Empress. Meanwhile, the real Emperor, Vespasian, lived in a modest home in the Gardens of Sallust.' He shook his head. 'It couldn't last. As long as Titus was merely co-ruler with his father, the senate could ignore his eastern lover, but as soon as Vespasian's health got worse and it looked as if Titus might become Emperor . . .' Sisyphus leaned back and poured himself another glass of spiced wine.

'What?' said Flavia and Nubia together.

'I'm a Greek,' said Sisyphus. 'We're not afraid of strong women. But the Romans. They suspect and fear a woman with power. Especially one from the East.'

He leaned forward and lowered his voice dramatically. 'The Senate forced Titus to choose between the great love of his life,' Sisyphus held up one cupped hand, 'and their political support.' He held up the other, and looked from hand to hand sadly, as if weighing two difficult choices.

'What does he choose?' asked Nubia, gripping Flavia's hand beneath the table.

'He's a Roman!' Sisyphus dropped his hands and puffed his cheeks dismissively. 'Of course he chose power over love. He told her she had to leave Rome.'

The girls sat back, disappointed, and Caudex made an odd clucking sound.

'But it was a difficult choice.' Sisyphus nodded slowly. 'They say Titus wept when he sent Berenice away, and that she wept as she went. They also say . . .' Here he leaned forward again '. . . that he promised to recall her and make her Empress as soon as the Mule-Driver died.'

'Who is the Mule-Driver?' asked Nubia.

'Vespasian, of course. The old Emperor. So when Berenice left six months ago, she only took two of her many slaves, only one chest of clothing, and she only went as far as Athens. She expected to be called back very soon, you see.'

'How many slaves did she have?' asked Flavia.

'Hundreds. All high-born Jewish women. They were Titus's gift to her. She also made Titus promise to be kind to all the male Jewish slaves in Rome.'

Flavia frowned. 'But our cart-driver said that Titus put thousands of the male slaves to work on the new amphitheatre.'

'Pah!' Sisyphus blew out his cheeks again. 'Of course they work; they're slaves. But they're well fed and their quarters quite comfortable. And do you know where Berenice's women live?'

The girls and Caudex shook their heads.

'In Nero's Golden House!'

'Oh!' breathed Flavia and Nubia and Caudex.

After a moment of reverent silence Nubia meekly asked, 'What is Nero's Golden House?'

'After the great fire here fifteen years ago Nero built the most amazing palace on the ashes. It covered three hills. There were gardens, vineyards, woods, even a lake. He made Rome his villa, the Palatine Hill his atrium, and the huge lake his impluvium. The people hated him for it.'

'Now I remember!' cried Flavia. 'Pliny mentions the Golden House in his *Natural History*, doesn't he? It was made of pure gold.'

'Almost,' said Sisyphus. 'The rooms were decorated with ivory, marble, silk and gold.' He made a dismissive gesture. 'Of course, Vespasian stripped most of that away and built his new amphitheatre on the site of the lake. But they say the Golden House still bears traces of its former glory, with scenes from Greek mythology painted on almost every wall, and gem-encrusted fountains and hidden corridors . . .'

'And that's where the Jewish women are?' asked Flavia.

Sisyphus nodded. 'They're somewhere in it. Not sure exactly where.'

'How would a person get in there?' said Flavia casually, picking a caraway seed from the table and crunching it between her teeth.

Sisyphus gave her a sharp look. 'My dear, they wouldn't,' he said. 'Unless possibly they were one of the Emperor's slaves, and a child or a eunuch at that.'

He yawned and stretched luxuriously. 'Oh dear, past my bedtime. Yours too, I'd wager. I'll show you to your rooms. You girls don't mind sharing, do you?'

Flavia shook her head and Nubia said, 'What is happening to Berenice now? The Mule-Driver is dead, yes?'

'Yes, indeed.' Sisyphus pushed back his chair and rose to his feet. 'Vespasian died almost three months ago.'

'And is Berenice coming back to the Titus?'

'Yes and no,' said Sisyphus with a smile. 'There's another story there, and a mystery as well. But I'm afraid it will have to wait until tomorrow.'

Early the next morning in the port of Ostia, before dawn had tinted the sky, Lupus rose, slipped on his best sea-green tunic and made his way stiffly downstairs to the fountain. Aristo had insisted that Lupus and Miriam sleep at Flavia's house. 'I don't want any more of you to go missing,' he had grumbled.

Now Lupus stood beside Flavia's fountain and scrubbed his face, neck and hands as best he could. He wet his hair and slicked it back with his fine-toothed wooden comb. Then he sat on the marble bench and waited.

Scuto and the puppies swarmed round him, wagging their tails and pawing his knees, pleading to be taken for a walk. Lupus ignored them. Even when Tigris fetched his new leather collar and dropped it hopefully on the bench, Lupus only scratched him behind the ear.

When Aristo came downstairs and saw Lupus waiting meekly for him, he smiled and gave the boy a nod. Without a word they left the house and made their way into town.

At the southern end of the forum, near the Temple of Rome and Augustus, was the basilica, a large brick building faced with marble and surrounded by columns. The law court occupied the spacious ground floor, with offices on the first floor and prison cells at the back.

A group of men, most of them wearing togas, had already gathered outside. Because they were all waiting to see different clerks and officials, the queue moved quickly. Lupus and Aristo saw the magistrate within the hour. A slave led them up a narrow marble staircase and along a gallery overlooking the law court below.

Bato's office was the next to last on the right: a small, bright room with an arched, west-facing window. The young magistrate sat in front of this window, writing at a table covered with wax tablets and scrolls. On the floor beside him were more scrolls in baskets. Lupus noticed a small personal shrine to Hercules in one corner of the office.

'How can I help you?' Bato glanced up briefly, then continued making notes on a piece of papyrus. There was no chair for visitors. Lupus stood beside Aristo on the other side of the table.

'I am Aristo, son of Diogenes of Corinth, tutor and secretary in the house of Marcus Flavius Geminus. We've come to inquire about Captain Geminus's neighbour, a certain Mordecai ben Ezra.'

Bato looked up. 'Oh, yes. The Jew. I'm afraid he's being held on charges of conspiracy. The evidence indicates he was harbouring a known assassin. We believe he's involved in a plot against the Emperor's life.'

'Impossible,' said Aristo. 'He's a doctor. A healer. In fact, the Emperor recently praised him for helping the victims of Vesuvius. And Simeon couldn't be an assassin. He's Doctor ben Ezra's brother-in-law. Simeon's sister was Mordecai's wife,' he explained.

Bato gave Aristo a steady look. 'I know what a brother-in-law is,' he said dryly. 'Do you know what a *sica* is?'

Aristo frowned. 'What?'

Bato leaned back in his chair. 'I visited the doctor the day before yesterday because I was concerned about his safety. I thought he might be the assassin's target. It never occurred to me he could be the assassin's accomplice. Yesterday, however, more information came to light. It seems there are at least three assassins on their way from Corinth. One was sighted four days ago in Rhegium. A third was seen yesterday, coming off a ship in Puteoli. All are Jewish. All – we presume – intend to kill the Emperor. And Simeon is one of them.'

Lupus and Aristo exchanged glances.

Bato tapped the end of his pen on his bottom teeth. 'Tell me, Aristo son of Diogenes, have you ever heard of the Jewish revolt?'

'Of course,' said Aristo. 'It led to the destruction of Jerusalem.'

Bato nodded. 'When the Jewish revolt began fifteen years ago, a dangerous new kind of rebel came to our attention. These men were Zealots, fanatically religious, refusing to accept Roman rule. They carried curved daggers hidden in their belts or cloaks. I managed to acquire one a few years ago.'

Bato rose and moved over to a small chest near his personal shrine. He lifted the lid and took out a dagger about the length of a man's hand. It was shaped like a sickle, with a razor sharp edge.

'This is a *sica*,' he said, walking back to his desk. 'Do you see how thin the blade is, and how sharp the point? No, don't touch it, boy!'

Bato raised the knife out of Lupus's reach and continued. 'A swift cut at the back of the neck like *this*,' Bato flicked the knife, 'severs the spinal cord and causes instant, silent death. By the time those around the victim realise what's happened, the killer has melted into the crowd.'

Aristo and Lupus exchanged glances.

'At first,' said Bato, resuming his seat, 'the *sicarii* – as these knife-men were known – only killed Jewish traitors and so-called Roman oppressors. Later, people began to seek them out and pay them to kill their personal enemies. And once they could be bought, they were no longer freedom-fighters, but mere assassins.' Bato's lip curled as he pronounced the final word.

'Most of them died in the destruction of Jerusalem and the siege of Masada, but a few survived. Their names are on our most-wanted list; they are enemies of the Emperor. Simeon may be the doctor's brother-in-law, but I can assure you, he is also an assassin.'

SCROLL XII

Lupus and Aristo emerged from the cool interior of Ostia's basilica and stepped into the heat and noise of the central forum on a busy morning. Bato had refused to set Mordecai free on bail. He had also refused to let them see Mordecai. He had even refused to let them give Mordecai a message.

Deep in thought, Aristo automatically turned for Green Fountain Street. Lupus brought him up short by gripping the hem of his tunic.

'What?' Aristo frowned.

Lupus tipped his head to the right and started towards the back of the basilica. Aristo sighed and followed him between the basilica's western wall and the temple of Venus, a space so narrow that sunlight never reached it.

'Ugh!' said Aristo. 'It stinks here. Can't people use the public latrines?'

Lupus ignored him and continued down the passage until he reached several small square openings in the thick brick wall.

'What's this?' Aristo frowned.

Lupus pulled out his wax tablet and scribbled:

WINDOWS FOR PRISON

'Can he hear me if I talk?'

Lupus nodded.

'How do you know?'

Lupus made bug eyes at Aristo. The meaning was clear: Not now; I'll tell you later!

Aristo put his mouth to one of the gaps.

'Mordecai? Can you hear me? It's Aristo.'

There was no reply.

'Mordecai?' Aristo spoke a little louder.

Suddenly they heard an accented voice. 'Aristo? Is it you?'

'Yes. I'm here with Lupus. Are you all right?'

There was a moment's silence. Then: 'It could be worse.'

'Mordecai. We've just seen Bato. Is it possible your brother-in-law Simeon is an assassin?'

There was another long pause.

'Many years ago,' came Mordecai's voice, 'when Simeon was young, he joined the *sicarii* for a time. But he told me he'd reformed and . . . Now I may have put my family in danger. Are Miriam and Jonathan all right?'

Aristo and Lupus looked at one another. There was no point adding to Mordecai's worries.

'Yes,' said Aristo. 'They're worried about you, but they're both fine.'

'Good.' Mordecai's voice sounded tired.

'Mordecai. Is there anything we can do? Anything we can get you?'

'No. Yes! If you should see Simeon, tell him to make himself known to the authorities. That is, if he's innocent.'

'I understand,' said Aristo. 'Anything else?'

'I could do with a wax tablet. Oh, and some of the Egyptian balm for my cellmate. He's injured.'

'You're not alone?'

'No . . . there's another prisoner in here with me. He's wounded.'

Lupus held up one of his wax tablets – he always carried at least two – and Aristo nodded.

'Mordecai. We're going to drop a tablet through the airhole now. Can you catch it?'

'I'm ready.'

Lupus stood on tiptoe and pushed his spare tablet through the opening.

'Thank you. I've got it,' Lupus heard Mordecai say.

'We'll bring you the balm as soon as we can.'

'Clean strips of linen, too, if you can find them.'

'Of course. Take care, Mordecai.'

'Shalom, Aristo. Shalom, Lupus.'

Flavia stepped out of the bedroom and stretched. Then she shivered with excitement. She was in Rome! It even felt different. Although it was not going to be as hot as the previous day, the early morning air was already warm. Humid, too. And there was a faint smell of meat roasting on charcoal: probably from the morning sacrifices.

She looked round the tiny courtyard of the children's wing. Seven bedrooms looked out onto what was little more than a light well. Splashing in the centre of this paved courtyard was an orange marble fountain. A few steps took her to this fountain and she splashed her face. Nubia joined her and they both drank from cupped hands.

'Oh good! You're up,' Sisyphus clapped his hands and stepped into the courtyard. He was wearing a leek-green tunic and matching leather ankle boots. 'Let's go have our breakfast in the ivy pergola. It's the perfect place to plan our next move.'

'You're going to help us find Jonathan?' Flavia looked at him in amazement.

'Of course.' He winked at Nubia. 'I haven't had this much fun in years. *Much* better than copying out the senator's speeches!'

He led them down a corridor, through a large atrium with a rainwater pool, and into the open space of a long inner garden. Although the garden was laid out with formal paths and knee-high hedges of box, it had become rather scruffy and overgrown. Flavia liked it: it looked lived-in. She noticed children's toys here and there: a leather ball, a wooden horse with one broken wheel, and a reed hoop.

'How many children does my aunt have again?' she asked.

'Six last count,' sighed Sisyphus, 'or is it seven? I can never remember. Children don't interest me until they learn to speak intelligently. And some of them never do. I like Aulus Junior, though. He's about your age: twelve, I believe.'

'I'm only just ten,' admitted Flavia.

'But my dear! You're so *mature* for ten. And terribly clever.'

Suddenly he stopped. 'Tell me. How old do you think I am?' He struck a pose with his hands on his slim hips and turned his face to show them his profile.

Flavia and Nubia looked at each other in dismay. To Flavia he just looked old, like her father, but she knew adults always liked to be thought younger than they really were.

'Um,' said Flavia, 'twenty-five?'

'Miss Flavia,' beamed Sisyphus, 'you're my friend forever!' He linked his arms into theirs and led them on down the path to a small arbour covered with thick ivy. They had to bend to enter and it took Flavia's eyes a moment to adjust.

'Oh, it's wonderful,' she exclaimed as she looked around.

Nubia nodded. 'House of Green,' she said.

A wooden trellis was covered in glossy ivy, so that they seemed to stand inside a miniature house with an ivy ceiling and walls. It was deliciously cool and full of a deep green light. There was just enough room for a small wrought-iron table and a stone bench on either side.

Breakfast was already laid out on the table: caraway seed bread, soft white goat's cheese and three cups of foaming black grape juice. And arranged carefully on a small silver plate were several sections of a pulpy fruit whose colour and scent Flavia recognised at once.

'Orange!' She clapped her hands and looked up at Sisyphus with delight.

'You and Lupus can't go to Rome,' cried Miriam. 'I'll be all alone!'

'I've asked Alma to come and stay here with you,' said Aristo. 'She'll bring the dogs with her.'

'I want to come with you!' said Miriam, tossing her dark curls and gazing defiantly at Aristo.

She looked very beautiful, and Lupus could tell Aristo was tempted. He was about to let Aristo know it was a bad idea when the young Greek shook his head.

'What if they release your father? And what if Captain Geminus returns from his travels? Or someone brings an important message?'

'You're right,' Miriam turned away. 'I just feel so useless!'

'You're not useless,' said Aristo. 'You can help us. Rome's a big city. Flavia has probably gone to stay with her aunt, but we've no idea where Jonathan is. Just tell us anything that might help us determine where he might have gone, and why.'

Miriam thought for a moment. 'Ever since he smelled that lemon blossom perfume, he's been depressed about mother's death. Flavia told me he blames himself.'

'For your mother's death? But surely he was just a baby when she died.'

'I know.'

'Anything else that might indicate where he's gone?' asked Aristo.

'Uncle Simi left for Rome yesterday morning; so presumably they went together.'

'How do you know Jonathan went to Rome?'

'His message on this wax tablet. Oh, you won't be able to read it: it's in Hebrew: "Gone to Rome" he says, and then "Please . . ." and the rest of the wax melted, though it's firm again now.'

Lupus picked up the red and blue tablet and examined it.

Aristo shook his head. 'If only we knew the rest of the message; it might help us find him.'

Lupus tugged the short sleeve of Aristo's tunic.

'What, Lupus?'

TABLET IS NEW wrote Lupus on his own wax tablet.

Miriam nodded. 'That's right. Gaius gave it to Jonathan for his birthday the day before yesterday.'

CHEAP WAX continued Lupus.

'Probably been mixed with some lard,' said Aristo. 'It happens.'

STYLUS PUSHED THROUGH

'What are you getting at, Lupus?'

MESSAGE UNDERNEATH?

'Of course!' Aristo snapped his fingers. 'Lupus, you're brilliant!'

'What is it?' asked Miriam.

'This tablet,' said Aristo, 'has only been used once and the wax was very soft. See where Jonathan's stylus pushed right through to the wood?'

'Yes . . .'

'If he pushed hard to write the whole message he might have scratched the wood underneath—'

'—so his message might still be there, under the wax which melted and then hardened again!'

Lupus nodded vigorously.

'So if we melt the wax and pour it off—' began Miriam.

Aristo finished her thought: '—we might be able to read the message hidden underneath.'

SCROLL XIII

Jonathan sat in the changing rooms of the Claudian Baths in Rome and waited.

He had soaked and oiled and scraped himself and it was his turn to guard their things while his uncle bathed. Earlier, on the way to the baths, Simeon had bought them new tunics: cream linen with a black vertical stripe from each shoulder to hem. They also had the precious barbiton, and a money purse with the last of their coins.

Jonathan had put on his new tunic. He had the money purse round his neck and the barbiton safe across his lap, so he closed his eyes. Because of all the wheeled traffic, their room had been noisier through-out the night than it had been during the day. It had been so noisy that when Simeon had made some remark, although he was only a few feet away on the second bed, Jonathan hadn't been able to hear him. He had barely slept and now he was exhausted.

But he must have dozed off, because something startled him awake. A good-looking Roman stood in front of him. The man had a big head, dark blue eyes and quizzical eyebrows. He wore a cream tunic with a black bar from shoulder to hem.

'Uncle Simeon?' Jonathan blinked sleep from his eyes.

Simeon nodded and rubbed his clean-shaven chin. 'It's amazing what a good shave can do.' He shouldered the barbiton and looked down at Jonathan.

'Come on,' he said. 'Time for us to visit the Palatine.'

Lupus pushed between Aristo and Miriam, eager to see what was happening on the kitchen hearth.

'Careful, Lupus,' Aristo warned. 'The coals are red hot.' To Miriam he said, 'Just melt the wax; make sure you don't burn the wood.'

'I know what I'm doing,' said Miriam. 'I cook every day.'

Chastened, Aristo was quiet for a moment. Then he said to Miriam, 'You've changed. You used to be such a shy little thing.'

'I'm only shy with people I don't know.' Miriam turned her head and they looked at one another for several long moments. Finally, Lupus jabbed Aristo with his elbow.

'What?' Aristo scowled down at Lupus.

Lupus pointed at the wax tablet, which was starting to smoke.

'It's burning,' Aristo cried.

'No, it's not.' Miriam calmly lifted the tablet off the heat with a pair of tongs and tipped it to one side. The liquid wax ran off it and was absorbed by the ashes of the hearth. Miriam replaced the tablet on the metal pan for a moment and then poured off the rest of the yellow wax.

'I can see marks,' cried Aristo.

Lupus nodded enthusiastically.

'Let's take it out into the sunlight,' said Miriam.

The three of them hurried out into the garden courtyard and Miriam tipped the rectangle of wood until she found the right angle of light and shadow to make the marks clear.

'Yes,' she said. 'I think I can read it.'

'What does it say?' said Aristo.

' "Gone to Rome. Please . . . don't worry. Simeon . . . is with me. He thinks . . . mother is . . . alive and a slave in the Golden House . . . We will try to save her." '

Miriam's face went pale. 'But father always told us mother was dead,' she said slowly. 'Simeon must have lied to Jonathan.' She gripped Aristo's hand and looked up into his face. 'Flavia was right: it's some kind of trap,' she said. 'You've got to help Jonathan!'

'Jonathan,' said Simeon, 'are you sure you want to do this? You don't have to come in with me. You can wait back at our rented room until I come out. *If* I come out.'

They stood by a fountain in the dappled shade of the umbrella pines on the Palatine Hill. Beside them, two marble sea nymphs poured splashing water from carved shells into a granite basin.

Jonathan pulled his new cream-coloured tunic away from his perspiring body. It had been a stiff climb up the Palatine Hill. He was wheezing, too.

'Just tell me again,' he said.

Simeon turned his head and looked straight into Jonathan's eyes.

'I believe,' he said, 'that your mother is still alive and a slave in the Golden House.'

Jonathan gazed back into his uncle's blue eyes and then nodded.

'Then I'll come in with you.'

'First you should know the full extent of my mission.'

'All right.' Jonathan sat on the cool granite edge of the fountain and waited.

'Three assassins,' said Simeon, 'have been sent from Corinth to the Palace of Titus.'

'Three?' said Jonathan.

Simeon nodded and reached into his leather belt. From a hidden slit he pulled out a curved dagger.

'Three,' he repeated, 'and I am one of them.'

SCROLL XIV

'Titus and Berenice,' said Sisyphus. 'were very wicked people. Before they met one another. And after.'

'What were they doing?' asked Nubia. Although breakfast was over and the plates cleared away, they lingered in the green coolness of the ivy pergola.

'My dears, you don't need to know the gruesome details. Suffice it to say the people of Rome called them "Nero and Poppaea".'

Flavia gasped.

Nubia frowned. 'What is Neronpopeye?'

'Nero was an evil Emperor,' said Flavia. 'Poppaea was his girlfriend. I know because pater told me some of the things they did. They were horrible.'

Sitting on the edge of the splashing fountain in the cool shade of the Palatine Hill, Jonathan grew pale as Simeon explained his mission.

'If they catch us before we reach the Emperor,' his uncle concluded, 'they may very well torture us. And afterwards they will certainly kill me, probably by crucifixion. You will most likely be enslaved. Are you still willing to come with me?'

Jonathan nodded and tried to speak, but his throat was suddenly too dry. He scooped up a handful of water from the fountain behind him and turned back in time to see Simeon toss the curved dagger underneath a myrtle bush and kick a thin layer of pine needles and dust over it.

'If they found that knife on me,' explained Simeon, 'I would be hanging from a cross before I could blink. Now our only weapons will be our wits.' He stood up and slung the barbiton over his shoulder.

Jonathan stood too. His heart thumped and he felt sick.

'Nervous?' His uncle looked down at him.

Jonathan nodded.

'Don't worry,' said Simeon. 'The guards won't think it odd. Anyone about to perform for the most powerful man in the Roman Empire would be nervous.'

'But my dears, let me tell you.' Sisyphus leaned forward. 'Since he became Emperor three months ago, the most remarkable change has come over Titus. He is completely reformed. For example. You've heard of Vesuvius?'

Flavia and Nubia glanced at each other.

'The volcano,' said Flavia.

'Precisely. A terrible disaster. Thousands left ruined and homeless. And do you know what Titus did? The man we all thought would tax us to death in order to pay for his orgies?' Sisyphus slapped his thigh and sat back on the bench. 'He used his own money to help the survivors!'

'Amazing,' said Flavia.

'Quite,' said Sisyphus. 'You can be certain a man has had a real change of heart when he opens his coin purse.'

'And you don't think he was just pretending to be good, to get the senators to like him?' asked Flavia.

'And for making the other people to like him?' added Nubia.

'Some people think that. But I don't. Let me tell you why I think Titus has really changed. Within a week of his father's death Berenice hurried back from Athens, ready to be Poppaea to his Nero. But do you know what happened?'

Flavia and Nubia shook their heads.

'He sent her away again! He had complete power. Could have made her his queen. Could even have kept her as his secret girlfriend. But he sent her away for the second time *without even seeing her*! Something has happened to him. I tell you, the man has changed.'

There was an urgent snipping noise outside the ivy pergola and Flavia pushed her head out.

'Caudex!' she said. 'What are you doing out there?'

'Just trimming the ivy.' The big slave blushed and looked down at his feet. 'And I wanted to hear the rest of the story.'

*

Somewhere on the Palatine Hill, slaves were building an extension to the already vast palace. Jonathan could hear the faint sounds of hammer, saw and workmen shouting. But here by the slaves' entrance it was peaceful, with only the twitter of birds and a slight breeze rustling the leaves. There was a shady porch, with cool marble benches and columns. Two soldiers stood guard, one either side of the double doors, but they kept a discreet distance.

A door slave had gone to find his superior.

'Remember,' Simeon told Jonathan as they waited for the steward, 'just bang the tambourine as you did last night; you'll be fine.'

Jonathan nodded and told himself this was his chance to make things right.

Presently a tall man with grizzled hair appeared in the open doorway. He had a large nose and bushy eyebrows.

'Good morning.' Simeon's voice was as deep and sweet as the barbiton. 'We're travelling musicians. We've come to play for the Emperor.'

'I'm sorry,' said the steward in a well-educated voice. 'We aren't allowing any strangers into the palace at the moment.'

'But I thought the Emperor enjoyed listening to new music,' said Simeon.

'Ordinarily, he does. But security is tight at the moment. I'm afraid it's impossible to gain access to the palace.'

Simeon turned away and then back. Things were obviously not going as he'd planned.

'Is it possible to speak to someone named Agathus?' he asked.

The door-slave looked from Simeon to Jonathan and then back. 'I am Agathus,' he said slowly.

Simeon glanced at the soldiers standing guard nearby. Casually, with the tip of his new sandal, he traced a symbol on the dusty threshold of the porch. Before Jonathan could see it, he scuffed it out.

But Agathus had seen it. He looked up at Simeon from under his bushy eyebrows and then nodded.

'There may be a way . . .'

'So how do we know whether Jonathan has been able to get into the Golden House?' Flavia asked Sisyphus.

'I've been thinking about that.' Sisyphus's dark eyes gleamed. 'We have to come at this problem from a different direction.'

'What do you mean?' said Flavia.

'We could waste valuable time merely trying to find out if Jonathan's been able to get in. I think we should assume he has been successful, and try to find out how we can get in to the part of the Golden House where the Jewish slaves are kept.'

'So you think we should learn more about the Golden House,' said Flavia slowly. 'Like whether there are any secret corridors or tunnels.'

'My dear, if Nero built it, there are bound to be secret corridors and tunnels. We just need to find out where they are.'

SCROLL XV

'Hurry, Lupus! The cart's leaving.'

Lupus looked up and down Ostia's main street. He could hear Aristo but he couldn't see him. He had just been approaching the mule-driver's fountain when he heard his tutor's voice calling.

'Quickly!' cried Aristo again. 'I've saved you a place.'

Then Lupus saw the cart. It was already moving into the shade beneath the arch of the Roman Gate up ahead. Lupus sprinted down the Decumanus Maximus, his sandals slapping the hot white paving stones. He dodged two giggling women with papyrus parasols and a carpenter carrying planks of wood. He nearly knocked over a slave carrying a jar of urine to the fullers.

Lupus ran past the columned shop-fronts on his left and the long water trough on his right and charged through the Roman Gate with its laughing soldiers. He emerged into the hot sunlight again and reached out to grasp Aristo's extended hand. Then he felt himself lifted up and onto the hard, wooden bench. The other men in the cart grinned at him. The driver – who'd been going slow – gave him a wink over his shoulder before turning back to flick his whip at the mules.

'Did you give Mordecai the balm?' asked Aristo in a low voice.

Lupus nodded, then turned to watch the white marble arch of Ostia's main gate grow smaller and smaller.

He was going to see Rome at last.

In an inner room of the Imperial Palace on the Palatine Hill a dough-faced man with greasy black hair was interviewing Simeon and Jonathan.

'My name is Harmonius,' he said. 'Agathus has recommended you but I want to satisfy myself that you are genuine. And the only way I can do that is to audition you. We're on alert against a possible assassination attempt, but the Emperor's headaches have been particularly bad. Music is one of the few things that gives him any relief. If your music can help him, then your reward will be great.' He folded his arms. 'But first you must show me whether you are real musicians or merely impostors.'

'There it is.' Sisyphus stood beside Lady Cynthia's private litter with his hands on his hips and squinted up at an enormous structure. 'The eighth wonder of the world.'

Flavia and Nubia leaned out of the litter and gasped at the sight of a huge oval building, white against the turquoise sky above Rome.

'Bulbus. Caudex. Have a little rest,' said Sisyphus.

The two door-slaves set the litter onto the hot paving stones and helped Flavia and Nubia out.

'It's the biggest building I've ever seen,' said Flavia tipping her head back and shading her eyes. 'It's colossal!'

'What is it?' asked Nubia.

'It's Vespasian's new amphitheatre,' said Sisyphus. 'When it opens in a few months there'll be gladiatorial fights, sea battles, beast hunts . . .'

'What is that twigs all over it?' asked Nubia.

'Scaffolding.'

'What are they doing?' asked Flavia. 'Painting it?'

Sisyphus shook his head. 'They're covering it with stucco, a type of plaster. They mix it with marble dust so that it sparkles like the real thing. When they've finished,' he said, 'the entire amphitheatre will look as if it's made of solid marble. Then they'll paint it and put statues in the niches.'

Flavia glanced at Sisyphus. 'There must be hundreds of slaves working on it,' she said.

'Thousands, my dear. Simply thousands. And almost every one of them a captive from Judaea, brought back by our illustrious Emperor Titus.'

By the end of Simeon's second song, two dozen slaves, scribes and soldiers of the Imperial Palace had crowded into the wide doorway to listen to the music. As the last note died away, they all broke into spontaneous applause.

Harmonius passed a handkerchief across his eyes. 'Extraordinary,' he whispered. 'I have never heard anything quite like that. Sir, you are an artist.'

Simeon bowed his big head modestly, and Jonathan breathed a secret sigh of relief.

'The Emperor has an official engagement this evening,' continued Harmonius, 'but his younger brother Domitian is having a small dinner party here in the palace, and I'm sure he would pay you just as well. Then you can perform for the Emperor tomorrow.' Harmonius stood. 'Now, if you would both like to rest and prepare yourselves, I will show you to your rooms.'

'Of course, there's more than one forum in Rome,' said Sisyphus, helping Flavia and Nubia down from the litter a second time. 'But when people say the Roman Forum, this is the one they mean.'

Flavia gazed open-mouthed at the buildings towering around them. She had never seen so many columns in one place. Somehow, she'd always imagined the Roman forum would be of pure white marble, but the roofs were red tile, almost all the statues were brightly painted, and there were dazzling touches of gold on most of the buildings.

Something else was not as she'd imagined. Apart from a few slaves going about their business and a boy driving a flock of goats between two temples, the forum was almost deserted.

'It's so empty,' she said. 'I thought it would be crowded with people.'

Sisyphus nodded. 'It usually is,' he said, 'but listen.'

The girls stood very still; Caudex and Bulbus, too. At first they could only hear the soft clanking of the goat bells growing fainter and fainter. Then they heard a muffled roar.

'I am hearing that earlier,' said Nubia.

'It's coming from the Circus Maximus,' said Sisyphus. 'Just the other side of this hill, which is the Palatine, of course. The races are under way. That's the sound of a quarter of a million people cheering for their teams.'

Flavia gasped. 'A quarter of a million?'

Sisyphus nodded. 'That's why Rome feels so empty. It's the *Ludi Romani*.'

Nubia frowned. 'What is the loo dee ro ma nee?'

'A twelve-day festival to Jupiter. With chariot races every day. That's where all the Romans are. Can't stand the races myself. All that noise, dust and heat. I much prefer a good comedy by Plautus. Or a musical recital. Now have a look behind you.'

'Great Neptune's beard!' exclaimed Nubia.

Flavia shrieked: 'What is THAT?'

Behind them towered an enormous gold statue of a nude man. It was almost as tall as the huge new amphitheatre which stood behind it.

'It's the sun god.'

'It doesn't look like the sun god.' Flavia squinted at the statue.

'You're absolutely right, my dear, it's not,' he hissed. 'It's actually a portrait of Nero which he erected to himself. But no Roman will give him the satisfaction of acknowledging that. Vespasian put some rays on his head and now we all call it the sun god.'

'He looks like a big pudgy bully.'

'Yes,' murmured Sisyphus. 'It is an excellent likeness. Anyway,' he continued. 'Here's me.' He gestured at a marble building with greyish green columns and bronze doors. 'The plans of the Golden House should be in there. They'll let me in because I work for Senator Cornix. But you won't be allowed.'

'What shall we do, then?' said Flavia.

'Thought of that already,' said Sisyphus. 'Bulbus, take the girls to Lady Cynthia's baths. You and Caudex wait outside.'

He turned to Flavia and Nubia. 'You're going to enjoy one of the great pleasures of Rome,' he said. 'A day at the baths. Have a manicure. Or a massage. Get your hair done. Just tell them you are Lady Cynthia's niece and put it on her account. I'll see you back at the house by the eleventh hour. Hopefully with some useful information.'

It was mid-afternoon of the same day when Harmonius led Jonathan and Simeon to the private dining room of the Emperor's younger brother. Domitian and his guests were just finishing their first course when

Jonathan and his uncle passed between pink columns to a low platform facing the diners.

Fifteen guests reclined on five couches, eating peppered wedges of a strange orange fruit which Jonathan had never seen before. It was still early, only the ninth hour. Outside, the city of Rome was sweltering. But the summer triclinium of the Imperial Palace was a cool oasis of greens and pinks. Across the entire back wall a sheet of glassy water hissed into a trough of pink marble. Potted palms and gardenias provided colour and fragrance, while six Egyptian slave-girls created a breeze by waving peacock-feather fans.

Jonathan recognised Domitian at once. He was a slimmer version of his older brother, but where Titus's hair was sandy, Domitian's was brown. He was stretched out on the central couch, between a bearded man and a lovely red-headed woman.

The woman was laughing throatily at something Domitian had said. Jonathan supposed she thought him handsome. He had curly hair and large brown eyes, but Jonathan didn't like his smirk.

When Simeon had settled the barbiton between his feet, he glanced over at Harmonius, who raised his eyebrows and nodded.

Simeon bowed his head for a moment, then found the beat of his heart on the deepest string. Gradually the diners grew silent. After a moment, Jonathan echoed the beat on his tambourine, damping it somewhat to make the instrument resonate more than jingle. Then Simeon added the melody and finally the words.

Jonathan didn't have to look at the diners to know they were moved. He felt a kind of stillness within the room. Finally, near the end of the third song, he did look up.

Some of the dinner-guests were smiling, and tapping the beat with their fingers. Others had closed their eyes to concentrate. But the bearded man had leaned forward and was speaking into Domitian's ear. They were both looking at Simeon, who was lost in his music.

Simeon strummed the last chord and when the applause died down, the bearded man said in a loud voice, 'Well played, Simeon!'

'Thank you,' said Simeon with his gap-toothed smile. And then froze.

Jonathan saw a look of panic flit across his uncle's face and he suddenly realised why. The bearded man had addressed him by name, not in Latin but in Hebrew. And Simeon had replied in the same language.

SCROLL XVI

'Oh Pollux!' Flavia heard Bulbus grumble, as they rounded a corner on their way back from the baths. 'Looks like we have more visitors.'

As Flavia leaned out of the litter to look, it tipped alarmingly to one side. She heard Bulbus curse as he tried to compensate for the sudden shift of weight.

'Stop the litter!' cried Flavia, and when Bulbus and Caudex obeyed, she leapt out and ran towards the two figures standing in the shade of the porch.

'Aristo! Lupus!' she cried and threw her arms around her tutor. 'I'm so glad to see you!' She let Aristo go and hugged Lupus, too.

'You girls are in big trouble.' Aristo tried to scowl.

Flavia tipped her head to one side. 'Then why are you smiling?'

'I'm not,' he grinned, and they all burst out laughing.

'Guards!' The Emperor Titus's younger brother slid off the dining couch and landed lightly on his feet.

Immediately, two soldiers stepped in from the garden and clanked to attention.

'Is your name Simeon ben Jonah?' Domitian asked Jonathan's uncle.

There was a terrible silence. The bearded dinner-guest eased himself from the couch and moved to stand beside Domitian. This time he spoke not in Hebrew but in Latin. 'Of course he is. I recognise him, even though he's cut his hair and shaved off his beard. Don't you know me, Simeon?'

Jonathan looked from the bearded man to his uncle. It was so quiet that he could hear the waterfall splashing into its trough at the back of the room.

'Yoseph ben Matthias,' growled Simeon, and rose slowly to his feet. Jonathan stood, too.

'Precisely.' The bearded man smiled round at the other diners, as if pleased that he had been recognised. 'But now I am the Emperor's servant and have taken his name. You may call me Titus Flavius Josephus.'

Domitian moved forward until his face was inches from Simeon's. Jonathan could smell the wine and garlic on Domitian's breath as he said, 'Josephus, are you sure this man is an assassin?'

'Oh yes,' said Josephus. 'I'm sure. Everyone knows Simeon the Sicarius.'

'Very well,' said Domitian, and turned away. 'Guards! Find out what they know. Then crucify this one. As for the boy . . . brand him and put him with the other Jewish slaves. And no need to bother the Emperor.'

★

Bulbus was lighting the oil lamps when Sisyphus stepped into the dusky light of the grape arbour courtyard.

'Ah,' he said with a smile. 'You must be the famous Lupus. Pleased to meet you at last. Flavia and Nubia have told me all about you. And you are Aristo?'

Aristo nodded. 'I hope you don't mind two more guests.'

Sisyphus raised his eyebrows and said something in Greek.

Flavia's tutor laughed and replied in the same language.

'Hey!' cried Flavia. 'Don't do that. I hate it when people speak a language I can't understand.'

'You should understand it,' said Aristo with a grin. 'We've been studying Greek together for over three years.'

Flavia scowled. 'I know. But I don't understand when you talk fast.' She turned back to the secretary. 'Sisyphus,' she said, 'Aristo and Lupus found a message left by Jonathan. We were right. Jonathan *has* gone to the Golden House. But not to get information about his mother. He actually thinks she's alive! He must have gone to search for her. But Jonathan's sister Miriam is sure their mother is dead. She thinks it's some kind of trick!' Flavia stopped to take a breath.

'Why would someone go to all this trouble to trick Jonathan?' asked Sisyphus.

'Maybe Simeon is trying to trick Jonathan into helping him kill the Emperor!' said Flavia.

'That is a very real possibility,' said Aristo. 'Nobody expects a deadly assassin to have a boy with him.'

'Did you find out how to get into the Golden House?' Flavia asked Sisyphus.

'Not yet,' he said. 'But I've brought some scrolls back with me. We can look at them tomorrow, as soon as it gets light.'

'Good,' said Flavia brightly. 'Now that we're all together, I'm sure we'll rescue Jonathan from the assassin's clutches in no time at all!'

'You're lucky,' said Agathus, as he and Jonathan watched a slave heat the branding iron in a brazier full of red-hot coals. 'If Josephus hadn't intervened they'd be torturing you by now.'

Jonathan sat shivering in his loin cloth. He didn't feel lucky. They had shaved his head and searched him for lice. They had opened his mouth to examine his teeth. They had stripped him of all his possessions, including the bulla which showed he was freeborn and his ruby ring. They had even taken away his lemon-scented handkerchief. The only thing they hadn't taken was his mother's signet ring, stuck tightly on his little finger.

Agathus saw Jonathan looking at the ring. 'It will come off soon enough,' he said. 'I imagine you'll lose quite a bit of weight in the next few days.'

Jonathan stared stupidly at the steward and then looked back at the metal rod glowing red in the coals.

A slave was about to brand his left arm with the Emperor's seal. Then he would become the property of Titus Flavius Vespasianus.

'Your friend's lucky, too.' said Agathus. 'He'll live. If he survives the torture.'

Jonathan felt ill. The bearded man named Josephus had persuaded Domitian not to kill Simeon but merely to put out his eyes and cut off his big toes. That way, Josephus had said, he'll be blind and lame and unable to hurt anyone, but we can still enjoy his beautiful music.

'Are you going to be sick again?' Agathus put his hand on Jonathan's bare shoulder.

Jonathan shook his head. 'Nothing left to throw up,' he muttered.

The slave was approaching with the branding iron.

Agathus squeezed Jonathan's shoulder and handed him a leather belt.

'Here, boy. Bite on this. The pain will be quite severe.'

Jonathan placed the leather strap between his teeth and then took it out again.

'My handkerchief,' he said, nodding towards his clothing at the end of the rough wooden bench. 'Can I bite on that instead?'

'I suppose, if I fold it several times . . .' The slave stopped and waited for Agathus to bring the cloth. Jonathan inhaled its lemon fragrance to give himself courage, then clamped it between his teeth and watched the red-hot end of the branding iron move towards his shoulder.

It was not the pain that made him pass out, but the smell of burning flesh.

SCROLL XVII

'Useless!' cried Flavia, throwing down the scroll. 'There's nothing here!'

It was late afternoon three days later.

Flavia and Sisyphus were in the senator's library. Scrolls lay spread across the table. Most of them contained architects' plans or accounts of Nero's reign.

Aristo and Lupus stepped wearily into the study. They had been prowling the Palatine Hill, disguised as a young patrician and his slave boy.

'Anything?' Flavia looked up at them with wet eyes.

Lupus shook his head and Aristo angrily pulled the toga from his shoulders. 'I don't know how citizens can bear to wear these things,' he said, tossing it onto a chair. 'They're insufferably hot.'

'It *is* one of the senator's winter togas,' murmured Sisyphus, rising and going to the chair. 'He's taken his light summer togas with him.' He shook out the toga and carefully began to fold it.

The light dimmed momentarily as two more figures appeared in the doorway.

'Nubia, Caudex!' said Flavia. 'Any luck?'

Nubia shook her head. They'd been trying to find an entrance to the part of the Golden House on the Oppian Hill.

'Big wall all round it,' grumbled Caudex and wandered off towards the kitchen.

'We'll never find him!' Flavia slumped into a chair and bit her lip to keep from crying. 'I'm a terrible detective.'

The others sat dejectedly at the big oak table.

After a while Sisyphus spoke. 'My grandmother, may Juno bless her memory, was a very wise woman. When I was a boy, I once lost a figurine that was very precious to me. I looked for it everywhere. Then one day she said, Sisyphus, if you stop looking for it, it might find you.'

'Did it work?' asked Flavia.

'As a matter of fact, it did. I went to visit a friend the next day and there it was. She'd borrowed my figurine without asking.'

'How does that help us?' sighed Aristo.

'Well,' said Sisyphus. 'Tomorrow is the last day of the *Ludi Romani*. I suggest we take the day off and go to the races.' He shuddered dramatically. 'Much as I hate them. If nothing else, it may give us a break and a fresh perspective.'

Lupus whooped. Nubia sat up straight, too. She longed to see the horses run. Flavia glanced at Aristo and he gave a small nod.

'All right,' sighed Flavia. 'I suppose it can't hurt.'

*

'What are you doing?' asked a little girl's voice in Aramaic.

Jonathan didn't even bother to look up. 'What does it look like I'm doing?' he replied in the same language.

'It looks like you're scrubbing the latrines.'

'Then I suppose that's what I'm doing.' He stopped for a moment and closed his eyes. The throbbing pain in his left arm seemed to be getting worse, not better.

'You're new here, aren't you?' she asked.

'Yes,' said Jonathan, trying not to retch at the smell. After a moment he said: 'Where is here, anyway?'

After they branded him he had passed in and out of consciousness. He vaguely recalled being taken some distance to a cubicle just big enough for him to lie down in. For two days an enormously fat female slave had left bowls of wheat porridge outside his door. This morning she had tossed a scrubbing-brush into his cell and told him to clean the latrines down the hall.

'You're in the Golden House,' said the girl's voice.

Jonathan snorted as he scrubbed the holes cut into the long wooden bench. 'Some Golden House.'

'My name's Rizpah. What's yours?'

'Jonathan.' Suddenly he stopped and said slowly. 'The fat lady said I'm supposed to be in isolation for a week until I'm no longer unclean. She told me nobody comes here at this time of day. So what are you doing here? And how did you get in?' He turned to peer at her in the dim light of a small, high window. 'You didn't come through the doorway . . .'

The little girl named Rizpah sat on the polished oak latrine behind him, between two of the holes.

Jonathan had never seen such a curious person.

She was tiny, the size of a five-year-old, but he guessed she was older, at least Lupus's age. She had perfectly straight white hair and her eyes were pink. Her skin was so fine that it was almost translucent. She wore a grubby black tunic with a white border.

'You're one of the Emperor's slaves, too,' he observed.

'Of course.' She swung her feet and drummed the wooden latrine with her heels. 'You're handsome. I like you.'

'Oh yes,' said Jonathan. 'Shaved head, festering brand on the arm, all covered with . . . I'm *very* handsome today.'

'What's it like out there?' she asked presently.

'Out where?'

'Rome.'

Jonathan peered at her. 'You've never been outside?'

Rizpah shook her head. 'I hate the sun. Anyway I like it here. It's cool and dark here. I've lived here in the Golden House all my life,' she added. 'Here I was born and here I'll die.' She seemed to be quoting someone.

'And they call *me* a pessimist,' muttered Jonathan. He resumed scrubbing. 'Any other gems to brighten up my day?'

'I know how *you* could get out of here.'

Slowly Jonathan put down his scrubbing brush and

turned to face her. 'Rizpah,' he said. 'I can't tell you how much that would brighten up my day.'

Nubia sat forward in her seat and looked over the rail down onto the race track below. Then she looked across the sandy track at the strange sculptures in the central divider. She especially liked the immensely tall needle of red granite in the middle of the central island, and the seven gold dolphins at one end.

Finally she looked around at the people behind her and across the track and on either side.

'I have never seen so many peoples,' she murmured.

'I know,' said Flavia, and then turned to Sisyphus. 'How did you get such good seats?' she asked. 'Right at the front by the turning post, *and* in the shade?'

'They're not mine. They're the Senator's,' said Sisyphus. 'He's got eight seats so that he can take Lady Cynthia and the howling brood. And we won't be in the shade for long, I fear. It's still early.'

'Behold!' cried Nubia. 'The horses.'

As the first of the chariots emerged from the shaded starting gates and moved into the sunshine for their parade lap, trumpets blared and a huge roar erupted from the onlookers. Nubia covered her ears, but as the first chariot approached she forgot about the noise and leant forward.

'Behold!' she cried. 'It is the Titus!'

'Yes,' shouted Sisyphus. 'Today is the last day of the festival, so the Emperor himself leads the procession.'

Titus rode in a golden chariot pulled by two magnificent white stallions. Dressed in purple with a gold wreath on his thinning hair, the Emperor himself held the reins. In the chariot beside him stood a rigid young man, dressed in golden armour. He seemed curiously pale and stiff to Nubia, and his eyes gazed ahead unseeing.

'Is that a statue?' shouted Flavia.

Sisyphus nodded. 'It's the famous gold and ivory statue of Britannicus. He and Titus were boyhood friends, until Nero poisoned him.'

Nubia leaned further over the rail. Now the different teams were approaching.

The Blues came first, each team of four horses stepping proudly and tossing their manes as if they enjoyed the adulation of the crowd. Next came the Greens, the Reds, and finally the Whites. Each chariot was trimmed in its team colours. As the third red team came nearer, Nubia gripped the rail.

'I like those horses.' Nubia brought her mouth close to Sisyphus's ear, to make herself heard above the continuing cheers of the crowd.

'Oh no, my dear.' He shook his head. 'Not the red team. Only sailors and cart-drivers support the Reds. You simply must support the Blues.'

Nubia frowned. 'But their horses are not so good.'

Sisyphus scowled. 'Oh, very well,' he said. 'If you insist.' He pushed along the row and stomped up the steps towards one of the arches.

'What did you say to him?' asked Flavia. 'I've never seen him get angry before.'

Nubia looked worried. 'I only said I am liking the Reds.'

Now the third red chariot was passing directly below them. Nubia saw that its driver was an African boy not much older than she was. He wore red leather and like the other charioteers, he had tied the reins around his waist.

She tugged at Flavia's sleeve.

'Why does he tie himself to horses? What if he is being dragged?'

'I don't know,' said Flavia.

'Nubia,' said Aristo, raising his voice to make himself heard above the cheering. 'Do you see what he's holding in his hand?'

Nubia saw the flash of bright metal. 'A knife?' she said.

'Exactly. If he gets pulled out of the chariot and dragged along he'll cut himself free.'

Nubia shuddered.

Some time afterwards – she had no idea how long – the young charioteer passed again, but this time his teeth were bared in a grimace of wild joy and he was driving for all he was worth, well ahead of the eight remaining chariots. It was the final lap. A huge wave of cheering swept the circus. Nubia felt her spirit lifted up and carried along by it and then she heard herself crying at the top of her lungs: 'Come on the Reds! Come on the Reds!'

She hadn't seen Sisyphus return, but she was suddenly aware that he was on his feet beside her and he was screaming for the Reds as loudly as everyone else.

'Great Juno's peacock, but it's hot! It's usually much cooler this time of year.' Sisyphus fanned himself vigorously with a papyrus fan and smiled at them. 'We should probably be going soon. Avoid the crush. Still, we've done very well today. We've made a tidy profit.'

'What do you mean?' asked Flavia absently, cracking another pistachio nut with her teeth. She had poured the nuts onto her lap and was studying the papyrus twist they had come in: it had faint writing on it.

'We've made nearly a thousand denarii. That's more than the rent I get for these seats.'

Flavia's head jerked up and she saw Lupus looking wide-eyed, too.

'We've made a thousand denarii?' she said. 'How?'

'Simple. I've been betting on all the horses Nubia recommended. So far she's been right about them all.'

Flavia, Aristo and Lupus stared at Nubia open-mouthed. She looked equally surprised.

'My dears. Where do you think I've been rushing off to before each race? The latrines?'

Aristo said something to Sisyphus in Greek and he replied in the same language. Abruptly he stopped and looked at Flavia.

'Why are you giving me that injured look?' Sisyphus said to her. 'Oh all right.' He lowered his voice. 'Aristo said he thought that only senators and citizens were allowed to sit in these seats. And I said he was correct, but that I have an *arrangement* with the steward. The senator rarely attends the races so these valuable seats would sit empty. If it weren't for us.'

'So you and the steward rent them out?' whispered Aristo.

Sisyphus nodded. 'We split the profits. But we only rent them to very respectable families who will behave themselves and *not lean dangerously over the parapet flicking pistachio shells onto the race track, Lupus.*'

Lupus sat back and grinned at them.

Sisyphus scowled at Lupus, but there was a twinkle in his eye as he turned away. Then he gasped. 'Great Juno's peacock! Is that Celer sitting over there by the Imperial Box? I thought he'd died years ago. Flavia! It's Celer!'

'Celer who?'

'Not Celer who. Who Celer. Marcus Vibius Celer. The architect. The man whose plans you've been studying for the past few days?'

'It's Celer!' cried Flavia. She leapt to her feet, scattering pistachio shells everywhere.

'Yes.' Sisyphus nodded. 'It's definitely time you lot went home. Can you possibly take them, Aristo?'

'I think I can find the way,' said the young Greek.

'It's easy,' said Flavia. 'We just follow the big aqueduct back up the hill.'

'As for me,' said Sisyphus, 'I'm going to pay my compliments to old Celer over there. He owes me a few favours. And if anyone knows about secret passages or entrances to the Golden House, it will be him. After all, he built it.'

SCROLL XVIII

Jonathan was moving through blackness with nothing to guide him but the hand of a small girl.

'How do you know where you're going?' Jonathan said into the void. 'And how did you find these tunnels?' He heard his voice echoing back from the moist plaster walls.

'I told you,' came Rizpah's voice. 'I've lived here all my life. There are tunnels everywhere. Some of them are blocked up now but most aren't. Mother said the Beast built them.'

'The Beast?' Jonathan's Aramaic was a bit rusty. His father always insisted on them speaking Hebrew at home.

'The Beast. Neeron Kesar.'

'Oh. You mean Nero.'

'That's what I said.'

'Rizpah. Is your mother here?'

'Of course.'

'Could I see her?'

She must have stopped, because he bumped into her.

'Sorry, Rizpah.'

'Jonathan.' He could tell from her voice that she was trying to be patient with him. 'Do you want me to get you out, or do you want to meet my mother?'

'Are there other women with your mother?'

'Of course. They weave wool in the octagonal room.'

'Rizpah,' he said into the void. 'I want more than anything to get out of here. But I came to Rome to find my mother. Her name is Susannah. Is there a woman named Susannah ben Jonah with the others?'

There was such a long pause that if he hadn't been holding her moist little hand he would have thought himself alone.

Finally Rizpah's voice came out of the blackness. 'There is a woman called Susannah the Beautiful. But she is not with the others. She weaves on her own.' He felt her hand clench in his as she added, 'They call her the Traitor.'

As Flavia and her friends emerged from the shaded exit of the Circus Maximus and stepped into the blistering heat of a Roman afternoon, they scattered a group of feral cats who had been scavenging a discarded lunch. Most of the cats fled, but one of them – a tortoiseshell – looked up at them with round eyes.

'Great Juno's peacock!' Flavia exclaimed. 'Feles!'

'What?' said Aristo. Lupus echoed the question with his bug-eyed look.

'Feles . . . driver of cart?' said Nubia.

'Yes! I'm so stupid!' Flavia hit her forehead with the palm of her hand. 'That cat reminded me of him. Feles told us his girlfriend is a slave in the Imperial Palace on the Palatine Hill. She might know how to get in. I should have thought of this days ago.'

'Never mind, you've thought of it now,' said Aristo. 'How do we find her?'

'We'll have to ask Feles. He stays at the Owl Tavern just inside the gate.'

'Which gate?'

'The gate with three arches by the big white pyramid.'

'That's the Ostia Gate,' said Aristo. 'It's not far.'

Lupus held up his wax tablet:

WHAT ARE WE WAITING FOR?

'Rizpah,' whispered Jonathan. 'I think I can see light up ahead.'

'It's the octagonal room,' came Rizpah's voice. 'That's where my mother is.'

They were crawling along a low tunnel. As they moved forward, the blackness brightened to grey and then gold. Presently they reached the square end of the tunnel.

Jonathan peered out, squinting as his eyes adjusted to the light. He found he was looking down onto a vast octagonal room full of women weaving at looms. The weavers filled the space below him and the five large alcoves around it.

Above the courtyard rose a vast domed roof, covered with rough concrete, lit golden by the light pouring through a large circular skylight. The beam of sunshine illuminated the wool-dust suspended in the air, and to Jonathan it looked like a fat gold column that had tipped to one side.

From somewhere to his left came the sound of falling water.

'What is this place?' whispered Jonathan.

'I think this used to be the Beast's dining room,' said Rizpah. 'My mother calls it the Pavilion, because when she first came there was cloth inside the dome and it looked like a big tent. I don't remember. I wasn't born then.' She pointed. 'That's my mother over there, the one with the fluffy brown hair. See? The one working on the red and blue carpet. Her name is Rachel.'

All the women wore black robes, as if they were in mourning. A few had pulled black scarves over their hair but most had left their heads uncovered.

'And Susannah the Beautiful?' asked Jonathan.

Rizpah looked at him with her pink eyes. 'She isn't here.'

'I know. But can you take me to her?'

Rizpah nodded. 'Yes. Do you want to see her now or talk to my mother first?'

'I'd like to see her now.' Jonathan's heart was pounding.

'Then we have to go further on,' said Rizpah. 'She's in a special place we call the Cyclops' cave.'

Flavia and her friends found the Owl Tavern between two lofty tenement blocks on a street so narrow that it probably only saw the sun at midday.

'I don't like it here,' said Aristo, pulling aside the curtain of the litter so that Flavia, Nubia and Lupus could climb out.

The smell of sour cabbage mingled with the sickly-sweet odour of human sewage. Flavia squealed as something dripped on her shoulder, but it was only some wet washing hung overhead.

'At least we have Bulbus and Caudex to protect us,' she said, trying to breathe through her mouth.

Aristo looked around. 'I still don't like it. Let's find this Feles quickly and get out.'

'Yes,' lisped the innkeeper a few minutes later. He was a hideously ugly man with a harelip and a lazy eye. 'Feles is here. Only he's not here. He took his girl to the races.' The innkeeper smiled and his lip split even further to revealed orange teeth, the result of pink wine stains on yellowing enamel.

'We've just come from there,' said Flavia, looking him steadily in his one good eye so that she wouldn't have to look at the rest of his face. 'The races should have finished by now.'

'Then he'll probably be back any moment. Shall I get you a jug of wine while you wait?'

'No,' said Aristo hastily. 'We must get back. But could you give Feles a message? Ask him to go to the house of Senator Cornix on the Caelian Hill. It's the house with the blue doors at the foot of the aqueduct.' He flipped the innkeeper a copper coin.

The others turned to go, but Flavia stayed a moment longer and forced herself to look back at the innkeeper.

'Please tell Feles,' she said politely, 'that Flavia Gemina needs his help.'

'Be careful, Jonathan,' said Rizpah, 'it's slippery here.' The space they were moving through now was not so much a tunnel as a channel. Water ran between them along a shallow concrete trough. On either side of the running water was a space just big enough for them to crawl on their bellies. Rizpah wormed her way expertly along the right-hand bank of the channel, Jonathan moved more laboriously on the left. They were heading towards a chink of light the shape of an eye.

Presently, the chink grew bigger and brighter and Jonathan could hear the sound of foaming water. The brand on his left arm throbbed and his elbows were raw from pulling himself forward along the rough concrete, but he ground his teeth against the pain and moved steadily on.

Abruptly the water fell away, splashing onto sculpted rocks and into a pool.

As his eyes adjusted, Jonathan found himself looking into a large vaulted room designed to resemble a cave.

The floor was polished black marble and the walls encrusted with shells, pumice and imitation pearls. Stalactites of sculpted plaster hung from the ceiling.

At the far end of this long, man-made cave he could see columns silhouetted against the bright inner garden beyond. The soft greenish-yellow light which filtered in from the courtyard was reflected off the pool and formed wobbling rings of light on the stalactites.

At the brighter end of this bizarre room a solitary woman sat before a loom. Jonathan could not see her face, because she had just turned her head towards the garden, but he saw that she wore the black robes marking her out as a slave of Titus. Her head was uncovered, and her black hair as smooth as silk.

Presently, the woman turned her head back towards the loom. When Jonathan saw her profile, his heart pounded so hard he thought he might die. She was beautiful, like Miriam, with the same dark eyebrows, straight nose and full lips.

He knew it was his mother.

As he watched, a man appeared in the garden, his stocky body silhouetted as he passed through the columns and approached the woman. Her head turned again, she rose and stood with her back to Jonathan.

The man walked to the woman and took her hands in his. She was as tall as he, and he looked directly into her face. The man shook his head and put his arms around the woman, patting her back as if to comfort her.

He was powerfully built, with a square head and sandy hair. And although he was not wearing his purple toga or his golden wreath, Jonathan knew the man embracing his mother was the Emperor Titus.

SCROLL XIX

When Flavia and the others returned from the Owl Tavern, they found Sisyphus waiting for them in the atrium.

'Where have you been?' His eyes were shining.

'To an inn near the big pyramid by the Ostia Gate,' said Flavia. 'Our cart-driver's girlfriend is a slave at the Imperial Palace and we were trying to find him.'

'Any luck?' Sisyphus giggled.

'No,' said Aristo, 'but by the sound of it you have.'

'Yes, yes, yes!' Sisyphus clapped his hands together. 'Miss Flavia. Do you remember the plans of the Golden House we pored over? How some of the walls were shown with double lines?'

'Yes,' said Flavia. 'A black line next to a red line. We thought that meant the walls were extra strong.'

'No, no, no! Celer told me the red lines mark the location of secret tunnels!'

'But that means,' said Flavia, her eyes wide, 'that there are dozens of tunnels all over the Golden House!'

'And remember we puzzled over one or two red lines wandering off into the gardens? Those must be the places where the tunnels lead from the inside out!'

'Or,' said Flavia, 'from the outside in!'

'Why didn't you tell me the Emperor and my mother were lovers?' said Jonathan to Rizpah.

They had wriggled back to one of Rizpah's secret dens, between the octagonal room and the Cyclops' cave.

'They aren't lovers,' she said. 'All the women think they are but I know they're not.'

'It looked that way to me.'

'They're just friends. He visits her and talks to her every day but he doesn't spend the nights. Sometimes I hide here and listen to them talking.'

'How long has this been going on?'

'Since Berenice left. Five or six months.'

Jonathan groaned and leaned back against the damp wall. All these years, he had believed his mother was dead. But she had been right here in Rome, less than fifteen miles from Ostia. And Titus, the greatest enemy of the Jews, had been with her daily for half a year: talking to her, holding her hand, gazing into her eyes.

Jonathan felt sick. He was finding it hard to breathe. He closed his eyes, calling to mind the day he had first met Titus on the beach south of Stabia, less than a month ago. On that occasion, Titus had hurried back to Rome as fast as he could. To be with her?

Jonathan opened his eyes.

Everything his uncle Simeon had told him made sense now.

Leaning against the opposite wall, Rizpah was watching him steadily. Light filtered in from somewhere above. He could see a pile of rags beside her, presumably her bed. Near it were a few flat loaves of black bread and a ceramic jug.

'Rizpah,' he said, still trying to breathe. 'There's something I've got to tell you. I have to tell someone and I don't know who else to tell.'

'Then tell me,' she said. 'But first, drink this.' She held out the clay jug.

He nodded and drank straight from the jug, long and deep, and came up gasping.

'And eat this.' Rizpah tore a piece of bread from the dark loaf and handed it to him.

'I can't. If I eat it I'll just throw it up.'

'No you won't.' Her tone was surprisingly firm. She pushed it into his hand. 'Eat it,' she said.

The bread was leathery but tasted of honey. It was good.

'And you need one more thing,' she said.

'What?'

'This.' Rizpah reached into the pile of rags and extracted a tiny ball of grey fluff. She placed it in Jonathan's lap. It was warm and it mewed.

'A kitten,' said Jonathan, and held up the tiny creature. The mother cat lifted her head from the bedding and studied Jonathan. After a moment she lowered her head again to attend to the rest of her litter.

Jonathan cupped the tiny creature in his hands and held it close to his filthy black tunic. As the kitten felt the warmth of his body and the beating of his heart it began to purr.

'It's impossible,' whispered Jonathan, shaking his head.

'What's impossible.'

'That something this tiny could make a noise so loud.'

And then, at last, he wept.

'Yes, I used to be a slave in the Golden House,' said Feles' girlfriend Huldah. 'But Queen Berenice didn't like me, so she sent me away to the Imperial Palace on the Palatine Hill. I much prefer being a slave there. I get one day a week off and I can meet Feles when I go to the markets.'

Feles and Huldah had arrived at the fifth hour after noon, just as dinner was being served.

Flavia frowned. 'But isn't the palace on the Palatine part of the Golden House? I mean, the plans showed . . . isn't the Golden House spread over three hills?'

Huldah shrugged and tore at her chicken leg with small white teeth. She was extremely pretty, with a curvaceous figure and slanting black eyes. 'Not sure,' she said with her mouth full. 'All I know is that we call it the Golden House. It's not on the Palatine. It's part of the Esquiline Hill. The one the other side of the new amphitheatre. We call it the Oppian.'

'The banqueting pavilion!' cried Sisyphus. 'Celer told me. It was an enormous complex full of nothing but dining rooms for Nero to entertain his guests and show off his works of art.'

Aristo nodded. 'So who exactly lives in the Golden House on the Oppian Hill?'

'It was Berenice's quarters,' said Huldah. 'Just far enough from the official palace to be discreet, but close enough for Titus to visit her. Or vice versa. After the destruction of Jerusalem she asked Titus to spare all the noble women of Jerusalem. So he did. We were his gift to her.'

Huldah sucked the last shreds of meat from her chicken leg and took a handful of olives.

'Berenice looked after us,' she said, refilling her wine cup. 'We wove beautiful carpets and told each other stories and sometimes we had music. Some of the women even have their children with them. They have their own slave school. And Titus let us observe the Sabbath and keep the feasts.' She spat an olive stone onto her plate and grinned. 'We only lacked one thing.' Here she slipped her arm round Feles and gave him a squeeze: 'Men.'

'Do you ever go back there?' asked Flavia.

Huldah snorted. 'You'll never get me back there.

Besides, once you're out of the Golden House, you can never go back. You're unclean, or something.'

'So nobody goes there?'

'Nobody but Titus and female musicians. He gets bad headaches and music is the one thing that helps. Oh, and sometimes we had child entertainers. But no men. We were like the Emperor's harem, except Berenice was the only one he ever visited.' She pouted.

'Why did Berenice send you away?' asked Sisyphus, then added in a conspiratorial tone. 'Or shouldn't I ask?'

Huldah looked up at him from under thick eyelashes and popped another olive in her mouth. Then she grinned. 'Why do you think? Berenice was jealous of me. I was fifteen, she was almost fifty. She saw Titus looking at me once. Then *ecce!*' Huldah spat the olive stone across the courtyard. 'I was out of there like a bolt from a ballista.'

Lupus guffawed.

Feles looked at Huldah. 'You are beautiful enough to be an empress, you know.'

Huldah shrieked and elbowed him in the ribs. 'Oh you!' She took a long drink of wine and as she wiped her mouth with the back of her hand the copper bangles on her arm jingled. 'I just love my little tomcat.' She squeezed Feles round the waist again and nibbled his earlobe. 'Couldn't do without him now.'

Flavia looked round the table. Aristo, Caudex and Bulbus had glazed looks on their faces. Even Lupus was staring open-mouthed at Huldah. Sisyphus winked at Flavia and she cleared her throat.

'Huldah,' she said, 'was there a woman among the slaves from Jerusalem named Susannah? Susannah ben Jonah? Something like that?'

Huldah scowled. 'There are two or three women named Susannah,' she said. 'And one they call Susannah the Beautiful. But she's much older than I am. And I don't think she's so very beautiful.' Huldah tossed her hair and turned to Feles. 'Let's go, tomcat,' she said. 'I'll get into trouble if I'm not back soon.'

Somewhere in a secret room of the Golden House, Jonathan dried his eyes. The tears had brought a kind of release. His mother was the Emperor's slave, but at least she was alive. And as long as she was alive, there was hope that he could save her and somehow bring her home.

He cradled the kitten in his left arm and felt its tiny, needle-like claws dig into the crook of his elbow. The pain was nothing compared to the throbbing of his branded shoulder. With his right hand, he slowly reached for another piece of bread.

'You were going to tell me something important,' said Rizpah.

Jonathan nodded and bit into the bread. 'Do you know Queen Berenice?'

Rizpah nodded. 'I've known her all my life, till she went away six months ago.'

'Is she nice?'

Rizpah shrugged. 'She was kind to us. But all she talked about was Titus and how one day she would be Empress. When Vespasian died and Titus became Emperor a few months ago she came back. But he wouldn't even see her. He sent her away for the second time in half a year.'

'Yes,' said Jonathan slowly, thinking about what Simeon had told him, 'that makes sense. Last month – that must have been after Titus sent her away the second time – Berenice went to Corinth. That's a seaside town in Greece where there are lots of Jewish slaves. She visited the slaves and pretended to be buying some as bodyguards for the Emperor. But really she was looking for assassins to send back here to Rome.'

'To kill Titus?' Rizpah frowned. 'But she loves him. Even though he keeps sending her away. Besides, if she killed him she'd never be Empress.'

'Not to kill the Emperor,' said Jonathan. 'Berenice hired three assassins to kill the woman she thinks he's fallen in love with.'

Rizpah's pale eyes widened. 'Your mother!' she breathed.

Jonathan nodded. 'My uncle wouldn't tell me all the details, but now I've seen for myself. Berenice must think that if my mother Susannah died, Titus would be sad for a while, but then he would send for her and things would be the way they were again. He'd make her his Empress. That's why she hired the assassins to kill my mother. What Berenice didn't know was that one of the assassins she interviewed was my mother's brother Simeon.'

'God must be looking after her,' said Rizpah.

'Yes. My uncle thought that, too. When Berenice asked him to go to Rome to kill a Jewish woman called Susannah the Beautiful, he suspected it might be his sister. So he accepted the job, risked his life, and came to warn his sister, if it was really her. He knows what the other two assassins look like. They each took different routes and I think my uncle got here first.'

'Why did your uncle disguise himself as a musician? Why didn't he just warn Titus about the other assassins?'

'Berenice told my uncle and the other two assassins that she had an agent in the palace – someone high up – but she wouldn't tell them who. She said her agent would be watching them and would kill them if they tried to warn Titus. And they would only be paid after they had done the job.'

Rizpah nodded and Jonathan continued,

'My uncle was trying to reach the Emperor directly without letting anyone else know who he was. But then Domitian caught us . . .' Jonathan stopped stroking the kitten. 'By now they will have cut off Simeon's big toes, so that he can't walk, and blinded him, so that he can't even point out the other assassins.' Jonathan hung his head. 'And it's all my fault. All of it.'

SCROLL XX

'Why is everything your fault?' Rizpah asked Jonathan.

Jonathan wiped his eyes with the back of his hand. 'We were living in Jerusalem when I was born. But my father knew of a prophetic warning that Jerusalem would fall. "When you see Jerusalem being surrounded by armies, you will know that its desolation is near." My father always quotes that,' added Jonathan. 'He took Miriam and me to a village called Pella where there were other . . . where he believed we would be safe. But my mother refused to go with us.'

'Why?' asked Rizpah.

'I'm not sure. All I know is that it had something to do with me.'

'But weren't you just a baby?'

Jonathan nodded. 'I was one and a half.'

'Then how could it have been your fault?'

'I don't know. But last week I heard my uncle tell my father that it wasn't his fault. He said "She'd made up her mind to stay because of Jonathan". I'm sure it was my mother they were talking about, because my father was crying.'

Jonathan felt Rizpah watching him as he stroked the kitten.

'And you're sure your uncle meant you?' she asked softly.

'Who else would he be talking about?' said Jonathan. 'Besides, I've always known it was my fault.'

'How?'

'I just know.'

'And that's why you risked your life to save her,' said Rizpah.

Jonathan nodded. 'I have to make it right,' he said. 'I have to find some way to rescue her and bring her home.'

'Here!' said Flavia, punching the scroll with her forefinger. 'This entrance by the lake leads to the big octagonal room. That's how we'll get in.'

'Oooh, it's exciting, isn't it?' said Sisyphus.

Flavia looked up at him.

'Sisyphus. You heard what Huldah said: only women and children can go into the Golden House.'

'No!' The scrolls on the table jumped as Aristo slammed his fist down. 'You can't possibly imagine I'm going to let you go down some tunnel all by your-selves? Absolutely not.'

'But Jonathan is our friend. We have to do some-thing!'

'Flavia.' Aristo passed a hand across his face. 'I care about Jonathan, too. But I cannot allow you to go in there on your own.'

'We probably won't even be able to get into the gardens,' said Flavia. 'But couldn't we just look? I promise we won't do anything unless you give permission. Please, Aristo?'

'Jonathan,' said Rizpah. 'Was your uncle the only one who knew what the other assassins looked like?'

It was dark in Rizpah's den, for night had fallen. There was just room for the two of them on the pile of rags with the kittens in between.

'Yes,' said Jonathan. 'But he described them to me. One is called Eliezar. My uncle said he's a big man with red hair and beard and a scar on his forehead. The other one is called Pinchas. He's small and dark and one of his eyes is half brown and half blue. It's a good thing men can't get in the Golden House.' He added.

There was a pause in which he could only hear the kitten purring. Then Rizpah said, 'That's not completely true . . .'

Lupus, Flavia and Nubia stood at the three points of an imaginary triangle and tossed a leather ball slowly back and forth. Aristo and Sisyphus stood nearby chatting quietly and staring out at the new amphitheatre. Lupus knew that to play trigon properly they should have been throwing the ball very rapidly as hard as they could. However, their focus was not on the game but on the gardens behind a thick wall.

It was early morning of the next day and they stood on the shaded slopes of the Oppian Hill. To their left and below them was the new amphitheatre, so close that occasionally Lupus could hear the voices of the slaves calling to each other on the scaffolding. To their right, rising up behind the other side of the wall, were tall umbrella pines, cypress and cedars: the gardens of the Golden House. They had found a place where the earth was highest against the wall and it was almost possible for Aristo to see over it.

When they were close enough to the wall to see the cracks in the yellow plaster, Flavia nodded at Lupus and he deliberately threw the ball over the wall.

'Oh dear,' said Flavia loudly, in case any guards were nearby. 'Our ball has gone over the wall. What shall we do? Slaves! Come here and help us!'

Aristo and Sisyphus glanced at each other and grinned.

'What do you require, mistress?' asked Sisyphus in a mock humble tone.

'Lift up my little brother so he can see where our ball went,' Flavia commanded.

Lupus felt himself lifted up by the two Greeks, each of whom had grasped a leg. As his head rose above the top of the wall, he found himself staring straight into stern eyes beneath a polished helmet. A woman guard!

'Aaah!' Lupus yelled and his arms flailed.

Startled, Flavia and Nubia squealed. Aristo and Sisyphus cursed as they tried to keep hold of Lupus. They managed not to drop him, but the three of them collapsed in a heap on the ground.

'Oh Pollux!' Sisyphus brushed himself off. 'Pine needles and dust all over my best mauve tunic!'

Lupus's brief glimpse had shown him that the gardens were terraced; the ground level was much higher on the other side of the wall. He, Aristo and Sisyphus scrambled to their feet and looked up at the face glowering down at them.

'What do you think you're doing?' The guard's voice was stern.

'Please, miss.' Flavia used her little girl voice. 'We were just playing and our ball went over.'

'Do you behold it?' Nubia asked.

Flavia added, 'Our slaves here were just lifting up my little brother so he could see where it went. It's his favourite toy. Isn't it, Lupus?' She looked pointedly at him.

Lupus employed one of his least favourite tactics. He burst into babyish tears.

'Oh dear! Don't cry, little boy! I didn't mean to frighten you.' The woman's head disappeared and a moment later she was back. The ball dropped onto the ground beside them. 'There's your ball. Now, you mustn't play here again. Do you know why?'

Lupus and the others shook their heads.

The guard attempted a friendly expression. 'Yesterday we caught a bad man trying to climb over this wall,' she said. 'A huge red-haired Jew with a very sharp knife. We think he was trying to kill the Emperor. So we're guarding this whole area very carefully. Now do you understand why you mustn't play here?'

Lupus sniffed and wiped his nose on the back of his finger. The two girls nodded meekly.

'We won't ever play here again,' lisped Flavia, and then asked in a tiny voice, 'what happened to the bad man?'

'Oh, he was a very bad man,' said the guard. 'They crucified him this morning at dawn.'

SCROLL XXI

The moment Jonathan woke up, his stomach clenched as he remembered the momentous thing he had discovered. His mother was alive.

He lay curled up on Rizpah's pile of rags and gazed up at the dim light filtering in from above. Next to him the kittens mewed. They were looking for their mother.

He could smell the salty dampness of the walls and the faintly sweet smell of cat's milk.

The mother cat stalked into the den. Rizpah followed her in on hands and knees.

'Good afternoon, Jonathan. You slept a long time.'

He yawned and winced as he used his left arm to push himself to a sitting position.

Rizpah handed him the jug and he brought it to his lips. It was buttermilk, thick and tart and delicious. It made him think of home. Of Ostia. He wondered what his father and Miriam and his friends were doing there now.

He handed Rizpah the jug, but she shook her head. 'I've had breakfast. Ages ago.' She sat cross-legged stroking the smallest kitten, a purring bit of black fluff.

Jonathan drank again and finally put down the empty jug. Rizpah ran her finger inside the neck of the jug and let her kitten lick the buttermilk off.

Jonathan gently took the grey kitten, which he had named Odysseus, and followed Rizpah's example. He laughed as he felt the kitten's warm tongue wetly sandpapering his finger.

'Rizpah,' he said after a moment. 'Don't you have any slave duties?'

'No. The guards aren't even sure I'm still here. My mother and the other women know I'm here but they'd never give me away. I can go places nobody else can and so I tell them what's happening. The guards used to look for me but they never found me.' She wiped her finger in the jug again and then added, 'They've been looking for you, too. But now they've given up.' She giggled. 'The women who run the slave school think you've fallen down the latrine pit.'

'There are women teachers?' said Jonathan, amazed. And when Rizpah nodded, he murmured. 'It's strange that there are no men here.'

'It was Berenice's idea. She didn't want any men around. After what happened.'

'What do you mean?'

'I mean what happened after the Romans finally took the city.'

'I still don't understand.'

'Jonathan,' said Rizpah. 'I am eight years old. My mother is Rachel. I don't know who my father is.

Neither does she. There are twenty-three of us here at the Golden House, all eight years old, all born in June.'

Jonathan frowned.

'All born in June,' repeated Rizpah, and added, 'Nine months after the legions entered the city.'

'Oh!' said Jonathan, and then: 'I'm sorry.'

'Don't be,' said Rizpah matter-of-factly, and kissed her kitten on the nose. 'Here I was born and here I'll die.'

'Rizpah,' said Jonathan. 'I need to see my mother. Now that they've captured my uncle, I'm the only one who knows about the assassins Berenice sent. I have to warn my mother. Is there another way to her room, apart from the fountain tunnel?'

Rizpah nodded. 'I've been waiting for you to ask me. I'll take you now.'

At the slave entrance of the Imperial Palace on the Palatine Hill stood a quintet of travelling musicians, three of whom were children. On their heads were flowered garlands entwined with ribbons. Each of the musicians wore a different coloured tunic. The flautist was a dark-skinned girl in yellow, the drummer a younger boy in green, and the girl with the tambourine wore blue. A handsome, curly-haired Greek in a red tunic played the lyre and a slender, dark-haired man in mauve shook a gourd full of lentils.

They had just finished a short musical piece and now

this colourful quintet gazed hopefully at a grizzled slave and a dough-faced man.

The two men looked at one another, nodded and beckoned the musicians inside.

Jonathan was following Rizpah through one of the tunnels back to the octagonal room when she jumped down into an immensely long, high corridor.

'This is a different way,' said Rizpah. 'I don't like it as much. It's too bright. But it's faster.' The dim vaulted corridor was covered with plaster and all the walls were painted with delicate frescos in purple, azure and cinnabar red. Some of the fresco panels on the wall of the corridor were the same designs as the carpets the slave women had been weaving. Even though the light was muted, Rizpah shaded her eyes against it.

'They call this the cryptoporticus. That means "secret corridor", but it really isn't secret,' she said. 'I don't think we'll meet anyone, but if we do, let me do the talking.'

'I'm afraid you men will have to wait here on the Palatine,' Harmonius said to Aristo and Sisyphus. 'The Emperor wants music at the Golden House immediately, but no men are allowed there. Only women and children. Don't worry,' he said, as the Greeks started to protest. 'You'll all be paid handsomely and you'll find your quarters most comfortable. When the children have finished they'll be escorted back here. Then you'll perform for Domitian.'

'But who will look after them while they perform at the Golden House?' said Aristo.

'My dear fellow, they're only going over to the Oppian Hill and they'll be under the Emperor's protection. What harm could possibly come to them?'

'He's still with her,' hissed Jonathan. 'Why doesn't he go away? Doesn't he have an empire to run?'

'I don't know,' Rizpah answered. 'Something must have happened. He looks upset. He usually only visits her first thing in the morning or last thing before dusk.'

Jonathan and Rizpah had approached the Cyclops' cave from ground level – through the garden – and had found a hiding place behind a glossy shrub with bright orange berries.

Jonathan watched his mother and the Emperor. They sat facing one another on elegant folding armchairs in the shade of the peristyle, halfway between the bright garden and the dim Cyclops' cave.

Jonathan strained to hear what they were saying but the sound of a fountain splashing in the garden made it impossible to distinguish anything apart from his mother's coughs.

'She's not well,' he muttered. 'She's coughing. If my father were here he would prescribe mallow boiled in milk. Or a tincture of rye-grass.'

Rizpah touched his arm reassuringly. 'All the

weavers cough,' she said. 'My mother says it comes from breathing the wool dust. Don't worry.'

'And now she's crying. Look! Titus has made her cry!'

'Shhh!' said Rizpah, 'If they hear you, they'll take you away and you'll never get a chance to warn her. Oh look! Here comes Benjamin.'

A dark-haired slave-boy approached the Cyclops' cave and waited discreetly outside. He was about Rizpah's age, and Jonathan could see by his shiny hair and spotless black tunic that he was not on latrine duty.

Presently Titus glanced over at him. The young slave bowed his head respectfully and said something. Jonathan caught the word 'musicians'.

Titus nodded, said something to Susannah and rose to his feet. He and the boy disappeared in the direction of the octagonal room.

Jonathan's mother watched them go, then she slowly stood and closed her eyes for a long moment. Presently she opened them again and moved into the sunlit garden, towards the very bush which hid Jonathan and Rizpah.

SCROLL XXII

'Great Juno's peacock!' exclaimed Flavia. 'Look at that.' She parted the filmy purple curtain at the front of the Imperial litter and the three of them rolled over onto their stomachs, gazing out in wonder.

Above and before them lay an immensely long palace built into a green wooded hill. It was fronted with a row of dazzling golden columns that blazed in the late afternoon sunlight.

'There must be a thousand of those columns,' breathed Flavia. 'Do you think they're solid gold?'

Lupus shook his head and made a painting motion.

'Just gilded? Still, that's a lot of gold paint . . . Now we know why they call it the Golden House.'

Above the yellow-tiled roof of this dazzling complex, on the crest of the hill, she could see fountains, a portico of smaller white columns and seven palm trees planted in a circle.

The bearers puffed as they carried the litter up marble steps between green terraces.

'Great Juno's peacock!' cried Flavia again. 'A peacock.'

'Behold! Its tail is spreading,' whispered Nubia. Flavia

could tell from Lupus's round eyes that he had never seen a peacock before. Somewhere behind the fragrant shrubs which lined the stairway, another peacock uttered its haunting cry.

Now the litter had reached the top of the marble steps, and the highest terrace came into view. Several long reflecting pools lay at the foot of the long portico, doubling the golden columns. A dozen exotic wading birds with curved beaks and orange-pink feathers stood in the pools among clumps of papyrus and floating water lilies.

Nubia uttered a word Flavia didn't understand.

'What?'

'Those birds are from my country,' said Nubia.

The four burly slaves carried the litter between two of the reflecting pools, then set it down beneath the portico. It was afternoon now and the golden columns threw dark shadowed bars across the walkway. As Flavia climbed down from the litter, she noticed for the first time that the bearers were female.

Holding her beribboned tambourine, Flavia followed one of the female bearers into a huge domed space.

'The octagonal room,' breathed Flavia, tipping her head back and putting up her free hand to keep the garland on her head. The immense dome and large circular skylight gave the room a breathtaking sense of space and light. Beneath the dome, dozens of dark-haired women worked at colourful tapestries. Some of them had already put down their shuttles, beaters and wool; they were beginning to form a semi-circle around a central platform beneath the dome.

'That's where you sit,' the litter-bearer said to Flavia, indicating the platform. 'Play half a dozen songs,' she continued in a husky voice, 'take a break, play six more, then we'll carry you back to the Palatine. Oh, and if the Emperor appears, you don't need to bow or acknowledge him in any way. Unless, of course, he approaches you. In which case, the correct way to address him is "Caesar".'

'All right,' murmured Flavia politely. She led the other two up to the platform where cushions were already set out.

'This is it,' she whispered to Nubia and Lupus. 'Keep your eyes open for Jonathan or Simeon. Or anything suspicious.'

As Susannah the Beautiful approached, Jonathan took a deep breath and stepped out from behind the bush.

'Oh!' she cried out and her hand went to her throat. Then she saw Rizpah and spoke in Aramaic.

'Rizpah! You frightened me. You mustn't leap out of the shrubbery like that.'

'I'm sorry, Susannah.' Rizpah shaded her eyes with both hands and screwed up her face against the brilliance of the garden.

'Who's this?' asked Susannah, looking at Jonathan with interest, but before either of them could answer, her eyes widened.

157

'Jonathan?' she whispered. 'Is it you?'

Nubia glanced at Lupus and Flavia to make sure they were ready. They nodded back at her and she lifted the flute to her lips.

First they played the 'Song of the Traveller', a song from Nubia's native land. Then they played 'The Raven and the Dove', a song their friend Clio had taught them. Under Nubia's fingers this popular song took on an exotic flavour.

Nubia set aside her flute to sing the 'Dog Song', while Lupus drummed, then she and Flavia took up their instruments again for the last two songs, both of which Nubia had composed herself. The first she called 'Sailing Song' and the second, her favourite, she called 'Slave Song'. She could never play this last without shedding a tear and when she looked up she saw that most of the women from Jerusalem also had wet cheeks.

Nubia felt a touch on her arm. Flavia nodded towards a man standing behind them on the extreme left, leaning against one of the golden columns.

The man's eyes were closed and his face turned up towards the diffused light of the dome.

Although he wasn't wearing his purple toga or golden wreath this time, Nubia recognised him. 'Titus?' she whispered.

Flavia nodded.

*

Jonathan tried not to cry out as his mother threw her arms round him, but he couldn't help flinching.

'Oh, Jonathan!' she drew back and looked at his shoulder in horror. 'I've hurt you. Dear Lord! Titus didn't say you'd been branded! Oh my poor son.'

'The Emperor knows about me?' said Jonathan, taking a step back. Although she had spoken to him in Aramaic he used Latin.

'Of course.' She followed his lead and replied in Latin. 'They look for you everywhere.' Her Latin wasn't very good. 'Simeon tells us how brave you've been, how you are willing to risk your life—'

'Simeon? He's all right? They haven't tortured and blinded him?'

'No, no.' Susannah stepped forward and took Jonathan's face between her cool hands. He caught a whiff of her scent. It was no longer lemon blossom, but something different: rose and myrtle. 'Your uncle Simeon is good,' she said. 'He is on the Palatine. Josephus warns Titus before they torture him.'

'Josephus!' Jonathan stepped back again, away from her touch. 'That's the name of the man who betrayed us.'

His mother let her arms fall to her sides. 'Josephus doesn't know Simeon comes to help,' she said. 'He thinks your uncle assassinates the Emperor. Josephus is loyal to Emperor.'

'And I see that you are loyal to the Emperor, too.'

'Jonathan. Do not hate Titus. He is good man.'

'He murdered thousands of Jews, destroyed Jerusalem and burned down God's temple!' cried Jonathan.

'And he is most sorry.'

'Oh. He's sorry. Well then. That makes it all right, doesn't it? So now you can kiss him and tell him it doesn't matter.'

'Jonathan. Please do not.'

He turned his head aside, fighting to hold back the tears. 'I came to find you. To warn you. To take you back to Miriam and father. And I find you in the arms of that monster . . .'

'Jonathan. You are dear, precious son. I am so sorry.' She took his hands. 'Please, my Jonathan. Tell me. How is sister Miriam? And father? And you?'

Lupus was watching one of the slave women closely. He had noticed her even before they began to play. The way she had walked to her cushion had attracted his attention. Was she Jonathan's mother? No. There was no look of Miriam or Jonathan about her face.

Perhaps he had seen her somewhere before?

As he drummed he let his gaze slide round the other women's faces. Most had their eyes closed or were weeping. But this woman's eyes beneath her black headscarf were cool and calculating; unaffected, even by the 'Slave Song'.

She must have felt his gaze, for as she looked at him she modestly covered the lower half of her face with her scarf. For a moment their gazes locked. That's odd, thought Lupus: one of her eyes is half brown and half blue.

SCROLL XXIII

'Alas! My heart is wretched.' Lupus heard Nubia whisper to Flavia. 'Because I have no more songs. They will know we are not real music players.'

'Don't worry, Nubia. We'll just play them again.'

Lupus saw that the Emperor was approaching their low platform. At the same time he noticed the woman with the strange eye had risen to her feet. Another woman – one with fluffy brown hair – gripped her hand, but the first woman shook it off and walked slowly towards the golden portico.

The Emperor was standing before them now, talking to Flavia. Lupus ignored him, turned his head to watch the woman move towards the columns. He knew there was something else strange about her.

Just before she disappeared from sight, a breeze blew up the hem of her black robes. Lupus saw a hairy and well-muscled calf, and below it, a soldier's sandal.

Rizpah must have slipped back into the shadows because Jonathan sensed that he and his mother were alone now. He sat on the chair the Emperor had occupied earlier and allowed her to hold his hands.

Jonathan reverted to Hebrew to tell his mother about his childhood without her, how they had moved from Pella to Rome and then to Ostia. He told her about Flavia, Lupus and Jonathan. He told her that Miriam was engaged to a Roman farmer who had probably lost everything in the eruption of Vesuvius. He told her his father was well, but lonely.

Finally, Jonathan told his mother how he had dreamed of her in the Cyclops' cave, waiting to be rescued.

'Mother. It was my fault that you stayed in Jerusalem and were taken captive. But now I can fix it. I think I can find a way for us to get out of here.'

'You do?' she said vaguely, and then: 'But, Jonathan, why do you think it was your fault?'

'Simeon said you stayed in Jerusalem because of me.'

'What?'

'I overheard Simeon tell father you stayed in Jerusalem because of me.'

His mother turned her head and stared into the Cyclops' cave.

'Then he knows.'

'What are you talking about? What did I do to make you stay?'

'No.' She looked back at him and he saw that her eyes were full of tears. 'It wasn't you, my son. Nothing was your fault. You were only a toddler. A dear, sweet little boy.'

'Then . . . I don't understand.'

His mother stood. She walked to her loom and reached out to touch the wool stretched taut across it.

'I did a bad thing, Jonathan. I never wanted you or Miriam or your father to know.'

'What? What did you do, mother?'

Jonathan's mother looked at him and then beyond him. He turned to see what she was looking at.

A figure stood in the bright garden, watching them through the columns. It was one of the Jewish slave women. She was dressed in black and had pulled her scarf across her face. It seemed one of the women of Jerusalem had come to offer her hand in friendship.

Then his mother's dark blue eyes opened in surprise. Following her gaze, Jonathan saw that the woman in black came not in friendship but in malice.

In her hand she held a curved, razor-sharp dagger.

'Aiieeee!' Lupus struck the assassin at the back of the knees.

'Oof!' The figure in black collapsed.

Lupus rolled aside to avoid being crushed, grasped the figure's headscarf and yanked. Long hair tumbled out as the assassin's head flew up and then cracked down hard onto the marble walkway.

Lupus's flowered garland had slipped down over his eyes. With a grunt of disgust he tore it from his head and threw it away. Luckily, the figure on the floor was stunned. Lupus saw long hair and heavy eye-liner, but the stubble on the assassin's cheeks confirmed what Lupus had suspected: it was a man. And although he was fine-boned with delicate features, he was tough. Already he was shaking his head and struggling to sit up.

The knife.

Lupus had to get the knife away from the assassin. He had just lunged for it when a foot stomped hard on the assassin's wrist. The knife spun across the shaded marble path and into the shadows of a cave-like room.

'Lupus! Give me your hand!' The voice was Jonathan's.

Lupus grasped an extended hand and was lifted to his feet.

It took him a split second to recognise the slave-boy who had helped him up. Jonathan seemed taller and thinner. His shaved head made his eyes look huge. And he had a strange expression on his face.

Lupus grunted and leapt back as the assassin struggled to his feet. Then for a second time he kicked the man hard in the back of the knees. The man went down again, this time onto all fours, his long hair screening his face.

'Jonathan!' Lupus heard a little girl's voice and the sound of metal on marble and suddenly Jonathan held the dagger in his hand. Someone in the shadows had kicked it back to him.

Still on all fours, the man in the black robes looked up. Jonathan was breathing hard, half crouching and holding the curved dagger in his right hand. Somewhere a woman was screaming. Lupus could hear the approaching slap of running feet on marble and the sound of a jingling tambourine.

So could the assassin.

He looked round, like a cornered beast, his long hair flying about his shoulders. Then he rose and turned and ran through the garden courtyard towards the vaulted rooms near the front of the palace.

Lupus ran after him.

Jonathan knew he had to get his mother to safety. As soon as he saw the assassin fleeing, he ran up to her. She was cowering in the shadows behind her loom.

'Come on, mother! I know where we can hide,' he said, then turned in amazement as he heard a familiar voice shout:

'There he is!'

As if in a dream he saw Flavia and Nubia run through the sunlit garden. They were both wearing flowered garlands with coloured ribbons streaming out behind. Flavia held a beribboned tambourine in one hand; it jingled as she ran. Neither of them saw him standing in the shadowed vault, gripping his mother's wrist.

Two muscular women in shiny breastplates came hard on the girls' heels and then the Emperor himself, red-faced and gasping.

'Titus!' whispered Jonathan's mother. She took a step forward, but Jonathan pulled her back, almost roughly. Still holding her by the wrist, he set off through several dim, empty rooms, pulling her after him.

'Where are we going?'

'Here.' He pulled her into a small triangular room. He remembered Rizpah telling him Nero had once used it to display a statue of a sleeping satyr, but now the room was empty.

Jonathan stopped, panting hard. 'We'll be safe here for a while. Then Rizpah will show us the way out.' Still holding her hand, Jonathan turned to his mother. 'First, tell me . . . what was the bad thing you did?' His breath came in wheezing gasps. 'Why didn't you . . . escape with us?'

His mother looked at him and then dropped her head.

'There was a man,' she finally said.

'A man?'

'I loved him.'

Jonathan realised he was still holding her hand. He dropped it.

'He was a famous freedom-fighter. His name was on everyone's lips. They called him Jonathan the Zealot.'

'His name was Jonathan?'

She nodded.

The odd shape of the room made him feel slightly unbalanced, and not for the first time, he wondered if he was dreaming.

'Am I . . . named after him?'

His mother hung her head and nodded again.

Jonathan felt cold. He could see each black and white chip in the mosaic floor with terrible clarity. Finally he took a deep breath and asked: 'Was Jonathan the Zealot my real father?'

SCROLL XXIV

'There he is!' shouted Flavia.

When Lupus had jumped off the platform she had followed him without hesitation. She hadn't even put down her tambourine.

She and Nubia had run down the colonnade after Lupus, the golden columns flashing by on their left. Suddenly Lupus had veered right, and they followed him across a hot, grassy courtyard, into a complex of brightly painted, high-vaulted rooms. There they lost him, until a woman's scream directed them to an inner garden courtyard. A moment later a long-haired man in black robes ran past, closely pursued by Lupus.

Flavia heard footsteps behind her and glanced back. Two of the muscular female litter-bearers and Titus himself had joined the chase.

'There he is!' she shouted to them again.

She followed Lupus through a large vaulted room and suddenly they were at the front of the palace again, at the golden portico.

Flavia stopped for a moment, hugged one of the golden columns with her left arm and looked around, panting. There! The assassin was splashing through the reflecting pool, sending the exotic pink birds into a panic. They squawked and flapped and tried to fly away, but in vain: their wings had been clipped.

Suddenly the man slipped and fell with a splash, then staggered to his feet. His black robes clung to his body and they could see his masculine build. Lupus was almost upon him now. Flavia gasped as the assassin swung round to strike Lupus a glancing, backhand blow.

'Lupus!' She pushed away from the column and ran to help him, Nubia close beside her.

Lupus had fallen into the pool. But a moment later he was up, shaking himself off like a dog, then resuming his pursuit of the assassin, who had doubled back and was running up marble stairs to the upper level. Flavia and Nubia were close behind Lupus now, close enough to see drops of water flying off his soaked green tunic.

Flavia took the stairs two at a time, her tambourine jingling with each step, trying not to slip on the scattered pine needles.

'Behold!' Nubia panted and Flavia caught a glimpse of the assassin turning to run along the long upper portico of white columns. Lupus was right behind him.

Hampered by his dripping black robes, the assassin was running awkwardly now; once he almost tripped. He stumbled along the portico, then veered between the columns and into a small, angular garden. Beyond a circle of palm trees in the centre of the garden, Flavia saw another portico with thick green woods beyond. Woods thick enough to hide any fugitive.

The assassin saw it, too, and made for it, heading towards the ring of palms.

Suddenly Flavia remembered the plans she had studied with Sisyphus. There was a click in her mind, like the sound of a wax seal being broken. She knew what the palm trees surrounded and which room was below them.

'Lupus!' she cried. 'The eye! It's inside the palm trees. Be careful!'

Lupus heard her, but so did the assassin. The man skidded to a halt, then whirled to face them, his long hair flying. He crouched and his eyes narrowed as he saw his closest pursuer was just a boy.

Flavia knew she had to act quickly, before the assassin could attack Lupus. She drew back her arm and threw her tambourine hard, like a discus, giving it a spin as it left her hand. Amazingly, it went exactly where she had intended: the beribboned tambourine struck the assassin a hard jingling blow on the chest, then bounced to the ground. The man staggered back, flailing wildly with his arms, trying to keep his balance.

Then he was gone.

Flavia and Nubia ran to the rim of the eye, the circular skylight in the dome. A shower of dust and gravel rattled over the side and disappeared into the octagonal room below. Lupus was breathing hard, hands on his knees, gazing down into the void below. The female guards and finally the Emperor himself came puffing up behind them.

'Careful!' cried Flavia. But they knew the layout of the Golden House and slowed down before they reached the rim of the circular gap.

If there had ever been glass in the skylight, it must have been stripped away, along with other precious materials. The man in black had plunged sixty feet and had hit the platform where they had been playing music a few minutes earlier. His long hair fanned out across his back, giving him the look of a jointed wooden doll which a child has thrown down in disgust. It was obvious from the impossible angle of his head that his neck was broken.

The assassin was dead.

In a triangular room somewhere near the back of the Golden House Jonathan asked his mother: 'Was Jonathan the Zealot my real father?'

'No.' His mother raised her head. 'You are Mordecai's son. I hadn't been unfaithful to him.' She lowered her eyes again. 'Not then.'

'Then how? When?'

His mother turned to face the plaster wall. There was a fresco of Venus on it and she reached up to touch the goddess's face.

'Jonathan was the first man I ever met who wasn't a close relative,' she said. 'I was fourteen and he was seventeen, a few months older than Simeon. The two of them had been throwing rocks at the Romans and some soldiers were chasing them. They ran into our house and I hid them behind my loom. Jonathan had hurt his hand so while Simeon went out of the room to see if it was safe, I dressed Jonathan's wound. While Simeon was gone, in only a few short moments, Jonathan kissed me and told me I was the most beautiful woman he'd ever seen. He said he wanted to marry me. He was young, brave, handsome . . . Even then his name was whispered by all the girls. I was dazzled.'

Jonathan felt unsteady and had to lean against the wall. His mother still had her back to him.

'A few days later,' she continued, 'my father said a man had asked to marry me. I was overjoyed. Then father told me he was a doctor, a man of twenty-seven, and my heart sank. I heard nothing more from Jonathan, so I married the doctor, your father. He was a kind man. We went to live in his house near the Beautiful Gate. Soon I had the two of you. I was not unhappy.'

'You were not unhappy,' repeated Jonathan dully.

'Miriam was born the year the rebellion started. It was the same year your father joined that sect. While everyone praised the bravery of Jonathan the Zealot, all your father talked about was loving our enemies.'

'Go on,' said Jonathan.

'One day, I was visiting my parents when Simeon

and Jonathan came in from one of their secret missions against the Romans. It was the first time I had seen Jonathan in nearly five years. I watched him from behind a lattice-work screen. "Have you heard?" Jonathan was saying to my father. "The Christians are leaving the city. Going across the Jordan, to Pella. I hope your son-in-law isn't one of them. Cowards!" My father didn't say anything but I could tell by the way he clenched his jaw that he agreed with Jonathan. "I should have accepted your offer to marry Susannah," he said to Jonathan. "I didn't want a Zealot as a son-in-law. But it would have been preferable to one of those madmen who think God had a son." That was when I realised Jonathan *had* asked to marry me.'

Susannah was silent for a moment. Then she continued. 'As soon as my father left the room, I stepped out from behind the screen. Jonathan ran to me and told me he had never stopped loving me and that he would die for me. We said many other things. When I finally returned home that day I found your father about to flee the city. He begged me to come but I refused, saying that my father had forbidden me to leave. I let him go. And I let him take you with him.'

'So you loved Jonathan more than you loved us,' said Jonathan in a flat voice. He felt sick.

'I don't think it was love.' His mother leaned her cheek against the wall. 'It was a kind of madness. The next week the gates of Jerusalem were closed and the armies of Titus encamped outside. Jonathan and I had a few weeks together, maybe a month. We lived secretly in your father's house, for I was still a married woman and adultery was a crime punishable by death. Then the famine set in. One day Jonathan went out and never returned. I heard later that he was killed fighting a man for a piece of dead mule. A brave death,' she said bitterly.

She turned to face Jonathan. Her eyes were dry.

'That's the reason I didn't come with you.'

'But now . . .' said Jonathan, 'now I've come to rescue you. To take you home.'

'Jonathan. My dear brave Jonathan. I can't come with you. I must stay here.'

'Why?'

'Titus needs me.'

'We need you! I need you. I came all this way to bring you home.'

'I can't.'

For a moment it was as if Jonathan was standing above the scene. He could see himself: thin, pale, his head shaved and an angry red brand on his arm. He looked like a slave. And his mother standing with her head bent before him. He saw that he was almost as tall as she was.

'Can you forgive me, Jonathan?'

He stared at her. He had risked his life to save her and now she refused to escape with him. Just as she had refused his father ten years earlier.

'Please, Jonathan?'

Slowly Jonathan shook his head. Then he turned and stumbled out of the room. He ran along the crypto-porticus, and although he was half blinded by tears, somehow he found the dark tunnels Rizpah had shown him. Like a mole, he made his way blindly along them until he found the darkest, most hidden place of all.

SCROLL XXV

'Flavia Gemina,' said the Emperor, mopping his brow.

Flavia glanced over at the Emperor in amazement. They were all walking back along the golden portico towards the octagonal room. The Emperor's sandy curls were plastered to his pink forehead and he was breathing as hard as a bull led to sacrifice.

'How do you know my name, Caesar?' she stammered.

'I have an . . . excellent memory.' Now he was mopping his chin and neck. 'I met you . . . at the refugee camp . . . south of Stabia . . . Your uncle – Flavius Geminus – was with you.'

'That's right,' said Flavia.

'And you're her slave-girl . . . Sheba.'

'Nubia.'

'That's right. Nubia.' He looked at Lupus. 'And Lupus. A most . . . unusual name.'

'That's amazing,' said Flavia. 'That you should remember our names.'

'Confession,' the Emperor said. 'Jonathan's uncle

Simeon . . . mentioned you . . . Told me you were the boy's friends.'

'Simeon!' cried Flavia. They had reached the octagonal room and she stopped beside one of the golden columns. 'He's an assassin, Caesar. He's going to kill you,' she gestured with her tambourine, 'like that man just tried to kill you.'

'No.' The Emperor smiled. 'But I appreciate your loyalty in telling me. Simeon came to warn me, not to kill me. You see it was his own sister – Jonathan's mother – he was sent to assassinate. That assassin intended to kill Susannah. Not me.'

'Yes, he did intend to kill you,' said a voice. It was a woman's voice, full of hatred.

The women of Jerusalem stood round the platform in the middle of the octagonal room, looking down at the dead assassin. One of them was kneeling beside his broken body and it was she who had spoken. She had dark, fluffy hair and narrow eyes full of hatred.

Titus walked to the platform and frowned down at her.

'My name is Rachel,' she said, rising to her feet. 'But you wouldn't know that, even though I've been your slave for nine years. His name was Pinchas. I only knew him a few hours but in that short time I could tell he was a brave man. One of our freedom-fighters. Berenice hired him to kill that traitor Susannah. But afterwards he was going to kill you, too. He was a true hero. You are a pig.'

Slowly and deliberately, Rachel spat in the Emperor's face.

Everyone gasped and stared at him.

Then Titus did something Flavia would never forget.

'You may not believe this, Rachel,' he said quietly, mopping his cheek with his handkerchief, 'but I would rather be killed than kill one more person. I am sorry this man is dead. And I am truly sorry,' he looked round at all the women, 'for what I had to do to your country. To your people.'

He looked round at them all. 'You are not my slaves but Berenice's. But she will not return.' He hung his head for a moment and Flavia was close enough to hear him murmur, 'I should have done this before.'

The Emperor raised his head again and continued in his commander's voice. 'I hereby set you all free. You may remain here as my freedwomen, under my protection, and begin to receive wages for your weaving. Or you may go. The decision is yours.'

He started to turn away, and then added, 'If you stay, I will allow you to marry. I believe Berenice was only trying to protect you by keeping you from men. Because whether you believe it or not, she loved you all. Her parting wish was that I watch over you.'

He turned away from the women of Jerusalem and said to Flavia and her friends, 'Come, Flavia Gemina. Let us find your friend Jonathan.'

But though they searched and searched, Jonathan was nowhere to be found.

Jonathan remained in his dark hole for a long time. There was barely enough room for him to sit, so he curled up and huddled there. Thoughts raced round and round his head, like chariots at the circus. Presently he slept and dreamt of his childhood. He woke and sought refuge in sleep again; the dreams were the most vivid he had ever had.

Someone regularly left a jug of fresh water outside the entrance, but nobody spoke to him and it seemed that he was alone for weeks.

What finally drove him out was the hunger.

He was sick and dizzy with it, and as he wormed his way along the tunnel he had to stop every few minutes and gasp for breath. Once or twice his throat contracted and he almost retched. He could taste the bitter juices of his empty stomach.

At last he staggered blinking into the cryptoporticus and stared towards the light in wonder.

A figure stood there. The filtered sunlight behind her made her white hair and her white tunic glow like an aura around her.

'Rizpah?' he croaked.

She nodded, and stepped forward. She handed him a jug of cold water. In the crook of her arm she cradled a grey kitten.

'How long have I been in there?' he asked her after he had drained the jug.

'Three days.'

'Only three days?' Jonathan slumped down onto the floor and leaned the back of his head against the cool plaster of the cryptoporticus. 'It feels like weeks.'

'No,' said Rizpah, sitting beside him. 'Only three days.'

'I'm ravenous,' he turned his head to look at her. 'Have you got any bread?'

'No,' she was stroking the kitten. 'No food today. We're all fasting.'

'What?'

'Today is Yom Kippur,' she said. 'The Day of Atonement. Everyone here in the Golden House is fasting. But don't worry. We'll eat this evening.'

He gulped some air and tried to stand. But he felt too dizzy and let his back slide slowly down the wall again.

'How is my mother?' he asked after a while.

'Waiting for you. They all are. The Emperor and your friends looked everywhere and finally they went away. I didn't tell them where you were but I told them you were all right.'

'Will you take me to her?'

'Of course.' She wrinkled her nose. 'But first you might want to visit the baths.'

'All right,' said Jonathan. 'You lead the way and I'll crawl after you.'

SCROLL XXVI

'Please, mother. Tell me why you won't come back to Ostia with me.' Jonathan sat facing his mother in the shaded peristyle by the Cyclops' cave. He had bathed in hot sulphur water and cold sea water. Now, dressed in a loose white tunic, he felt clean and new, though the brand on his left arm throbbed and his stomach was empty as a pit.

His barefoot mother was also dressed in white: a long linen tunic, unbelted because leather could not be worn on the Day of Atonement.

'Tell me why you can't come home with me,' he repeated.

She nodded. 'I'll try to explain,' she said and took his cold hands in her warm ones. 'After the famine set in, the nightmare began. My lover Jonathan died, as I told you, fighting over a dead mule. After that, I went to stay with my parents. About this time Simeon became a Christian like your father. He renounced the Zealots and came to stay with us. Simeon and I watched our parents slowly weaken and die. There was nothing we could do to help them. We cooked belts, sandals, even scrolls. My mother died first, then my father. As my father lay dying I held him in my arms. He looked up at me and said, "I know you committed a sin which demands the penalty of death. God forgive me, Susannah, I could not stone my own daughter." I wept when I realised he knew what I had done. "Atone for your sins," he whispered. "Obey the Lord and follow his commandments." I nodded. "I promise I'll be good from now on." He died smiling.'

Susannah squeezed Jonathan's hands and he looked up at her.

'Jonathan,' she said. 'I know God spared me for a reason. I honoured my father's dying wish. I have spent most of the past nine years at my loom in silent prayer. Somehow I knew you had all survived. I prayed for you every day. I prayed for everyone I knew, even Titus.'

Jonathan nodded. He could smell her rose and myrtle perfume.

'Then, last year, Titus sent Berenice away. But I know he missed her because he used to come back here and wander through the rooms she had occupied. One day he walked through the octagonal room. Most of the women turned their faces away, but I smiled at him as I prayed for him. The next day he summoned me into his presence.'

Jonathan swallowed. His heart was pounding.

'I think at first that he wanted me to take Berenice's place. But we ended up talking. It became a regular occurrence. He especially likes hearing about our

Torah. He is intrigued that our God is a moral one. Titus has committed many great sins, as I have. He does not fully believe, but he is beginning to.'

Jonathan looked at her. 'Then he's not your lover?'

She looked at him and for the first time he saw complete openness in her eyes. 'No. We are not lovers. Only friends.'

Jonathan breathed a sigh of relief. That meant she had changed. That meant there was hope. Hope that she might yet come back to them.

'Jonathan,' she was saying. 'I am atoning for my sins. For letting my father down, my husband, my children. I would dearly love to come home to you but I believe God has led me here, to the most powerful man in the world, for such a time as this. Do you understand?'

Jonathan shook his head. 'Not really.'

She squeezed his hands again, and looked down at them. 'My ring!' she exclaimed. 'Jonathan, where did you find my ring?'

Jonathan looked in surprise at the sardonyx ring on his little finger.

'Oh,' he said. 'I was looking through your things, trying to find out what happened to you. I found this,' he slipped it easily off his finger. 'And I found love letters that father wrote to you. Beautiful love letters quoting the Song of Solomon.' Suddenly a terrible thought occurred to him. 'Or did Jonathan write them?'

'No.' Tears filled her eyes. 'Your father wrote those letters to me.'

Jonathan nodded and hung his head so she would not see his face.

Presently he slid the ring onto the forefinger of her left hand. 'Here,' he said. 'Take it. Promise me you'll wear it. And whenever you catch sight of it, will you think of me?'

'I have thought of you every day,' she whispered. 'Every day since the last time I saw you, looking over your father's shoulder, waving goodbye to me with your chubby hand.'

The octagonal court had been cleared of looms. There were too many diners for couches, so long tables had been brought in and every chair and stool available. It was just past dusk and a hundred candles and oil lamps filled the deep blue of the domed room with stars of light.

Two hundred slave women and twenty-four children, all in white, sat at long tables, ready to eat the food set before them. Jonathan sat between Rizpah and the slave boy called Benjamin. On Rizpah's right was her mother Rachel – the woman with fluffy brown hair who had spat in Titus's face. She sat quietly and gazed thoughtfully at the candles.

Jonathan's stomach rumbled fiercely as he caught a whiff of roast chicken and coriander. He was dizzy with hunger.

There was a murmur at the table as two figures in white entered the room through the golden columns: a man and a woman.

Jonathan knew the woman was his mother, but the man didn't look like Titus.

'Is it Titus?' Jonathan peered into the gloom. 'I can't see clearly in this light.'

'No,' whispered Rizpah, 'It is a tall, slim man.'

'Uncle Simeon!' cried Jonathan.

His uncle stepped into the lamplight at the head of the table, and gave Jonathan his radiant gap-toothed smile.

'Before Susannah recites the blessing,' Simeon said in his deep voice, 'I have some news to give you. Titus has just made me steward of this house. As you know, the Emperor set you free three days ago. You are now his freedwomen, under his protection for as long as you choose. You will be given quarters here and elsewhere, and you will be allowed to marry.'

He looked round at them all. 'You are probably wondering who I am. My name is Simeon ben Jonah. Susannah here is my sister. For half a year you have shunned her for befriending the Emperor. But today is the day when God wipes our sins from his memory and writes our names in his scroll of life.

'Will you forgive her, at last, and receive her back into your company?'

There was a positive murmur and then Rizpah's mother stood and looked around at them all. 'None of us is without sin,' she said. 'We forgive you, Susannah.' Rachel smiled at Susannah and Simeon, then resumed her seat.

Jonathan's mother remained standing. She lifted her veil and covered her head, and she looked so much like Miriam that Jonathan wanted to cry.

'Blessed are you, O Lord our God, who gives us bread to gladden our hearts and oil to make our faces shine,' she recited as she lit the special candles. 'Let us eat and be glad,' she added with a smile.

As Jonathan began to eat, he felt his spirits lift.

'It takes so little,' he said.

'What?' said Rizpah. Her pale eyes looked pink in the lamplight.

'A few bites of food make us happy again. Food is a wonderful thing.'

'Yes,' said Rizpah. 'Food is wonderful.'

Jonathan took a mouthful of chicken. 'I suppose you'll be leaving here with your mother. After what she said to the Emperor today. You'll miss your tunnels, won't you.'

'Oh, I don't think we'll be leaving here,' said Rizpah with a smile, and glanced at her mother. 'Not if your handsome uncle is remaining as steward. No,' said Rizpah, popping a bean into her mouth, 'Here I was born and here I'll die.'

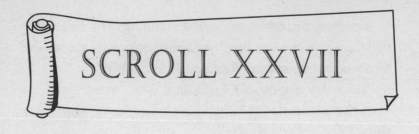

SCROLL XXVII

'Caesar,' said Jonathan, and rose from the couch.

'No don't get up, Jonathan. Sit. I need to talk to you.'

It was late morning of the Sabbath. Jonathan had spent the night in a luxurious guest room on the Palatine Hill.

Jonathan sat back down on the edge of the couch and the Emperor sat beside him. For a moment Jonathan and the Emperor Titus both looked at the painting on the wall opposite. The fresco showed the return of Odysseus in the moment where he discards the disguise of a beggar to reveal his true identity.

'I have fought in many battles,' said Titus presently, 'and many have called me brave. But what you did in coming here to find your mother, risking torture and possibly death – that was remarkable.'

Jonathan looked down. 'Thank you,' he said.

'Jonathan. Your mother is teaching me so much.' The Emperor looked down at his hands, at the thick fingers covered with rings. 'She is a very wise and beautiful woman.'

Jonathan kept his eyes down.

The Emperor reached out his right hand and almost touched the brand on Jonathan's left shoulder.

'I'm sorry about this, Jonathan.'

Jonathan looked away and shrugged. 'I belong to you. I'm Caesar's slave now.'

'No.' The Emperor fished in a pouch at his belt and pulled out Jonathan's ruby ring and bulla. 'You are not my slave.' He held them out to Jonathan. 'I release you from servitude to me and I grant you not only your freedom, Jonathan, but your citizenship.'

Slowly, Jonathan took his ring and bulla. Roman citizenship was a precious and sought-after gift.

'You're too young to receive it now, but I will bestow that honour upon your father. Then your whole family will be citizens. By the way, your father is no longer in prison.'

'My father was in prison?'

'The magistrate in Ostia took him in for questioning. Your friends told me and I sent word that he be released at once. As a Roman citizen he will of course have special privileges. This sort of thing should never happen to him again.'

'Thank you.'

The Emperor removed one of the rings from his little finger. 'Take this ring, too. If anyone questions the brand on your shoulder, mistakes you for my slave, show them this. It proves that you are no longer a slave but under my protection. And if you should ever need anything, you have only to come to the Palatine and present that ring. I will see you at once.'

Jonathan nodded and glanced at the Emperor. He could see his eyelashes and the mixture of green, gold and brown in his hazel eyes. For the first time he saw Titus as a man and not the Emperor.

'Thank you,' said Jonathan. And he took the ring.

Beneath the grape arbour in the house of Senator Cornix, Sisyphus the Greek secretary took the message from Bulbus and thumbed the parchment open. The seal fell off and rattled onto the table like a small wax coin.

Flavia picked up the disc of red wax and studied it as Sisyphus scanned the message. Titus's seal was the boar of the tenth legion, the legion he had commanded in Judaea. Underneath it were the letters IMP TITVS CAES VESP.

'It's in Titus's own hand,' said Sisyphus, raising his eyebrows. 'He thanks us for our loyalty and devotion to him and to the Roman Empire. He says that our friend Jonathan is rested and well,' Sisyphus looked up in surprise, 'and already on his way back to Ostia.'

SCROLL XXVIII

Jonathan lay on a rush mat between Flavia and Nubia and looked up at the chinks of turquoise sky gleaming through the lattice of branches. Tigris was curled up at his feet panting gently with his pink tongue. It was the next to last day of September, and the three friends were back in Ostia, lying beneath a shelter woven of branches in Jonathan's garden.

'So,' said Flavia quietly. 'Your mother is alive.'

'Yes. You and Nubia and Lupus saved her life.'

'So did you. If you hadn't gone to Rome . . .'

Jonathan grunted.

'And your father doesn't know?' whispered Flavia.

'No,' said Jonathan. 'He doesn't know she's alive. She asked me not to tell him. Yet.'

'I hope we can go back to Rome again one day,' said Flavia. 'I'd like to meet her.'

'I have a feeling,' said Jonathan, 'that we'll go back.'

Flavia reached up and brushed a green palm frond with the tips of her fingers. 'So what's this thing called again?'

'A succah. The word means shelter. It's supposed to

remind us of the time the Jewish people wandered in the desert. Before we found the promised land.'

'So this is another festival.'

'Yes. We call it the Feast of Tabernacles. A tabernacle is a tent or a shelter like this.'

'What are those dates hanging from roof?' asked Nubia.

Jonathan grinned. 'They're for you.'

Nubia sat up and reached for one.

'And we're going to eat dinner in here tonight?' said Flavia.

'Yes.' Jonathan sat up. 'Miriam's cooking my favourite stew again. I didn't eat much of it on my birthday.'

Flavia sat up too, hugged her knees and inhaled. 'I like it in here. It smells lovely.'

'And you can see the sky,' added Nubia.

'Yes,' said Jonathan. 'You're supposed to be able to see the stars at night.' He reached up and pulled a few grapes from a cluster hanging above his head.

'You sleeping here?' asked Nubia, her amber eyes gleamed with interest.

Jonathan nodded. 'It's the full moon tonight.'

'Can we sleep here, too?' cried Flavia.

'I'll have to ask father but I think he'll say yes. It's big enough for us all.'

'Do you *all* sleep out here?'

'Of course. For eight nights we eat and sleep in the succah. Me and Miriam and father and Lupus.'

Nubia frowned. 'Where is the Lupus?'

'He had a visitor just before you arrived. A man in a green tunic with his hair all oiled and combed back. He looked like one of Felix's men. They went off towards the harbour.'

'Hey!' cried Flavia. 'Two weeks ago Lupus told us that Felix was looking for something for him. Maybe he's found it.'

'He did indeed,' said a voice from outside the shelter.

'What is it, Father?' Jonathan emerged from the succah, followed by Flavia and Nubia. Mordecai was thin and pale, but smiling. He held a tray with cups of mint tea on it and gestured with his bearded chin towards the front of the house.

They all saw Lupus step into the bright inner garden, hand in hand with a small dark-haired girl.

'Great Neptune's beard,' breathed Jonathan. 'It's Clio.'

'Clio!' Flavia squealed with delight and ran to hug the little girl. 'You weren't buried by the volcano!'

Clio grinned and shook her head.

'It's thanks to her we survived,' said a woman's voice. 'She insisted we all clamber over the landslide and walk to Neapolis.'

'Rectina!' said Flavia. 'You're alive, too! And all eight of Clio's sisters?'

Rectina nodded and smiled. She was a tall, elegant woman with beautiful dark eyes.

'Where are they?' said Flavia, looking behind

Rectina, and then stopped as she saw a man and a girl standing in the shadowed corridor. Flavia's heart skipped a beat and she barely heard Rectina's answer: 'My husband and Vulcan and the girls are all in Stabia, helping with the relief operations.'

Flavia nodded vaguely at Rectina and moved past her. 'Hello, Pulchra,' she said. 'Hello, Patron.'

'Flavia darling,' cried the blonde girl. She stepped forward and managed to kiss Flavia on both cheeks without touching either of them. For a moment they looked into each other's eyes. Then they both grinned and hugged each other tightly.

'Jonathan!' Pulchra thrust Flavia aside and rushed forward into the sunshine.

Flavia staggered and laughed and watched Pulchra hug Jonathan. Then she turned back to the man standing in the shadows. He was tall and tanned, with dark eyes and prematurely grey hair.

'Hello, Flavia Gemina,' he said. 'Are you well?'

'Very well,' said Flavia, touching her hair to make sure it was tidy.

Publius Pollius Felix was wearing a sky-blue tunic and a short grey travelling cloak. He looked even more handsome than she remembered. Flavia swallowed. 'Were you the one who found Clio? Was that what you were looking for? For Lupus, I mean?'

Felix nodded and smiled at the group of friends in the sunlit garden, all chattering and hugging and writing on wax tablets. 'I had my men looking everywhere. Then

194

one day I had to visit my estate at Pausilypon and I rode into Neapolis to do some business. A colleague there told me the story of a woman and her nine daughters who had escaped the volcano on foot. I knew it had to be them.'

'They walked all the way to Neapolis?' Flavia pulled a myrtle twig from her hair and let it drop on the ground behind her.

Felix nodded. 'It's only about four miles. But they made the right decision. By the worst stage of the eruption, they were safely out of danger. Now they are reunited, and helping me with the relief operations. Tascius and Rectina have adopted two more orphans.'

'Girls?' asked Flavia.

Felix smiled. 'One of each, actually.'

'Hey,' said Flavia, looking back over her shoulder at the happy crowd. 'Where's Miriam?'

'I brought your uncle Gaius back with me,' said Felix, half turning towards the atrium. 'I believe Miriam is greeting him.'

'Oh,' said Flavia. And then, '*Oh!*'

Felix gave her an amused glance.

'Hello, Patron.' Jonathan stepped forward and held out his hand.

'Hello, Jonathan.' Felix grasped his hand. 'Are you well? You look . . . older.'

'I am older,' said Jonathan. 'I celebrated my eleventh birthday a few weeks ago.'

'Congratulations.'

'Patron, I would like to invite you and Pulchra to dine with us this evening under the succah.'

Felix looked over Jonathan's shoulder at the shelter woven of palm, myrtle and willow. Beside it, Nubia was introducing Clio to Pulchra.

'It looks like it might be an interesting experience,' said Felix. 'Pulchra and I would be honoured to stay for dinner.'

Jonathan looked around his succah with satisfaction. He had built it well. In a few days it would begin to grow stiff and yellow and the fruit would wither, but for now it was good. The branches were green and supple and fragrant. The fruit hanging from the woven canopy was ripe and full of sweet juices. And there was room for everyone. They sat on embroidered cushions around the octagonal table and sipped their watered wine and chatted as they waited for the dessert course.

His sister Miriam looked beautiful in her white tunic. Whenever he looked at her now, he saw his mother. Miriam and Gaius were speaking softly, as lovers do, oblivious of everyone else.

Clio was dressed in a bright orange tunic, chattering away to Lupus, describing their escape from Vesuvius in great detail and with vigorous arm movements.

Mordecai and Rectina, both in dark blue, sat next to each other. They were discussing useful ointments for baby skin irritation.

Nubia sat straight in her prettiest yellow silk tunic.

She was demonstrating some fingering on her cherry-wood flute to Aristo.

On Jonathan's left sat Flavia. She was wearing her best pale blue tunic and Nubia had arranged her hair. A strand had already escaped and Flavia kept brushing it out of her eyes as she told Felix about how she and Sisyphus had discovered the tunnels in the Golden House.

'Jonathan,' purred a voice in his ear. 'Is it true you saved the Emperor from an assassin?'

He turned to look at Pulchra and smiled.

'We all had a part in it.'

'Will you tell me about it?' She was wearing a pink silk tunic and pink ribbons were braided into her yellow hair. She smelled of lemon blossom.

'Some day,' said Jonathan. 'Not yet. But I would like to play you a song I wrote.'

'You've learned to play!' Pulchra opened her blue eyes in delight and clapped her hands.

'Let's say I'm learning.' Jonathan smiled as he reached behind his cushion and lifted up his bass lyre.

'A Syrian barbiton!' Felix sat up with interest and Jonathan remembered he was a keen musician. 'Where did you get it?'

'My uncle bought it in Rome, and he gave it to me,' said Jonathan. 'He taught me how to play, but so far I can only play one song. Would you like to hear it?'

'Yes!' everyone cried.

Jonathan settled the instrument and gripped the

smooth bulb of the sound box between his bare feet. Already it felt right, as if it were part of him.

'I wrote this song myself,' he said, looking around at them. 'I call it "Penelope's Loom".'

Jonathan closed his eyes and found his heartbeat. Then he speeded it up and began to play.

FINIS

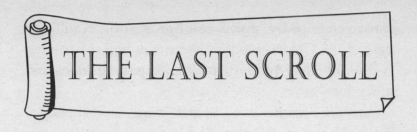

THE LAST SCROLL

In the spring of AD 70, nine and a half years before this story takes place, four Roman legions surrounded the rebellious city of Jerusalem. The commander was Titus, son of Rome's new Emperor, Vespasian. Jerusalem should have withstood the siege for years, but weakened by the fighting of those inside, it fell in months. Those few months were among the most terrible in the history of the Jewish people. Thousands were crucified as they tried to escape. Those who remained in the city suffered terrible famine. Finally, the Temple of God was destroyed, Jerusalem razed to the ground, and the survivors killed or enslaved.

Titus returned to Rome in triumph with thousands of Jewish slaves. It is probable that many of them were put to work building Vespasian's new amphitheatre. This monument came to be known as the Colosseum, after the colossal statue of Nero which stood nearby.

Nero had died a year before the fall of Jerusalem. His opulent Golden House only survived another thirty-five years before it became the site of Trajan's baths. Nobody knows exactly what it was used for during those years. Today, if you visit Rome, you can still visit part of the Golden House. There you will see painted rooms, a long cryptoporticus, an octagonal pavilion and a 'Cyclops' cave'.

Simeon, Susannah and Rizpah were not real people. Titus, Domitian, Josephus and Berenice were. You can read more about them in history books.

THE DOLPHINS
OF LAURENTUM

ITALY IN AD 79
(after the eruption of Vesuvius)

N

Rome

Ostia
River Tiber
Laurentum

Neapolis

Misenum
Surrentum

Herculaneum
Pompeii
Stabia

Sicily

Towns destroyed in the
eruption of Vesuvius
are shown in grey

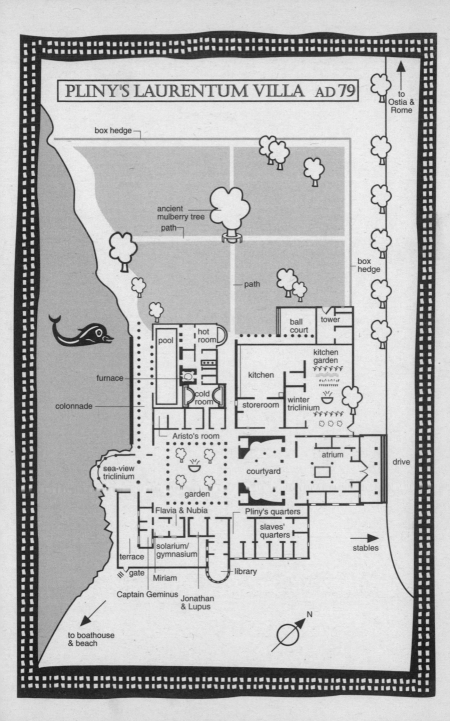

PLINY'S LAURENTUM VILLA AD 79

to Ostia & Rome

box hedge

ancient mulberry tree
path

path

box hedge

pool

hot room

ball court

tower

furnace

cold room

kitchen

kitchen garden

colonnade

storeroom

winter triclinium

Aristo's room

sea-view triclinium

garden

courtyard

atrium

drive

Flavia & Nubia

Pliny's quarters

slaves' quarters

terrace

solarium/ gymnasium

library

stables

gate

Miriam

Captain Geminus

Jonathan & Lupus

N

to boathouse & beach

To Jan-Theo, Bill, Barbara,
Eric, Silvano, Domenico
and all my other cyber-buddies
from the Ostia website

SCROLL I

Lupus was drumming.

He sat on the wooden floor of the small bedroom and played his goatskin drum: one beat with his right hand, another with his left. His eyes were closed but in his head he clearly saw the pattern he was making. The hits were small black pebbles, the no-hits were white pebbles. He played the pattern, built up the white and black pebbles and then entwined them in a plait. Just like the black and white mosaic chips in the floor of the triclinium downstairs.

When he wove drum patterns, it drove everything else from his mind. And that was good. The mosaic rhythm lifted him up and carried him along. He was only aware of the ache in his forearms and the tingling in the tips of his fingers and the pattern unwinding in his head.

'Lupus!'

The voice had been calling him for some time now.

He opened his eyes.

Jonathan was sitting on his low bed, tuning a Syrian barbiton.

'Enough warm-up,' said his friend with a grin. 'Let's play.'

Lupus nodded and looked at Jonathan hard. Sometimes, when he'd been drumming, it was as if he'd been dreaming. And when he stopped it was like coming out of a trance: everything looked strange.

His friend Jonathan looked strange.

Maybe it was because Jonathan's hair, once thick and curly, was now shorn to a soft dark stubble. Maybe it was because he'd lost weight, and his dark eyes looked huge in his face. Maybe it was because the brand on his left shoulder was still red and swollen.

Jonathan ben Mordecai had recently turned eleven. He seemed older than his age. Lupus felt older than his own eight and a half years, too. He hadn't felt like a child since his tongue had been cut out.

Lupus watched Jonathan settle the smooth wooden bulb of the instrument between his bare feet and support the long neck with his hands, one over, one under.

He heard the deep note as Jonathan began to thumb the fattest string. The sound was sweet and round. It needed a drumbeat that sounded not like pebbles, but like something softer, rounder, more muted.

Lupus picked up the new drumstick he'd found at Flavia's.

He gave the drum an experimental tap and nodded

in satisfaction at the sound. Perfect. He found the beat and started to weave a new pattern, holding the drumstick in his right hand and using the palm of his left.

'Lupus!' Jonathan was staring at him in horror.

Lupus stopped drumming and gave Jonathan his bug-eyed look: What?

'What on earth are you using as a drumstick?'

Lupus held up the sponge-stick and shrugged, as if to say: It's a sponge-stick.

'Where did you get it?'

Lupus tilted his head towards Flavia's house next door.

'Lupus. Do you know what that is? I mean, what it's used for?'

Lupus shook his head.

Jonathan sighed. 'I know you used to be a half-wild beggar-boy,' he said. 'But you've been living with us for nearly four months now. You're practically a civilised Roman. You're sure you don't know what that sponge-stick is used for?'

Lupus shook his head again. And frowned.

Jonathan leaned forward and grinned. 'It's for wiping your bottom after you've been to the latrine.'

'Flavia!' bellowed a voice from the latrine. 'Where's the sponge-stick?'

Flavia Gemina looked at her ex-slave-girl Nubia.

They shrugged at one another, got up and went out of their bedroom onto the balcony.

'I don't know, Uncle Gaius!' Flavia yelled down into the sunny courtyard garden. 'Isn't it there? In the beaker of vinegar?'

'No!' came a grumpy voice from the latrine.

Flavia leaned further over the polished rail and called out, 'Do you want me to grab you some leaves from the fig tree?'

'I'll do it!' said Alma the cook, coming into view. She peered up at the two girls suspiciously.

'You two aren't wearing eyeliner, are you?'

'Um, no!' Flavia hastily pulled Nubia back into their room. Not only were they wearing kohl around their eyes, but they had done up their hair and put on all the jewellery they owned. They were trying on their outfits for Miriam's betrothal supper, although the date had still not been set.

Nubia was wearing a peach shift over a lemon-yellow tunic. 'Flavia . . .' she said slowly, as she brushed her finger against the wine dregs at the bottom of an empty wine-cup, 'what is betrothal supper?'

Flavia was smoothing her own grey silk shift over the sky-blue tunic and admiring the combination. 'Well, it's usually when the parents arrange the marriage of a man and a girl. There's a celebration banquet and the man holds the girl's hand in front of everybody and then he gives her a ring. After that they set the date for the wedding. Alma told me the wedding might be a week later, or a month later or even ten years later, if the couple are very young when they're betrothed. Sometimes the girl is younger than we are.'

Flavia sat beside a small oak table on a folding stool. Nubia sat on a similar stool, facing her former mistress.

'Do you think Miriam and Gaius will wait a year or two later?' Nubia leaned forward and brushed her finger lightly over Flavia's cheekbone.

'I don't think so. First, because of the volcano. Aristo says it reminded everyone that they won't live forever. And second, because they're passionately in love. Alma says it's a bad omen.'

'The volcano?'

'No, that they're in love. She says marrying for love is always a bad idea.' Flavia peered into her highly polished silver mirror. 'No. That's too dark. Brush a bit off.'

Nubia thumbed the wine dregs off Flavia's cheek, leaving just the hint of a blush.

'That's better,' said Flavia, and stroked some of the powdered wine onto Nubia's cheekbone. Then she leaned back on her stool and narrowed her eyes.

'No. Your skin's too dark. It doesn't show up,' said Flavia. She sat forward again. 'Where you grew up, do the parents choose your husband or do you?' she asked.

Nubia covered her smile with her hand. 'We choose, and our parents say yes or no.'

'Now do my mouth,' said Flavia, pushing her lips out.

'Oh, very nice!' came a voice from underneath Flavia's low bed.

'Jonathan!' Flavia squealed and the silver mirror clattered to the floor. 'How long have you been under there?'

Jonathan wriggled out from underneath the bed and grinned up at her. His nutmeg-coloured tunic was grey with fluff and there was brick dust in the stubble of his cropped hair.

'You need to remind Alma to dust under the beds,' he remarked, standing up and brushing off the dust balls.

'Stop!' cried Flavia. 'You'll get our clothes dirty!'

Jonathan ignored Flavia. 'Come on, Lupus,' he said. 'You can come out now.'

'Lupus is under there, too?' Flavia and Nubia exchanged horrified glances. Flavia stood up and folded her arms. Have you two been spying on us? We finished lessons over an hour ago. How long have you been under there?' she repeated.

'Not long.' Jonathan helped Lupus to his feet. Lupus grinned at them. He was wearing his favourite sea-green tunic and had slicked his dark hair back from his forehead with laurel-scented oil. Because Lupus couldn't speak, he always carried a wax tablet with him. Now he opened this tablet with a flourish and thrust it in the girls' faces:

SURPRISE!

With his other hand he held out the sponge-stick.

'Where did you find that?' cried Flavia. 'And how did you –?'

'Shhh!' said Jonathan. 'We don't want anyone else to know about our secret entrance.'

'You mean you came in through the wall?' Flavia's grey eyes widened.

Jonathan nodded. 'My bedroom is right next to yours. Whenever I can't sleep I pick at the plaster. I haven't been sleeping very well since we got back from Rome and I've picked off quite a bit of it. Lupus and I spent all day yesterday getting the mortar out from between the bricks and we've made a way through.'

'Jonathan! How exciting! Let's not tell anybody else,' Flavia breathed. 'Not even your father or Miriam.'

'That's why I've been telling you to be quiet.' Jonathan rolled his eyes.

Flavia sucked a loose strand of her light brown hair

thoughtfully. 'We'll have to think of a secret signal for when we want to come through. How about three taps on the wall?'

Jonathan shook his head. 'Everybody knocks three times,' he said. 'How about four? One for each of us.'

'Excellent idea,' said Flavia.

Lupus gave them a thumbs-up.

At that moment they all heard four distinct raps at the front door of the house. The friends looked at each other, wide-eyed.

'You two stay here. Out of sight!' hissed Flavia. She and Nubia rushed back to the balcony and peered down into the garden.

Flavia's uncle Gaius was standing by the fountain, washing his hands. As he shook the drops from his fingers and turned towards the entrance of the house, Caudex the door-slave staggered into the garden, half-carrying and half-supporting a beggar.

The man wore a tattered tunic and had bandages instead of sandals on his feet. His legs were covered with red sores. His hair was matted and his beard ragged. The beggar was tall, but painfully thin. From her vantage point on the balcony above, Flavia couldn't make out his expression, but it looked as though he was drunk.

'Caudex,' she scolded, starting down the stairs, 'what on earth are you doing? You can't just let any –'

Alma screamed.

'Great Jupiter's eyebrows!' exclaimed Gaius, and rushed forward to help Caudex.

Scuto was sniffing the beggar's legs and wagging his tail.

'All lost,' the stranger croaked. 'Ship sunk and everything lost.' As Flavia reached the bottom step, he lifted his head and looked at her. His eyes above the peeling, sunburned cheeks were the same grey-blue as hers, and already tears were filling them.

'Pater!' Flavia gripped the railing with one hand. 'Pater, is it you?'

'Yes, my little owl,' said the sea captain Marcus Flavius Geminus.

Then he collapsed.

SCROLL II

Jonathan's father, Doctor Mordecai ben Ezra, looked up at the people crowding into the bedroom doorway.

'He's still unconscious,' said Mordecai, straightening up from the bedside of Flavia's father. 'From the looks of him, he's suffering from hunger and exposure. It's obvious he's been shipwrecked.'

The doctor rinsed his hands in the copper bowl which his daughter Miriam held.

'I would guess that the cuts on his legs and feet were made by sharp coral.' Mordecai dried his hands on the linen towel over Miriam's arm. 'And I'm afraid they're infected. If we don't act immediately,' he glanced at Flavia's father and lowered his voice, 'we may have to amputate his feet.'

Mordecai spoke Latin with an accent and Nubia didn't understand the word he had just uttered. 'What is amputate?' she asked Flavia.

'Cut off.' Flavia's face was very pale.

'Just tell us what to do.' Gaius stepped forward and looked down at his unconscious twin brother.

'Will you go to the market with Miriam, Gaius? I'll

make her a list of healing foods. She'll know which stalls are most likely to have them. Also, when he wakes up, he'll need lots of liquids. Alma, can you make him chicken soup?'

'Of course, Doctor Mordecai.' Alma looked relieved to have something to do and retreated from the dim bedroom.

'Just broth, to start,' called Mordecai after her. 'Plenty of garlic.'

'Right you are,' came her voice, already halfway downstairs.

'Aristo, can you buy some strips of linen? His wounds will need a fresh dressing.'

'Right away,' said Flavia's tutor, a young Greek with curly hair the colour of bronze. He, too, hurried out of the room.

'Flavia. Nubia.' Mordecai turned to the girls. 'Go down to the beach and fill some buckets with sea-water, as clear as possible.'

The girls nodded.

'When you get back you must sponge his feet and legs with the seawater. It won't be a pleasant job, I'm afraid.'

'That's all right, Doctor Mordecai,' said Flavia and then turned to Nubia. 'Is that all right?'

Nubia nodded.

'Better take Caudex as your bodyguard,' added Mordecai.

'What about us, father?' asked Jonathan. 'What can we do?'

Mordecai looked at the boys, his heavy-lidded eyes as dark as the turban above them. 'You have the most unpleasant job of all,' he said. 'I want you to search the gutters of the meat market. Bring me back some nice young maggots. And make sure they're still alive.'

Nubia stood on Ostia's hot beach for a moment, just where the small waves washed up onto the shore. She liked the feel of the water sucking the sand from under her feet. It tickled. And it was deliciously refreshing to have the blue water cooling her legs. She had changed back into one of her ordinary tunics – the faded apricot one – because it was short enough to allow her to wade in up to her knees.

She used to hate the sea. For most of her life she had lived in the desert. Her first glimpse of the sea had been at the port of Alexandria, when the slave-dealer Venalicius angrily pushed a girl from her clan into its blue depths. The girl had still been chained and she had drowned before Nubia's eyes.

But now that Lupus had taught her to swim, Nubia was no longer afraid of the sea. She moved forward, beyond the little waves that foamed up onto the sand, and lowered the wooden bucket into the water. When it was full, she turned back to the shore.

Her puppy Nipur was sniffing something on the beach. Since the volcano, bits of flotsam and jetsam had been washed ashore almost daily, some of it very unpleasant. Flavia was already there, her bucket filled, also staring down at the object.

'What is it?' said Nubia, splashing back towards the beach.

'Only a medusa,' said Flavia.

'A what?' Nubia looked at the transparent blob with its tangle of greyish-white strings.

'A jellyfish. Don't touch it! It can still sting, even though it's dead. They call them medusas because the tentacles look like Medusa's snaky hair.'

Nubia nodded. Flavia was one of the cleverest people she knew. She was always reading scrolls and knew almost as much about Greek mythology as their tutor Aristo.

Scuto came up to investigate, his tail wagging and his new ball in his mouth. He gave the jellyfish a quick sniff and then retreated. He knew from experience what they could do.

'Filled your bucket?' said Flavia.

Nubia nodded.

'Then let's get back.'

'I can't believe how hot it is for October,' said Jonathan, as he and Lupus slipped behind the stalls of Ostia's meat market.

Lupus grunted. The air above the white stone pavement shimmered with heat and the stench of blood and rotting meat filled his nostrils.

Jonathan's puppy Tigris strained at his rope lead, nose down, urgently following an invisible trail.

'Good boy,' said Jonathan. 'Find the maggots! Ugh! It smells revolting here. Still, I suppose it's good maggot weather.' He ignored an over-the-shoulder glare of a fat pork butcher and scratched the stubble on his head. 'I wonder why my father wants maggots? I don't know of any balms or medicines which have maggots as an ingredient . . .'

Tigris barked, startling a group of feral cats who had been scavenging in the gutter. The cats scattered, then turned to watch the boys from a safe distance. Lupus squatted to examine the object of their attention. Tigris came forward to sniff it and Lupus gently pushed the puppy away.

'Ugh!' Jonathan lifted Tigris into his arms. 'Why did God make flies? And maggots . . .' He gazed down at the rotting chicken leg. Dozens of white maggots writhed in the rancid meat.

Lupus pulled out his handkerchief, a rather grubby one that smelled faintly of lemon blossom, and carefully wrapped the chicken leg in it. Then he stood and nodded.

'Well done, Tigris,' said Jonathan, and kissed his puppy's nose. 'You're a good maggot-hunter.'

Lupus patted Tigris, too, and the boys started back towards Green Fountain Street.

As Lupus and Jonathan made their way through the crowded forum, Lupus glanced warily around. In his begging days he had learned to be constantly alert, always aware of his surroundings and any possible danger. Old habits died hard.

It was almost noon and the forum was crowded with people finishing their day's work before returning home for a light meal and short siesta. It was still as hot and heavy as summer and a layer of charcoal smoke from the morning sacrifices hung over the forum. Everyone blamed the eruption of Vesuvius two months earlier for the unusually hot autumn and lack of rain.

On Lupus's left rose the gleaming white temple of the Capitoline triad: Jupiter, Juno and Minerva. On his right stood the basilica where only a few weeks earlier Jonathan's father Mordecai had been imprisoned for hiding a suspected assassin. According to Miriam, they had officially released Mordecai by having a scribe announce that he had been cleared of blame and was free to go.

A similar ceremony was taking place now on the steps of the basilica. Lupus glanced over to see who was being released.

The prisoner was a barrel-chested man in a filthy

grey tunic. His head was wrapped in linen strips, stained with dried blood. He was facing the scribe and the magistrate with his back to Lupus, but as he turned Lupus's stomach writhed as if it were as full of maggots as his handkerchief.

The man gazing around the forum with a blind eye and a twisted smile was the person Lupus hated most in the world: Venalicius the slave-dealer.

SCROLL III

'Venalicius is here in Ostia!' cried Jonathan, and rushed past Caudex to cry out again, 'Flavia! Where arc you?'

'Upstairs in pater's room,' came Flavia's voice.

Jonathan took the wooden stairs two at a time, with Lupus and the dogs close behind him.

'Flavia!' Jonathan cried, then stopped as he saw she had her finger to her lips.

Marcus Flavius Geminus was sitting up in bed and Jonathan's father was standing beside him with a razor-sharp blade.

'Hello, Jonathan. Hello, Lupus.' Marcus's voice was little more than a whisper.

'Hello, Captain Geminus,' said Jonathan. 'Welcome home.'

Lupus nodded his greeting.

Jonathan glanced down at Flavia and Nubia, who were sponging Marcus's wounded feet. Then he wished he hadn't.

'Not a pretty sight, is it?' whispered Captain Geminus.

Jonathan swallowed and tried to smile.

'Did you get the . . . what I asked for?' said Mordecai.

Lupus nodded and held out his handkerchief.

Jonathan stared at the razor in his father's hand.

'You're not going to amputate his feet, are you?'

Mordecai smiled. 'No, I was just about to shave him. But now I have something more important to do.' He put down the razor and turned to Captain Geminus. 'I must ask you to put aside your prejudices, Marcus. I have used this method before and it is remarkable. I would like to put maggots in the infected wounds on your feet.'

'Ugh!' squealed Flavia. 'No!'

'Flavia,' croaked her father. 'Let the doctor finish.'

Mordecai took a deep breath. 'The maggots eat the dead flesh . . . the rotting flesh. But they do not eat the healthy skin. In a few days the maggots will be fat and the remaining flesh will be whole and healthy and ready to heal.' Mordecai opened Lupus's handkerchief and nodded with satisfaction. 'I will only do this,' he continued, 'if you consent. However, I must warn you, I believe it is either maggots or amputation.'

They all looked at one another and the four friends breathed a collective sigh of relief as Captain Geminus whispered, 'Maggots, please.'

'What were you in such a hurry to tell us?' Flavia

asked Jonathan a short time later. Mordecai had applied the maggots to her father's wounds and bound his torn feet loosely with strips of clean linen. Shaved and shorn, her father had drunk a bowlful of chicken soup and was now fast asleep in his darkened bedroom.

Downstairs in Flavia's cool, marble-floored triclinium Doctor Mordecai, Aristo and the four friends were sipping mint tea.

'We wanted to tell you that Venalicius is here,' Jonathan said. 'Lupus and I just saw him being set free on the steps of the basilica.'

'Venalicius!' Flavia and Nubia stared at one another in horror. 'But he was arrested in Surrentum after he tried to buy freeborn children as slaves. Why is he back in Ostia?'

Mordecai put down his cup of mint tea. 'They brought him back here to stand trial,' he said. 'Ostia is his home and his base of operations.'

'You knew about this?' said Flavia.

Mordecai nodded.

'You knew Venalicius was in Ostia?' Jonathan stared at his father.

'Yes. I knew.'

Lupus gave an odd choking sound, and Aristo patted him on the back.

Because Lupus was tongueless, sometimes food and drink went down the wrong way. Apparently not this time, thought Flavia, for Lupus writhed away from Aristo's patting and pointed at Mordecai accusingly.

'Yes, Lupus,' said Mordecai quietly. 'As I think you've just guessed, my cellmate last month was Venalicius.'

'What?' cried Flavia.

'Last month,' repeated Mordecai. 'While you were in Rome. You remember that I spent a week in the basilica after I was arrested? Well, I wasn't alone.'

Aristo said something to Mordecai in Greek and the doctor replied in the same language.

Lupus stared at them in disbelief, then snarled and lifted his empty cup as if to smash it against a wall. Jonathan caught the younger boy's wrist and said:

'Whoa, Lupus! What's the matter?'

Lupus gave Mordecai a withering look, slammed his cup onto the table and stomped out into the garden.

'Why were you speaking Greek and what did you say?' asked Flavia. She stared out into the bright garden at Lupus, who was pacing angrily back and forth under the dappled shade of the fig tree.

'Last month,' said Aristo, 'Lupus and I brought Mordecai some medical supplies, when he was being held in the basilica. I just asked Mordecai if he had used them to bandage Venalicius' ear, the one Lupus nearly cut off.'

'And I said that I had,' added Mordecai. 'That

sometimes an act of kindness speaks more than a thousand words, and that no man is beyond redemption until he dies.'

'I'm sorry, Flavia,' said Aristo. 'I know you hate it when I speak Greek. But Lupus hates Venalicius so much that he tried to kill him last month. I was trying not to upset him.'

'It didn't work,' remarked Jonathan.

'Do you know,' said Flavia slowly, 'I think Lupus understood every word you said!'

Lupus needed to get out of the house. He needed to breathe. He needed to think.

He knew Scuto's lead hung just inside the kitchen doorway. Alma smiled at him from the hearth as he pulled it off its nail. It was rare that Scuto actually went on the lead, but its jingle always alerted him that it was walk-time.

Immediately four wagging dogs appeared at Lupus's feet: big black Ferox, the two smaller black puppies and medium-sized Scuto, ball in mouth.

'Are you going to take the dogs out, Lupus?' called Flavia from the triclinium.

Lupus nodded and glanced over at them. They were all watching him, probably talking about him, too.

'Thanks, Lupus,' called Jonathan.

Lupus ignored them and unbolted the back door.

Flavia's house was built against Ostia's town wall, and the back door was built into this thick wall. It led straight into the graveyard and for security reasons there was no latch on the outside.

Jonathan – whose house was virtually a mirror image of Flavia's – had invented a small wooden wedge to prop his door open. He had made a similar one for Flavia's house. Lupus now kicked this wedge into place and let the door almost close behind him. Then he stepped outside the town into the hot afternoon.

Scuto and the two puppies had already raced through the door and now sped through the golden grasses towards their favourite umbrella pine. Ferox, still recovering from a knife wound to the chest, limped beside Lupus as he made his way past the tombs of the dead towards the Laurentum Road.

Once, not so long ago, Lupus had tormented Ferox by slinging stones at his rump. But Ferox's wound had made him gentle. He had either forgotten or forgiven the offence. Lupus ruffled the top of Ferox's head and the big dog rolled his eyes back and panted. His tail went steadily back and forth.

Strange, thought Lupus, how a wound can make a gentle creature fierce and a fierce creature gentle.

Presently they reached the road and Ferox squatted in some horse grass to do his business.

Lupus discreetly turned away. He closed his eyes

for a moment and inhaled the spicy scent of the sun-bleached grasses and pine resin. The buzzing of the cicadas was thin and brisk. Autumn was coming. His heart had stopped pounding and he no longer felt quite as sick as he had when Mordecai had confessed showing kindness towards Venalicius.

A moist nose butted his knee in mute appeal. It was Scuto. Flavia had brought her dog a ball as a souvenir from Rome and he was besotted with it. Scuto dropped this ball in the dusty pine needles at Lupus's feet, then backed away and gazed up at Lupus expectantly.

Lupus picked up the ball and threw it hard towards the dunes. Scuto and the two puppies pursued it joyfully and Ferox ambled across the road after them.

As Lupus followed, he allowed himself to remember his first ball. It had also been leather, sewn from two pieces of pigskin and filled with dried lentils. His parents had given it to him on his sixth birthday, a beautiful mild day in the middle of February, two and a half years ago.

Lupus and his father had stood before the bright sea, laughing and tossing the ball back and forth. With each catch they had taken a step away from one another. Eventually his father had become a dark silhouette against the dazzling water behind him. Then Lupus's mother had called them and presently half the village had gathered beneath their grape arbour to feast on suckling pig. Lupus still remembered the salty sweetness of the meat, roasted on a spit and glazed with honey, a rare delicacy on the island. That was when he still had a tongue and could taste food.

He remembered how happy his father had been that day: half closing his green eyes and showing his white teeth whenever he laughed. And his mother Melissa. So beautiful and full of love.

A few months later all that had been taken from him by the man who called himself Venalicius. Lupus's heart started pounding again. He bent to pick up Scuto's ball, then threw it with a grunt of rage, as hard as he could. He and Ferox followed the dogs and presently they topped a dune with a view of the water.

Lupus clenched his fists and stared out at the Tyrrhenian Sea, its blue so deep it was almost black. Many times before he had promised the gods he would get revenge. This time he silently vowed to do something about it.

SCROLL IV

The next day, Lupus paid a visit to the Baths of Thetis. He knew most of the people who visited this baths complex. In his begging days, before he had consented to live with Jonathan, the bath attendants had let him sleep by the furnace and scavenge scraps of food left behind by the clientele.

Sometimes a young changing-room slave had given Lupus a few coppers to help him guard the clothes. Now this same slave – his name was Umidus – stared down at Lupus with a frown.

'Lupus? Is it you?' Umidus's voice was muffled; he had a cleft palate and could only speak with difficulty.

Lupus nodded and took out his wax tablet:

NEED SOME HELP?

Umidus scratched his big head. 'I hardly recognised you. You look like a young gentleman! And you can read and write? I wish I could!'

Lupus dropped the tablet and gestured round at the

changing-room, then rubbed his forefinger and thumb together.

'You want to earn a few coins? All right. You can keep any tips you get.'

Lupus nodded with satisfaction. He didn't want Umidus to suspect his real reason for coming – to hire an assassin.

It was here in the Baths of Thetis that Lupus had first seen the man named Gamala.

The Gamala family had lived in Ostia for many generations, and were well-respected. But the man who called himself Gnaeus Lucilius Gamala was not a native of Ostia. He was a foreign relation of the Gamala family. He spoke Latin with an accent. Some said he came from Judaea, others said Syria. But everyone knew he had done something criminal before settling down in Ostia; the scars of the whip on his back were there for all to see. Recently Lupus had developed a theory. He reckoned Gamala had been a *sicarius*: a member of the elite Jewish assassination squad.

Lupus was about to test this hunch. He remembered that Gamala usually came in with the first wave of male customers.

As the gong began to clang noon, the double doors of the baths opened and the first group of men entered the pale blue changing-room. Lupus's heart beat faster as he saw the person he was waiting for.

Gamala was tall and lithe, with thick black hair, a nose like an eagle's beak and keen brown eyes. He was alone, accompanied by neither friend nor slave, and he moved over to his usual niche with a fluid grace. Once there, he stripped off, folded his tunic, and placed it in the cube-shaped recess in the blue wall. His belt and money pouch went on top. Before he turned to go, he tossed Lupus a small copper coin.

As Gamala strode towards the palaestra for a pre-bath workout, Lupus studied the pale scars on his retreating back. He counted twenty separate strokes before Gamala disappeared through the arched door-way.

Lupus knew the whip-marks were not proof that Gamala was an assassin. Punishment for that crime was crucifixion. But they indicated that he might have been a Zealot, a Jew who had rebelled against Roman rule in Judaea. Lupus also remembered what Jonathan had told him recently: even a retired *sicarius* never feels safe without his weapon.

When the changing-room was empty, Lupus stepped up onto the plaster-covered bench which ran round the room. He leaned into Gamala's niche and began to examine the contents. Behind him, across the black and white mosaic floor, Umidus the bath-slave uttered a cry of protest. Lupus looked over his shoulder and gave a small shake of his head to say: Don't worry; I'm just looking.

Quickly, Lupus patted Gamala's tunic, sandals and coin purse. It was only when he examined the last item that he found what he was looking for. Cleverly concealed in a secret pocket of Gamala's leather belt was a small knife. It was razor-sharp and curved like a sickle.

Flavia sat in a chair beside her father's bed and gazed down at his face. He had slept through the whole night and most of the morning, then woken at noon to take some more chicken broth. Now he was sleeping again.

The room was dim and relatively cool. Quiet, too, now that most of Ostia was taking a siesta. The only sounds she could hear were the faint strains of Jonathan practising his barbiton next door and the thin buzz of the cicadas from the umbrella pines.

Every morning over the previous two weeks Flavia had stood before the household shrine and vowed that if the gods brought her father back she would be a good, dutiful Roman daughter.

But it seemed the gods had returned a different father from the one who had sailed away. This father looked frail and helpless. His eyelashes lay pale against his sunburnt skin and his cracked lips were slightly parted in sleep. He looked like a boy.

Or maybe she was the one who was different.

So much had happened in the two months since he had sailed out of Pompeii's harbour. She had been to Stabia, Surrentum and Rome. She had survived a volcano, pirates and assassins. She had witnessed death and birth, grief and joy. People her father had never even met – Vulcan, Clio, Pulchra, Sisyphus, even the Emperor himself – had become her friends.

And she had met *him*.

Flavia looked down at the object she held carefully in her lap.

A dutiful Roman daughter should marry and have children. Soon her father would be thinking about arranging a suitable match for her. How could she tell him she would never marry? That she would never give him grandchildren? That her heart belonged to someone she could never have?

Flavia sighed, and lifted her eyes. The thread of afternoon light around the curtained doorway blurred, then cleared as she let a few hot tears spill onto her cheek. She felt very old and very wise.

With another deep sigh she turned her gaze back to the cup and to the image of the handsome god painted inside.

Jonathan stopped playing his barbiton and frowned. He thought he heard his sister shouting. But he wasn't sure. He didn't think he had ever heard her raise her voice before. He heard a man's voice, too, but he knew his father had gone out to see a patient.

'We'll never get married!' came his sister's voice distinctly from the garden.

Slowly Jonathan lifted the barbiton from his lap and set it beside him on the bed. Three steps took him to the bedroom doorway.

'Of course we will.' Jonathan recognised the voice of Flavia's uncle Gaius. 'Just as soon as I find somewhere for us to live.'

Jonathan moved quietly to the rail of the balcony above their inner garden.

Below him, Miriam and Gaius stood face to face in the shade of the fig tree.

'With what money?' Miriam cried. 'You have hardly any left. Why won't you use my dowry? I have twenty gold coins.'

'I don't want to use your dowry,' said Gaius. 'That's your security.'

'But I don't want security. I want to be married to you and I want us to live in our own house. A house with a garden.'

'I refuse to live on your money.' Gaius ran his hand through his light brown hair. 'I have my pride.'

'Oh!' cried Miriam in disgust. 'You and your masculine pride.' She turned away from him and hung her head so that her dark curls hid her face.

Gaius sighed and touched her shoulder. 'Miriam,'

he said. 'I love you more than anything in the world. I've waited my whole life to find someone like you, waited till I'm an old man.'

'You're not an old man.' Miriam turned back to him and tried not to smile. 'You're only thirty-one.'

'I'm an old man,' repeated Gaius with a grin, pulling her into his arms. 'And I should be able to take care of you, to provide for you . . .'

Miriam lifted her face and for a moment Jonathan saw how beautiful his mother must have been at fourteen.

Gaius's grin faded. 'I love you so much,' he whispered. And lowered his head to kiss her.

Jonathan watched with a mixture of horror and fascination. Should he step back into his room? But what if they noticed the movement and accused him of spying on them?

He needn't have worried. They were oblivious to everything except each other.

Lupus's head jerked up. He must have dozed off. He was sitting in the pale blue changing-room of the Baths of Thetis, waiting to hire an assassin.

Had he missed Gamala? No. A quick glance showed the man's clothes still in his niche.

Lupus stood and stretched and looked round for Umidus. The young bath-slave was sitting across the room on the plaster bench that ran right round the wall. His head was tipped back and his open eyes stared unseeing at the circular skylight of the domed ceiling.

Lupus took a step forward and found his knees were trembling.

Umidus the bath-slave appeared to be quite dead.

SCROLL V

As Lupus stared down at the dead bath-attendant he heard someone chuckling behind him.

He whirled to find himself face to face with a probable assassin.

'You think he's dead, don't you?' said Gamala, towelling his hair. 'Have a closer look.' He turned and walked over to his cubicle.

Lupus looked down at Umidus. Was the slave still breathing? He glanced back at Gamala, who was slipping on his tunic.

'Gave me quite a fright once, too,' said Gamala with a grin. 'But he's just sleeping. I knew another man like that once. In Judaea. Slept with his eyes wide open. His wife couldn't take it. She divorced him in the end.'

Lupus looked back down at the bath attendant. Although the young slave's eyes were wide open, Lupus could now see his chest rising and falling gently. He breathed a sigh of relief.

'He probably just had a late night. Let him sleep.' Gamala sat on the bench and began lacing up his sandals. The changing-room was still deserted.

Lupus suddenly realised that if he were going to act, it must be now.

His heart thumping, Lupus approached Gamala. With his left hand he gripped the leather pouch which held all his worldly wealth: two gold coins, each worth a hundred sestercii. In his right hand he held his wax tablet. On it he had drawn a sickle-shaped knife and underneath he had printed in his neatest writing:

HOW MUCH TO KILL VENALICIUS THE SLAVE-DEALER?

*

'We had to leave Pliny's body on the beach,' said Flavia from her seat at the table.

It was dinner time. She and her friends were telling her father about the eruption of Vesuvius six weeks earlier.

'The sulphur fumes would have killed us if we hadn't left right away,' added Jonathan. 'I nearly died.'

'And Frustilla did die,' said Gaius, who was reclining next to Miriam.

'Poor old Frustilla.' Captain Geminus put down his bowl of chicken soup. After nearly a day and a half of sleeping he had asked to dine with the others. Caudex had carried him downstairs and propped him up on cushions. 'And poor Admiral Pliny. What a way to die.'

'But he died a hero,' said Flavia, taking a bite of salad and sucking the honey and vinegar dressing from her fingers.

Beside her Lupus nodded his agreement, and Jonathan explained: 'Pliny went to Herculaneum to try to save Rectina and then when he couldn't reach the shore he headed south to Stabia. That's where we were.'

'Yes.' Captain Geminus nodded sadly. 'Pliny could have gone back to the safety of the harbour at Misenum. There's no doubt that he was a brave man. I'm sorry I never got to know him better.'

Scuto and the puppies had been sitting attentively below the dining couches hoping for scraps. Suddenly they barked and scampered out of the triclinium.

A few moments later the golden light of late afternoon dimmed as Caudex stepped into the door-way.

'Man here to see you,' he mumbled to nobody in particular 'Says his name's Pliny.'

'I'm terribly sorry to interrupt your dinner,' said the man who called himself Pliny.

This was not the Pliny she knew, thought Nubia, but a much younger man. She noted the soft fuzz on his upper lip, and guessed he was probably about the age of her eldest brother Taharqo, who was seventeen.

But the youth did bear a strong resemblance to the old admiral: he was short, with the same keen black eyes and pale, rumpled eyebrows. And the set of his small mouth was the same. However, unlike Admiral Pliny, this young man was slim. And he had hair: a thick brown mop of it, which he combed over his forehead.

'You haven't interrupted us.' Gaius slid off the couch and extended his hand. 'We've just started.'

'Please join us,' said Captain Geminus, trying to sit forward, then sinking back onto his cushions.

'That's very kind of you,' said the young man, looking round at them all. 'Allow me to introduce myself. I am Gaius Plinius Caecilius Secundus. I believe you knew my uncle and were with him when he died.'

'You're Pliny's nephew!' cried Flavia.

The young man inclined his head. 'I am indeed the admiral's nephew.'

Nubia nodded to herself. That made sense.

'What a coincidence!' Captain Geminus tried to sit up again and this time he succeeded. 'We were just talking about your uncle, saying how brave he was.'

'Yes,' said the young man and Nubia saw his black eyes grow moist. 'That's why I've come. To hear of his last hours. My uncle's scribe Phrixus said you were all with him at the end.'

'Please,' said Gaius. 'Wash your hands and join us.

Caudex, would you bring the copper basin? And a fresh napkin?'

But Miriam was already on her feet. She smiled at young Pliny and he stared at her open-mouthed. Flushing slightly, Miriam hurried out of the triclinium.

'I'm Gaius Flavius Geminus,' said Flavia's uncle. 'I own – or rather *used* to own – a farm in Stabia. That's my brother Marcus, whose hospitality you're enjoying.'

Captain Geminus gave young Pliny a weak smile from the dining-couch.

'This is Mordecai ben Ezra,' continued Gaius. 'He is the doctor who treated many of your uncle's sailors for burns and cuts. And this,' said Gaius, as Miriam came back into the dining-room, 'this is his daughter Miriam.'

Nubia saw the young man's neck flush as he dipped his hands in the basin Miriam held.

Although Miriam was only fourteen, her beauty was fully developed. Nubia thought she looked particularly lovely this afternoon: she wore a faded lavender tunic with a matching headscarf that allowed her black curls to spill up and over. On her wrist gleamed a silver and amethyst bracelet.

Gaius finished the introductions and invited Pliny's nephew to join him on the central couch beside Miriam.

'Alas! That might not be good idea,' Nubia whispered to Flavia. They watched the young man clamber somewhat awkwardly onto the couch and saw him grow pink as Miriam lowered her slender form next to his.

'Thank you.' Young Pliny accepted a bowl of salad from Alma.

'What would you like to know about your uncle's last hours?' asked Gaius. 'Anything in particular?'

Pliny fished a radish out of his bowl. 'My uncle's scribe Phrixus was with him the whole time. He told me most of what happened. I just wondered if you could add any details. I am writing up an account of his last hours.' He turned to Lupus. 'Are you the boy who brought Rectina's message to my uncle?'

When Lupus nodded, Pliny said, 'You and the blacksmith did an extraordinary thing.'

'But if Lupus hadn't brought the message your uncle might still be alive,' said Jonathan through a mouthful of cucumber, and then stopped crunching as he realised what he'd said.

'No, no,' said Pliny's nephew. 'My uncle had already decided to investigate the phenomenon. This boy's arrival persuaded him to go in a warship, which was a much more sensible means of conveyance.'

Nubia whispered to Flavia, 'I am not understanding him.'

'He said if Lupus hadn't come along, Admiral Pliny would have taken a small boat instead of a big one.'

'Oh,' said Nubia.

'Why didn't you go with your uncle?' Flavia asked

244

the young man. 'Didn't you want to help him investigate?'

'My uncle had asked me to compose an imaginary letter from Cicero to Livy,' said Pliny. 'I was busy working on that.'

Jonathan raised his eyebrows. 'A mountain ten miles away had just exploded and you stayed in to do your homework?'

Pliny flushed and looked down into his salad bowl, then back up at Jonathan. 'I intend to climb the ladder of honour all the way to the top. Law is the first rung of the ladder. To become a successful lawyer, I must show self-discipline. My assignment seemed important at the time. Besides, when my uncle set out, it wasn't even clear which mountain the smoke was coming from.' He looked around at them all. 'As it happened, I was able to help my mother and the terrified peasants around us. But I very much regret that I couldn't have been with my uncle in his last hours.'

'I don't think there's anything you could have done for him,' said Mordecai gently. 'Your uncle was obviously asthmatic and the fumes were so dense . . . But he was courageous to the end.'

'Phrixus tells me that my uncle actually slept for several hours.'

'Yes!' Jonathan nodded vigorously. 'I had to pass his room on the way to the latrine and I could hear him snoring. Even over the noise of the volcano!'

'What courage!' cried Pliny.

Lupus appeared to have a choking fit but Flavia and Jonathan patted his back until it subsided. Luckily young Pliny didn't notice their amused reaction. His gaze had strayed to Miriam again.

Over the course of the meal, Nubia observed that the young man kept looking at Jonathan's sister. Once he even closed his eyes and inhaled. Somehow she knew it was not the pine-nut and honey omelette he was sniffing.

Near the end of dinner, when the air was cooler and the scents of the garden filled the dining-room, Alma brought in the dessert course of peppered figs and cheese. She was just going out again when the dogs ran barking to the front of the house a second time. Once more, Caudex stood in the wide doorway of the dining-room.

'Another man to see you, master,' he growled. 'Don't like the look of this one.'

Flavia saw her father and uncle exchange glances and then Gaius said, 'I'll go.'

A moment later Gaius was back, looking grim. A short man with greasy black hair and a jutting chin stood beside him, unrolling a papyrus scroll.

'This is an official notice for Marcus Flavius Geminus, sea captain,' he read in a loud, nasal voice. 'From the bankers Rufus and Dexter. Unless you pay the amount of one hundred thousand sestercii by this time tomorrow your house and all its possessions will be seized and sold to pay off this debt.'

'What?' said Marcus, struggling to rise from the couch. 'That's insane! I can't possibly pay that amount. My ship was lost. The cargo, too.'

'Was you insured, sir?' said Greasy-hair.

'No, that is . . . I can raise the money . . . but you must give me time. There was no time limit on that loan.'

'Afraid that's not entirely true, sir. According to this, the amount is payable at the lender's discretion. And that's now.'

'But . . . you can't do that!'

For the first time in her life, Flavia saw panic in her father's eyes.

'Marcus, let me handle this.' Gaius turned to Greasy-hair. 'Where do your employers operate from?'

'I'm only the messenger,' sneered the man, 'I have lots of employers.'

'I mean the bankers Rufus and Dexter. Where can I find them?'

'Banker's stall on the west side of the forum, opposite the little circular temple. But this states quite clearly,' said Greasy-hair with a smirk, 'that unless you pay one hundred thousand sestercii, they're possessing your house tomorrow.'

SCROLL VI

'Great Neptune's beard!' said Marcus, after the messenger left. 'I'm ruined.'

Mordecai rose from his couch, looking grave. 'Gaius, this is the worst thing for your brother. His mental state must remain positive. Is there anything you can do to stop this happening?'

Gaius pushed his hand through his fair hair. 'A month ago I could have paid his debts. But since Vesuvius erupted . . .'

'What about Cordius?' suggested Flavia. 'Your patron?'

'Yes!' said Marcus, then his face fell. 'No. He's away at his estates in Sicily. He always goes to oversee the grape harvest and remains there until the Saturnalia.'

'Or Senator Cornix?' suggested Aristo. 'By the looks of his town-house in Rome, he has money to spare . . .'

Captain Geminus shook his head. 'There's bad blood between us . . .' he murmured.

Flavia took a deep breath. 'Publius Pollius Felix might help us,' she said. 'He's rich. And powerful.'

'He might,' said Gaius, 'but he's in Surrentum. Even if I sent a messenger at dawn it would be a week before I heard anything back.'

'We have to do something!' Flavia blurted out. 'I don't want to leave our house. I love it!' She bit her lip, aware that she wasn't helping.

Sensing her distress, Scuto placed a paw on her leg. Flavia slipped off her chair and put her arms around Scuto's woolly neck. From the couch behind her young Pliny spoke.

'If the worst happens, you can always stay with me. I owe you a debt for your kindness towards my uncle in his last hours. I've inherited his Laurentum villa. It's only a few miles down the coast and I've room enough for all of you.' Here he glanced at Miriam. 'I'd be most honoured if you would be my guests. All of you,' he repeated.

'That's very kind of you,' said Gaius, 'but –'

'– it might be an excellent idea,' Mordecai said to Pliny's nephew. He turned to Gaius. 'May I have a word with you in private?'

'Of course, doctor.' The two of them rose and went out towards the study.

There was an awkward silence in the dining-room as everyone looked at one another. When they realised they could hear Mordecai's accented voice in the study, repeating the phrase 'must remain positive', Jonathan began to hum a little tune, then asked Pliny's nephew if he would like more peppered figs.

A few minutes later Gaius and Mordecai returned.

'Secundus,' said Gaius to the young man.

'Please call me Pliny.'

'Pliny,' said Gaius, 'your offer has come at a good time. My brother needs to recover his strength. And it would be best for the children not to be exposed to this unsettling business. We accept your kind offer. Mordecai and I will stay in Ostia and try to sort out this matter. But can you take Captain Geminus and his household and put them up at your Laurentum villa?'

'My great pleasure,' said the young man. 'Er . . . does that include the doctor's daughter?'

'An excellent idea,' said Mordecai. 'Miriam is almost as skilled as I am. She can look after Marcus. Monitor his progress.'

'And me?' Aristo narrowed his eyes at Pliny. 'Shouldn't I go too?' He looked at Captain Geminus. 'Don't you want me to continue the children's lessons?'

'Lessons?' said Pliny. 'To keep the children occupied? What a good idea.'

'It's an excellent idea,' said Flavia's father from his couch. 'We mustn't interrupt their education just because disaster has struck.'

'Jonathan and Lupus will come, too, won't they?'

Flavia unwrapped her arms from Scuto's neck and stood up.

Mordecai glanced at Gaius, who nodded. 'Of course,' said Mordecai. 'I think it would be better if you all went. Things here could get . . . difficult. Caudex and Alma can stay at my house with Gaius. There will be room if the boys go with Marcus and the girls.'

Gaius turned to Pliny. 'I can't thank you enough for your kind offer,' he said. 'Surely the gods sent you today.'

Pliny glanced at Miriam again and Flavia heard him murmur: 'I am almost tempted to agree.'

Lupus woke instantly. Something was wrong.

It was just before dawn. Through the latticework screen of the bedroom window, the sky showed as grey diamonds in the solid blackness of the wall. It was not the steady sound of Jonathan's breathing that had woken Lupus, but something else.

It came again: four urgent taps on the wall. Their secret signal!

Lupus grunted and threw off the linen sheet that half covered him. He quickly slipped on the tunic he had been wearing the day before and shook Jonathan by the shoulder.

'Mmmf. Whuzzit, Rizpah?' mumbled Jonathan. Tigris's head appeared from beneath Jonathan's sheet as the tapping came again. Lupus dragged the bed away from the wall – with Jonathan and Tigris still in it – and started to pull out the bricks.

'Ow!' Jonathan winced as he lifted himself up on his branded left arm. 'What are you doing, Lupus?'

But Lupus already had one of the bricks out, and now hands were pushing from the other side, widening the hole.

'Jonathan! Lupus!' came Flavia's voice from the other side. 'They're here!'

'Who?' said Jonathan, groggily slipping on his own tunic, back to front. 'Who are here?'

'Bailiffs. Two men, one with a scribe's pen. They're making a list of all the things in the house so that we don't take them.'

'They can't do that, can they?' Jonathan yawned again and helped pull out bricks. The diamonds in the window were already a lighter grey and as Lupus got down on his belly, he could see Flavia's face: a dark smudge with darker smudges where her eyes were. Tigris padded over to investigate and touched noses with his brother Nipur, sniffing from the other side.

'I think they can take almost everything,' hissed Flavia. 'My things, too! And Nubia's! Can we hand them through to you?'

'Of course,' said Jonathan. 'Tigris! Get back!'

'This is the most important one,' whispered Flavia. 'Quickly, before they come upstairs.'

As Jonathan lifted Tigris out of the way, Lupus took the object Flavia had thrust through the wall. It was a smooth, flat ceramic cup with small handles. Suddenly he knew what it was: the elegant Greek kylix which the rich patron Felix had given to Flavia the month before. Lupus put it carefully on the bed and reached for the next object.

More things were coming through: Nubia's flute, her tigers-eye earrings in their original pouch, a silver mirror, two scrolls and Flavia's tambourine.

'Flavia!' said Jonathan suddenly. 'What about all that gold in your store room? The gold you were keeping safe for your father's patron?'

'It's all right,' said Flavia. 'After we caught the thief, Cordius took it back.'

She pushed a large wad of material through the gap. As Lupus put it on the bed he saw it was several silk tunics rolled together.

'They're coming!' hissed Flavia. 'I have to put my bed back. Can you close the gap?'

'Yes!' whispered Jonathan. He was still holding Tigris.

Lupus quickly replaced the bricks. He was just about to fit the last brick into its space when he heard voices and saw the flickering yellow light of an oil-lamp illuminate the floor beneath Flavia's bed. He glanced over his shoulder at Jonathan and then put his eye to the diamond-shaped space where the last brick would go.

Lupus could see the calves of Flavia's legs, silhouetted against the torchlight. Clever girl. She was sitting on the bed.

'We'll make note of all the items in here, too,' said a man's voice.

'Ready,' came the reply, presumably from the scribe.

'Two beds; two folding stools, wood with bronze lion-feet; one oak table. On the table: two wooden combs; two bath-sets; three clay oil-lamps; three scent bottles, one ceramic, one glass and one rock crystal.'

Lupus heard the scraping of items on a table.

'Three necklaces . . . just glass beads,' continued the bailiff, 'one make-up box, six brass hairpins, four ivory hairpins, seven bone hairpins . . . That's everything on the table.'

There was a pause and the torchlight flickered.

'Got a chest here . . . looks like it's made of cedarwood, full of clothes. Two woollen mantles –'

'You can't take our clothes!' Lupus heard Flavia cry.

'I'm afraid we can,' said the scribe's voice. 'They're valuable property.'

The bailiff continued: 'We also have one bronze standing oil-lamp, one woven rug, one slave-girl –'

'No!' cried Flavia fiercely. 'Nubia is not a slave. I set her free last month and my witness is Publius Pollius Felix. Don't you dare put her on that list!'

There was a pause and then the bailiff continued.

'Two watchdogs: one medium-sized mongrel with pale brown fur and one black mastiff puppy.'

'Mongrel!' Flavia's voice sputtered with fury. 'He's not a . . . anyway, the dogs belong to our next-door-neighbour, not to me.'

'Both of them?' Lupus could hear the sneer in the bailiff's voice. 'I find that hard to believe.'

'Yes,' Flavia lied. 'Both of them.'

'We can verify that later. Now, if you girls don't mind moving, we'll just have a quick look under the beds.'

SCROLL VII

'Jonathan, it was terrible!' Flavia's face was red and blotched. 'They just came right in as if they owned everything already. And they tried to take Nubia. And Scuto and Nipur!'

'I know. We heard everything.' Jonathan patted Flavia on the back. Dawn was just breaking and they were in Jonathan's house, sitting on the striped silk divan in his father's study.

Lupus scribbled something on his wax tablet and held it up:

AT LEAST WE GOT BRICK BACK IN

Flavia blew her nose and nodded.

Nubia added, 'It is good you make that hole in the wall yesterday.'

Jonathan gave her a rueful smile. 'Yes, it was.'

Flavia blew her nose again. 'Is my kylix safe?'

'Yes, we've got your precious cup,' said Jonathan.

'And I've got the mint tea.' Miriam came in with a tray of steaming beakers.

'Thank you, Miriam.' Flavia smiled through her tears. 'Mint tea always makes me feel better.' She warmed her hands on the side of the beaker and then took a sip. 'Mmmm. Nice and sweet.'

'Better?' asked Jonathan.

'A little,' said Flavia, and took another sip of the fragrant brew. 'Where's your father?'

'He went next door, just after you arrived. I think he's helping Gaius supervise the rest of the inventory.' He slurped his own tea.

'Oh, Jonathan!' Flavia's lip began to tremble. 'What are we going to do? Our beautiful house with its secret garden. And Scuto's jasmine bush. And the fig tree.'

'And fountain,' added Nubia.

'And pater's study and all my scrolls . . .'

Jonathan could tell she was about to cry again. He had to do something.

Suddenly he jumped up from the divan. 'Wait! A brilliant plan!'

'Yes?'

'That's what we need,' said Jonathan, sitting down again. 'A brilliant plan.'

There was a moment of silence. Then everyone laughed.

'Oh, Jonathan!' Flavia said. 'What would we do without you?'

He shrugged and grinned at her.

Flavia thoughtfully ruffled Scuto's fur. 'You know,'

she said presently, 'there's a mystery here. I think there's someone behind all these bad things that are happening.'

'Behind your father's shipwreck?'

'No. Behind Venalicius being set free and the bankers wanting to take our home.'

'Who?' said Nubia. 'Venalicius?'

'Maybe. I don't know. But I have a few ideas about how we could find out. What time did Pliny say he was sending the carruca to pick us up?'

'He said he would send it around noon,' said Jonathan.

'Then we only have a few hours. We'll have to work fast.'

'Uncle Gaius, can we go to the forum with you this morning?'

Flavia's uncle frowned at her as he tore a piece of bread from the disc-shaped loaf. The bailiffs' dawn visit had left him in a grim mood. 'Why?'

'We want to help,' said Flavia honestly.

He sighed. 'I don't think so, Flavia. I have to go to the barber's first and there's nothing for you to do there. And the bankers won't be impressed by two girls tugging the hem of my toga.'

'We won't be any trouble. Please can we come, Uncle Gaius? Nubia's good at seeing things and I'm good at getting ideas.'

Her uncle's face softened. 'Very well,' he said. 'But no toga-tugging.'

Not for the first time, Lupus stood beside Aristo in the office of Ostia's junior magistrate, Marcus Artorius Bato. This time Jonathan was with them, too. It was a small bright room with an arched window that over-looked the red-tiled roof of the temple of Venus next door. Lupus inhaled. Bato's office smelt of ink, wax, and papyrus, with a faint undertone of stale incense. Scrolls and wax tablets covered the large table and filled baskets underneath. In one corner was a small personal shrine to Hercules. The young magistrate tipped his chair back and eyed the trio with amuse-ment in his pale eyes.

'These your bodyguards?' he asked Aristo.

'My pupils,' replied Aristo coolly. 'I'm giving them a lesson in Roman justice. Trying to explain how bailiffs can seize a shipwrecked captain's goods the day after he returns home.'

Bato scowled and let his chair fall forward. 'Oh, that. Captain Geminus obviously didn't read the codicil. Nasty business.'

'How do you know about it?' Aristo raised an eyebrow.

'My superior, Aulus Egrilius Rufus, mentioned it to me. But that has to do with bankers' contracts, not Roman law. Nor Roman justice.'

'I see. Then would Roman justice be allowing a known kidnapper and slave-dealer to be set free without trial?'

'Venalicius!' Bato almost spat the word out. 'That man is a disgusting, vile worm!'

Lupus grunted his agreement. He was beginning to like Bato.

'So how is it that a "vile, disgusting worm" is wandering around Ostia?' asked Aristo quietly.

'You tell me,' said Bato. 'What else could grease Rufus's palm enough to let that scum slip through his fingers?'

'Money?' said Aristo.

'Yes, and lots of it.' Bato leaned forward and lowered his voice. 'A heavy pouch full of gold convinced Rufus that Venalicius – we don't even know if that's his real name – could walk free until enough witnesses were brought to trial.'

'But there are plenty of witnesses that he kidnapped freeborn children!' cried Jonathan.

'Who?' Bato snorted. 'You?'

'Well . . . yes!'

'How old are you?'

'I was eleven last month,' said Jonathan.

'No good, I'm afraid. Witnesses can't be children or slaves. Only adult Roman citizens.'

'Pollius Felix!' cried Jonathan. 'The Patron. He's a

citizen. And a friend of the Emperor's. He'll testify. He was here in Ostia a few weeks ago.'

'By Hercules!' Bato slammed his fist onto the table and several papyrus scrolls rolled over the edge and onto the floor. 'Rufus told me Felix was out of the country. In Alexandria. This is bad. Very bad.'

Lupus scribbled something on his wax tablet and showed it to Aristo.

'Rufus,' said Aristo, reading Lupus's tablet. He looked up sharply at Bato. 'You said your superior is named Rufus. Is he related to the banker Rufus? Of Rufus and Dexter?'

Bato nodded and sighed. 'They're one and the same man.' He shook his head wearily. 'Never trust a banker turned politician.'

'Flavius Geminus!' The short man behind the banker's stall leapt to his feet, knocking an abacus onto a pile of silver coins. With his narrow face and long front teeth he reminded Flavia of a rat.

'Yes?' said Gaius. Flavia could see that her uncle was surprised to be recognised so far from home.

'We all heard you were shipwrecked and at the gates of Hades.'

'Oh,' said Gaius, and a look of realisation crossed his face. 'Oh, you think I'm –'

'Pater!' said Flavia loudly. And before her uncle could protest, 'Pater, imagine that! He thought you were practically dead. You know: very *weak and helpless* and at the gates of Hades. But you're not, are you *pater*?'

'Er . . . no! As you can see,' said Captain Geminus's twin brother, 'the reports of my condition were exaggerated . . . that is, you can see that I broke my nose when the boat crashed . . . er, I mean *ran aground* on some rocks but, but otherwise I feel fine. In fact, I feel like a new man.' He stood a little taller and brushed an invisible speck of lint from his toga.

'And . . .' He glanced at Flavia and she nodded back at him encouragingly. 'And what do you think you're doing? Threatening to take my home away! Sending your bailiffs at dawn, terrifying my . . . my daughter and the rest of the household!'

'I'm sorry, Captain Geminus,' said the rat-faced banker, recovering himself somewhat. 'But there's been a run on our reserves and we've been forced to call in our loans.' He licked his thin lips and glanced nervously round the forum, as if he were looking for someone to back him up.

'Great Neptune's beard!' Gaius banged his fist on the banker's table and caused the coins to jump. Beneath the table a watchdog began to bark.

'We're within our rights.' The banker took an involuntary step back and licked his lips again. 'Tell you what. I'll give you an extra week to come up with the money. But you still have to vacate the premises by sundown this evening and hand over the key. We don't want objects going missing.'

'Very well,' growled Gaius and started to turn away.

Flavia tugged her uncle's toga and when he bent down she whispered in his ear.

'Writing,' said Gaius, turning back. 'I want that in writing.'

The banker glared at Flavia. 'Very well,' he said between clenched teeth. 'I'll draw up a document now.'

As Flavia and her uncle watched the banker scribble his promise on a scrap of papyrus, Nubia heard a sound which made her skin crawl: the clink of chains. She slowly turned and looked out between the columns into the bright forum.

There. On a low wooden platform in the shadow of the great white temple across the forum. A dozen slaves, all chained at the neck just as she had once been.

Her hand went involuntarily to her throat and she left the cool shadows of the colonnade to cross the hot, open space. People began to move with her: sailors, merchants, soldiers, a few women. The slave-dealer had not yet announced the auction but the jingle of iron links could mean only one thing. Some of the people jostled her, but she felt none of them, saw none of them.

Nubia heard Flavia calling her name but her feet refused to stop. They took her across the forum.

Now the slave-dealer – a man she didn't recognise – was beginning to summon buyers. 'Step closer, Ostians! Examine the fine flesh on show today.'

Nubia stared.

She had been sold naked, but these men wore white loincloths.

She had been thin and covered with sores, these muscular young men were smooth and oiled.

She had not dared to raise her eyes in her shame. These men looked straight ahead, proudly – almost arrogantly – above the heads of the crowd.

The slave-dealer, a tall, dark-haired man in a toga, stepped onto the platform. 'Young men in their prime!' he called. 'They're not cheap but they're quality . . . Suitable to be trained as gladiators, bodyguards, litter-bearers . . . Each one has a reserve price of twenty-five thousand sestercii. Step up! Have a good look before the sale next week!'

Most of the chained men had olive skin and strong noses; Nubia guessed they were from Syria or Judaea. But two had skin as black as hers. And one of them, she saw as she finally arrived at the foot of the platform, one of them was her eldest brother Taharqo.

SCROLL VIII

Lupus's thoughts were as tangled as seaweed in a net, but the deep blue interior of the carruca had begun to calm him. The carriage Pliny had sent for them had a cedar frame covered with blue silk curtains. These curtains were drawn against the hot noonday sun and created a deep blue light which filled the interior of the carriage, flickering gently as shadows and sunlight passed overhead. It was almost like being underwater, thought Lupus.

Captain Geminus lay on the cushioned bench which ran along the left-hand side of the carruca. The rocking motion of the well-sprung carriage had put him to sleep, so the others spoke in low tones.

Lupus sat forward and listened to Nubia. She was telling them how she had seen her older brother in the slave-market.

'Are you sure it was your brother?' Jonathan asked her in a whisper.

Nubia nodded. In the blue light her lemon-yellow tunic looked green.

'Did someone buy him?' asked Miriam softly.

Nubia shook her head and Flavia explained, 'The auction's not until the Ides, in three days.' Flavia had perched beside her father to make sure he didn't slip off the bench.

'Did your brother recognise you, Nubia?' asked Aristo.

'Alas! I do not think so.' Nubia hung her head. 'The slave-seller had the whip.'

'If the slaves don't keep their eyes straight ahead,' explained Flavia, 'then he whips them.'

'Maybe we could buy your brother and set him free!' suggested Jonathan in an excited whisper.

'They're starting the bidding at twenty-five thous- and sestercii,' said Flavia, and added: 'Each.'

'Oh.'

Flavia looked at Aristo. 'What did you find out at the magistrate's? Is it true the bailiff can take our house?'

Aristo leaned forward, and kept his voice low. 'I'm afraid your father didn't read the whole contract when he borrowed the money. He didn't read the part in small writing at the end: the codicil.'

'Oh,' said Flavia, and glanced down at her father's thin face. 'He's not very good at that sort of thing.'

'I usually advise him, but this time he didn't consult me,' said Aristo. 'He can be a bit impetuous.'

Flavia gave him a rueful smile. 'It runs in the family,' she said.

Lupus showed Jonathan his wax tablet.

Jonathan nodded and turned to Flavia. 'Bato also told us why they let Venalicius go.'

'Why?'

'He bribed them.'

Aristo explained: 'They claim there are no witnesses. Venalicius gave the chief magistrate Aulus Egrilius Rufus an amount of money to let him go until they can find enough witnesses for the trial. If he runs away, he forfeits the money.'

'Rufus!' cried Flavia, and then covered her mouth with her hand as her father stirred. 'Rufus?' she said again. 'He's one of the bankers who wants to take our house away!'

'We know,' said Jonathan. 'Was he the one you saw at the forum today?'

'No,' said Flavia. 'That was Dexter. He's horrible. He has a face like a rat.'

'And he has big watchdog,' added Nubia.

'Did he say why they were being so mean to your father?' said Jonathan.

'He said they didn't have any money or reserves or something . . . but wait! You just said Venalicius gave them a huge bribe to let him out until the trial. So they were lying when they said they didn't have any money.'

'Either that or their debts are so big that even Venalicius' bribe wasn't enough to cover them,' suggested Aristo.

'Oh,' moaned Flavia. 'My head hurts just thinking about it. And I feel a bit sick.'

'Me, too,' said Jonathan. 'It's bumpier now. I think we've left the main road. Can you open the curtains, Lupus? The ties are by you.'

Lupus scowled. He liked the underwater effect caused by the sun shining through the blue silk. It helped him think. And he needed to think up a way to raise one hundred thousand sestercii.

'Lupus,' hissed Flavia. 'Please open the curtains.'

Reluctantly, Lupus untied one panel of the filmy fabric and pulled it back. Behind him was the sea, glittering in the hot October sun. A faint breeze filled the interior and caused the silk walls to balloon.

'Oh, that's better.' Jonathan burped gently.

'Behold!' said Nubia and pointed to a butter-coloured villa further along the coast, just visible through some pines. 'House of Pliny.'

Lupus sighed. There was no way he could ever come up with one hundred thousand sestercii. And without that money it would be very difficult for him to fulfil his vow to take revenge on Venalicius.

Difficult, but not impossible.

Nubia had been to Pliny's Laurentum villa once before. A few months earlier, the four friends had helped rescue its previous owner, Admiral Pliny. On that occasion the old man had invited them to dine in his triclinium overlooking the sea.

It was in this same triclinium that they now settled down to eat. The serving girls had put linen dining-slippers on their feet and poured water over their hands. As the sun began its dazzling descent, they waited for the slaves to bring in the first course.

Nubia gazed around the room. On three sides, spiral columns of pink marble framed the sparkling sea. The columns rose from a low marble wall about as high as her waist. Beyond this sparkling white parapet was a dizzy drop to the rocks and sea below. On the remaining side of the triclinium, two green pillars flanked a tunnel of sunny and shaded courtyards which stretched all the way back to the double doors through which they had entered.

Nubia's eyes kept returning to an object in the dining-room that had not been there before. Against one of the green marble columns stood a life-sized statue of the hero Perseus.

The story of Perseus was one of the first myths Nubia had ever heard. Later she learned that heroes in Greek and Roman stories were always having to go on long journeys, usually to defeat a monster and bring back something as proof.

Perseus had to bring back the head of a creature named Medusa. Once she had been a beautiful woman, but she had boasted of her beauty to the gods. As a punishment, they had made her so hideous that anyone who looked at her turned to stone. Perseus avoided her terrible gaze by using his shield as a mirror, and cut off her head without looking directly at her.

The bronze statue in Pliny's triclinium showed the moment after the deed. Perseus, his handsome face averted, was holding up his gory trophy. Medusa was shown with her mouth open in a silent scream of rage and her snaky hair writhing as if still alive. From the hero's left arm hung a shield, round and curiously flat. Nubia looked closer. The shield was coated with a thin layer of silver, polished to mirror brightness.

Pliny noticed her gaze. 'My uncle loved beautiful things,' he said. 'That statue is one of his most recent purchases.'

Jonathan narrowed his eyes at it. 'Isn't it a bit . . . gaudy?'

'It's Hellenistic,' explained Pliny. 'The Hellenistic Greeks adored the overly dramatic. It's not particularly to my taste, either.'

Pliny reclined beside Miriam on the central couch. Flavia's father lay on the couch to his right, propped up with several cushions. Occupying his own couch on the left, Aristo rarely took his eyes off Pliny and Miriam.

The slave-girls were serving the appetisers now: prawns glazed with honey and cumin. Nubia took one from the dish and ate it thoughtfully. She wondered why Pliny kept glancing at the shield on the statue.

Suddenly she had the answer: he could see Miriam's face reflected in its mirror-like surface. Pliny had a double view of Miriam: her profile as well as her front view.

'I'm only here for another week or so,' Pliny was saying, 'then it's back up to Rome, where I'm studying to be a lawyer.' He looked away from the shield and glanced round at them all. 'But I wanted to make notes about my uncle's last hours while it was still fresh in my mind. I'm a historian, too, you see. And architect; I'm designing an extension to this villa.' He dabbed the corner of his mouth with his napkin. 'I've already drawn up my own plans,' he added, and glanced at Miriam. 'Would you like to see them?'

Without taking her eyes from her plate, Miriam nodded politely.

'*I'd* like to see your plans,' said Jonathan, sucking some honey sauce from his fingers. 'I design things, too.'

Pliny nodded at Jonathan. 'I'll show you tomorrow.'

'Delicious,' said Marcus from his couch. 'Those were delicious prawns. It's good to be back in civilisation.'

'Thank you, Captain Geminus. They're very fresh. One of the local fishermen caught them just this morning.' Pliny smiled at Flavia's father. 'Tell me, are you feeling better?'

'Much better, thank you.'

'After dinner I usually have one of my freedmen read to me from one of the classics. But your experience must rival that of Odysseus . . . will you tell us how you were shipwrecked?'

'Yes!' cried Flavia. 'You said you'd tell us when you felt stronger.'

'Only if you don't mind,' said Pliny.

'Not at all,' said Flavia's father. 'Though I am hardly Odysseus.' He lay back on his cushions.

'I believe the volcano caused the wreck, though we didn't know it at the time. It was the last week of August, and we had left the port of Alexandria the day before, having taken on a full cargo of spices. We were making the run to Crete. That's the most dangerous part of the voyage because it's across open water.

'Suddenly, without warning, an enormous wave was upon us. At one point it was no further than you are from me.' He looked up at them with something like awe in his expression. 'It was like a cliff of green glass and I could see fish swimming in it above my ship.' He paused for a moment, shaking his head.

'There was no time to tack. The wall of water struck the *Myrtilla* amidships. It was terrifying. One moment my ship was beneath us, the next she was gone. Thank Jupiter my crew and I were all on deck.

We found ourselves floating among flotsam and managed to cling to bits of timber.'

His eyes filled with tears. 'In only one respect am I like Odysseus,' he said quietly. 'I lost all my men. When it grew light again, they were gone.' For a moment he was silent.

'After a day or two,' he continued presently, 'I was washed up onto a rocky island inhabited only by birds. I survived for a few weeks by killing the birds and eating them raw.'

Nubia tried not to shudder.

'I must have become delirious,' said Captain Geminus, 'because the next thing I remember is lying in the bottom of a Cretan fishing boat. A few days later we met a Syrian merchant ship on its way from Rhodes to Rome. The fishermen persuaded them to take me aboard. The Syrians let me sleep in the galley. They lived on a meagre diet of porridge, but they shared what they had with me. There was nobody willing to attend to my wounds and we made slow progress because many harbours were damaged by the earthquake and the wave. We finally reached Ostia a few days ago.'

'Surely the gods were watching over you,' said Pliny.

'Yes.' Flavia's father stared up at the high blue plaster ceiling of the dining-room. Patterns of light reflected from the sea outside flickered across its surface. 'I pray that some of my crew survived. But my ship and its cargo of spices lies at the bottom of the sea. There's no doubt of that.'

Nobody spoke for a long time.

'My entire fortune was invested in those spices,' added Flavia's father. 'If only I could recover it!'

Pliny nodded gravely. 'If we could bring up just a fraction of the treasure that lies beneath the sea then we would be rich beyond our dreams.' He chewed his last prawn thoughtfully. 'There's even a wreck here at Laurentum. They say the ship was carrying casks of gold and the weight of the treasure sank it.'

'Here?' said Flavia, her eyes bright with interest. 'A sunken treasure near here?'

Pliny nodded. 'Just there. Do you see those rocks? The ones with the cormorants on them? The birds drying their wings?'

They all nodded and Nubia shaded her eyes with her hand.

Lupus pushed back his chair with a scrape of iron on marble and ran to the low parapet that surrounded the triclinium.

'When the water is clear you can see the wreck lying there, seemingly within your grasp. But it's an illusion.'

'Why doesn't someone dive down and get it?' asked Flavia, pushing her own chair back and standing up.

'The water is deeper than it looks,' said Pliny.

'Several local fishermen have tried. As far as I know, the only one to reach the wreck never came back up. According to the peasants round here, a terrible monster guards the treasure.'

'Oh.' Flavia slowly sat down again.

The serving-girls were bringing in the main course – fried veal in a raisin and cream sauce – so Lupus returned to the table. As he sat down Nubia glanced over at him. She saw a curious look in his eyes.

Triumph.

SCROLL IX

Flavia rubbed her teeth with her tooth stick and studied the mosaic seahorse on the floor. She and her friends had been given small but attractive rooms around a green courtyard near the sea-view triclinium. Each room had a different sea creature on the black and white mosaic floor.

Flavia sipped some water from a small jug and rinsed her mouth, then swallowed. 'I wonder if there is such a thing as a seahorse,' she said to Nubia, who was sitting on the bed with Nipur, searching for ticks in his fur.

'We have a dolphin on our floor,' said Jonathan. He and Lupus stood in the doorway. 'And Aristo has a crayfish.'

'It's a beautiful villa,' sighed Flavia.

'Lupus has something exciting to tell us,' said Jonathan.

Flavia looked at the younger boy with interest. Lupus's sea-green eyes were bright as he held up his wax tablet.

I CAN DIVE

'You can dive?' Flavia frowned. Then her eyes widened. 'In the sea?'

Lupus nodded and added another word with his stylus.

I CAN DIVE DEEP

'Deep enough to reach maybe some treasure?'

Lupus nodded.

'How?' said Nubia. 'Fishermen couldn't do it. How can you?'

I USED TO DIVE FOR SPONGES

'You did?' Jonathan stared at Lupus. 'You never told us you were a sponge diver.'

A shadow flickered across Lupus's eyes and he wrote:

MY FATHER WAS A SPONGE DIVER

'Oh,' they said.

Then Flavia asked a question none of them had dared to ask before.

'Lupus. You told us once that your parents were dead. Were they murdered?'

Lupus scowled and gave an impatient nod.

Then he underlined the first sentence he had written and held up his tablet:

I CAN DIVE DEEP

Flavia turned to the others. 'Do you realise what this means?' she whispered. 'If we could bring up even one chest of that gold, then I could pay father's debts. Maybe even buy him a new ship.'

'And I could give your uncle enough money to buy a house with a garden,' said Jonathan, 'so he could marry my sister.'

'I could buy my brother from slave-market,' said Nubia, her amber eyes bright with hope. 'And set him free!'

Flavia turned to Lupus. 'What about you, Lupus?' she asked. 'What would you buy if we get the sunken treasure?'

He etched one word on the tablet and showed it to them:

REVENGE

*

'What on earth is wrong with all of you this morning?' scowled Aristo. 'Jonathan confused Scylla with Charybdis, Flavia's sums are off by a mile and you've completely forgotten your Greek vocabulary. Well, all except for you, Lupus. Even you seem distracted, Nubia.'

'We're all thinking about the treasure,' said Flavia.

Aristo sighed. 'Flavia. You heard what Pliny said at dinner last night. There's no way we can dive that deep.'

'But Lupus is a spongy diver,' said Nubia.

'What?'

'Lupus used to dive for sponges,' said Flavia, hopping up and down in her chair.

'No. I'm sorry. I don't believe it.' Aristo folded his arms. 'There are very few places around here where sponges grow.'

Lupus stared back at him for a moment. Then he wrote on his wax tablet, pressing so hard that the stylus crunched the wood beneath.

I'M NOT FROM HERE!

'No?' said Aristo. 'Then why don't you tell us where you're from?'

Lupus wrote on his tablet and held it up. He had written a word in Greek.

ΣΥΜΙ

'What?' said Flavia, snatching the table and peering at it. 'SYMI? What's a Symi?'

Aristo said something to Lupus in Greek and Lupus folded his own arms and nodded.

'I don't believe it,' repeated Aristo.

'What?' they all cried.

'He's Greek. Lupus is Greek.'

'You're Greek?' Jonathan asked Lupus in disbelief.

Lupus nodded.

Aristo slowly unfolded his arms. 'And you used to dive for sponges on the island of Symi?'

'His father is spongy diver, too,' said Nubia.

'That actually explains a lot,' said Aristo.

'So Lupus can dive for the treasure,' said Flavia. 'And all our problems will be solved!'

Aristo leaned forward, resting his elbows on the cool marble surface of the table. 'Lupus. Do you really think you can reach depths a strong young fisherman couldn't?'

Lupus nodded emphatically.

'Well, then . . .' Aristo leaned back. 'That would benefit us all. If we could pay off Captain Geminus's debts . . .'

'So can we cancel today's lesson?' asked Jonathan eagerly.

'Not cancel . . .' Aristo's brown eyes gleamed, '. . . so much as modify. Flavia, you could do some research on wrecks and salvage. Maybe Jonathan can help me design some equipment to lift the treasure chests, if Lupus really *can* dive that deep. And we should investigate the wreck right away. But first we'd better ask Pliny's permission.'

They told Pliny as soon as he returned from his morning walk.

'By Hercules!' said the young man. 'What an excellent idea! We'll split any treasure you find. I can supply you with a rowing boat and I'll put one of my people at your disposal. How's that?'

'Excellent,' said Aristo. 'We should get started immediately, while the weather lasts. It's almost the Ides of October. This fair weather could change any day.'

'I'll get someone to show you where the boats and fishing tackle are kept,' said Pliny. He clapped his hands and when a boy in red appeared he said, 'Ask our new freedman to join us.'

'Yes, master.'

A few minutes later a handsome young man in a red tunic came into the room. He had dark hair and eyes and wore a soft cone-shaped hat on his head. When he saw Flavia and her friends his face brightened.

'Phrixus!' Flavia cried. 'How are you?'

'Free, Miss Flavia.' He pointed to the hat on his head. 'Young master Pliny gave me my freedom yesterday morning. I'm a citizen now and my new name is Gaius Plinius Phrixus.'

Pliny's eyes sparkled and he turned to Flavia. 'After you told me of his bravery and of his devotion to my uncle . . . well, I could scarcely do anything else!'

'Congratulations, Phrixus!' they all cried.

Phrixus nodded and smiled at them, but Flavia saw there were still shadows of grief beneath his eyes.

'How are you, Jonathan?' asked Phrixus as he led them out of the sea-view triclinium across a bright, sheltered terrace. A dozen terracotta flowerpots filled the hot air with the scent of violets and the buzz of bees.

'I'm well now, thank you.'

Phrixus opened a gate in the yellow plaster-covered wall and the dogs jostled through it in front of them.

'You suffer from asthma like my master, but you lived,' Phrixus said quietly as he led them down some sandy wooden steps towards the beach.

'I almost didn't,' said Jonathan.

'Jonathan was unconscious for three days,' Flavia told Phrixus.

'Did you go back to the Pliny?' asked Nubia as they reached the level beach. 'I mean, the old Pliny?'

Phrixus nodded and they all stopped as he turned to them. 'Tascius and I found his body two days after the eruption. He was lying on the sailcloth, just where we left him on that dreadful night. He looked so peaceful, as if he were sleeping.'

The young freedman turned and moved quickly

across the dunes. His conical hat blew off and Jonathan picked it up and dusted the sand off and ran to catch up with him.

Phrixus took the hat with a grunt of thanks and pushed it under his belt. He was heading towards a boathouse set into the low sandy cliffs near the shore. Further along and set back from the boathouse was a dense row of mulberry trees. Jonathan could just make out the red roof-tiles of a neighbouring villa through the leaves.

The dogs came running up from the water to join them, then surged ahead as they saw where everyone was going. Jonathan and his friends followed them into the dim interior of the boathouse, a brick vault built into the sandy cliff.

The dogs ran back and forth, noses down and tails wagging, delighted to discover such new and unusual scents. In the cool gloom of the vaulted space, Jonathan inhaled deeply. The boathouse had a musty perfume all its own: briny wood, pine-pitch and canvas, with undertones of kelp, mould and candle wax.

Jonathan liked it. As his eyes grew accustomed to the gloom, he saw several small boats in various states of disrepair on the sandy floor of the boathouse. And ranged along the inward curving wall were many other interesting objects.

As the others helped Phrixus push the biggest boat

out of the gloom into the bright sunshine, Jonathan and the dogs investigated these other items. He had not brought his wax tablet, so he made a conscious effort to memorise them, using a method his father had taught him:

> one small rowing boat (good condition)
> one medium rowing boat (hole in stern)
> one half-built rowing boat, still on its frame
> useful planks of wood
> several coils of rope
> three oak buckets (one filled with assorted fishing hooks, some quite big)
> seven fishing nets
> twelve cork floats
> an old sailcloth
> a small iron anchor (rusted)
> a broken trident (middle prong missing)
> four old oars (different sizes)

Presently Jonathan was aware of Flavia calling him from the beach and he came squinting back out into the bright sunshine, followed by the dogs. Although it was October and there was still a haze of volcanic ash in the air, the midday sun was hot.

The others were pushing a sky-blue fishing boat into the water, and its keel rasped on pebbly sand until it bobbed on the water. Phrixus and Aristo jumped into the boat. They took Tigris and Nipur, and after some manoeuvring the young Greeks lifted Scuto aboard, too. The four friends clambered in after the dogs.

Most of Jonathan's cream-coloured tunic was soaking wet but he didn't mind: it cooled him off.

Ball in mouth, Scuto sat in the bows as lookout. Tigris and Nipur ran from one side of the boat to the other, making it rock.

'Stop it, Tigris,' said Jonathan. 'You, too, Nipur. You're making me feel seasick.'

Aristo laughed. His face was shining. 'My family used to have a boat,' he said, 'before Fortuna abandoned us.'

The puppies settled down as Aristo took one oar and Phrixus took the other. Soon the boat was moving out to sea, heading for the rocky island with the cormorants. The water was calm with a dusty skin on its surface, and as the young men pulled on the oars, the boat surged ahead with a quick rustle of water, like a knife cutting green silk.

Jonathan closed his eyes for a moment. He could feel the living motion of the boat and the sun hot on his head and shoulders. His tunic was nearly dry.

'Pliny's villa looks so beautiful from here.' Flavia's voice.

Jonathan opened his eyes and twisted round.

The butter-yellow villa on the shore stood out

against the dark green woods behind it. He could see its columns and arches and red-tiled roof, its sea-view triclinium and the square tower rising at one end of the complex. The highest floor of this tower had large arched windows which let the sky show through like a tile of blue turquoise. As he looked, he saw the dark shape of a distant figure step into one of these blue spaces.

'I see the Pliny,' said Nubia, who had the sharpest eyes of all of them. She waved and they saw the figure wave back.

'Who's that with him?' said Flavia, and Jonathan saw the silhouette of a second figure join the first.

'It's Miriam,' said Aristo, and his jaw clenched as he pulled on the oar.

Presently they stopped rowing and Phrixus stood up in the boat.

'I came out here with the admiral once,' said Phrixus. His handsome face gleamed with sweat and there were patches of damp on the armpits of his red tunic. 'We discovered that if you position the boat in a direct line between the tower and Cormorant Island and those three umbrella pines on the promontory . . .' he peered down into the water and pointed in triumph, '. . . you will find the wreck!'

'Careful!' cried Jonathan. The boat had tipped alarmingly as his three friends and Scuto all eagerly leaned over the port side.

'I can't see anything!' said Flavia.

Lupus grunted and pointed. He had stripped down to his loincloth and his back next to Jonathan was smooth and hot and brown.

'I think I am seeing the boat,' said Nubia.

'It's down deep,' said Phrixus. 'The water isn't as clear as it usually is. You can see it as a dark shape against the sandy bottom.'

Jonathan gazed down into the water. It was clearer than the water had been off the coast of Surrentum but he still couldn't see anything that looked like a wreck. Beside him, Lupus scooped up a handful of seawater and wet the back of his neck. Then with two handfuls he splashed his face. He took several short panting breaths, followed by a long deep one. Jonathan could actually see his ribcage expand when he inhaled.

Finally, Lupus opened his wax tablet and scribbled something on it. Then he handed it to Jonathan.

PRAY AGAINST SHARKS!

With that, he was over the side, as smoothly as an eel from a fisherman's bucket. He made barely a splash.

'How will he breathe?' cried Nubia.

'He won't,' said Aristo. 'He'll hold his breath.'

Jonathan watched his friend sink deeper and deeper.

And suddenly he saw the wreck. He hadn't seen it because it was so deep. He looked at the others and shook his head.

'It's too far down,' said Jonathan. 'He'll never reach it.'

Lupus felt the weight of the water resist him from below and push him from above. Using his arms and legs, he propelled himself down from green to blue to darker blue. It was the slowest way to descend, but this was just a practice dive. Later he would use his special sponge-diving techniques for a quick descent.

The wreck was very deep, so he set himself the goal of just touching it. The pressure in his head was growing, so he pinched his nose and gently blew.

Presently he felt the desire to breathe. But he was not even halfway there. He was badly out of practice.

Still, he had set himself a goal and he would achieve it. Down and down he went, kicking and pulling at the water with his arms. Deeper and deeper into the blue depths.

Nubia let out her breath in a gasp and sucked in a lungful of air. Flavia realised she'd been holding her breath in sympathy with Lupus. He must be desperate to breathe by now. The three friends exchanged anxious looks and bent further over the side.

'There!' said Flavia. 'I think I see him coming up. Or is it? It looks too small . . .' Suddenly she screamed.

A severed head bobbed like a ball on the surface of the water.

SCROLL X

Nubia leaned over the side of the boat, stretched out her hands and lifted the dripping object from the water.

It was the carved wooden head of a woman. It still bore traces of paint: red on the parted lips and black on the eyes which stared blankly over Nubia's shoulder, like a soothsayer gazing into the future.

'It must be part of the ship's figurehead,' said Aristo.

Suddenly there was an explosion of spray and Lupus was gasping in the water before them.

'Lupus!' they cried.

Aristo held out his hand and pulled Lupus up into the boat. Lupus grinned at them, pushed back his dripping hair and reached for his wax tablet.

'You did it,' said Phrixus. 'You reached the ship. That's amazing. Very few of the local fishermen can dive that deep.'

Lupus wrote on his tablet.

FRONT OF SHIP LOWEST

Then he added something

THINK I SAW CRACK IN HULL

'Did you go inside?' asked Flavia. 'Did you see the treasure?'

Lupus shook his head and wrote

OUT OF PRACTICE. HAVE TO TRAIN.

Nubia frowned. 'How do you train?'

Lupus sucked in a big breath and flicked his fingers up, one after the other, starting with the little finger of his left hand. When all ten were up he started again on the next beat. Jonathan caught on and started to count:

'. . . twelve, thirteen, fourteen, fifteen . . .'

Nubia and Flavia joined in.

They had reached one hundred by the time Lupus opened his mouth to suck in a lungful of air.

After that, Lupus's three friends took turns diving to see if they could reach the wreck, too. But the water was colder at this depth and its chill made Jonathan wheeze and Nubia shiver. Flavia was still the weakest swimmer of the four. The feel of the water closing over her head made her panic. She also found it impossible to keep her eyes open under water. It didn't seem natural.

'You'd better be the one who dives, Lupus,' she said

through chattering teeth, as she towelled off. 'And we'll help you all we can.'

'What can we do?' Jonathan asked.

Lupus flipped open his wax tablet.

I NEED ROPE he wrote

AND BIG FLAT HEAVY ROCKS

AND MAYBE FISHNET

'I saw rope and fishing net in the boathouse,' said Jonathan.

'And there are rocks further up the shore,' added Phrixus. He squinted up into the turquoise sky. 'But it's already well past noon. I suggest we have lunch and then get everything prepared for a proper dive tomorrow. Will that give you enough time to train?' he asked Lupus.

Lupus nodded and wrote:

I HOPE SO. I WANT THAT TREASURE.

*

Lupus leapt out of the boat first and waded through the waves towards young Pliny, who was hurrying down the beach with Miriam. The two of them were shaded by her papyrus parasol. Scuto and the puppies splashed into the water after Lupus, then ran barking back and forth between the converging groups.

Lupus held up his dripping prize.

'By Hercules!' exclaimed Pliny, his dark eyes bright with pleasure. 'You've recovered the head of the goddess. May I keep it?'

Lupus nodded and Pliny took the head.

'Aphrodite, the foam-born,' said Pliny softly. 'Venus emerges from the sea and comes to Laurentum.' He slapped Lupus's back. 'Thank you, Lupus. I must confess, I didn't think you could do it. But you're a real urinator!'

'He's a *what*?' said Flavia, out of breath.

Pliny laughed at the expression on their faces. 'Urinator. It means "diver". We should celebrate.'

'But we didn't get the treasure,' said Jonathan. 'Lupus only barely reached the wreck.'

'He has to train himself to hold his breath for even longer,' added Flavia, pulling the towel around her shoulders.

'Phrixus and I are going to adapt the boat for diving,' said Jonathan.

Nubia added, 'Aristo and I are looking for heavy stones on the beach this afternoon.'

'And I,' announced Flavia, 'am going to research the dangers of the deep. Can I use your uncle's library?'

'Of course,' said Pliny. 'It's close to your room.' He

put the figurehead under his left arm and joined Miriam beneath the shade of her papyrus parasol again, touching her elbow lightly to direct her back up towards the villa. Suddenly he stopped and turned to look at them. 'How would you all like to have a banquet on the beach this evening, to celebrate Lupus's success?'

They all nodded, especially Lupus.

'Good.' Pliny glanced at Miriam. 'Tonight is the Meditrinalia, when we drink the new wine mixed with the old and thank the gods for their provision. Several years ago my uncle and I celebrated the feast down on the beach. It will be just like old times. I'll tell the kitchen slaves to slaughter a pig at once.'

It was autumn, the time of year when the hours of daylight grow shorter. And so it was almost dark by the time they finished their supper of spit-roasted pig, flat bread and chickpea stew. The sun had set and the sky was filled with a blue so vibrant that it seemed to sing. The sea was black and the embers of the fire glowed red.

As a pretty slave-girl named Thelma handed out fig-cakes, Phrixus appeared and set a beautiful Greek mixing-bowl on the sand. The krater had red figures of the wine-god Dionysus and his female followers dancing across the surface. Pliny rose from his reclining position and took two silver jugs. From one he poured a stream of wine into the krater. It gleamed ruby red in the firelight.

'This is last year's wine,' he explained with a smile. Then he emptied the other jug into the big krater. This wine was so dark it was almost black. 'And this,' he said, 'is the new.'

Flavia peered into the krater and watched the two colours mix. Then she settled down onto her stomach in the soft sand, rested her chin on her hands and gazed at the handsome god Dionysus. On this vase he was shown bearded, with his head thrown back in joy.

Pliny bent and dipped a flat silver bowl – a patera – in the krater. Then he tipped the patera, and a stream of red wine spattered onto the sand.

'*Novum vetus vinum bibo,*' he recited, '*novo veteri morbo medeor.* I drink new and old wine, and am healed of new and old disease.' He dipped one of the jugs into the mixing-bowl, poured the blend of new and old into a small silver cup, and handed it to Flavia. She rose up onto her knees to accept it. Pliny nodded her towards her father. 'Captain Geminus,' he said, 'to you the first mixed wine of the Meditrinalia.'

Still on her knees, Flavia shuffled over the sand, holding the cup carefully out before her. Her father was propped up on a cushioned litter. Even though it was a mild night, he had a blanket around his thin body.

As he leaned forward, Flavia supported the back of

his neck with her left hand and held the cup to his lips with her right.

'Thank you, my little owl.' He wiped a dribble of red wine from the corner of his mouth and leaned back against the cushions.

Meanwhile Pliny had filled other wine cups and Thelma was taking the blended wine round to the others, who sat or reclined on old carpets spread over the sand.

Presently, Phrixus and Thelma went back to the villa and Pliny sat down near Miriam. He sipped his wine and made a face. 'On the Meditrinalia the wine is supposed to have beneficial effects,' he said. 'But today it's more like the worst kind of medicine. It's been a terrible harvest.'

'It's not too bad,' said Captain Geminus. 'And it was a wonderful meal.'

'Would you like another fig-cake, pater?' asked Flavia.

Her father shook his head and closed his eyes. 'I wish I had more energy,' he murmured. 'I slept all day and yet I still feel tired.'

'Sleep is one of the best healers,' said Miriam, leaning over to pull the light blanket up around his shoulders. 'That's why my father wanted you to get away from Ostia. So you could rest and sleep. Then your body can heal itself.'

Captain Geminus nodded, his eyes still closed.

Flavia smoothed his hair from his forehead, struck again by how frail he looked.

'Play something nice, please, Nubia,' whispered Flavia. 'Something to help pater sleep.'

Nubia smiled and nodded. She took out the flute she wore on a cord around her neck and after a moment she played the 'Sailing Song'. Soon Lupus found the beat on a piece of driftwood with his spoon.

Flavia saw that both Aristo and Pliny were watching Miriam as they sipped their wine. She had closed her eyes and tipped her head back. Her long white tunic and her arms and throat looked pink in the red light of the coals.

As the last notes died away, a figure emerged from the darkness: Phrixus. He pushed seven torches into the soft sand around them. When the torches were lit, a golden circle of light surrounded the young diners.

'Phrixus,' said Pliny, as the freedman turned to go. 'Will you bring my lyre down to the beach?' He turned to the boys. 'You brought instruments, too, didn't you?'

Jonathan nodded. 'My barbiton and Lupus's drums. They're in our room.'

'And a tambourine please, Phrixus!' Flavia called out.

Phrixus was back with Thelma a few minutes later. They stepped into the circle of flickering torchlight and handed out the instruments, then vanished discreetly back into the darkness.

Pliny took the lyre in his left hand and fitted it against his left shoulder. Using a small ivory wand, he strummed some chords with his right hand.

'I don't have a very good singing voice,' he said, with a shy glance at Miriam. 'But I would like to sing for you, too. This is part of a Greek epic I composed when I was fourteen years old. I set it to music myself.'

SCROLL XI

Pliny cleared his throat and began to sing in Greek. It was a rather formal song and Nubia noticed he did not seem able to sing and strum at the same time. Once or twice she could tell he'd hit a slightly wrong note. But when he finished everyone clapped politely. Pliny bowed his head.

'A dithyramb!' Aristo's curls gleamed like copper in the firelight as he nodded. 'Very good.'

'Thank you.'

'I lost my own lyre in the eruption,' said Aristo, holding out his hand. 'May I?'

'Of course.' Pliny passed his instrument to Aristo, then held out the ivory wand.

'No thank you,' said Aristo. 'I just use my fingers.'

For a few moments the young Greek made some minor adjustments to the tuning. Then he turned to Nubia.

'Shall we play "Slave Song"?'

Nubia nodded and put the flute to her lips. She and Aristo looked at each other and began at precisely the same moment. Nubia had composed the song herself.

It had no words, but the image which had inspired it was that of a slave-girl sitting on the back of a camel, travelling in a caravan towards an oasis. Lupus drummed a steady beat, which Jonathan echoed with the low notes of his barbiton and Flavia with the muted jingle of her tambourine.

They finished softly and when the last notes died away there was no applause, just the crackling of the torches and the sighing of waves on the beach. Miriam's cheeks were wet and she wiped them with her fingers.

'Remarkable,' said Pliny at last. There was a strange catch in his voice. 'I have never heard anything like that. I remember now. My uncle spoke about you. I didn't make the connection before. Nubia, you are an exceptional musician. So are you, Aristo.'

Pliny stood and they all looked up at him. He was wearing a spotless cream tunic, with a broad purple stripe on each side. Flavia noticed he had trimmed his brown hair. The new haircut made his head look quite round.

'Excuse me,' he said. 'My hands. They're a bit sticky from the fig-cakes. I'm just going to rinse them.'

He moved quickly out of the circle of torchlight and down to the water.

Scuto ambled after him, tail wagging slowly. After a moment Flavia put down her tambourine and followed him, too.

For a few moments the three of them stood side by side on the shore and stared out over the water. Scuto raised his nose to test the sea breeze. The night was moonless and very dark apart from the breathtaking sweep of a hundred million stars blazing overhead.

It occurred to Flavia that it hadn't really been fair of Aristo to play the 'Slave Song' after Pliny's stiff dithyramb. Especially with all of them playing, too. But Pliny had been gracious in defeat.

'That was a very nice dinner,' Flavia said at last. 'Thank you for arranging it. And for having us all to stay.'

Pliny glanced sideways at her and she saw his eyes gleam wetly in the starlight. 'That's kind of you,' he said. For a moment she thought he was going to say something else. But he merely repeated, 'That's kind of you.'

Flavia bent to rinse her hands in a salty wave.

'Oh!' she cried. A greenish light fizzed in the water as she swished her hand.

'What?' Nubia had come up quietly behind them.

'Look!' breathed Flavia. As she pulled her hand through the black water it left a trail of greenish-yellow light which immediately faded. Scuto growled.

'Phosphorescence,' said Pliny. 'Nobody knows what causes it, but on dark nights the sea often burns with cold fire. It's harmless – or so my uncle told me.'

'Fox fur essence?' repeated Nubia, with a frown.

'Everybody! Come quickly!' called Flavia. The others – except for Flavia's father – rose and moved down to the water.

'Look!' said Flavia. She drew her hand through the water again and showed them the glowing trail her hand made.

Behind them, Lupus uttered a whoop, stripped off his tunic and ran splashing into the inky sea.

The black water shimmered yellow-green as he churned it with his hands and the drops he threw at them were like wet emeralds, fading even as they fell. Nubia laughed and walked into the water, too, looking behind her to see the brief trails of green light her legs made in the black water. The dogs barked at this strange behaviour.

It was a mild night and the water was deliciously warm. Soon all four friends were swimming and splashing in the shallow water.

When they swam, they left trails of fizzing light, and when they stood on the sandy sea bed to splash each other, the phosphorescence lit their laughing faces pale green.

Presently Lupus struck out into deeper water and turned on his back. It was a trick he had been trying to teach the others: to float on the water as if it were a supporting mattress.

'How do you do that?' asked Flavia in frustration,

watching as the other three floated on the silky surface of the water.

'Just relax,' Jonathan's voice came from her right. 'Make your hands like fans, with the fingers together, and keep them moving just a little.'

Flavia lay back and tried to relax, but water suddenly filled her mouth and she coughed.

'You might want to keep your mouth closed,' suggested Jonathan.

Flavia tried again. And again. At last, just as she was about to give up, she realised she was floating. Her hands had found the right motion.

Lupus was showing off, spitting a stream of water up from his mouth as if he were a spouting killer whale. The jet of water glowed yellow-green for a brief instant.

Flavia carefully turned her head and looked to her left, towards the shore. Miriam and the two young men were walking back up to join Flavia's father.

Just inside the circle of torchlight the puppies were wrestling. But Scuto remained close to the water, an alert shape silhouetted against the fire, watching to make sure no harm came to his mistress. Flavia smiled to herself and idly wondered what harm could possibly come to her here in this magical cove on such a glorious night.

At that very moment she felt the water push against her back, as if something had swum beneath her.

'What was that?' Jonathan's voice in the darkness sounded alarmed.

And then Nubia's trembling voice:

'Something touch me. Something big!'

SCROLL XII

Something unseen was moving in the black water beneath Flavia.

She panicked. Her body went rigid and her arms flailed. Black salty water filled her mouth as she sank down beneath the surface. She was drowning!

Then something strong and lithe and smooth pushed her up into the cool air and towards the beach. Flavia coughed out water and then filled her lungs with air. There was an odd wet sigh, and in the dim light of the green-gold phosphorescence, she saw a smiling face turn away.

It was a dolphin!

Flavia's toes touched softly corrugated sand. The dolphin had pushed her to shallow water. With her head and shoulders safely above the water, Flavia turned gasping to watch the others.

Three or four dolphins swam round her friends, describing luminescent loops and curves in the black water. Flavia could hear strange clicks and creaks and whistles: the dolphins were speaking to one another. They had their own language!

Her friends were laughing, and now Lupus – fearless as ever – clutched at a dolphin's dorsal fin as it swam past and managed to hold on. He whooped as it pulled him through the water.

Another dolphin was swimming in languid circles around Nubia and Jonathan, who were laughing and treading water.

Flavia felt a gentle nudge. A dolphin was beside her. Tentatively she reached out her hand and touched the dolphin's glistening back. It was like nothing she had ever felt: velvety but slippery at the same time. The dolphin circled and came close to her again, squeaking and smiling. Even in the dim starlight she could see that his dark eyes were full of intelligent humour. This time he tipped his dorsal fin towards her.

On impulse she grasped it as he passed.

Suddenly she was being pulled through the water towards Nubia and Jonathan. She squealed with delight as their startled faces sped past her. The water parted foamy green as her dolphin curved round and raced back towards the shore. Nubia whooped like Lupus.

Soon Nubia and Jonathan had found dolphin rides too, and all four of them were being pulled round the cove in phosphorescent trails.

Flavia didn't know how long they stayed in the water with the dolphins.

Once, she looked up and saw people standing on the shore watching, but they didn't seem important.

She didn't want to leave this vibrant, smiling creature so full of power and joy. Not yet.

Later, the four of them somehow found themselves splashing back up through the little waves onto the shore, where they were greeted with barking dogs and linen towels and questions. But they were all too exhausted to speak. Wrapped in their towels, Flavia and her friends trudged up the sandy beach to the villa, fell into their beds and were instantly asleep.

The next morning at lessons Jonathan felt deeply relaxed. For the first time since his return from Rome, he had slept soundly, without dreams.

Once or twice his father had treated him to a massage at the baths. Afterwards every muscle in his body had felt soft and loose. He felt like that now: refreshed and calm.

They had all slept late, rising when the sun was well above the horizon. His three friends had a kind of stillness about them, too. Lupus usually drummed on his thigh or his wax tablet and had to be told to stop fidgeting. But this morning he sat quietly. Flavia seemed calmer than usual and Nubia had a dreamy look in her amber eyes.

'Come on, you lot,' Aristo was pleading. 'We're diving for the treasure later and this calculation will help us determine the approximate depth of the wreck. Lupus. Do you know the answer?'

They were sitting at the table in the sea-view triclinium. It was another hot morning, with a soft haze over the calm, milky blue sea. Lupus was gazing out towards the horizon. Without looking at Aristo he shook his head.

'Jonathan,' said Aristo. 'How about you? Here. Take the abacus. Work it out.'

Jonathan took the abacus slowly. For the first time he noticed the weight of it. The polished acacia-wood beads on the copper wires looked like berries. Nutmeg-coloured fruit. A harvest of numbers. An autumn crop of sums.

'Jonathan!' Aristo passed his hand over his face. 'You're all even less focused than you were yesterday. What's got into you?'

'Dolphins,' said Pliny, coming into the bright room and pulling up a chair. 'They have a strangely calming effect on those who swim with them. Or so I'm told. Maybe this will interest you all.'

He carefully set a ceramic cup on the marble-topped table. Jonathan put down the abacus and leaned forward with interest, as did the others. The cup was a Greek kylix. Inside, the design showed a man holding a lyre and riding a dolphin.

'It's Arion!' cried Flavia.

'It is indeed,' said Pliny, and Aristo gave her a nod of approval.

'Please, Aristo,' said Nubia. 'Tell us story of Arion?'

Miriam had just come into the room.

'Your father's sleeping,' Miriam said to Flavia and then smiled at Aristo. 'Don't let me interrupt. Please tell your story.'

'Arion,' said Aristo, 'has always been special to me, because he was a lyre player from Corinth.'

'Just like you!' said Nubia. Aristo smiled and nodded. His skin was bronzed from their previous day in the sun and Nubia thought he looked very handsome in his fawn-coloured tunic.

Aristo cleared his throat and continued: 'Arion played the lyre so beautifully that Periander, the young king of Corinth, invited him to be court musician. The two men became close friends. They hunted together, dined together, played music together.'

'What instrument was the king playing?' asked Nubia.

'Um . . . Periander played the aulos, a wind instrument with reeds and two pipes. A very difficult instrument indeed, but one well worth learning. Periander was good, but Arion was better. In fact, he was the best musician in the world. It was said that if a man glanced at a girl while Arion was plucking his lyre then that man would fall in love with her instantly.'

Lupus barked with laughter, and when they looked at him curiously, he jerked his thumb towards the big bronze statue beside him. Medusa's already hideous face was shown contorted by a grimace of death.

'Well, it probably didn't work in every case,' admitted Aristo with a smile. 'But music is a powerful love potion.'

'Did it work the other way round?' asked Flavia. 'I mean, if Arion was playing and a girl looked at a man, would she fall in love with him?'

'Absolutely,' said Aristo. 'The only problem was that most girls looked at Arion when he played and so most of them fell in love with him!'

'Lucky Arion!' said Flavia.

'Not really,' sighed Aristo. 'He had lovesick girls following him everywhere. That was why he decided to leave Corinth for a while. He heard there was to be a musical contest in Sicily, with a fabulous prize for the winner. So he asked Periander's permission to go.

' "Absolutely not!" said Periander. "First, I have a bad feeling about your going; second, you might not win, and third, I'll miss you!" "But I'm a musician," said Arion. "I have the heart of a wanderer. Besides, if I win the prize I'll be rich and famous!" In the end he persuaded Periander to let him go.'

Aristo leaned back in his chair. A sea breeze ruffled his curly hair.

'He went, he played, he won. But on his way home, Arion discovered that the Corinthian sailors – men from his own town – were plotting to throw him overboard and steal his prize. "Take my gold," Arion pleaded, "but let me live!" "Absolutely not," said the wicked sailors. "First, you'll tell King Periander; second, he'll hunt us down; third, what good is gold if we live in fear for the rest of our lives?" "At least let me play my lyre one last time. After that, you can kill me." The sailors looked at one another and shrugged. They had never actually heard the greatest musician in the world play. "All right," they said.

'So Arion put on his best tunic, perfumed his long hair and went to the stern of the Corinthian ship. There he played the most joyful song he knew, hoping to change the sailors' hearts. But in vain. Their hearts were hardened by their lust for gold. The sailors approached him, brandishing sharp knives. With a prayer to Apollo and the sea-nymphs, and still holding his lyre, Arion jumped into the deep blue sea.'

Aristo picked up Pliny's cup from the table and tipped it so they could all see the image painted inside.

'Arion's beautiful music had not touched the sailors' hearts but it had attracted many creatures of the deep. As Arion sank beneath the waves, a friendly dolphin rose up with the musician on his back. The sailors were too busy counting their gold to notice.'

Lupus grunted his approval and Aristo smiled as he finished the story.

'And so Arion returned to Corinth, riding a dolphin

and playing his lyre. King Periander welcomed his friend with tears of joy, punished the wicked sailors and set up a bronze sculpture of Arion riding his dolphin. I have seen the sculpture with my own eyes,' added Aristo, putting the cup back on the marble-topped table. 'It's on the shore, at the very spot where the dolphin was said to have brought Arion safely home.'

After Aristo finished the story of Arion, everyone was quiet for a moment.

'Of course,' said Jonathan wistfully, 'nobody could actually *ride* a dolphin.'

'Why not?' said Aristo. 'You came close last night. And there are so many tales of shipwrecked sailors being carried to safety by dolphins that I think there must be some truth in the myth.'

Flavia looked at Pliny. 'Your uncle wrote about a dolphin who let men ride on it and then the governor wanted to honour it so he poured perfume on it but it made the dolphin sick. Where was that again?'

'In Hippo, on the coast of Africa,' said Pliny. 'What my uncle didn't put in his account, because he thought it too fanciful, was that the dolphin was friends with a particular young boy. He used to carry the boy back and forth across the lagoon so he could attend lessons. One day the boy caught a fever and died. The dolphin waited and waited and when he realised the boy wasn't coming back he purposely beached himself and died, too. They burned both bodies on the pyre.'

'Alas! That story is too sad.' Nubia's amber eyes filled with tears.

Lupus was writing on his wax tablet:

THAT CUP IS A BIT LIKE YOURS

He showed it to Flavia.

'Mine's older,' said Flavia. 'It's black-figure.'

'You have a black-figure kylix?' said young Pliny, his dark eyes widening with interest.

Flavia nodded. 'It shows Dionysus and the pirates, after he's changed them into dolphins.'

'By Hercules,' said Pliny. 'I'd give anything to see it. I collect Greek cups.'

'I have it here,' said Flavia brightly. 'I'll go and get it.'

As she ran out of the dining-room, Jonathan picked up Pliny's kylix. He held it carefully because he knew such things were worth a fortune. Only last month he had broken a Corinthian perfume flask.

His fingertips stroked the flat interior of the cup, smooth as silk where it was covered with black glaze, slightly rough where the shape of dolphin and rider let the orange-red clay show through.

Flavia came back into the triclinium and carefully placed her own kylix on the table.

'By all the gods!' breathed Pliny. 'It's the work of Exekias.'

'Who?' said Flavia.

'The most famous Greek vase painter of all.' Pliny turned the cup reverently in his hands. 'This is a masterpiece. Where did you get it?'

'Publius Pollius Felix gave it to me,' said Flavia, and Jonathan noticed she was blushing. 'It's my most precious possession.'

An hour later, when the day was hottest and the water calmest, the four friends and Phrixus made their way down to the beach. The dogs ran ahead, sniffing and watering as they went. Today was the day they hoped to recover the treasure.

Nubia glanced back at the villa. She could see several figures in the sea-view triclinium. Flavia's father sat propped up on a couch so that he could benefit from the sea breeze and enjoy the view. Pliny and Miriam and Aristo were also with him. Aristo had promised to catch up with them in a minute.

Nubia turned back and scanned the water. She hoped the dolphins would be there so she could swim with them again. Perhaps today one of them would let her ride his back.

But no fins broke the glittering expanse of water.

Nubia sighed. She felt strangely calm. The others seemed different too, especially Lupus. Something about his eyes had changed. They seemed softer, more open. For the first time since she had met him he had the eyes of a boy, not of a wary adult.

The dogs had run ahead to investigate an old fisherman who was pulling a battered yellow fishing boat up onto the beach beside their sky-blue one.

'Hello there!' The fisherman waved to them. He was short and stocky, his thin white hair a startling contrast to his chestnut brown skin. There were dark stains of octopus ink on his sun-bleached tunic.

As they drew nearer, he grinned, revealing several missing teeth. 'Want any fish for your kitchen today, Phrixus?' he called in a gravelly voice.

'What have you got, Robur?' said Phrixus. 'Anything special?'

'Yes, indeed.' The fisherman reached into the boat and held up a dripping basket. It was full of small silver fish, so fresh that some of them were still twitching. 'Look at these anchovies. There's a great shoal of them further out. Red mullet, too. And herring. I've never seen anything like it. Must be something to do with the volcano.'

'Did you see any dolphins out there?' asked Flavia.

Robur scowled and spat on the sand. 'Didn't see any,' he said. He lowered the basket of fish back into his boat. 'I hate the things. They eat all my fish. Especially my anchovies.' He caught sight of something in the boat and his face brightened. 'Have a look at this fine fellow.' He took an object from the boat and walked towards them, holding it out before him.

At first, Nubia thought it was a brown ball with pinkish-brown ribbons hanging from it. Then she looked closer. And recoiled.

She could see the round suckers on the octopus's tentacles and its human-looking eyes, frozen open in death.

Beside her, Lupus had been scratching Nipur's head. Now, as he stood upright, he stared directly into the blue eyes of the dead octopus.

Lupus opened his tongueless mouth. And screamed.

SCROLL XIII

As the inhuman scream died away, Jonathan turned and saw that Lupus was breathing in short, panting gasps.

'What is it, Lupus?' Jonathan knew what it was like to struggle for breath. He put his hand lightly on his friend's back and felt him trembling. But Lupus did not answer. He continued to stare straight ahead, unable to take his eyes off the dead creature in the fisherman's hand.

Instinctively Jonathan stepped between Lupus and the octopus.

As if a spell had been broken, Lupus turned and ran off up the beach. Scuto and the puppies bounded after him.

'I'm sorry,' the white-haired fisherman said to them. 'I didn't mean to frighten the poor lad.'

'Better get it out of sight,' said Phrixus quietly. 'Come on, Robur, show me what else you've got.' The two men stepped back to the yellow boat to inspect the rest of the catch.

When they were out of earshot, Jonathan turned to the girls.

'Did you see that?' he whispered. 'I've never seen Lupus frightened before!'

'I know,' said Flavia. 'He was almost . . . paralysed with fear.'

Nubia added, 'Like person when they see the head of Medusa.'

Flavia nodded. 'Yesterday in the library,' she said, 'I was looking through the ninth scroll of Pliny's *Natural History*. He says no sea creature is more savage than the octopus. It can grab a man with its suckers and then pull him apart.' She shuddered.

'But that octopus wasn't very big . . .' said Jonathan.

'And Lupus is seeing many terrible things,' added Nubia.

'You're right,' said Flavia slowly. 'Why should the sight of a dead octopus upset Lupus so much?'

'I have no idea,' said Jonathan. 'No idea at all.'

Lupus wiped his nose with the back of his hand and rubbed the tears from his cheeks. Then he stooped to pick up a large pebble. With an angry grunt, he hurled it into the water. The dogs thought it was a game and raced into the surf after it.

Lupus picked up another stone and threw it, and another. How could he avenge his father's death if he cried like a baby at the mere sight of a dead fish?

He shuddered at the memory which rose up before his eyes: an octopus lying in a pool of blood, staring at him with dead eyes. Eyes as dead as . . . No!

Lupus picked up another stone and hurled it. His right shoulder ached now, but he didn't mind the pain. Swimming with the dolphins had made him forget. He could not afford to forget. Not until he had revenge.

And to get revenge, he needed that treasure.

Followed by Scuto and the puppies, Lupus stalked back along the beach towards them. Nubia saw immediately that his eyes were hard again.

Lupus went straight to the sky-blue fishing boat and tried to push it into the water. Nubia and the others hurried to help him. The dogs scrambled in eagerly, before the ship's prow had even touched the water.

'Did I hear someone cry out?' asked Aristo, coming across the hot sand to help them launch the boat.

'Dead octopus. Gave Lupus a fright,' grunted Phrixus, as he put his shoulder to the skiff.

Nubia saw Lupus give Phrixus such a fierce glare that the freedman stopped pushing. But now the sky-blue fishing boat was afloat, bobbing on the water, gradually moving out with each small receding wave.

Phrixus pulled himself into the boat first, then Aristo, and they held out their hands to the others. Nubia chose Aristo's hand and let his strong arm lift her up and in. She smiled her thanks up at him, but his brown eyes were staring over her head, back towards the villa.

Lupus's heart had stopped pounding by the time they reached the site of the wreck. And his breathing had returned to normal. That was good. Nothing must break his concentration. As Phrixus released the iron anchor, Lupus stripped down to his loin cloth and tied the hemp cord around his chest under his arms. When he needed to surface, he would give three sharp tugs and Aristo would pull him up.

Lupus stepped over the side of the boat onto the new plank which Phrixus and Jonathan had fixed to the boat's hull. It seemed sturdy enough. He sat, legs dangling in the water. From here it was easy for him to bend over and scoop up handfuls of seawater. He wet the back of his neck, then his face, and took several short breaths.

Then he held out his hands. When Aristo had placed a flat, heavy rock in his open palms, Lupus filled his lungs one final time and slipped forward into the clear blue water.

The weight of the rock pulled him down and Lupus felt the sea close over his head and the weight of water above him, stuffing his ears and nose with pressure. A thousand silver bubbles peeled themselves away from him and rose up, as if he were a snake shedding his old skin. He opened his eyes to see a shoal of bright fish darting towards him, then veering away, as one.

It was nearly midday and the sun was almost directly overhead. At first, the water was bright and warm. But as he continued to sink the water grew cooler, darker, heavier. Presently, the water rushing past him was deep blue. And cold.

As he continued his downward plunge, Lupus tipped the flat rock so that it carried him closer to the wreck. He saw what he had not noticed the day before: the tattered remains of the ship's sail flapping in the underwater current.

As Lupus released the heavy weight-stone, he stopped sinking. Fighting his body's natural buoyancy, he kicked out and swam towards the wreck, a black shape against the blue water around it. The ship's front – its prow – had impaled itself in the sandy bottom. It was a merchant ship, like the one Flavia's father had owned, so there were no banks of oars, just the two steering paddles at the back. Above these, the figurehead tipped forward like a decapitated sentry about to topple onto the mast.

Another shoal of fish approached, gleaming like pewter in the murky light. They flickered away, each turning at precisely the same instant.

By the time he found the crack in her hull his lungs were ready to burst. He must get back up. Three sharp tugs on the cord around his chest.

As he rose up through the water, Lupus mentally marked the hull's breach in relation to the fluttering shreds of sail.

Don't breathe in yet, he told himself. Breathe out. Breathe out bubbles.

Water warmer, lighter now.

There was his goal above him, the water's bright undulating skin, with the darker shape of the boat floating far above him. Still a long way away.

Must breathe. But not yet.

The water's increasing warmth and brightness told him just a little longer.

Must breathe, must breathe, must breathe.

Not yet, not yet, not yet.

NOW!

Lupus broke the surface of the water and sucked in air. As the roaring in his head grew quieter he heard his friends shout: 'One hundred and twenty-three!'

'Lupus,' cried Flavia. 'You stayed under twenty counts longer than yesterday!'

Lupus nodded, still gasping for breath. He felt dizzy. A few strokes took him within reach of them.

Hands lifted him into the boat, a towel enveloped him, dogs licked him and his friends patted him on the back. He waited until his teeth stopped chattering.

Then he took his wax tablet and – his hand still trembling from the effort of the dive – he wrote:

FOUND GAP AGAIN

NEED TO MAKE MORE DIVES

SCROLL XIV

Lupus knew what the others did not: you never made more than seven dives a day.

Six dives was enough to leave even the strongest man gasping like a fish on the bottom of the boat. Seven made your nose and ears begin to bleed, that was the warning sign. And after eight dives, maybe nine, the cramps gripped you, softly at first, then more fiercely, until the pain was excruciating and the only relief came with death.

On his first dive, he had found the hull's breach.

On his second he squeezed through the gap and into the dark belly of the ship. He realised now why no man had got inside the wreck before. The gap was very narrow, like a crack in a giant cup.

On his third dive, he found a great pile of amphoras filling the upended front of the hull. He pushed them aside, the round ones more easily than the long ones. But he found no casks or treasure-chests.

Back up in the sunlight, Lupus noticed blood on the towel. Not from his ears or nose, but from his hands, where he had pushed the amphoras aside. The barnacles and shells which had attached themselves to the rough clay were razor sharp.

He needed a break: to breathe and to think. The others were asking him questions, but he shut out their voices and concentrated on breathing slowly and deeply. Was there really gold in the wreck? There were no chests. No strongboxes. Only amphoras. Suddenly Lupus remembered the trick that Captain Geminus's patron had once used to hide some gold: he had poured the coins into amphoras, where nobody would think to look for them.

Lupus dived again, and on this – his fourth dive – he found some smaller amphoras. He knew the big ones usually contained grain or wine. If there was gold in some of the amphoras, it would be in smaller ones like these, because of the weight.

Lupus wasted his fifth dive trying to break one of the smaller amphoras. He needed to know what was inside. He didn't want to end up with a jar full of fish sauce, nutmegs or olives. None of those things were of use to him. Only gold could buy Gamala's swift cut to the base of the neck. He tried to smash one amphora with another, but the jars were well-made and the water made his movements too sluggish to be effective.

On his sixth dive, he was just feeling the urge to breathe when he found a small amphora with a broken neck. He needed to start back up soon. But first he would see what was inside.

Cautiously he lowered his hand into the jar. A shiver of pleasure ran through him as his hand grasped small, heavy discs. Lupus pulled out a fistful of what he had been praying for. Even in the deep blue gloom of the hull the glint of gold was unmistakable.

Stupid! Why hadn't he brought a pouch or bag? Every sponge-fisher knew to bring his sponge net. No time now. Desperate for air. Get it next dive.

He pushed through the breach and started up. He had never left it this late. But with his hands balled round the coins he couldn't tug his lifeline and he couldn't swim properly. He had to let the coins drop.

Lupus opened his hands and tugged his cord, then frantically began pulling the water to bring himself up. A shower of gold discs drifted past his kicking feet towards the sandy bottom.

But Lupus no longer cared. He had only one desire: to reach the surface and breathe.

Nubia wrapped the towel around Lupus and rubbed vigorously. His brown shoulders were shivering and his teeth chattering. Instinctively she felt something was wrong. He should be leaving himself more time to recover between dives. There was a strange, feverish look in his eyes. Now he was already pushing the towel away, looking for something in the bottom of the boat: his tablet pouch. He emptied out the wax tablets and tied it round his left wrist.

'Did you find the gold?' asked Flavia, her eyes gleaming.

Lupus nodded.

Suddenly Nubia uttered a cry of horror. A slow trickle of bright red blood was oozing from Lupus's left ear. As he turned to look at her she saw his nose was bleeding, too.

'Behold, the blood flows from your nose and ears!'

'Oh, Lupus!' cried Flavia, clapping her palms to her cheeks.

Lupus wiped his nose with his arm and saw the smear of blood there. He shrugged, stepped out onto the board, sat with his legs in the water and splashed his face. Nubia knew he was preparing to dive for the seventh time.

But before he could slip into the water again, strong arms lifted Lupus back into the boat. 'Oh no you don't,' said Aristo quietly. 'I grew up beside the sea and I'm no fool. There is no way I'm letting you dive again today.'

That afternoon at dinner Lupus sat sullenly at the table and refused to eat his food. Nubia decided he was still angry because Aristo had stopped him diving for the gold. She noticed that he kept staring at the statue against the wall, particularly at the Gorgon's agonised face, frozen horribly in the throes of death.

His mood affected everyone.

Finally Nubia had an idea. She knew drumming often brought Lupus a sort of peace.

'Shall we play music?' she suggested when the dessert course had been cleared away. If Lupus joined in he might feel better.

Aristo shot her a keen glance. 'Good idea,' he said and turned to their host. 'May we play?'

'Of course,' said Pliny. He clapped his hands. 'Phrixus! Bring our instruments, will you? And there's another lyre in the storeroom.'

Phrixus returned a few moments later and handed out the instruments. When Lupus refused to take his goatskin drum, Phrixus set it on the table beside him.

Nubia glanced at Aristo and mouthed 'Song of the Traveller'. It had a strong beat. Aristo nodded and began to play. Nubia sang, Jonathan thumbed the bass notes on his barbiton and Flavia jingled her tambourine.

Lupus ignored them.

When the song ended, Nubia looked at Aristo. He raised his eyebrows at her and she knew which song he wanted her to play: 'Slave Song'.

She nodded back and kept her eyes on him. They began together.

Presently Jonathan came in on the barbiton and then Flavia softly on tambourine, but the music longed for the drum. Nubia had to close her eyes to concentrate.

The first time she had played it, even though she

had played solo, the song had brought her a deep release. She had known then that it was something special.

Later, when Aristo and her friends had learned to play the song, it had become something even more wonderful. But without the drum it sounded wrong.

Nubia felt a strange tightness in her throat. She tried to swallow but that didn't help, so she stopped playing and opened her eyes. Aristo stopped, too, and the song trailed off. He gave a small shake of his head and nodded towards Lupus's place at the table.

It was empty.

The slaves looked up with interest as Lupus entered the kitchen. It was a large, dim room with a vaulted ceiling and a coal hearth along one entire wall. The grey plaster walls were smoke-streaked and in places the brickwork showed through. Despite its drabness, the laughter of the kitchen slaves and the scent of dried herbs gave it a cheerful feel.

One of the figures detached himself from the group and came over. Lupus was surprised to see it was Phrixus.

'What is it, Lupus? What do you want? Buttermilk? Soup?'

Lupus shook his head. He had been expecting to mime his requests but Phrixus could read, so he unflipped his wax tablet and wrote:

In one corner of the kitchen was a stone sink full of water. Phrixus took a clay beaker from the shelf, filled it with water and handed it to Lupus. Then he passed the boy a ceramic bowl of grey salt with a bone spoon in it.

Lupus stirred three spoonfuls of salt into the water and drained the beaker.

'That will make you terribly thirsty,' said Phrixus.

Lupus nodded at him to say: Yes, I know.

Then he wrote a list on his wax tablet:

ALMONDS

DRIED FISH

OLIVE OIL

MORTARIUM

Phrixus raised an eyebrow when he saw the list and then called out: 'Rosa! Bring us some almonds, dried fish, and olive oil. Oh, and a mortar and pestle.'

A plump kitchen slave with red hair hurried to get the items. She dimpled prettily as she set them on the wooden table.

Lupus grunted his thanks and put a handful of

330

almonds in the large, flattish bowl. It was made of fired clay with bits of pottery grit embedded in it. Using a heavy marble pestle he ground the almonds to paste, then gradually began to add the dried fish.

Rosa and Phrixus watched with interest and soon the other slaves had gathered round. Lupus's forearm was already beginning to ache from the grinding. He switched to his left hand.

'What is he making?' asked Rosa.

'I can't wait to see,' said Phrixus.

When the fish and almonds were ground together, Lupus began to add olive oil.

Now his left arm was aching so he switched back to his right.

'Take over the grinding, would you, Rosa?' asked Phrixus with a smile.

The slave-girl took the pestle from Lupus. As he added the oil, she continued grinding. Her forearms were strong and muscular. Soon the mortarium was full of a viscous light-brown liquid.

'What on earth?' Phrixus asked Lupus.

Lupus sighed and picked up his wax tablet again.

SPECIAL MEAL FOR DIVERS he wrote.

Phrixus nodded, and then winced as Lupus poured the whole mixture into the empty water beaker and carefully tipped it down his throat.

Something woke Flavia from her dream of swimming with dolphins.

It was the deepest hour of the night. The ceiling above her was only just visible in the flickering light of a small clay night-lamp.

From across the room, Nubia's breathing was slow and steady. Everything else was silent.

Then Flavia felt it. Along the length of her back where it rested on the mattress. The merest trembling, first a purr, then a growl, then stillness again. Had she imagined it? She heard Nipur whine and felt Scuto's cold nose gently butt her hand.

No. She had not imagined it. The dogs had sensed it, too. She patted the bed beside her. 'Come on, boy,' she whispered. 'You can come up just this once.'

Scuto didn't need to be told twice. The narrow bed creaked as he lifted himself onto it, then turned in a circle to make a place. Flavia had to move right over until she was almost falling off but she didn't mind. She turned on her side, slipped her arm around Scuto's warm, woolly neck and gave him a reassuring squeeze.

Just as there had been tremors before the volcano erupted, this must have been one after. She wondered how much stronger it would have felt for those living near Vesuvius. And in Surrentum.

Presently she drifted back to sleep and into an

unsettling dream in which she was standing on Green Fountain Street in front of her house. She was locked out. When she stepped forward and banged the knocker, strange eyes appeared in the peephole: the brown eyes of a woman.

When Flavia awoke the next morning she had forgotten all about the tremor.

Aristo came into the triclinium as the slaves were serving breakfast. He sat heavily on one of the wrought-iron chairs and stared out through the pink spiral columns towards the sea.

Nubia looked up from her cheese and figs. 'Are you unhappy, Aristo?' she asked.

He turned back to the table and looked at the girls. 'Last night I had a bad dream,' he said. 'I can't remember what it was, but when I got up and opened my bedroom curtain the first thing I saw was a slave-girl crying.'

'And?' said Flavia, taking a sip of pomegranate juice.

'When I asked her what was wrong, she said she had been cleaning fish for supper this afternoon and she found one with no heart.'

Flavia slowly put down her cup.

'What does that mean?' asked Nubia.

'It's a bad omen,' said Aristo.

'Very bad,' said Flavia. 'The day Julius Caesar was

murdered, the soothsayers found the lamb had no heart.'

'And that's not quite all,' said Aristo. 'I asked her what sort of fish she had been gutting, and she said it was the fish called "lupus".'

SCROLL XV

'Maybe we shouldn't let Lupus dive today,' said Flavia to Aristo. 'If the omens are bad, he could be in danger.'

There was an angry grunt from behind them. Jonathan and Lupus had just come into the room. The younger boy had his hands on his hips and it was obvious from the scowl on his face that he had heard Flavia's last remark.

'She's right, Lupus,' said Aristo. 'You could be in danger.'

Lupus was already writing on his tablet. He strode forward and slammed it down on the marble table.

I DON'T BELIEVE IN OMENS

'Besides,' said Jonathan, 'I've invented a special float-rope that means Lupus will only have to make one more dive.'

'Really?' said Aristo. 'Show us.'

'Here are my plans,' said Jonathan, opening his wax

335

tablet and putting it on the table. He bent over and leaned his elbows on the cold marble.

'What's this line with little circles on it?' asked Flavia.

'That's my invention. I call it a float-rope. A few days ago I noticed about a dozen floats in the boat-house, for keeping the fishing nets from sinking.'

'I know what they look like,' said Flavia. She pressed her two fists together: 'They're about this big, round and light brown.'

'That's it. They're made of cork, a kind of bark. Well, yesterday, after we got back, Phrixus and I attached the cork floats to the end of a long rope. I used the abacus to calculate the depth of the wreck. I think it's about eighty feet deep. So I've made the float-rope a hundred feet, just in case my calculations are off.'

'Your calculations are excellent,' said Aristo, study-ing the figures on Jonathan's wax tablet.

'And Lupus and I have been doing a few tests in the heated swimming pool of the baths this morning,' said Jonathan, standing up straight. 'We tried pushing cork floats under the water. It's almost impossible to hold them down.'

Aristo frowned. 'If the floats are so buoyant, how will we get a dozen of them to a depth of eighty feet?'

'I've thought of that,' said Jonathan. 'The anchor is the only thing I could think of heavy enough to pull the float-rope down and keep it there. We attach the float-rope to the anchor with hemp cords. When Lupus cuts these cords the float rope will immediately rise to the surface, bringing the amphora with it.'

'Jonathan,' said Aristo, 'that's a brilliant invention.'

Jonathan flushed with pleasure. 'The most difficult part,' he said, 'will be for Lupus to get the gold-filled amphora to the float-rope, but the water should make it less heavy than if it were in the air. You taught us that.'

It was Aristo's turn to flush. 'You've actually applied something I taught you, Jonathan. That's the sign of a true engineer.'

'And look,' said Jonathan, 'Lupus drew me a picture of the amphora with the gold in it. The neck is broken but it still has one handle. So Phrixus and I attached this big fishhook to the float-rope. All Lupus has to do is slip the handle of the amphora over the hook. He doesn't have to tie a knot or anything.'

CAN WE TRY IT OUT? wrote Lupus on his wax tablet.

Aristo glanced out through the pink columns. 'Very well,' he said. 'Against my better judgment. But I want to wait an hour or so to see if that bank of clouds on the horizon is coming or going. Agreed?'

They all nodded.

337

'Get out your wax tablets,' Aristo said. 'Let's go over Jonathan's calculations.'

'Do we have to do sums, Aristo?' moaned Flavia. 'Couldn't you just tell us a quick story? Like yesterday?'

'Another story maybe of dolphins?' added Nubia.

'Well,' said Aristo with a slow smile, 'there is one more myth about dolphins. It's the story of Neptune and Amphitrite.'

'Neptune, the god of the sea, had a thick beard as green as kelp and swarming with sea creatures. Little scuttling crabs in particular.'

'Ewww!' said Flavia, and the others laughed.

'And as Flavia has just demonstrated,' continued Aristo, 'this seething green beard was not very attractive to females. So when Neptune fell in love with a beautiful sea-nymph named Amphitrite, she ran away from him. She did not want to kiss a man with a kelpy beard, even a god!'

Flavia and Nubia glanced at one another and Nubia giggled behind her hand.

'But Neptune was passionate about Amphitrite, so he devised a plan. He would win Amphitrite's heart by building her a palace made of pearls and coral and sea-gold. When it was finished, he told all the creatures of the sea to search the watery realms of his kingdom for Amphitrite, most beautiful of the nymphs.'

'What did she look like?' asked Nubia resting her elbow on the table and her chin in her hand.

'What did she . . . ? Oh. Well, let's see. She was very beautiful with a slender body as white as marble. Her eyes were violet, the colour of the sky at dusk.' Aristo had a dreamy look in his eyes. 'Her lips were pink as coral and her teeth as white as pearls. Her hair was beautiful: glossy, and thick, and curly . . .'

He trailed off as Miriam came quietly into the dining-room.

'You were describing her hair,' said Flavia, with a mischievous gleam in her eyes. 'Glossy and thick and curly . . .'

'And green!' said Aristo. 'Her hair was green.' He glanced over at Miriam, who was leaning on the parapet, and he coloured slightly. 'Anyway, Neptune loved Amphitrite and was so intent on having her as his wife that he offered a reward of immortality to whoever found her.'

'What's immorality?' asked Nubia.

'Er . . . immortality means you live forever, like the gods on Olympus.'

'Stop interrupting him,' said Jonathan mildly. 'I want to hear the rest of the story.'

'There's not much more to tell,' said Aristo. 'Delphinus the dolphin found Amphitrite hiding near the Atlas Mountains. He told her that she could live in a palace made of pearls and coral and sea-gold. If she came back. And he said that Neptune had promised not to kiss her too often. Amphitrite missed her sea-nymph friends and she liked the idea of living in her own palace. So she climbed onto Delphinus's smooth grey back and the faithful dolphin carried her home.'

'Someone else who rode a dolphin!' cried Flavia.

Aristo nodded. 'Neptune married Amphitrite and made her his queen. They were very happy together and had lots of little green-haired sea-nymphs. As for Delphinus, he was made Neptune's official messenger. But whenever he wasn't working, he was allowed to frolic in the foamy waves. And when, after a long and happy life, Delphinus the dolphin finally died, Neptune turned him into a constellation and set him in the sky, to comfort sailors at night.'

'The gods always do that,' said Jonathan. 'Same with Hercules. They promise you immortality and then they make you into a constellation: cold stars in the big black sky. That's not how I want to spend eternity.'

Miriam had been leaning on the marble parapet, gazing out over the water. Abruptly she turned to them with excitement in her violet eyes. 'The dolphins must have heard you talking about them,' she cried. 'They're back again!'

It wasn't until she was swimming towards the dolphins that Flavia realised someone was missing.

'Where's Lupus?' She stopped to tread water and look around.

'He's back on the beach, under the big parasol. With Aristo and the dogs.' Jonathan turned onto his back and floated for a moment. 'It looks like he's practising his breathing.'

'But why isn't he coming with us? He loved swimming with the dolphins!'

'Dolphins are making Lupus soft inside,' said Nubia, who had also stopped to float.

'I think Nubia's right,' said Jonathan. 'Lupus seemed different after we swam with the dolphins. It was the first time I've ever seen him sit still, without fidgeting.'

'Yes,' said Flavia, trying to float like the other two. 'And he didn't look as . . . tough as he usually does.'

'Then he saw octopus,' said Nubia. 'And the tough comes back.'

Jonathan nodded.

'Maybe,' said Flavia slowly, 'that's the way he wants to be. Maybe he doesn't *want* to be soft inside . . .'

Suddenly she squealed with delight. She had caught sight of four grey shapes speeding through the glassy water beneath them. One of them leapt high in the air and the three friends laughed as he splashed down again, drenching them with salty spray.

Lupus lowered his head and then lifted it again.

With red-rimmed eyes, he watched the dolphins pull his friends in joyous circles through the water.

One of the dolphins swam alone. Every so often it leapt high into the air and flipped, scattering drops of water like diamonds, then splashed back into the sea. Lupus knew the dolphin was trying to attract his attention.

Would it be so terrible if he forgot about his vow and ran down to the water to swim?

No. Swimming with the dolphins had made him feel soft. And weak. And if he grew weak he would not be able to avenge the murder of his parents.

Vengeance was his duty. His duty as a son.

Lupus sat up straighter and crossed his legs. Then he closed his eyes to the sight of his friends and their dolphins swimming in the glittering blue sea. He took several quick breaths. Finally he blew all the air from his chest and took a breath so big it made his ribs ache.

Then he began to count.

SCROLL XVI

'I think I had the same dolphin as before,' laughed Flavia. She spread her linen towel just outside the shade of Lupus's parasol so that the hot sun would dry her. 'I tried to ride my dolphin like Arion, but I kept slipping off.'

'My dolphin used his nose to pull me,' wheezed Jonathan as he flopped down in the shade beside Lupus. 'I was patting his nose like this and he started swimming and I was being pulled along and I was yelling stop, stop and then I was yelling no, don't stop!'

'And my dolphin is pushing my feet from underneath,' said Nubia.

'That was amazing!' said Flavia, unpinning her wet hair and attacking the tangles with a fine-toothed comb. 'Did you see it, Lupus?'

Lupus shook his head.

'When Nubia put her feet together and made her body stiff, her dolphin came from underneath and pushed her right up out of the water!'

Lupus nodded, but kept his eyes on the horizon.

343

Flavia stopped combing for a moment and glanced over at Aristo. He frowned and shook his head.

'So,' said Flavia, as she resumed combing her hair, 'it's turned out to be a beautiful day. The clouds are gone and the water's lovely. Are we going to try for the treasure again?'

Lupus sat on Jonathan's boat shelf and prepared himself.

He had wrapped a strip of clean linen around his ears so the water would not get in and make them bleed.

He had swallowed his diver's concoction earlier in the day and had also been drinking lots of fresh water after his morning beaker of salted water.

He could now hold his breath for a count of one hundred and eighty. Almost twice as long as two days ago.

He knew exactly where the small amphora of gold was. He'd been dreaming about it all night.

Jonathan's special float-rope was ready, attached to the anchor which would pull him down faster than any stone.

He had a sharp knife to cut the cords attaching the float-rope to the anchor, once he'd hooked the amphora onto it.

He even had a pouch which he could fill with gold, in case the amphora was still too heavy to lift.

Nothing could go wrong.

Lupus leaned forward on his bench and wet his face and then the back of his neck. After a moment he slipped into the water and swam to the anchor, which Phrixus had lowered just below the surface. Lupus checked that the float-rope was securely attached, then put his feet on either side of the V-shaped bottom of the anchor and gripped its T-shaped top.

Still holding this rough iron bar, Lupus took several short quick breaths until he felt almost dizzy. He forced the air from his lungs and breathed in as much as he could. Then he sucked in a bit more. And a bit more. When he felt his lungs would burst he nodded at Phrixus.

Phrixus tapped the wooden peg from the winch.

The anchor plunged down into the sea.

Lupus had never descended so quickly. The cold blue depths of the water swallowed him whole. He gripped the anchor tightly and closed his eyes for a moment. It felt as if his stomach had leapt into his throat.

He opened his eyes to see the wreck already rushing up to him. They had judged it well. He let go of the anchor and watched it continue its plunge to the sandy bottom.

His lungs did not feel like bursting any more. They felt good: full of air, and he had as yet not the least desire to breathe.

But as he swam towards the wreck he frowned. The gap in the ship's hull had changed shape and it was bigger. Much bigger. How could this have happened? Something was wrong.

Lupus easily swam through the breach. As he scanned the deep blue interior of the hull, he cursed inwardly.

All the amphoras had shifted position. It was as if Neptune had picked up the ship, given it a shake and put it down again. What could have caused this?

Lupus swam back and forth – touching, pushing, shoving the amphoras – until threads of blood drifted up from his fingertips. He searched desperately for the small amphora with the broken neck. Or even one like it. But the only amphoras he could see were almost as big as he was.

All his work for nothing! If only Aristo had let him make that last dive yesterday, at least he would have a pouch full of gold.

His heart was pounding now and he felt like howling with frustration. His anger had used up the last of his air. He must regain his calm. He would simply keep diving until he found the small amphora. Or one like it. But now he needed to get back to the surface.

He turned and kicked back towards the breach. But as he started to pull himself through the gap in the hull something in the black water stroked his ankle.

Was it seaweed? Rope?

The thing around his ankle tightened and as Lupus felt the grip of living flesh his stomach clenched. As soon as he turned his head, he saw its eyes gleaming in the shadows behind the amphoras.

Octopus! An enormous one! He clutched the rough timber on either side of the gap, tried to pull himself through to safety.

But the powerful tentacle was stronger than he was. Lupus felt his bleeding fingers begin to slip. Another moment and the octopus would pull him back into the dark belly of the wreck.

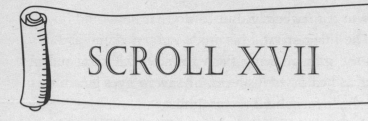

SCROLL XVII

'He's taking a long time,' said Flavia.

Jonathan tried to concentrate. He was counting for Lupus: '. . . one hundred and eighty-one, one hundred and eighty-two, one hundred and eighty-three . . .'

'I think I feel a tug,' said Aristo.

'Then pull him up!' cried Flavia.

Aristo shook his head. 'If I start pulling when he's still inside the ship, it could make him hit his head on the beams and knock him unconscious.'

As Lupus lost his hold on the wreck he thought quickly. If the octopus drew him deeper the other tentacles would grip him. Then he would be lost. Quickly he looped part of his hemp lifeline around a projecting timber of the hull. That would buy him a moment or two.

With the octopus pulling his leg and the lifeline cutting into his armpits, he reached for the razor-sharp knife at his belt. He knew from experience that he could not pull off an octopus's tentacle. The only way was to cut it cleanly. But to do that he would have to cut his lifeline first.

Part of his mind was screaming for air. But another part was calm. He had one chance.

Lupus fumbled for his knife and cut the lifeline. Then, as he felt himself being pulled deeper in, he twisted and hacked at the tentacle round his ankle.

The octopus reacted instinctively. A cloud of black ink mingled with its blood and even as the other arms writhed towards him out of the gloom, Lupus frog-kicked out through the gap.

He was desperate for air now. He couldn't inhale, but at least he could exhale. The bubbles rose and he followed them up, tugging at the water, kicking desperately with his legs. Up towards the light. But now, instead of growing lighter it seemed to be growing darker. And colder. He had lost his bearings. He slowed and stopped. Was he going up or down?

Lupus didn't know any more. There was no lifeline to guide him. He only knew one thing: that he had to breathe.

And so he did.

'Two hundred and ten!' yelled Jonathan, a look of alarm on his face.

'Pull, Aristo!' cried Flavia, and Nubia nodded.

'I think you're right,' said Aristo. He pulled the line. 'It's stuck . . . It's . . .' He tugged again. 'Now it seems to be coming up quite easily,' he said in surprise.

A few moments later they all stared in dismay at the hemp lifeline. There was nothing attached to its end.

As the water filled Lupus's lungs, a deep calm settled over him. He floated in a blue-green world, peacefully aware of the beauty around him. A shoal of golden fish flickered past him and then another, silver this time, like a ball of quicksilver that shifted and melted as it moved.

Lupus smiled. Something was coming towards him from the sapphire depths. The pale smiling face was strangely familiar. Lupus laughed as Neptune's messenger gently nudged him.

It was Delphinus, coming to take him home.

SCROLL XVIII

Flavia's eyes were red with weeping. Jonathan had his arm around her but his face was white as chalk. Nubia was dry-eyed. She sat stiff-backed in the boat and stared fixedly at the water.

At last Aristo surfaced and shook his head. He pulled himself dripping back into the boat.

As Phrixus tossed him a towel, Flavia burst into tears again. 'It's all my fault!' she sobbed. 'It was my idea to dive for sunken treasure. Oh Aristo! How will the gods ever forgive me?'

Aristo shook his head and pulled on his tunic.

Suddenly, a chattering laugh bubbled up from the water. Nubia rose slowly to her feet and Flavia looked up at her.

'Behold!' whispered Nubia. Then she burst into tears.

They all turned to see a sleek dolphin nudging Lupus's body towards the boat.

Jonathan took charge.

'Let me,' he said as they pulled the boy's dripping body into the boat. 'I know what to do.'

Aristo nodded and stepped back. They all watched as Jonathan knelt beside Lupus and tipped the boy's head back so that his tongueless mouth was open and his chin pointed to the sky.

Jonathan put his mouth over Lupus's and blew. Then he took his mouth away and pushed on Lupus's chest. Then he blew. Then he pushed. Then he blew.

After a while he looked up fiercely. 'Pray!' he commanded, and lowered his mouth to Lupus's again.

Presently some water gurgled out of the corner of Lupus's mouth. The boy shuddered, then coughed and was sick onto the folded canvas beneath him.

Jonathan sat back, trembling. Flavia hugged him and then hugged Lupus and then hugged Nubia and then hugged Jonathan again. Aristo wrapped Lupus in the towel and held him tightly.

After a time, Aristo passed Lupus back to the girls, who cradled the semi-conscious boy on their laps.

Aristo and Phrixus gripped the oars and pulled towards home.

The dogs stood at the prow, tails wagging, and Jonathan sat at the rudder, trying to steer through a blur of tears.

'Lupus almost died,' whispered Flavia to her friends, as they trudged across the hot sand. Aristo went before them, carrying Lupus up the beach towards the villa.

'He *did* die,' said Jonathan quietly. 'When I breathed my spirit into him his heart had stopped.'

'How did you know what to do?' asked Flavia. 'I mean, how to breathe some of your spirit into him?'

'I saw my father do it once. He saved a little boy. We were at some friends. Their three-year-old fell into the impluvium and drowned, but father brought him back to life.'

'Will it hurt you?' asked Nubia. 'Losing some of your spirit?'

'I don't think so,' said Jonathan. 'I ask God to breathe his spirit into me every day. That should fill up any gaps.'

'What do you think happened down there?' asked Flavia. 'Why didn't Lupus come up sooner?'

'Look at the marks on his leg,' grunted Aristo, over his shoulder. He stopped to let Phrixus open the villa gate and the three friends examined Lupus's legs.

'Behold!' cried Nubia. 'White circles on his leg!'

'Octopus?' said Flavia.

Aristo nodded grimly. 'And a big one, judging by the size of those marks.'

Lupus groaned.

'He must have been terrified down there,' murmured Jonathan.

Phrixus held the door open and they followed Aristo up the steps and into the hot, violet-scented terrace which led to the sea-view triclinium.

Still carrying Lupus, Aristo stepped into the bright dining-room.

Then he stopped dead in his tracks. Flavia and the others almost bumped into him. But they stopped, too, when they saw what Aristo was staring at.

Miriam and Pliny were standing close together by one of the pink spiral columns. She had her hands on his shoulders and she was kissing him.

SCROLL XIX

'Miriam!' cried Flavia. 'What are you doing? You're engaged to Uncle Gaius!'

Miriam whirled to face them and her cheeks flushed.

'I wasn't doing anything,' she stammered. 'I was just thanking Gaius for a gift.'

'Where's Gaius?' asked Jonathan, looking around.

'Gaius is my first name, too,' said Pliny, with a modest cough. 'And your sister is right. She didn't do anything wrong. She merely gave me a chaste kiss on the cheek.'

Pliny put his hand protectively on Miriam's shoulder, but it fell away as she stepped towards Aristo.

'What's wrong with Lupus?' she asked.

'He almost drowned,' said Aristo.

'Dear Lord,' whispered Miriam.

'Will he be all right?' asked Pliny.

Aristo gave him a curt nod.

'Jonathan saved his life,' said Flavia. 'He breathed some of his spirit into Lupus and brought him back from death!'

'Oh Jonathan!' Miriam ran to her younger brother and hugged him. 'I'm so proud of you.'

Lupus groaned and Aristo muttered, 'Boy's getting a bit heavy, here. Where shall I put him?'

'Put him in Captain Geminus's room,' said Miriam. 'There's an extra couch and I can tend them both. Follow me.'

'Lead on,' said Aristo through clenched teeth, and followed her out through the green marble columns.

'And suddenly Lupus coughed and was sick, and then he was alive again!'

Flavia was telling her father about Lupus's near-death experience. 'We think it must have been a giant octopus!' she whispered, with a glance towards Lupus's couch. Nubia stood near Flavia, who had perched on Captain Geminus's bed.

Flavia's father was propped up on half a dozen soft cushions. He smiled at the girls and closed his eyes for a moment.

Miriam had closed the latticework shutters against the late afternoon sun and the light spread a pattern of bright hexagons over his blanket.

'Is the sunshine in your eyes?' Flavia asked him.

Marcus opened his eyes again and shook his head. 'No. It's fine. It's a good room here. Very quiet and peaceful. And Miriam's a good nurse.'

Nubia looked over at the other couch. Miriam was

sitting beside Lupus and spooning chicken soup into his tongueless mouth. She was wearing a pink tunic with a pale green mantle wrapped round her slender waist. She had tied up her dark curls with a mint-green scarf. It covered the part of her scalp where some of her hair had been burnt away.

Lupus turned his head aside when he had eaten enough and closed his eyes. Miriam stood and put the half-empty soup-bowl on a bronze table beside his couch. Then she approached Captain Geminus and the girls.

Up close, Nubia could see Miriam's new earrings. They were fat little dolphins, with eyes like daisies.

'Are these the Pliny earrings?' whispered Nubia, touching one with her forefinger. It was heavy and she could tell it was made of pure gold. 'They are so beautiful.'

Miriam stood still and allowed the girls to examine them. 'He gave them to me because you all had your dolphins and he thought I would like some, too.'

'Why didn't you come down to the beach with us?' asked Flavia. 'You would have loved swimming with the dolphins.'

'I don't know how to swim,' said Miriam quietly. 'Besides, I'm looking after the invalid.'

'Don't call me that,' grumbled Flavia's father. 'You know I hate that word.'

Miriam laughed and showed her perfect white teeth.

Nubia sighed. Everything Miriam did, even her slightest gesture, was breathtaking. It was no wonder so many men were in love with her.

Suddenly Jonathan's head appeared in the doorway. He was breathing hard. 'Come quickly!' he gasped. 'You've got to see this. Aristo and Pliny are having a fight in the ball court!'

Built against the grain-tower between the garden and a colonnade was a sunny ball court. Flavia and her friends stopped in the deep shade of the colonnade and stared into the bright sunken courtyard. The ball court had smooth red plaster walls on three sides and a hard earth floor. Black lines were painted in various places on the walls and floor and Flavia knew they were markers for the ball, to tell whether it was in or out.

She had seen women playing the game once in the baths in Rome, and she knew that Aristo and Pliny were not doing it right. The ball and their wicker bats lay forgotten in one sunny corner and the two men were rolling on the floor.

At twenty-one, Aristo was older, stronger, and taller, but seventeen-year-old Pliny had obviously mastered some useful wrestling moves. He had his knee on Aristo's neck and was squashing the young Greek's face into the dirt. Flavia clapped her hand over her mouth.

'Admit it,' demanded Pliny, whose face was quite pink. He was twisting Aristo's arm back. 'You cheated!'

Aristo gasped and tried to speak. Pliny eased up a little.

'No!' spat out Aristo, and suddenly writhed under him. 'I did not cheat!'

After an undignified scuffle, the positions were reversed: Aristo, hair and tunic covered with dust, now gripped their host in a complicated twist of arms and legs. '*You* cheated!' He wrenched Pliny's arm. 'You're trying to buy her affection with gifts. Admit you love her.'

'Never!' gasped Pliny, and even though he was in the submissive position he cried, 'why don't *you* admit you love her!'

'Freely!' cried Aristo, throwing up his hands in a dramatic gesture and letting Pliny fall forward onto the hard earth. 'I admit I love her. I'm not a coward like you! I admit it for the world to hear. I love Miriam!'

Beside her column, Miriam uttered a choked cry.

Slowly, Aristo and Pliny turned their heads towards the shaded colonnade.

'Oh,' said Aristo with a sheepish grin. 'Hello, Miriam!'

SCROLL XX

'What,' said Miriam, 'are you two doing?'

Aristo had just helped Pliny up off the ground. Now he was attempting to brush some of the dust from his host's tunic.

'Um . . . We were just practising some wrestling moves,' he said. 'Pliny was showing me one called the Spartan Shoulder-pull.'

'He's a very quick learner,' said Pliny. He slapped Aristo's back in a gesture of manly affection, and the dust which puffed up started them both off coughing.

Miriam walked slowly down the steps and into the bright courtyard. She stopped in front of them.

'You weren't practising.' She looked from one to the other. 'You were fighting over me. Weren't you?'

Pliny dropped his head.

Aristo gazed straight back into her eyes. 'Yes.'

'I am not,' said Miriam coldly, 'some garland to be won in a wrestling match. I'm a woman. I'm betrothed to Gaius Flavius Geminus – or will be if he ever gets round to it – and I love him!'

'I'm very glad to hear that,' came a voice on the other side of the court.

'Uncle Gaius!' cried Flavia. All heads turned to look at the man who had stepped out from behind a mulberry tree.

Miriam turned to look up at him, too, a look of astonishment on her face.

Gaius smiled at her and opened his arms.

But instead of running into them, Miriam uttered a cry of disgust and rushed up the steps and into the shadowed corridor towards her room.

The girls found the curtain drawn across the doorway of Miriam's bedroom. Flavia scratched softly at the pale blue plaster on the wall outside.

'Go away, Gaius!' came Miriam's voice. 'I don't want to see you now.'

'It's us: Flavia and Nubia.'

There was a pause.

'Can we come in?'

Another pause. Then a very quiet: 'Yes.'

Miriam was standing by the window with her back to them.

'Miriam,' said Flavia softly. 'What's wrong?'

For a long moment Miriam was quiet. Then she turned around. Her eyes were full of tears.

'I miss Frustilla,' she said.

'Frustilla?' said Flavia.

'Old cook of Uncle Gaius,' whispered Nubia. 'Who died of fumes.'

'I know that,' Flavia said to Nubia. She turned back to Miriam: 'Why her? Why do you miss Frustilla?'

'Because she was so wise and kind. She told me all sorts of things that father never told me.' Miriam sat on her bed and stared down at her hands. 'Frustilla would have known what to do about all these men who want me.'

'But don't you like the attention?' said Flavia. She sat on one side of Miriam and Nubia on the other. 'You're so beautiful,' continued Flavia, 'I wish I were . . .'

'I *hate* being beautiful!' said Miriam, with such vehemence that Flavia recoiled. 'And don't envy me. You least of all, Flavia. Everyone loves you because of who you are. Not because of how you look. It's awful to have men stare at you as if they're starving and you're some tasty morsel of bread dipped in gravy . . .'

'I'm sorry, Miriam,' said Flavia. 'I didn't realise—'

'I hate them fighting over me when they don't even know me. They make me out to be some kind of goddess, when I'm only human. Frustilla knew that. She would have known what to do and . . . I miss her. I miss her so much.' Tears welled up in Miriam's eyes and spilled onto her cheeks.

Flavia started to say something but Nubia put her finger to her lips. Flavia nodded and put her arm around Miriam, whose whole body shuddered with sobs.

Presently, when Miriam's tears subsided, Nubia said, 'You are loving Gaius because part of him was Frustilla?'

Miriam raised her head and looked at Nubia with swollen eyes. 'I love him,' she sniffed. 'But I also loved Frustilla and the farm and the garden . . . I was happy there.'

Flavia passed Miriam her handkerchief. 'So it's harder to love him on his own? When he's poor and doesn't have Frustilla or the farm and the garden?'

Miriam looked at Flavia and bit her lip. After a moment she nodded. 'Is that wrong?' she said, and tears welled up in her eyes again.

'I don't know,' said Flavia. 'I only know Uncle Gaius loves you for who you are, not just what you look like.'

'I know,' said Miriam. 'But there are other things . . . There's your faith . . . his faith. It's so different from ours. He worships dozens of gods and ours is only one of them.'

Flavia didn't know what to say. So she put her arm around Miriam's shoulders again, and gave her a squeeze.

As she did so, she was almost certain she heard footsteps outside in the corridor. Footsteps going quietly away.

'Uncle Gaius, why did you come here? Is everything all right?'

Flavia's uncle turned from the parapet of the violet-scented terrace. His eyes were shadowed.

'No,' he said. 'Everything's not all right.' He looked at the three friends. 'Where's Lupus?'

'He's sleeping,' said Jonathan, coming out of the triclinium into the sunshine. 'He nearly drowned today. He'll be all right, but he needs to rest.'

'Poor boy.' Gaius shook his head. 'He's the reason I came. I need to talk to you. But not here. Somewhere private. And open. I need some air.'

'We can go into the big garden,' suggested Flavia.

Her uncle nodded, so Flavia led the way back through the triclinium, down another long terrace with the sea on their left and the baths on their right. The sun was low in the sky now and the mulberry and fig trees cast bluish shadows back across the bright green lawn and rosemary borders.

Near the centre of the garden stood an enormous and ancient mulberry tree whose trunk was encircled by a marble bench. Gaius made for this tree. He brushed some ripe mulberries from the marble seat and sat down on it. Flavia and Nubia sat on one side of him and Jonathan sat on the other.

Gaius pulled a scroll from his shoulder bag and turned to Jonathan. 'Bato the magistrate came to see your father yesterday,' he said. 'Apparently Lupus tried to hire an assassin a few days ago.'

'What?' they all cried.

Gaius nodded. 'A man named Gamala. He used to be a member of the *sicarii*, a group of Jewish assassins. Somehow Lupus found out and approached him in the baths a few days ago. He asked this Gamala how much he would charge to kill Venalicius. Luckily Gamala is a friend of Bato's. He played along: named some ridiculous amount which Lupus could never hope to raise . . .'

Flavia jumped up from the bench. 'But Uncle Gaius! He does hope to raise it. That must be why he wants the gold so badly. He wants to hire someone to kill Venalicius.'

'But why does Lupus hate Venalicius so much?' said Jonathan. 'I mean, we all hate him. But this is ridiculous!'

Suddenly Flavia knew. 'Venalicius must be the person who killed Lupus's parents and cut out his tongue!' she whispered.

Gaius nodded. 'Correct. It's all here.' He tapped the scroll.

'What is?' Flavia frowned and sat down again.

'The story of how Lupus lost his tongue,' said Gaius.

Flavia stared at him, then took the scroll and examined it. It was a slender roll of papyrus, without a central rod, sealed with a red disc of wax.

'Hey!' Jonathan exclaimed. 'That's my father's seal.'

Gaius nodded.

'Why is my father's seal on Lupus's story?'

'Venalicius must have told him,' cried Flavia, 'when they were imprisoned together.'

'Correct again,' said her uncle. 'Venalicius confessed everything to Mordecai. Jonathan's father swears that Venalicius has repented of his former ways. That he wants to make up for his bad deeds . . .'

'I don't believe it!' cried Flavia.

Jonathan frowned. 'Why didn't my father tell us this before?' he asked.

'Venalicius' change of heart is very recent, and this information about Lupus is very . . . private. I think Mordecai hoped that Lupus would tell you himself one day, in writing. But when we found out that Lupus tried to hire an assassin . . . that is very serious.'

'And dangerous,' added Jonathan.

'Exactly,' said Gaius. 'You've got to talk him out of it. Mordecai thought you might have a better chance of convincing him if you knew the whole story.'

'Do you know the whole story?' asked Flavia.

'I know enough,' said Gaius, getting to his feet. 'Mordecai told me the gist of it. But he thought you should hear a fuller account.'

He handed the scroll to Jonathan and looked up

366

into the fading sky of dusk. Above them a huge flock of starlings had begun to wheel and swoop.

'It's getting dark,' said Gaius. 'I have to get back to Ostia and return my horse to the stables. And I have an early morning meeting with Rufus and Dexter, the bankers.'

Have you found out any more about why they're trying to take our house?'

'Not yet,' said Gaius. 'Rufus has been in Rome on business. He only just got back. Good luck with Lupus. I hope you can help him.' He glanced towards the villa and for a moment Flavia thought he was going to say something else. But he only shook his head and strode towards a gap in the box hedge. Flavia and her friends followed him and waved as he rode off down the tree-lined drive. But he did not look back.

Jonathan sat back down on the marble bench between the girls. They all looked at the scroll in his hand.

'That's it,' whispered Flavia. 'The story of how Lupus lost his tongue.'

Jonathan nodded and took a deep breath. Then he put his thumb under the edge of the scroll and slid it up the textured papyrus towards the wax disc. He felt a pop as the seal broke. Slowly, the scroll unrolled itself in his lap. It was not a very long sheet, only about the length of his arm. He quickly scanned the text.

Flavia looked puzzled. 'Why are you starting at the end?'

'What? Oh, Hebrew is written right to left. We start our scrolls from the other end.'

Flavia peered over his shoulder. 'Your father wrote it in Hebrew? Why?'

Jonathan shrugged. 'I guess to make sure nobody else could read it, even if it was opened.' He frowned at the scroll. 'That's a strange rubric,' he said.

'What is a rude brick?' asked Nubia.

'The rubric is the heading. The title.' Jonathan pointed: 'Here. In red ink. It says *The Story of Philippos* . . . I don't understand that.'

'But you understand the Hebrew?' said Flavia.

'Of course.'

'Then read it, Jonathan. Please.'

Jonathan cleared his throat and began to read, translating from Hebrew to Latin as he went along.

SCROLL XXI

The Story of Philippos

My appreciation of beauty has been the greatest curse in my life. If only I had been born blind, like other people, I might have been happy.

Perhaps it was because my mother Elena was so beautiful. She was the most beautiful woman on the island of Symi.

Or perhaps it was because my father was so ugly. He was a sponge-diver with crooked teeth and small black eyes. His huge nose was a shapeless mass squashed across his face. Even from a very young age I couldn't bear to see them together.

Luckily my father was often away with the other men of the island, diving for the best sponges, so my mother and I spent many happy days together alone. I would sit and watch her weave and listen to her sing. Whenever my father came home, I ran out of the house onto the beach. When father sailed away again, I would return to my mother.

The summer I was seven, we barely saw my father. And it seemed to me that my mother grew even more beautiful. Her belly grew like a ripe fruit. Sometimes, when I rested my head on it, I felt something stir inside.

Then one day, my father returned.

He embraced my mother. Presently he saw me and lifted me up. 'How's little Philippos?' His breath stank of garlic and there were tiny black dots on the leathery skin of his nose and cheeks.

I thought he was horrible and shrank away. He laughed.

Suddenly my mother cried: 'The baby! It's time!'

Soon the house was full of women in black. My father and I were pushed outside. We sat beneath our grape arbour with the men from the village and listened to my mother's screams. At last she grew silent. The women brought out my baby brother and presented him to my father.

Then they told us that my mother was dead.

I hated my father. It was his fault she had died. The baby's, too. Sometimes I tried to smother it, but my father always caught me and beat me.

As my little brother Alexandros grew older, I realised that he had my mother's beauty. When people saw him, their eyes lit up. But their faces remained blank when they looked at me. Then one day I discovered the reason why. For the first time in my life I saw my own reflection.

I will never forget that day. I knelt over the puddle of rainwater for a long time, not believing what I saw.

I, Philippos – who was so aware of beauty – looked like my father. It was a cruel joke of the gods.

I hated myself and everyone around me. Perhaps my hatred made me even uglier. Gradually people had nothing to do with me at all. Only one person on the island befriended me. A little girl named Melissa, about my brother's age.

Because she was kind to me, I wanted to get her a gift. Something special. But the people of my island were so poor that we could not afford mirrors or silk or even the very sponges which we dived for. Then one day I found a bed of oysters. Although my father had made me dive the full seven dives that day, I decided to dive again. Diving was something I was good at. I would dive once more and get a pearl for Melissa.

I ignored the warning of the gods and made eight dives. Nine. Ten. I brought up oysters, but none of them had a pearl. Then my vision grew red: my left eye had filled with blood. The pain of losing the sight of one eye was terrible, but not as bad as the pain I felt when I ran to find my reflection in the water. A horrible monster glared back at me. A face that would make children cry and men turn away.

I was thirteen years old.

The injury meant I couldn't risk diving again. Now I was useless. Good for nothing. Melissa was still kind to me but I could see she was repelled by my blind eye. I decided to end my life and so I climbed a cliff above jagged rocks. But my courage failed me and I crept back down again.

Not long after that, my father sold me to slave-traders. He needed the money, he said.

On that day, I vowed revenge.

Twenty years later I returned to Symi, a rich man with my own ship.

But I had not forgotten my vow.

Unseen, we dropped anchor in a secluded cove and I went alone to my father's house on the beach. It was dusk. I hid behind a trellis twined with honeysuckle and waited for darkness, my knife in my hand.

It was not my father who came out of the house, however, but a beautiful woman. She had been a little girl the last time I saw her, but I knew it was Melissa.

Standing there behind the honeysuckle I prayed to Venus, vowing that if Melissa would have me, I would become the kindest of men and renounce my evil ways. I would stop dealing in slaves and use my money to help the poor and unlovely. Even as the thought occurred to me, I felt my spirit lift.

At that moment a young man and a little boy ran up from the beach. The boy sat down to eat and the man kissed Melissa.

As I recognised Melissa's husband, I felt something like a blow to my heart. It was my younger brother Alexandros. The gods on Olympus had played another cruel joke on me.

That night my brother and his son went fishing. When they were gone, I went into the house after Melissa. Vengeance was in my heart, but she turned away my wrath with kind words and we talked all night.

When her husband and son returned in the morning, something made Melissa scream. Before I could explain that I hadn't hurt her, Alexandros overpowered me and took my knife. I fought back and in the struggle he cut off my ear.

The searing pain drove me mad and gave me new strength. I won back the knife and used it. The boy threw himself at me, but I easily knocked him to the ground. Soon Alexandros lay on the floor, too. I stood panting, and stared down at my brother's dead body. There was no room for remorse now.

'If you ever tell anyone of this,' I warned Melissa through a screaming haze of pain, 'I'll kill you, too.'

'I won't tell,' she sobbed, but then my good ear heard a voice ring out:

'I'll tell on you! You're Uncle Philippos!'

My nephew must have been about five or six. A brave boy. But foolish.

'No, you won't tell,' I said. I took the knife and cut out his tongue before his mother's eyes. Then I said to her: 'I'm taking the boy with me. If anyone comes after me, he dies.'

SCROLL XXII

Jonathan stopped reading for a moment and swallowed hard.

'I feel sick,' whispered Flavia. The others nodded.

'I don't understand,' said Nubia presently. 'Who is Philippos?'

'Philippos,' began Flavia, but her voice caught. 'Philippos,' she attempted again, 'must be Venalicius' real name. He is Lupus's uncle. The one who killed Lupus's father.'

'And cut out Lupus's tongue,' said Jonathan.

Nubia was still frowning. 'This story is written by Venalicius?'

'In a way,' said Jonathan. 'I suppose my father wrote it down as Venalicius told it to him.'

'Is there any more?,' asked Flavia, swallowing again.

'A little,' said Jonathan. 'Listen.'

I left Melissa weeping and sailed away with my nephew. He was ill for many days but hatred made him strong and he recovered. When we docked in Ostia he escaped. I was almost sad. He had begun to remind me of myself at that age.

*

Flavia had been watching Jonathan's finger move from right to left as he read the story. When he stopped again, she pointed. 'What's that? Did you read that bit?'

'It's just another rubric. It says:

I, Mordecai, servant of the living God, wrote this story as it was told to me on the fifth day of Tishri in the first year of the Emperor Titus. I wrote it as accurately as I could and without making judgment. May God have mercy on my soul and on his.'

As Jonathan read these words a movement caught Flavia's eye.

'Lupus!'

The boy had stepped out from behind the mulberry tree. He was wearing a clean tunic and his arms hung loose beside him. In one hand he held a wax tablet.

'Lupus, we're sorry,' said Jonathan. 'We just wanted to help you.'

Flavia braced herself for Lupus's fury. But he did not run away or scream or tear up the scroll. Instead, he took a single step towards them.

'Are you angry that we read the scroll?' asked Nubia.

Lupus shook his head.

'Were you behind the tree the whole time Jonathan was reading?' whispered Flavia.

Lupus nodded. Flavia noticed one of his eyes was very bloodshot and swollen.

Jonathan pointed to the wax tablet in his hand.

'Talk to us,' he said.

Lupus stared down at the tablet. After a while he opened it and wrote:

HE TOLD ME HE KILLED MY MOTHER TOO

'Oh Lupus,' said Flavia, and knew instantly that she had made the mistake of letting him see the pity in her eyes.

He turned and fled out of the garden towards the beach.

Lupus stood on the beach and watched the blood-red sun sink into the sea.

Could his mother still be alive? Somewhere out there on a Greek island far away? He felt sick with hope.

Suddenly he saw something which almost made his knees collapse beneath him.

To the right of the setting sun was a huge black hole.

Part of the sky was missing. And part of the sea. It was as if the vista before him was a red and blue tent and someone had burned a hole in the cloth, revealing the darkness beyond.

Lupus closed his eyes for a moment, then opened them again.

The black hole in the fabric of the cosmos was still there; shifting and moving slightly, as if a wind from the void beyond was blowing through it.

In that instant, as he looked, Lupus remembered what he had seen when he had breathed under water.

The dolphin's smiling face had faded. The world around him had grown cold. Finally he had been surrounded by a terrible darkness.

Now his body was trembling uncontrollably and his teeth chattered. He could not take his eyes from the horror of the hole in the universe. Was it coming for him now? Maybe death could not be cheated. Maybe the hole would grow bigger and bigger until it swallowed him in its blackness.

As he stared, unable to turn his eyes away, the hole seemed to shift and grow lighter. Then he saw it for what it really was.

It was a huge flock of starlings, hundreds and hundreds, perhaps thousands of them, wheeling and turning in flight above the water.

Birds. Not death. The hole was only birds. His knees gave way and he sat heavily on the still-warm sand.

Lupus knew that this moment had changed his life forever.

Now he knew what Hades was like. And he knew

he should be there now. For the first time Lupus wondered how he had been brought back from death.

And why.

'I think I've solved the mystery,' said Flavia to the others. 'The mystery of why Rufus and Dexter are trying to take our house.'

'Go on,' said Jonathan.

It was almost dark. A thousand starlings had flown in from the sea in a long dark ribbon, and were now roosting. The great mulberry tree above them quivered with birds.

'This is what I think happened,' said Flavia. 'After we captured Venalicius in Surrentum, Felix must have sent him to Ostia to stand trial.'

'That makes sense,' said Jonathan.

'And we know that your father and Venalicius were in a cell together for over a week, and that they talked about very . . . personal things. I think that's when Venalicius realised how much the four of us had to do with his arrest.'

'My father wouldn't betray us!' cried Jonathan.

'Not on purpose. But remember what Uncle Gaius said? If your father believed that Venalicius wanted to become good, he might tell Venalicius about himself and about us.'

'I don't believe Venalicius wants to be good,' said Nubia fiercely.

'Me neither,' said Flavia. 'People don't just change like that.'

'Sometimes they do,' said Jonathan. 'I've seen it.'

Flavia shook her head. 'It's far more likely that Venalicius took advantage of your father by *pretending* to be good. That way he could find out more about us in order to get revenge. After your father was set free, I'll bet Venalicius bribed Rufus to help him seize my father's possessions.'

'Why?' said Jonathan. 'Why would Venalicius do that?'

'To get revenge on us,' said Flavia. 'And to get money. They could sell our house.'

'Or,' said Nubia, and clutched Flavia's hand, 'Venalicius could be living in your house himself!'

It was dark now but Lupus remained on the shore, sitting cross-legged in the sand. Stars began to prick the deep violet dusk in the west. Behind him lay a deeper darkness. Before him was the sea.

He wanted to weep, but he couldn't. Deep within, a small, cold voice was speaking to him. Revenge, it said. That is what you were brought back for.

Jonathan had always told Lupus that God spoke to him in a small voice, like a clear thought.

This was a very clear thought.

It spoke again: Revenge.

Lupus shivered.

Somewhere, out in the cove, he heard a deep sigh and a soft splash. Then a whistle. He knew it was his dolphin. Delphinus was calling to him.

Come and swim with me, the dolphin seemed to whistle. Forget the voice that said Revenge.

Come and play.

But the dolphin's call came from outside himself, and Jonathan always said God was within.

Lupus could not move. Presently he heard the dolphin's chattering laugh and a resounding splash. Delphinus had done one of his flips.

Lupus longed to swim with his dolphin and be free. But he also wanted to do what was right and avenge his father. He wanted to rid the world of a monster. If he didn't, who would?

Delphinus whistled again, plaintively. The whistle was fainter. He was swimming away.

Lupus got to his feet. Don't go, he wanted to cry out. Wait! But he couldn't call, because he had no tongue. He would never speak again. The reminder of what his enemy had done to him gave the voice inside him greater strength. Now it seemed to fill his head.

Revenge, the voice seemed to shout. Revenge.

And the other voice – the dolphin's – had gone.

The Ides of October dawned warm and soft, with a milky haze floating like a blanket on the water. It would be another hot still day. In the garden courtyard a slave was standing over a pile of burning leaves. Despite the pleasantly acrid scent, autumn had not yet arrived at Laurentum.

Jonathan turned from his bedroom door and looked down at Lupus, still fast asleep in his bed. He had not heard his friend come in the night before and had been hugely relieved to find him there in the light of dawn.

Tigris was curled up at the foot of the boy's bed. Lupus was curled up too, with his knees right under his chin, and even in sleep he seemed to frown.

Jonathan tried to imagine what it must have been like for Lupus to have witnessed the murder of his father at the age of six. Would he ever be free of that anger and pain?

Jonathan closed his eyes. 'Please, Lord,' he whispered. 'Please help him get better.'

Lupus's eyes opened, and Jonathan gasped.

'Lupus! Your eye! It's all red and swollen!' He was going to add, 'like Venalicius' in the story!' but he swallowed the words.

Lupus sat up in bed. He blinked and rubbed his swollen eye, then shrugged. He slipped on his sea-green tunic, laced up his sandals and pulled a comb through his tousled hair. Then he tied the strip of linen around his head, covering his ears. Without looking at Jonathan, he stood and walked out of the room.

'Lupus, wait!' Jonathan followed him. Tigris stretched and trotted after them.

'Lupus!' said Jonathan. 'We need to talk. I don't mean *talk* . . . I mean . . . you know what I mean. You have to forgive him, Lupus. Otherwise you're only hurting yourself. I know it doesn't make sense but I know what I'm talking about. Lupus! Wait up! Where are you going? What do you want in the kitchen? What are you –? Why are you grinding up that disgusting dried fish? Don't tell me you're still after the treasure? Lupus, you nearly got killed by a giant octopus and drowned yesterday. Please tell me you're not going to dive again today!'

'Good morning, pater,' said Flavia, coming into the dim bedroom with a cup of hot milk mixed with spiced wine. Scuto padded after her.

She put the steaming cup on her father's bedside table. 'I've brought you a breakfast poculum.'

'Flavia.' Captain Geminus stretched and pushed himself up on his cushions. 'Good morning, sweetheart.'

'How do you feel?'

'Better, thank you, my little owl.' He took the cup and sipped. 'Mmmm,' he said. 'Yes, I feel much better today.'

'You need a shave,' observed Flavia. She wandered over to the east-facing window and pushed the lattice-work shutter. Bright morning light flooded the room. The sun had been up for two hours.

'It's going to be another hot day,' she murmured sleepily. She had been awake long into the night, thinking about Lupus.

She turned and padded across the room, opened the larger west-facing window, and stretched.

Abruptly she stopped, her arms pointing stiffly towards the ceiling.

She had heard something. The wet clop of oars from across the water.

Carefully, she gripped the window ledge and leaned out, scanning the low fog which blanketed the water.

Suddenly a figure rose up from the mist, looked around, then sank down again.

'Someone's out there.' Flavia frowned.

'What?' said her father.

Flavia leaned out a little further and gasped.

To her extreme right a ship was moving slowly towards Ostia. Within moments, it would be out of sight. But now its sail was still visible above the blanket of fog. The sail was striped yellow and black, like the colouring of a wasp.

It was the slave-ship *Vespa*.

SCROLL XXIII

'Help!' cried Flavia, running down the corridor. 'Venalicius and his men are after the treasure!'

She collided with Nubia, rushing out of the sea-view dining-room.

'Venalicius!' gasped Nubia, pointing back the way she had come. 'Behold his ship is there.'

'I know!' said Flavia. 'And I just saw a man in a rowing boat right where the treasure is. The ship must have brought him.'

'What is it?' said Miriam, pushing aside her bedroom curtain.

'Venalicius!' cried Flavia. 'I think he's after the treasure!'

'But how?' cried Pliny, coming up behind Nubia. He held a small bunch of grapes. 'How could he possibly have known it was there?'

'What's all the noise about?' asked Aristo, coming out of his bedroom across the courtyard.

'We think Venalicius is after the treasure!' cried Flavia.

Aristo stepped through the columns. 'Where's Lupus?'

'I tried to stop him,' gasped Jonathan, running into the courtyard. 'But he wouldn't listen. He saw Venalicius' ship too, He's down on the beach. And he has his knife with him.'

Lupus ran onto the beach just in time to confirm that it was the sail of the slave-ship *Vespa* disappearing behind the promontory. His sharp eyes scanned the low-lying fog and he saw what Flavia had seen, a dim figure looking about, then disappearing into the blanket of mist.

A grim smile spread across his face.

This time he was ready. He had his knife, as well as his sling and a pouch with some stones in it.

If he got to Venalicius soon he wouldn't have to bother diving for the gold. He wouldn't need to pay an assassin; he could do the job himself.

There was a small rowing boat in the boathouse. He would have to take that unless – yes! The old fisherman's boat was there on the shore, and Robur was sitting beside it, his head bent over something.

'Morning, young lad!' Robur looked up from mending his net. 'Where are you off to in such a hurry?'

Lupus pointed out to sea and then pointed at Robur's boat and himself and back out to sea.

'You want me to take you out?'

Lupus nodded vigorously.

'But I've only just brought her in. Nothing much out there today. The fish aren't biting in this fog.'

Lupus flipped open his wax tablet and wrote

I'LL PAY YOU

He held up the tablet.

'Sorry,' said Robur. 'Can't read.'

Lupus rubbed his thumb against his fingertips to signify money.

'Want to hire me, do you?' Robur put the net aside. 'You don't look rich, but I suppose if you're one of Pliny's house-guests you can afford it. Twenty sestercii.'

Lupus didn't have time to bargain but he knew if he agreed straight off, the fisherman might think he didn't really have the money. So he shook his head and held up both hands.

'Ten sestercii? Don't make me laugh.' Robur stood up. 'Eighteen. I'll take you out for eighteen.'

Lupus knew he should have gone for twelve sestercii, but the others would be here any minute. He had to get to Venalicius before they stopped him. So he nodded and held out his hand.

Robur squinted suspiciously at him for a moment, then shrugged and grasped Lupus's hand in his leathery paw.

They shook on it.

'He didn't take the little rowing boat . . . it's still in the boathouse,' Jonathan was wheezing as he reached the others by the water's edge. The mist made his asthma worse.

'And the big boat is right here,' said Pliny. He squinted out to sea. 'Too misty. I still can't see anything . . .'

'Here!' cried Flavia. She had been walking up and down the shore with her head down. 'The sand's been scraped here as if someone just pushed a boat out.'

'Behold!' cried Nubia, who had been following her. 'Small bare footprints. Not yet rubbed out by the foamy waves!' The dogs bounded up to investigate.

'And big ones, too,' said Flavia. 'That fisherman we saw a few days ago, the one who frightened Lupus with his octopus . . . What was his name?'

'Robur,' gasped Jonathan, still breathless. 'I'll bet he's taken Lupus out in his boat!'

'Quickly, then,' cried Pliny. 'Let's get this one in the water. Aristo, will you help me row?'

'Of course.' Aristo already had his shoulder to the boat.

As the sun shone down on the sea, it began to burn away the mist. Lupus, leaning over the prow, was only vaguely aware of its warmth on his back.

Behind him, Robur stood at the stern, using the big paddle to move them forward. Lupus could hear the clop and drip as the fisherman twisted it in the water, but his whole being was intent on searching the wisps of shredded fog ahead. Presently the mist thinned and he dimly saw a boat with two figures sitting in it.

Lupus turned and indicated the boat to Robur, who nodded, his black eyes gleaming.

'Looks like Phrixus has decided to catch his own fish,' chuckled the old fisherman. 'Who's that with him?'

Lupus turned back and peered at the figures in the boat. Robur was right: one of them was Phrixus, holding a line of some sort. He had lifted his head now, had seen them, and the rising sun showed the look of surprise on his face. He turned to the person in the boat beside him: a man wearing black robes and a dark turban.

Lupus stared.

The man in the boat with Phrixus was Jonathan's father Mordecai.

As he continued to stare, a figure broke the surface of the water nearby. It lifted its head to speak to Mordecai and Phrixus, then saw the direction of their gaze and turned to look at the approaching fishing boat.

The man's head was wrapped in strips of white linen, but his horrible blind eye was unmistakable.

Lupus's jaw dropped.

Mordecai and Phrixus were helping Venalicius dive for the treasure!

'I heard something!' said Flavia.

'Me too,' said Pliny, and stopped rowing for a moment. 'Shhh, everyone!'

'Good thing we left the dogs on the beach with Miriam,' murmured Jonathan.

'Hear that?' said Aristo. 'We're on the right track.'

'The plop of oar in water,' whispered Nubia, and the others nodded.

Lupus watched Venalicius disappear beneath the surface. He was diving again. He was trying to get their treasure!

Grimly, Lupus turned to Robur and pointed to the anchor. It was a large iron one, shaped like the Greek letters *psi* and *tau* stuck together. He mimed hanging onto it.

It could only be dropped once, like yesterday. He would have to make this dive count.

'You want me to drop anchor with you on it?' said Robur in astonishment. Lupus nodded.

'All right, but I hope you know what you're doing . . .'

Lupus was already stripping off his tunic, strapping a belt around his waist. His knife hung from it, and a leather pouch. This time he would be prepared. He didn't need a lifeline.

'Lupus, wait!' Mordecai shouted across the water. 'He's helping us! Venalicius wants to help!'

'It's true!' yelled Phrixus.

Lupus started his breathing exercises, splashed water on his face and neck, ignored Mordecai's ridiculous cries as he climbed out onto the anchor. He gave Robur a nod, then took a final deep breath as the anchor fell away.

He plummeted down, and gooseflesh sprang up all over his skin. The water was colder in the middle of the morning, and darker. As the pressure mounted he was aware of his left eye throbbing.

Down he went, gripping the cold iron anchor, and finally he saw the wreck, a black shape speeding up to meet him. At the right moment he pushed away from the anchor and let it continue on down.

He kicked out towards the wreck and as he came closer he saw his uncle Philippos, also known as Venalicius the slave-dealer.

'Father!' cried Jonathan. 'What are you doing here? Where's Lupus?'

The three boats had converged above the wreck; Jonathan and his friends in the sky-blue fishing boat, Robur in his battered yellow craft, and Mordecai and Phrixus in a red rowing boat Jonathan had never seen before.

'Venalicius is trying to recover the treasure for Lupus!' called Mordecai.

'WHAT?' yelled Jonathan and Flavia together.

'It's true. I've been trying to tell Lupus.' The boat rocked slightly as Mordecai stood up in it. ' Venalicius came to the house yesterday and asked me to baptise him.'

'What is baptise?' asked Nubia.

'A kind of ritual to wash away your past,' Jonathan told the girls. He turned back to his father: 'Has Venalicius really converted?'

'Without a doubt,' cried Mordecai. 'Gaius told us Lupus was risking his life trying to recover some treasure and Venalicius offered to dive for it himself. To prove his remorse.'

'No!' cried Nubia. 'Venalicius is evil.'

'She's right!' called Flavia. 'It must be a trick!'

'You're all missing the point,' cried Jonathan. 'Even if Venalicius has turned good, Lupus doesn't know that. And he probably doesn't care. He has a knife and he intends to use it!'

Lupus did not need to use his knife.

Framed by the breach, Venalicius was writhing desperately in the grip of a giant octopus. As the slave-dealer struggled, his good eye spotted Lupus and he held out one arm in a gesture of supplication.

If he hadn't been underwater, Lupus would have

laughed out loud. Instead, he gave his enemy the rudest gesture he knew and started up for the surface. How fitting that Venalicius should be killed by his own greed.

As Lupus swam away from the struggling pair, something blocked his ascent. Lupus looked up. It was Delphinus, the dolphin who had saved his life. The whimsical face passed inches from his and Lupus felt velvet-smooth skin caress his shoulder.

He waited until Delphinus had passed, then kicked for the surface again, but with a powerful twist of his body the dolphin again blocked his way. This time the fish nudged him gently back down. Back towards the man still struggling in the grip of the octopus. The dolphin seemed to smile and Lupus saw the look of intelligence in its deep blue eye.

Delphinus didn't know Venalicius was evil. He only knew someone needed help, as Lupus himself had needed help the day before. Lupus shrugged at the dolphin, as if to say, what can I do?

Delphinus opened his mouth in a smile and even underwater, Lupus heard him click. A few silver bubbles rose from the dolphin's head. Delphinus swam towards Lupus again, tipping his dorsal fin as he passed. Instinctively, Lupus caught hold of it and felt a joyful surge as the dolphin pulled him strongly back down towards the wreck.

But then the joy faded and Lupus's stomach

clenched. Venalicius was still alive and writhing in the grip of the octopus.

Lupus wasn't sure which of the two monsters repelled him most.

Delphinus swam close to them. As he passed, Lupus let go and kicked towards Venalicius and the octopus. He still didn't know what he was going to do.

He pulled the knife from his belt and glanced back at Delphinus, who was making another pass. He heard the dolphin's echoed plea, sweet and mournful.

Lupus made his decision.

He steeled himself, for what he was about to do was repulsive. But it was the only way.

He swam forward and sank his blade deep in the brute's eye.

SCROLL XXIV

Phrixus started pulling. 'I just felt three tugs on Venalicius' lifeline!' he said.

'But where's Lupus?' cried Flavia.

They all leaned forward and fixed their eyes on the dripping rope as Phrixus pulled it faster and faster.

Suddenly two heads broke the surface, both clinging to the same lifeline.

'Lupus!' cheered Flavia and Nubia. 'You're alive!'

'Lupus!' cheered Jonathan. 'You didn't kill Venalicius!'

Venalicius the slave-dealer squirmed on the couch of the sea-view triclinium. Blood oozed from his nose and the bandage wrapped round his head had blossoming stains of red, too. The girls squealed with horror and Mordecai hovered with a moist sea-sponge.

'Dear God, what is it?' he muttered. 'What on earth is happening to him?' He tried to staunch the flow.

Lupus knew. He had once seen a sponge-diver writhe and bleed like this after his tenth dive. Shortly afterwards paralysis had set in and the man had died. Lupus clenched his jaw hard to stop himself smiling. He had only saved Venalicius to please Delphinus. Now he was glad to see his enemy dying in agony.

'Lupus.' It was Miriam, standing beside her father; she had been watching him. 'Do you know what's wrong?'

Lupus sighed and wrote something on his tablet:

HOW MANY DIVES?

Mordecai squinted at the tablet. 'How many dives did Venalicius make this morning?'

Lupus nodded.

'I don't remember exactly,' he said. 'Ten or twelve.'

Phrixus nodded. 'We couldn't find the exact place, because of the fog. And the water was still very dark,' he explained. 'It took him several dives just to find the wreck . . .'

Venalicius' body convulsed again and he stifled a scream. Lupus knew the pain would only get worse, and that it would only be relieved by death. There was nothing anyone could do.

Lupus looked at Mordecai and slowly shook his head.

'Lukos?' cried Venalicius. 'Where's Lukos?'

'Who's Lukos?' Flavia was biting her thumbnail and shivering. She had her other arm around Nubia.

Lupus stepped forward. Venalicius saw him and clutched Lupus's wrist.

'Lukos,' the dying man gasped. 'I'm sorry.' He writhed and tried not to cry out. 'So sorry for what I did to you and the others.'

Venalicius began to weep tears of blood.

Flavia screamed and buried her face in Nubia's shoulder.

Lupus shuddered with revulsion and looked up from the dying man's twisted face. At that moment, Mordecai moved aside to dip the sponge in a bowl.

And Lupus found himself gazing directly into the eyes of Venalicius as a young boy.

SCROLL XXV

Lupus stared over the writhing body of the slave-dealer into the face of Venalicius as a child. The boy was about his own age, with a swollen eye and a linen band round his head and an ugly face full of hatred. What was happening? Was the madness of the deep upon him too?

Then he saw what he was looking at.

Himself.

He was looking at his own face, perfectly reflected in the mirrored shield held by the statue of Perseus.

With a terrible clarity Lupus realised that he was becoming the person he hated most: Venalicius.

No one else saw what he saw.

Mordecai was sponging the slave dealer's face and Miriam held the bowl. Flavia and Nubia were trying not to look. Jonathan, Aristo and Pliny were staring at the dying man in horrified fascination.

'Mother?' whispered Venalicius, looking up at Miriam. 'Mother? Is it you?' He tried to smile but only succeeded in contorting his face into a horrible grimace. Miriam glanced at her father and tried to smile down at the dying man.

'He's losing his sight,' whispered Mordecai.

'Lukos!' cried Venalicius suddenly. 'Where is my nephew?'

He tried to look round but his neck was paralysed. His good eye swivelled in its socket until it found Lupus.

'Please. Lukos. Forgive me?' The tears on Venalicius' cheek were no longer bloody, but the spark of life in his eye was fading fast.

Lupus did not feel the least desire to forgive. He was glad his uncle was dying. Perhaps if he refused the dying man's wish Venalicius would go to that place of utter darkness. That would be good. Lupus wanted Venalicius to suffer for eternity. He had saved Venalicius from the octopus. Surely that was enough.

He looked up again into the cold eyes of the boy reflected in the mirrored shield. His hatred made him like his enemy. And he did not want to become another Venalicius. That was too high a price to pay for revenge. He did not think his dead father or his living mother would want that.

'Forgive me, Lukos. Please.'

Lupus looked down at his hated enemy and gave a curt nod.

'Thank you.' Venalicius closed his eyes, smiling.

Suddenly Lupus felt a huge release. As if something

dark had pulled itself away from him and flown out between the spiral columns. And with the release came tears. Tears of relief, because his burden had been so great, and he was only a boy.

Venalicius was trying to speak but his paralysed lips barely moved. Lupus bent forward and his hot tears fell on the slave-dealer's face.

'Help . . .' said Venalicius, speaking in the language of his mother. 'Help the children . . . the ones I took.' And with his dying breath, still in Greek, Venalicius uttered one final word. To Lupus it sounded like:

'Rose.'

They burned his body the next day.

Gaius and Bato had travelled down from Ostia together. Mordecai pronounced Venalicius dead of natural causes and Bato made an official confirmation. The young magistrate offered to take the body away but Lupus held out his wax tablet.

HE WAS MY UNCLE

WE WILL PERFORM THE RITES

Pliny's slaves had already built the pyre on the shore and prepared the body. It lay in a litter on the terrace. Now four slaves dressed in black lifted it up.

In silence Lupus led the way across the terrace and

down through the gate towards the beach. It was a heavy, overcast day with a scent of rain in the air. A breeze ruffled the black garments of the slaves who carried the body. Behind them limped Captain Geminus, on his feet for the first time, steadying himself on his brother's arm. Mordecai and Miriam came next, followed by Nubia, Jonathan and Aristo. The dogs – including Gaius's huge hound Ferox – sensed the solemnity of the occasion and hardly wagged their tails at all.

As the procession slowly moved out of the triclinium, and Pliny moved to take up the rear, Flavia touched his arm.

'I have something to ask you,' she said.

He looked at her and then at the departing group.

'It will only take a moment,' said Flavia.

Pliny nodded.

Flavia held out the Dionysus kylix.

'How much will you give me for it?' she said, as calmly as she could.

Pliny slowly took the cup.

'Something like this,' he said, 'is impossible to value. It's worth whatever the buyer is willing to pay.' He caressed the cup with his fingertips and looked at her. 'Are you trying to raise a specific sum?' Even as he asked the question she saw understanding dawn on his face.

'Ah.' He tipped his head back and closed his eyes.

'One hundred thousand sestercii?' he asked without opening his eyes.

'Yes,' Flavia managed to say.

Pliny winced. His eyes were still closed. 'I haven't yet inherited my uncle's wealth. But I think I can raise that amount.' He took a deep breath and opened his eyes again. 'Very well, Flavia Gemina.'

Flavia exhaled with relief. When she thought she could speak with a steady voice she said,

'Can you find a way of paying my father's debts without him knowing it was me? If he knew, he would feel . . .' she couldn't think of the right words.

'Of course,' said Pliny. 'I understand. Bato and I will arrange it. We will be very discreet. No one else will know.'

'Thank you,' Flavia whispered and turned to follow the others. Quickly. So he wouldn't see the tears.

'Flavia.' He stopped her with a hand on her shoulder. 'You know I'll take very good care of this cup.'

'Yes,' said Flavia, without turning her head. 'I know.'

The body was burning fiercely when suddenly the heavens opened and the rain began to fall. It was a soft, autumn rain and they were not too wet by the time they ran back into the triclinium, shaking out their cloaks and brushing drops from their tunics.

Pliny's kitchen slaves had already laid out the funeral banquet. It was midday and the meal would serve as both breakfast and dinner. They settled down to the meal of cold ham, pickled fish and chickpea pancakes.

As usual, Nubia and her friends sat at the table. The dogs had all gathered underneath; they knew the best place for tasty morsels. The remaining seven adults reclined on the couches: Aristo and Bato on one couch, Miriam and her father on another, and Pliny flanked by the Geminus brothers on the central couch. The welcome rain had led to a discussion of the effect of the volcano on weather patterns and the Roman economy.

Nubia looked out through the pink columns at the pearly grey sky. She was not listening to the adults' conversation but to the music of the rain as it drummed on the parapet, dripped from the eaves and gurgled in the gutters. It seemed to be telling a story as it muttered rhythmically. If only she could understand its song.

She kneaded Ferox's warm neck with her toes, just the way he liked it, and heard him sigh with pleasure. Then she turned back to her cold ham.

'I've just had some very good news,' Bato was saying to Captain Geminus, who reclined beside him on the couch. 'An anonymous benefactor has promised to pay your debts in full. Your house is safe.'

Nubia frowned. 'What's an ominous –'

'It means someone has given him lots of money but we don't know who,' Jonathan whispered.

'Praise the gods,' whispered Flavia's father, and Nubia saw him drop his head to hide the emotion on his face. She wondered who had been so generous.

'It turns out Rufus and Dexter really needed the money,' said Gaius. 'One of their biggest loans was to a man who died in the eruption. He lost his entire estate as well as his family. They may not be good bankers, but at least they're not crooks.'

Bato sipped his wine. 'The volcano hit some people very hard.'

'It did indeed,' murmured Gaius, with a quick glance at Miriam, reclining beside her father.

There was a moment of silence and then Aristo said to Marcus, 'But it's wonderful news that the house is safe.'

'It's not all good news, I'm afraid,' said Gaius. 'I went to the slave sale in the forum yesterday. I'm afraid your brother was sold, Nubia. A representative from the school in Capua bought the whole lot for one hundred and fifty thousand sestercii.'

Nubia put down her pancake. She felt numb.

'What school in Capua?' said Jonathan.

Gaius looked at him. 'The gladiator school.'

Flavia said, 'Maybe we could buy him back . . . if we dive for that treasure and –'

'No!' cried Aristo, Pliny and Gaius together.

'No more diving for treasure!' said Flavia's father. 'It's too dangerous.'

And Pliny added, 'I think the gods have made it very clear that they don't want that wreck disturbed.'

'Besides,' said Jonathan, 'father says that if Lupus dives again soon he could lose the sight in his left eye.'

They all looked at Lupus, who put down his cup and looked back at them.

'Your eye looks a little better,' said Miriam. 'The swelling's going down.'

'No diving for a few months, though,' said Mordecai. 'Swimming is permitted. But no diving. Understood?'

Lupus nodded and resumed drinking the warmed poculum they had made specially for him.

'Also,' said Captain Geminus, 'it looks as if autumn has finally come. There'll be no diving or sailing now for several months.'

'That reminds me,' said Mordecai, lifting himself a little higher on one elbow. 'I have some very good news for Lupus. Before we left Ostia, Venalicius took me to the forum and we drew up a will in the presence of witnesses. I think he had a premonition of his death.'

They all looked at Mordecai. 'He left you everything, Lupus, including his ship. You are now the owner of the slave-ship Vespa.'

Lupus stared back at Mordecai.

'I guess Venalicius really did turn good in the end,' murmured Flavia.

'Told you so,' said Jonathan.

Nubia felt a strange tangle of emotions: anger, relief, confusion.

'You are not old enough to officially inherit yet,' Mordecai was telling Lupus, 'so the money has been left in trust to me, as your guardian, until you put on the toga virilus at sixteen. As for the *Vespa*, I will do whatever you like with it. Sell it, burn it, whatever.'

Nubia's heart was pounding. She looked at Lupus and he looked back at her.

After a moment he wrote something on his wax tablet.

Jonathan picked it up and read it out for all to hear:

I WOULD LIKE TO RENAME THE SHIP
AND LET FLAVIA'S FATHER USE IT FOR HIS
VOYAGES

Nubia felt a wave of relief wash over her. Yes. Let that ship which had caused so much misery be used for good.

Mordecai smiled. 'A wise decision,' he said. 'And as owner, half the profits will go to you. Is that correct, Marcus?'

But Flavia's father seemed unable to speak.

'Pater!' cried Flavia. 'Did you hear that? Lupus is going to let you sail his boat!'

'Yes,' said Captain Geminus at last. 'I heard.'

'By Hercules,' said Jonathan. 'You're rich, Lupus.'

'What will you be naming her?' asked Nubia quietly.

Lupus thought for a moment. Then he smiled.

DELPHINUS he wrote.

'You should really give a ship a girl's name,' said Flavia. 'Otherwise it's bad luck.'

Lupus pursed his lips. Then he used the flat end of his stylus to rub out and the sharp end to make a small change.

DELPHINA

They all laughed and Lupus added:

WE WILL CLEAN HER UP & GET A NEW SAIL A WHITE ONE WITH A DOLPHIN ON IT

'I am glad,' said Nubia. 'I am hating that black and yellow one.'

SCROLL XXVI

The sun came out and glazed the wet columns and dripping roof-tiles with gold.

'Come on,' said Pliny. 'I have something I want to show you. All of you,' he added, looking at Miriam. 'It's not far, half a mile up the drive. We'll take the carruca.'

Pliny took the reins with Aristo on one side and Phrixus on the other. The rest of them squeezed onto the benches on either side. Ferox lay on the floor at his master's feet, and as Pliny flicked the reins and the horses moved off, Scuto and the puppies zigzagged behind the cart, sniffing the shrubs either side of the drive.

'All this land belongs to me now,' said Pliny, over his shoulder. He shifted the reins to his left hand and indicated with his right. 'It's mainly pasture for the sheep and cattle.'

He turned and pointed through the umbrella pines towards the sea. They could see the red rooftops of other villas.

'Most of that land belongs to my neighbours. But

here, where our drive meets the main road, we have a small plot of land and a lodge. My uncle tried to grow exotic vegetables and vines here once, when he was researching volume twelve of his *Natural History*.'

Pliny pulled the reins and the carruca rocked to a halt.

'Here we are,' he said. 'This little vineyard and those three olive trees belong to us. And there's the lodge.' He handed the reins to Phrixus, jumped down and walked round to the back of the carruca.

Scuto and the puppies were sniffing the dripping vines with great interest and Ferox joined them as Pliny helped the others out of the carriage.

Flavia could smell the musky scent of fox, and the rich aroma of damp earth. Somewhere in one of the olive trees a bird let forth a sweet trill. The early afternoon sun washed the wet vine leaves with liquid gold.

Flavia smiled at Pliny as he helped her down, then she took her father's arm, allowing him to lean on her. The boys ran ahead to explore the lodge and the rest of them strolled through the dripping vine rows after them.

Pliny fell into step beside Gaius, who walked ahead of Flavia and her father.

'The vines have gone a bit wild,' Pliny said. 'But at least they've been harvested.'

He stopped and uttered an oath. 'By Hercules!

Those peasant boys and their graffiti! What is today's youth coming to?' He glanced at Gaius and started walking again. 'As you can see, the lodge has suffered the lack of a tenant. But with a little work . . . and look! It has its own well.'

Jonathan and Lupus appeared between the two wooden columns of the small porch. 'It smells like something's died in here,' yelled Jonathan. 'We're trying to find the carcass!' They disappeared again.

Flavia's uncle Gaius stopped and fingered one of the grape leaves. 'They're getting the blight. You want to attend to this quickly, before it spreads.'

'No,' said Pliny, stopping and turning to Gaius. '*You* want to attend to it quickly.' He spread his hands, palms out. 'I need a tenant farmer and I think you would do very well. It needs a bit of work but I'm sure you're up to it. You and Miriam may have the lodge and land rent free. All I ask is that you give me half your output of wine each year. And that you invite me to the wedding.'

Gaius stared at him, then his face broke into a delighted smile.

Pliny smiled, too. 'Do you accept?'

'Oh Uncle Gaius!' cried Flavia, squeezing her father's arm in her excitement. 'Say "yes". You'd be so close to us and we could visit you and Miriam and it would be so wonderful.'

'Of course! I can't begin to . . . I mean –' Gaius

turned to Miriam and swallowed. 'Miriam, do you like it?' He gestured towards the lodge. Ferox had lowered himself into a patch of sunlight beside the well and was panting gently with his eyes half closed.

Miriam did not turn to look at the lodge. Her shining eyes had not left Gaius's face.

'Yes,' whispered Miriam, taking his hand in hers. 'I like it.'

Lupus had never written so much in his life.

When they had returned to Pliny's villa, he had gone into the library and found papyrus and ink. Now his hand ached and he was developing a callous on the ink-stained middle finger of his right hand. But he had finished. He had written it out. And it felt . . . not good. But better. Better to know his friends would finally know what had happened. He put the sheet of papyrus on the bedside table where Jonathan would be sure to see it. Then he walked down to the beach.

Maybe the dolphins would be there.

FATHER AND I HAD BEEN OUT NIGHT-FISH-ING. WE CAUGHT LOTS OF GOOD FISH AND ONE OCTOPUS. MOTHER HATED OCTOPUS. I USED TO TEASE HER. I COULD MAKE HER SCREAM BY HOLDING ONE UP WHEN SHE DIDN'T EXPECT IT. MAYBE FATHER DIDN'T KNOW THAT.

WHEN WE GOT BACK AT DAWN, FATHER WENT INSIDE AND MOTHER SCREAMED. I SAW THAT A MAN WAS THERE. HE AND FATHER WERE FIGHTING. THERE WAS A KNIFE IN THE MAN'S HAND BUT THEN FATHER TOOK IT AND PUSHED THE MAN AGAINST THE WALL. I KNEW HE WAS MY UNCLE PHILIPPOS THEY SOMETIMES TALKED ABOUT.

MY UNCLE SCREAMED AND GOT THE KNIFE BACK SO I JUMPED ON HIM. I TRIED TO PULL HIM AWAY BUT THEN I WAS ON THE FLOOR AND ALL I COULD SEE WAS THEIR FEET AND A DEAD OCTOPUS WAS LYING IN THE BLOOD STARING AT ME.

THE ROOM WAS ROCKING LIKE A BOAT. I FELT SICK. THEN FATHER WAS ON THE FLOOR TOO. HE WAS SO WHITE AND THERE WAS SO MUCH BLOOD AND I SAW MY FATHER'S EYES. THEY WERE DEAD LIKE THE OCTOPUS.

I HEARD A VOICE SCREAMING YOU KILLED HIM YOU KILLED MY FATHER! I'LL TELL ON YOU! IT WAS ME. THE VOICE WAS ME.

MY UNCLE TURNED AND CAME TOWARDS ME. HE HAD THE KNIFE IN HIS HAND. I DON'T REMEMBER WHAT HAPPENED NEXT.

LATER IN THE BOAT SOME SAILORS SAID
THAT I WOULD DIE IF THEY DIDN'T STOP
THE BLEEDING. DO YOU WANT TO LIVE
THEY ASKED ME. I NODDED. I WANTED TO
LIVE SO I COULD KILL MY UNCLE.

YOU HAVE TO BE BRAVE SAID THE SAILOR.
BRAVER THAN YOU'VE EVER BEEN IN YOUR
LIFE. THIS SPOON IS RED HOT FROM THE
COALS, SAID THE SAILOR. I HAVE TO PUSH IT
AGAINST THE PLACE WHERE YOUR TONGUE
HAS BEEN CUT OUT. THE ONLY WAY I CAN
DO THAT IS IF YOU OPEN YOUR MOUTH AND
LET ME. DO YOU UNDERSTAND?

SO I OPENED MY MOUTH BECAUSE I
THOUGHT IT COULDN'T HURT ANY MORE
THAN IT ALREADY DID BUT I WAS WRONG.

Nubia stood by the parapet and gazed out over the
water as Mordecai read the message Jonathan had
found by his bed.

'I think it's good he shared this with you,' said
Mordecai, as he finished. 'It means the healing can
begin.'

'Incredible to think what he's been through,' said
Aristo quietly. 'How he lost his family.'

'We're his family now,' said Flavia firmly. 'And now
that he has his own ship we can go and rescue all the

children that Venalicius captured. Rose and the others. Can't we, pater?'

Marcus gave her a weak smile. 'Lupus is the owner now. He can do what he likes.'

'I think Lupus will be all right,' said Jonathan.

'I think Lupus will be very all right,' said Nubia from the parapet. 'Behold!'

They all moved to the marble half-wall and gazed out over the blue Tyrrhenian Sea.

Far out in the water, silhouetted against the setting sun, they saw a sight none of them would ever forget.

It was a boy riding a dolphin.

FINIS

THE LAST SCROLL

Pliny the Younger is the only real person in this story. He was Admiral Pliny's nephew, aged seventeen when he witnessed the eruption of Vesuvius in AD 79. Many years later he wrote about the eruption in a letter to the Roman historian Tacitus. Pliny the Younger is famous today because of the letters he wrote. He published most of them in his lifetime, hoping that they might bring him lasting fame. He got his wish.

In another of his letters, Pliny the Younger describes his beautiful seaside villa on the coast at Laurentum near Ostia. His description is so captivating that many people over the centuries have tried to find or recreate Pliny's 'Laurentine villa'. There is a site a few miles south of Ostia called Villa di Plinio, but scholars are not sure whether this was really Pliny's villa or not.

My plan at the front of this book is based on many speculative plans and on the seventeenth letter in Pliny's second scroll.

In ancient times, sponge-divers were often crippled or even killed by their profession.

THE TWELVE
TASKS OF
FLAVIA GEMINA

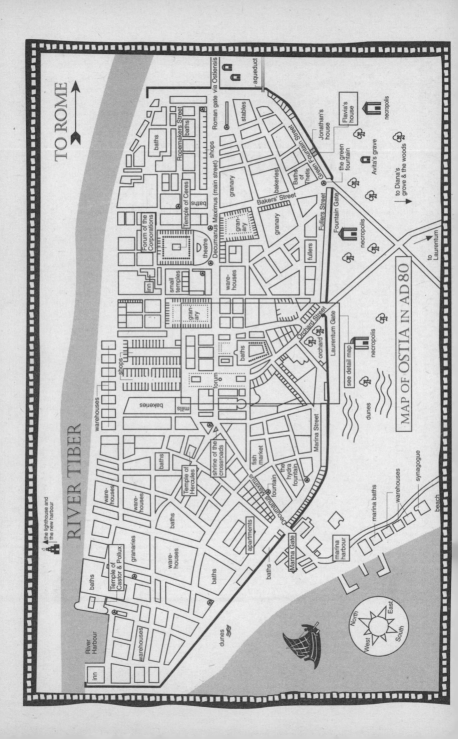

TO ROME

RIVER TIBER

the lighthouse and
the new harbour

River Harbour

inn

baths

Temple of
Castor & Pollux

granaries

ware-
houses

ware-
houses

warehouses

warehouses

baths

ware-
houses

baths

baths

Temple of Hercules

shrine of the
crossroads

apartments

Marina Gate

baths

marina harbour

marina baths

warehouses

synagogue

beach

Decumanus Maximus

fountain

the hydra fountain

fish market

shops

bakeries

mills

forum

granary

Forum of the
Corporations

Temple of Ceres

baths

theatre

small temples

inn

Decumanus Maximus (main street)

Ropemakers Street

baths

shops

Roman gate via Ostiensis

stables

aqueduct

granary

granary

granary

Bakers' Street

bakeries

fullers

warehouses

baths

Orchard Street

orchard

Laurentum Gate

see detail map

dunes

necropolis

Marina Street

Fullers Street

Fountain Gate

necropolis

necropolis

Green Fountain Street

Baths of Thetis

Jonathan's house

Flavia's house

necropolis

the green fountain

Avita's grave

to Diana's grove & the woods

to Laurentum

dunes

North
West   East
South

MAP OF OSTIA IN AD 80

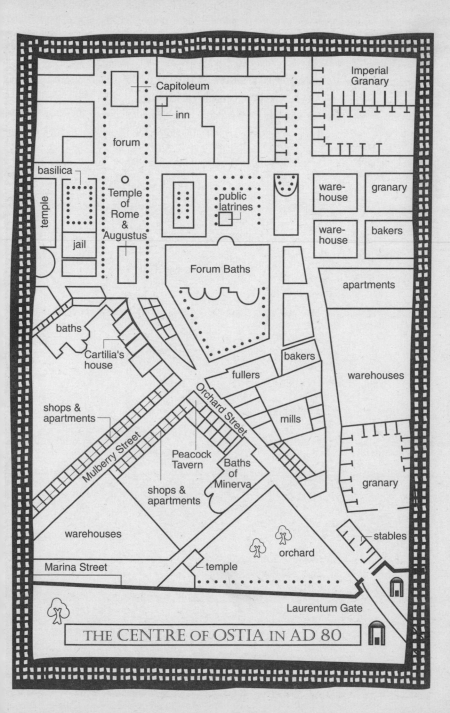

THE CENTRE OF OSTIA IN AD 80

To my sister Jennifer,
who loves wisely and well

SCROLL I

The day Flavia Gemina learned she was to be married began like any other winter day in the Roman port of Ostia.

When Flavia awoke, shortly after dawn, the sky showed as pearly pink diamonds through the lattice-work screen of her window. She could hear rain gurgling in the gutters and there was a delicious fresh-ness in the air: the smell of rich earth and wet brick. Flavia snuggled deeper under her woollen blanket and wormed her feet beneath her dog Scuto's warm bulk. Today was the day of her uncle's betrothal feast and tomorrow they were preparing for the festival of the Saturnalia, which would last five days. So there would be no lessons for a whole week.

Presently, the scent of spiced wine and scalded milk brought Flavia padding downstairs to the kitchen, her blanket wrapped round her. Scuto trailed behind, tail wagging absently.

'Good morning, dear,' said Flavia's old nurse Alma, pouring hot milk into a ceramic cup half-filled with spiced wine. 'Cheese or barley?'

'Both, please,' said Flavia. 'And a little pepper. Does pater have his poculum yet?'

'Yes,' said Alma, sprinkling cheese and barley onto the steaming liquid. 'I took it to him a few moments ago.' She passed a cube of cheese over a silver grater so that melting curls covered the surface of the drink.

'There you are, my dear.' Alma handed the poculum to Flavia.

'Thanks,' murmured Flavia and sipped the warming drink. She ate some of the cheese-coated barley floating on top and reflected that she liked a drink she could chew. The barley made her think of Pistor the baker. She and her friends had spent most of November trying to discover who had been stealing his poppy seed rolls. Flavia liked mysteries, and in solving Pistor's case she had proved to herself that she really was a detective.

Her blanket still trailing behind, Flavia took her spiced drink out of the kitchen and along the peristyle to her father's study. On the other side of the red-based columns, rain fell softly on the inner garden. The fig tree had lost its leaves but the shrubs nodded under the rain's caress. Scuto wandered over to the quince bush to perform his morning ablutions.

'Morning, Caudex.'

'Morning, Miss Flavia.' The big door-slave was standing on a small wooden stool, winding spirals of glossy ivy round the columns.

'That looks nice.' Flavia nodded her approval.

Caudex grunted.

On this mid-December day the rooms of the house were dimmer than usual. But in the study, a standing

422

oil-lamp added its golden glow to the pearly light filtering in from the garden. Beside the lamp was a copper brazier filled with glowing coals.

'Morning, pater.'

'Good morning, my little owl.' Marcus Flavius Geminus sat hunched over his desk, his toga draped round his shoulders like a blanket. He shot her a fond but distracted smile.

Flavia curled up on the old leather chair, tucking her feet up and pulling her blanket around her. For a moment she warmed her hands on the cup as she watched her father work.

She was still not used to his short hair. Two months ago the doctor had cut off his matted, lice-ridden locks, but at that time her father had been too weak to dedicate his hair to the sea god. So last week he had shaved off the new growth and offered it at the Temple of Neptune to thank the god for sparing his life in a shipwreck. Now, his short hair and the new lines on his forehead made him look older. His face reminded Flavia of her grandfather's death mask in the household shrine.

Next door in the atrium, she could hear the rain gushing from lion-mouthed terracotta gutters and splashing into the pool beneath the skylight. From upstairs drifted the sound of flute and lyre. Flavia's ex-slave-girl Nubia and their tutor Aristo practised together every morning before breakfast. Aristo said he found it easiest to compose music straight after waking.

Scuto padded into the study from the garden, leaving wet pawprints on the marble veneer floor. He sighed and sank heavily beneath the brazier. Soon the comforting smell of wet dog filled the room. It occurred to Flavia that, like her father, Scuto was also getting old.

'Pater?' Flavia took another sip of her hot spiced drink.

'Yes, sweetheart,' he said absently, his head bent over a papyrus tally sheet.

'Pater, have the sands of time just about run out for you?'

He gave her an amused glance. 'I'm only thirty-one,' he said. 'I trust I have a few years left.' He looked back at his sums and frowned.

'Pater?'

'Yes, Flavia?'

'Pater, are we poor now?'

Her father sighed and put down his quill pen and turned to face her.

'I mean,' said Flavia, 'they won't take our house away, will they?'

'No, my little owl. They won't take the house away. A gift from an anonymous benefactor saved our house.'

Flavia nodded. Her father still didn't know that she herself was the unknown donor.

'As for our daily living expenses,' he said, 'I may have to sell the divine Vespasian. Titus, too.'

'Oh no!' said Flavia, looking at the marble busts of the current emperor and his scowling father. 'I like them. I like things just the way they are. Don't change anything.'

He sighed. 'My only other option is to ask my patron Cordius to lend us enough money to see us through the winter.' Her father shook his head. 'Usually at this time of year I've plenty of cash on deposit with my bankers. But I'd invested everything in that cargo of spices and when it went down with the *Myrtilla* . . .' His voice trailed off and he stared down at the sheets on his desk.

Flavia could guess what he was thinking. Her father had named his ship after Flavia's mother, Myrtilla, who had died in childbirth seven years previously. Now he had lost both Myrtillas.

'But you can use the ship Lupus inherited, can't you?' said Flavia in her brightest voice.

'Yes.' Her father smiled. 'But the *Delphina* needs some work done to her before the sailing season begins. And we'll need to perform the purification ceremony. That means purchasing a bull: another vast expense.' Her father's chair scraped on the marble veneer floor as he pushed it back. 'Flavia.' He stood.

'Yes, pater?'

'Flavia, you must be very discreet. You must not let anyone know that we are in debt. If people know we're struggling financially, they'll take advantage of us. I may even be stripped of my rank as an equestrian. We must behave as if we are prosperous, but without spending anything more than is absolutely necessary.' Her father tugged at the folds of his toga to make them hang properly over his shoulder.

'I understand, pater,' said Flavia with a sigh. She had been planning to ask him for money to buy

Saturnalia gifts for her friends, but now that looked impossible.

Her face brightened as Nubia appeared in the doorway, holding a steaming cup.

'Good morning, Nubia!'

'Good morning, Flavia.' Nubia sipped her drink and watched her puppy Nipur romp into the study. He was pure black, almost as big as Scuto and still growing. He greeted Flavia and her father with wagging tail and acknowledged Scuto with a brief sniff. Then he hurried back into the garden to see if the rain had brought out any snails.

A young man appeared beside Nubia in the wide doorway. Their tutor Aristo was a handsome Greek with intelligent brown eyes and curly hair the colour of dark bronze. Today he was wearing a thick, oatmeal-coloured tunic, leather boots, and a short red cape. A net was slung over his left shoulder and in his right hand he held a light spear.

'I'm just off hunting,' he said. 'I'll be back in time for . . .' He took a deep breath. 'I'll be back by the seventh hour.'

Captain Geminus gave Aristo a grateful look. 'May Diana give you luck with the hunt,' he said. 'I believe we ate the last of your friend's quail pie yesterday afternoon.'

'I'll try to catch us a big boar for the Saturnalia.' Aristo disappeared towards the back door.

'I'm off now, too,' said Flavia's father. 'Going to the barber and then to see my patron Cordius. I'll be back in a few hours. Oh, Flavia. Hercules the wall-painter is coming today to make a start on the new fresco in the dining-room.'

'A wall-painter? I thought you said we had to be careful with our money.'

'He's doing it *gratis*. He owes me a favour,' said Flavia's father, and added, 'I gave him free passage to Sicily last year. Besides, it will give the impression that we're well off. He doesn't celebrate the Saturnalia so he'll be working here over the next week.'

'Imagine not celebrating the best festival of all,' murmured Flavia.

'Goodbye, sweetheart.' Flavia's father bent to kiss her forehead. 'Goodbye, Nubia.' He disappeared into the atrium and a moment later Flavia heard the front door close and the bolt fall into place.

Nubia lingered in the peristyle, looking anxiously towards the back door. 'I hope Aristo is joking,' she said. 'I hope there are no foaming boars in the woods today.'

'He looked sad,' remarked Flavia. 'And the music you were playing was sad, too.'

'I know. He is wretched because of today, because he is still loving Miriam.' Nubia shivered.

Flavia opened her blanket. 'Come and sit beside me, Nubia.'

Nubia squeezed onto the chair and pulled her side of the blanket round. 'It is most chilly,' she said.

Flavia knew that Nubia was used to the dry desert heat, not damp Italian winters. And this winter was particularly damp and cold. Everyone blamed the weather on the volcano which had erupted at the end of August. Flavia's nurse Alma said it was just laziness: 'They'll be blaming Vesuvius for everything that happens over the next twenty years,' she had grumbled. 'I've known colder winters.'

But Nubia obviously hadn't. She was still shivering.

'You should wear more than one tunic,' said Flavia, putting her arm round Nubia's shoulder and rubbing briskly. 'Like the divine Emperor Augustus. He used to wear five tunics in the winter.'

'Yes. I will do that.'

'And we'll go to the baths later,' promised Flavia. 'After we've been to the market.'

'Good,' said Nubia. 'I will sit in the steamy sudatorium.'

A loud knocking on the front door brought Scuto to his feet and Nipur in from the garden. They skittered across the study and into the atrium.

Flavia heard Caudex grumbling in the peristyle, so she called out, 'We'll get it, Caudex!'

Leaving the blanket on the chair, she and Nubia went into the atrium and past the rainwater pool to the oak door with its heavy bolt. Scuto and Nipur were scrabbling at the wood. They could smell their friend Tigris on the other side.

The door swung open to reveal two boys and a puppy standing in the shelter of the porch. They were dripping wet and their breath came in excited white puffs.

'Just come from shopping in the forum . . .' Jonathan, the taller of the two, suffered from asthma. 'You'll never guess . . . what happened!' he gasped. 'The whole town is . . . talking about it! Ship from Alexandria . . . delayed by storms . . . carrying animals for the games . . .'

Lupus – the younger boy – was making marks on a tablet, nodding as he wrote. He had no tongue and a wax tablet was his main form of communication.

'Animals . . .' Jonathan was leaning on the door frame. 'Wild, ravenous beasts . . . the lion knocked the trainer . . . off the gangplank and . . . all the animals escaped!'

'A lion?' breathed Flavia. She and Nubia exchanged wide-eyed looks.

'Other animals, too . . .' Jonathan was still breathless.

'What animals?' asked Nubia.

'You tell them, Lupus,' gasped Jonathan.

This was the moment Lupus had been waiting for. He held up his wax tablet and Flavia squealed as she read what he had written:

ESCAPED ANIMALS!!!
LION
CAMELOPARD
ELEPHANT
AND A GIANT MAN–EATING BIRD!!!

SCROLL II

'A giant man-eating bird?' cried Flavia. 'Like the Stymphalian bird Hercules had to kill in the myth?'

Lupus nodded emphatically. One of his eyes was slightly bloodshot.

'Did you behold it?' Nubia asked.

'No,' said Jonathan, stepping into the atrium. 'But Decimus the scroll-seller's son did. He said the bird was twice as big as a man, with a huge body, a long neck and evil yellow eyes.'

Lupus followed Jonathan into the atrium and bared his teeth fiercely.

'Oh, yes,' said Jonathan, 'and lots of sharp teeth!'

'A bird is having teeth?' said Nubia.

Jonathan shrugged. 'According to Decimus.'

'Have they caught any of the animals yet?' asked Flavia. She closed the door and made sure the bolt was down.

'No,' said Jonathan. 'That's why we came straight here. To warn you not to walk the dogs or go gathering ivy like yesterday. Apparently the elephant headed straight down the Decumanus Maximus towards Rome but the other animals ran along the beach towards the synagogue. They may have reached

430

Laurentum by now. Or maybe they're hiding in the woods.'

'Oh, I wish I'd seen the elephant running down the main street!' said Flavia.

'Aristo!' cried Nubia. Her fingers were digging into Flavia's arm.

'What about him?' said Jonathan.

'He is hunting,' said Nubia. 'In the woods.'

'And all he has to protect himself,' cried Flavia, 'is a javelin and a net!'

Nubia's eyes were as round as gold coins. 'We must warn him!'

'Are you crazy?' said Jonathan. 'A bird as big as Ostia's lighthouse and a man-eating lion and a camelopard . . .'

'What is a camelopard, anyway?' asked Flavia, leading them along the corridor towards the kitchen.

Lupus shrugged and Jonathan said: 'I don't know. I thought you might.'

'We'd better look it up in Pliny's *Natural History*,' said Flavia. 'But first, do you two want a hot poculum?'

The boys nodded and followed her into the kitchen.

'Alma!' said Flavia. 'There are some wild animals loose in the woods. They ran off a ship this morning!'

'Oh dear, oh dear,' Alma tutted. 'Not the first time that's happened. You'd better not go into the woods today. Barley or cheese for you, Wolfie?'

Lupus shook his head. Although the name Lupus meant 'wolf', Alma was the only person he allowed to call him 'Wolfie'.

The friends lingered in the small kitchen, unwilling to leave the warmth of the glowing hearth. Alma didn't seem to mind. As the boys sipped their drinks, she turned back to her mortarium and continued grinding chestnuts into flour.

'So tell us what happened again,' said Flavia. 'How did the animals escape?'

Jonathan put his cup down and wiped a cheesy pink moustache from his upper lip. 'Well, they think the ship from Alexandria was delayed by storms. Everyone was amazed to see a ship sail into the harbour in December. They must have run out of food. Decimus said the animals were ravenous.'

Lupus roared.

'Yes,' said Jonathan. 'Decimus and his father were just setting up their bookstall in the forum when they heard this enormous roar, coming from the direction of the river harbour. They ran to the Marina Gate just in time to see the giant bird run past. And then the lion. Decimus's father said he thought the lion was a Nubian lion.'

Flavia frowned. 'A Nubian lion? What does a Nubian lion look like, Nubia? Nubia?'

Jonathan, Lupus and Flavia looked round the small red kitchen and then out through the ivy-twined columns into the wet green garden.

But Nubia was nowhere to be seen.

'She always does that!' said Jonathan, hitting his forehead with the heel of his hand. 'I wish she'd teach me how to disappear like that.'

Lupus nodded.

'Nubia!' called Flavia. 'NUBIA!'

All they heard was the steady sound of the rain on the terracotta roof tiles.

'She's probably just gone upstairs to put on some more tunics,' said Flavia. 'Let's look for her.'

But as they headed for the stairs, Jonathan glanced towards the back door.

'You don't think . . .' he murmured. The others followed his gaze. The back door of Flavia's house was built into the town wall; it led directly into the tombs of the necropolis and the woods beyond. As the three friends moved closer, they could see by a thread of light that it was wedged open.

'Oh no!' cried Flavia.

'She wouldn't be foolish enough to . . .' Jonathan shook his head. 'I mean, why would she go into the woods when she knows there might be savage beasts lurking there?'

'Aristo!' cried Flavia. 'She's gone to warn Aristo!'

Lupus barked, then gestured round the garden and shrugged dramatically, his palms to the sky.

'You're right, Lupus. She's taken the dogs with her.'

Jonathan turned to them grimly. 'Lupus, you get your sling. I'll get my bow and arrow. We've got to go after her.'

'Well, you're not going without me,' said Flavia. 'Just wait while I get my cloak.'

Nubia followed the three dogs into the woods. The rain was lighter under the shelter of the umbrella pines

433

but already there was cold mud squelching between her toes; she was only wearing her house sandals.

'Aristo!' she called. 'Aristo, come back!'

She knew he must be somewhere nearby; he had only left a few moments ago. 'Aristo! There are wild beasts!'

Her heart was thudding against her ribs and her teeth were chattering. It was not the cold that made her tremble as much as a strange feeling in the pit of her stomach.

Nubia stopped and tried to still the chattering of her teeth so she could listen. Then, as her father had taught her, she reached out with all her senses, not just her sense of hearing.

Presently she had the impression that she should go straight ahead and a little to the left. She knew that this feeling – however vague – was her intuition, so she obeyed it. She moved forward, not calling out now, just listening. The dogs sensed her mood and followed her quietly. Like shadows, they slipped between the rain-glazed trunks of the pine trees. The fine drizzle had stilled all birdsong; the woods were utterly silent.

Then she heard it. A rustling in some myrtle bushes up ahead. Something was moving towards her. Something big.

Cautiously, Nubia moved forward and peered round the wet trunk of an acacia tree. And gasped.

SCROLL III

Lupus was several paces ahead of his two friends when suddenly Scuto exploded out of the woods.

'Here's Scuto!' said Jonathan.

But Flavia's dog did not stop to greet them. He ran yelping back towards the town walls. Flavia and Jonathan turned and watched him with amazement.

'I've heard the expression "tail between his legs" before,' Flavia said. 'But I'd never actually seen it until now. Look! Here come the puppies!'

The two puppies raced past the three friends after Scuto. Then Nubia emerged from the woods, her cloak flapping behind her.

'Run!' she cried. 'Big bird is pursuing me!'

Lupus's jaw dropped as a huge black and white bird loped out of the woods and stopped to regard him with an enormous long-lashed eye. It had a long white neck and muscular legs. The huge bird clacked its beak and ambled towards him.

'Aaaaah!' Lupus yelled. He turned and ran as fast as he could back towards the safety of the town. He didn't need to urge Flavia and Jonathan to run. They were well ahead of him.

*

'Man-eating bird!' screamed Flavia, bursting through the back door into her inner garden. 'A giant man-eating bird is after us!'

She stood panting and held the door open. Nubia and the dogs were already inside. Lupus charged through a moment later and Jonathan came last, wheezing and gasping. Flavia kicked the wedge out of the way, slammed the door and pressed her back against it.

'Are we all safe?' cried Flavia, breathing hard.

They looked at one another and nodded. The dogs crowded around the gasping friends, snorting and wagging their tails.

'Flavia! What on earth is this commotion!' Her father stepped out of the triclinium and into the garden. The rain had stopped and it was brighter now, although the leaves were still wet and dripping.

'You come in covered in mud, yelling like a fish-wife—'

'Pater!' cried Flavia. 'Oh pater! A giant bird . . . a Stymphalian bird! It was the most terrifying thing . . .' Her voice trailed off as she saw a figure emerge from the study behind him. It was a woman Flavia had never seen before.

Her father turned to the woman.

'Flavia,' he said somewhat stiffly. 'This is Cartilia Poplicola. Cartilia is a friend of my patron Cordius, and she's recently moved back to Ostia from Rome.'

The woman was slender and not very tall, only about Jonathan's height. She had brown eyes and dark hair, pinned up in a simple knot at the back. She wore a cream-coloured stola and had wrapped a brown palla round her shoulders. The smile on her face seemed stiff and unnatural.

Flavia disliked her at once.

Her father turned to Cartilia: 'That's my daughter Flavia,' he sighed. 'The one covered in mud.'

Flavia looked back at her father. 'I can't help it, pater. I slipped when I was running away from the Stymphalian bird!'

'Don't be silly, Flavia. You know there's no such thing as a Stymphalian bird. If you're trying to embarrass me—'

'No, pater. It's true. I'm not lying! Am I, Nubia?'

'Nubia's just a slave, Flavia,' said her father quietly, with a rapid glance at the woman. 'I'm sure she'd say whatever you told her to say.'

'Pater!' cried Flavia, 'I *did* see a Stymphalian bird! And Nubia's not my slave any more. I told you I set her free three months ago when—'

'Flavia!' Her father clenched his jaw. 'I want you to take Nubia and go to the baths right now. There's something I need to discuss with you . . .' he glanced at Cartilia again, 'and I refuse to talk to you when you're in such a filthy state.'

With a sigh of relief, Nubia descended into the circular pool full of hot water.

'. . . he might as well have called me a liar,' Flavia was saying behind her. 'He's never spoken to me like that before.'

Nubia nodded and walked to the deepest part. The water in the caldarium of the Baths of Thetis was hot and milky green and smelt of lavender oil. It was wonderful. She sat on the underwater marble shelf and let the steaming water come up to her chin. Then she closed her eyes to let the delicious warmth sink in.

Flavia imitated her father's voice. 'I'm sure Nubia would say whatever you told her to!'

Nubia opened her eyes and looked at Flavia, also neck deep in the pool. Flavia's face was quite pink and one or two strands of light brown hair had come unpinned and clung to her neck.

'And he called you a slave! When will he get it through his head that I set you free?'

Nubia closed her eyes again. She knew that when Flavia was upset it was best just to let her talk.

'At least he doesn't treat you like a slave. If he did, I would . . . well, I wouldn't take it!' Flavia paused for a moment and Nubia heard the soothing slap of water against the marble edge of the bath.

'And who was that woman anyway?' muttered Flavia.

Presently, two fat matrons came down the steps into the pool and the water level rose noticeably.

'Come on,' grumbled Flavia. 'Let's go to the hot rooms.'

Nubia pushed through the warm water and carefully followed Flavia up the slippery marble steps. Even though the air in the caldarium was warm, her wet body immediately felt cool. She slipped her feet into the wooden bath clogs. Then, taking up her towel, she hurried into the laconicum after Flavia.

That was better. The laconicum was her favourite room of the baths. It was small and smelled of pine. She liked it when it was so hot and dry she could hardly breathe. It reminded her of the purifying heat of the desert. These past few weeks, sitting in the laconicum or the sudatorium was the only time she felt really warm.

Flavia couldn't take the intense heat of the laconicum, so presently they moved on to the sudatorium. Nubia didn't mind. The sudatorium was hot, too, and steamy. She led Flavia up the tiered marble seats to the one nearest the top: the hottest. She sat and relaxed against the warm marble wall. She wanted to stay here for a long, long time.

'Pater was fine this morning,' continued Flavia. 'But when we came back – after the bird chased us – it was as if he'd changed. He *looked* like pater, but he was acting like someone else! It made me think of how Jupiter disguised himself as Amphitryon . . .'

Nubia frowned. Then nodded as she understood the reference.

Hercules.

In lessons yesterday, Aristo had begun to tell them how Jupiter had disguised himself as Hercules' father, Amphitryon, so that he could spend the night with Hercules' mother. Nine months later Hercules had been born. Nubia sighed. Sometimes she found the Greek myths utterly mystifying.

'Maybe,' breathed Flavia, '. . . maybe Cartilia is a venefica and has bewitched pater.'

'What is veiny fig?'

'A venefica is a sorceress who uses potions to enchant people: a witch,' said Flavia, then added, 'I'll bet she's enchanted pater.' There was a long pause and then Flavia said in a small voice. 'I wonder what he wants to talk to me about . . .'

'Flavia,' said the sea captain Marcus Flavius Geminus. 'Come here.'

Flavia went to her father. He stood in the atrium before the household shrine. Flavia had put on her best blue shift and grey leather ankle boots. She wore a dove-grey palla round her shoulders and although her hair was still damp from the baths, she had pinned it up in a simple knot.

For a moment the two of them stood looking at the shrine. It was a wooden cupboard with doors at the front. Inside were the death masks of the Geminus family ancestors. On top of this cupboard were two small marble columns, topped by a wooden pediment and roof, to make it look like a miniature temple.

When she was younger the lararium had seemed huge to her. Now she was as tall as it was. Flavia saw the offerings of the day: a honey cake and a small hyacinth-scented candle. Painted on the wooden back panel of the shrine was a man with a toga draped over his head, the representation of the Geminus family genius. Flavia knew the genius protected the continuity of the family line. The household lares either side of him were shown as windswept young men in fluttering tunics who poured out offerings of wine and grain. Flavia saw the familiar clay statuettes of Castor and Pollux, and of Vesta. At their feet coiled a bronze snake – the protective spirit of the house.

Once, when she was little, her father had found her playing with the sacred images, making up a story in which Castor and Pollux were fighting off the snake who was trying to bite Vesta. Her father had told her they were not toys, but important protectors of the house and family.

Some families worshipped daily at their household shrines. Before his shipwreck, Flavia's father had occasionally lit a candle at the beginning of the day, and made sure the food offering was fresh. But since his return he had become more observant. Now he lit a stick of incense and bowed his head for a moment in prayer.

Presently he turned to her. 'Flavia. Do you know the meaning of the word "piety"?'

'Um, I think so. Aeneas was pious. That meant he was . . . um . . . dutiful.'

'Yes, that's right. Being pious means honouring the gods, your family and the household spirits.'

She nodded.

'I know I haven't been the best father to you. I've been away a lot recently. You've had Alma to feed you, Caudex to protect you and Aristo to educate you . . . but you've obviously felt the absence of a father's discipline. You are very independent and,' he glanced down at her, 'strong-willed.'

Flavia nodded and swallowed.

Her father took the wooden statuette of Castor from the lararium and examined it. 'You have disobeyed my orders on several occasions, sometimes endangering your life. And lately you've been running wild. Today was a clear example of that.'

Flavia hung her head.

'I love you very much, Flavia. Perhaps too much. I've allowed you to make all sorts of decisions without any reference to me, even though I am the paterfamilias: the head of this family.' He sighed. 'For example, three months ago you set your new slave-girl free on your own initiative—'

'—but Pollius Felix said—'

'—I do *not* want to hear that name again!' her father shouted, and Flavia recoiled at the vehemence in his voice. 'We can't finish one day without you mentioning him. Felix may be a rich and powerful patron, but he is not your father. I am!'

Tears stung Flavia's eyes. Her father hardly ever shouted at her.

He put Castor back and turned to look at her. 'Flavia, I am trying to raise you up to be a pious young woman. But you run all over Ostia with a Jew, a beggar-boy and a slave-girl, claiming to see giant birds, claiming to solve mysteries, claiming to be some sort of detective! It has to stop.'

'What?' Flavia's eyes widened in horror. 'What has to stop?'

'I like to think I'm a modern man. I've let you wear a bulla, arranged for you to be educated, entrusted you with a certain measure of independence. But recently I've been criticised for raising you too much like a boy and it seems . . . well, it seems that my critics may have some reason.'

'Who?' said Flavia. 'Who criticises you?'

He turned to look down at her. For a terrible moment he seemed like a stranger and Flavia wondered again if someone had bewitched him.

'I'm afraid,' said her father, 'I'm afraid that from now on I must forbid you to leave the house for any reason, unless you have my express permission.'

Flavia opened her mouth, but no sound came out.

'I've also been thinking,' said her father, putting his hands on her shoulders, 'that it's time we started planning your betrothal. You will soon be of marriageable age and I believe . . .' For the first time during their interview he smiled at her: 'I believe I've found a suitable husband for you.'

443

SCROLL IV

'A husband?' gasped Flavia. 'But pater! I'm only ten years old.'

Her father's smile faded. 'This would just be a betrothal. I wouldn't expect you to marry him for five or six years yet.'

Flavia tried to swallow, but her throat was too dry.

'He's a senator's son,' said her father. 'Of very good birth. Lives in Rome.'

Now Flavia was trembling.

'Apparently he's very studious,' continued her father. 'He loves books as much as you do. And he's your age.'

'My age!' wailed Flavia. 'No, pater! Don't make me marry a baby.'

'Flavia! This would be an excellent match for you. Besides, it's your duty to marry. And to have children. It's . . . it's piety!'

'No. I can't.' Her heart was banging against her ribs. 'I won't marry him!'

Her father sighed. 'Then we'll find someone different. Someone older.'

'No! I don't want to marry anybody!'

'What?'

'I'm never going to get married!'

'Flavia, you're my last burning coal. If you don't marry and have children you'll be snuffing out your descendants. You'll be snuffing out *my* descendants.' He gestured at the lararium. 'You'll be dishonouring our family genius!'

Flavia swallowed hard. 'I'm sorry pater, but I can't,' she whispered. 'I love someone I can't have, so I'm never, ever getting married.'

The look on her father's face was not one of anger. It was one of stunned amazement.

Blinking back tears, Flavia ran out of the atrium and up the stairs to her bedroom.

Jonathan put down the clay doll of a woman he had been examining and picked up one of a gladiator.

He and Lupus were shopping in Ostia's main forum. The market was busy. Ostia's population halved during the months when sailing was impossible. But today it seemed that all the remaining twenty thousand inhabitants were taking advantage of a lull in the rain to buy gifts for the Saturnalia. Men were buying silver, women were buying pickled fruit, slaves and poor people were buying the cheapest gift: candles. And everyone was buying sigilla, the dolls which were the traditional gift of the mid-winter festival.

'Hey!' cried Jonathan, and Lupus started guiltily. He'd been lifting the tunic of a girl doll to see what she looked like underneath.

But Jonathan wasn't looking at Lupus. He was examining some sigilla at another stall. 'Look at these ones. They're animals. And they're made of wood, not clay.'

Lupus put down the sigillum he'd been examining and pushed past a soldier to see.

'Look!' cried Jonathan. 'It's the man-eating bird!'

The stall-keeper laughed. 'That's an ostrich. They don't eat meat. Rumour is one's running around Diana's Grove, outside the Laurentum Gate.'

'So *that's* what it was. Hey!' Jonathan turned to Lupus. 'We should buy this for Nubia.'

Lupus nodded and reached into his coin purse. Jonathan put a hand on his arm.

'Don't use your own money,' he said, then lowered his voice. 'Father gave me fifty sestercii to buy presents for everyone. For Flavia, Nubia and Miriam. And you, too, of course. Which one do you like? The wolf? Now what shall we get for Flavia?'

Suddenly Lupus grabbed Jonathan's belt and pulled the older boy after him.

'Watch it!' said a man in a yellow tunic as Lupus shoved past him.

'Sorry, sir,' Jonathan said to the man, and to Lupus: 'What is it?' Lupus pointed to the sigilla at the next stall. These were also wooden. And painted. Lupus held one up and Jonathan caught his breath. The small jointed doll wore a purple toga and gold wreath. It looked just like the Emperor Titus, whom Jonathan had met two months before.

'Don't touch!' said a voice. 'The Emperor costs two hundred sestercii. That's real gold leaf on the wreath.'

'These are amazing!' said Jonathan, taking the Emperor doll from Lupus and carefully replacing it. He looked up at the merchant, a young man in his late teens with hair so fair it was almost white. 'Did you paint them?'

'No,' said the young man. 'A friend of my father's. He sells them up in Rome. He let me bring some to sell here in Ostia. They're images of real people, you know.'

Lupus tugged Jonathan's tunic and pointed excitedly to a painted doll of a stout bald man.

'That's admiral Pliny,' said the young man. 'He died last summer but he used to live around here. He came to our stall in Rome once or twice.'

'We knew him,' murmured Jonathan, and picked up another figure he recognised: Titus's younger brother Domitian. He felt a jab in the ribs and scowled. 'What is it now, Lupus?'

Lupus held up one of the dolls.

Jonathan took it wide-eyed, then looked at Lupus.

'I don't believe it,' he whispered. 'Is it him?'

Lupus grinned and nodded.

'Shall we buy it for Flavia?' he said.

Lupus nodded again.

'How much is this one?' asked Jonathan casually.

'Oh, I don't know who that is. He's only wearing a toga. No gold leaf. Not a senator. Probably a poet. Or somebody's patron. I can let you have it for forty sestercii.'

Jonathan nodded and reached for his coin purse. 'We'll take – ouch! That was my foot, Lupus!'

Lupus elbowed Jonathan aside and held up both hands.

'Ten?' said the young man to Lupus. 'Don't make me laugh. I couldn't sell it for less than thirty.'

A quarter of an hour later the boys left the stall with five dolls: a wolf for Lupus, a gladiator for Jonathan, an ostrich for Nubia, a woman with a removable bead necklace for Miriam – and the man in the toga for Flavia.

Lupus had negotiated the lot for fifty sestercii.

'Sorry I can't tell you more about the man in the toga,' Peromidus the stallholder called after them. 'I've no idea who he is.'

'It doesn't matter.' Jonathan grinned at Lupus and added under his breath: 'We do.'

Nubia was patting Flavia's back when she heard four hollow taps on the bedroom wall.

It was their signal to open the secret passage between their two houses.

Nubia pulled Flavia's bed away from the wall and began to pull out the loose bricks. Bricks were disappearing from the other side, too.

Scuto and Nipur sniffed the growing gap and wagged their tails.

'Hey!' came Jonathan's voice. 'Is Flavia crying?'

'Yes,' said Nubia. 'Her father is telling her to get married. And no more being a detective.'

'What?' Jonathan's voice was still muffled. 'Why?'

Nubia pulled another brick out. 'He says she must be dutiful Roman girl and sit inside. And she mustn't be running all over Ostia with a Jew, a beggar-boy and a slave-girl!'

'Poor Flavia!' came Jonathan's voice.

Presently a hand holding a wax tablet appeared. On it Lupus had written:

I'M NOT A BEGGAR
I'M A SHIPOWNER!

Finally the breach was big enough for Tigris and the boys to wiggle through. They sat on Flavia's bed, beside Nubia, and the wooden frame creaked alarmingly. Flavia's face was still pressed into the pillow. Outside, it had started to rain again.

'Your father says you can't go out any more?' said Jonathan. 'Don't worry, Flavia. You'll think of something. You always do.'

Flavia rolled over on her back and looked up at them with red and swollen eyes.

'Want to hear a joke, Flavia?' said Jonathan brightly.

Flavia blinked at him, then nodded.

'How many detectives does it take to light an oil-lamp?'

Flavia shook her head.

'Four!' cried Jonathan. 'One to solve the mystery of how to light it, and three to . . . um . . . do what she says!'

Nobody laughed, but Flavia sat up.

'OK, it's not a very good joke but . . . What I'm trying to say is that we can still solve mysteries. You can be the brains and we'll do the legwork.'

'No,' sniffed Flavia, wiping her nose on her arm. 'You don't understand. I'm a terrible daughter. I've disappointed pater and now I'll never be a detective again.'

'Flavia,' said Jonathan. 'Lupus and I bought you a present for the Saturnalia, but I think you need it now.' He glanced at Lupus who nodded and disappeared back through the hole in the wall. 'It might cheer you up,' said Jonathan.

Lupus reappeared through the gap. In his hand he held a wooden sigillum of a man wearing a toga.

'Look,' said Jonathan with a grin, handing the figure to Flavia.

Flavia took the figure and stared at it in wonder.

Nubia looked too. She saw the blue tunic and white toga, the hair which might have been grey or white-blond, the dots of black paint for the eyes.

Flavia looked up at Jonathan, open-mouthed.

'It's a little doll of the Patron. Of Publius Pollius Felix,' said Jonathan. 'Isn't it good?'

'Oh Jonathan!' Flavia hugged the little doll tightly. 'It's wonderful.' And she burst into tears.

Flavia must have fallen asleep because the next thing she knew, Nubia was gently shaking her awake.

'Flavia,' said Nubia, 'Aristo is safely back. He was not eaten by a lion.'

'Good,' mumbled Flavia, and pulled the blanket up to her chin. The bed was warm and cosy. 'What time is it? Have I been asleep?'

'Yes. It is almost time for the betrothal feast. You must get dressed.'

Flavia blinked up at her window. She could tell from the light in the room that it was early afternoon.

'Oh!' She groaned and let her head fall back on the pillow. 'I can't go. I'm too miserable.'

'But Flavia. We have been waiting many weeks for this day. It is the big betrothal day of Miriam.'

'No,' said Flavia, 'you go without me.' Noble tears welled up in her eyes. She kept her face to the wall and waited for Nubia to persuade her, but there was only silence.

Flavia glanced over her shoulder.

The room was empty.

She sat up, injured. Was that all? Wasn't Nubia going to try harder to convince her? Then Flavia heard her father's feet stomping up the stairs. She quickly lay down again and hugged her new doll so that he wouldn't see it.

'Flavia.'

'Yes, pater,' she said in a meek voice.

'Get up and get dressed. This is one of the most important days of your uncle's life and you will not spoil it for him.'

'Yes, pater,' said Flavia. She slipped the Felix doll under her pillow and turned to him. 'Will you ask Nubia to come up, please?'

'I am here,' said Nubia, putting her head into the doorway.

Captain Geminus scowled. 'I want you girls downstairs as soon as you're ready. We're late as it is.'

'Yes, pater.'

Nubia stepped into the doorway. She was already dressed in a long peach shift worn over a lemon-yellow tunic. Around her hips she had knotted a salmon-pink, red-fringed scarf. And over her shoulders she wore a faded orange palla that had once belonged to Flavia's mother. Nubia wore her tigers-eye earrings and all her copper bangles. Her short hair had been braided in neat rows running back from her forehead.

'Nubia! You look beautiful! Who did your hair?'

Nubia smiled shyly. 'Alma. I am telling her how and she does it very well.'

'And you've stained your lips!'

Nubia nodded. 'With juice of blackcurrants, like we practised. Alma helps.'

'It should have been me that helped you. And now I don't have time to get ready myself.' She picked up the polished silver mirror from her bedside table.

'Oh!' she wailed. 'I look terrible! My face is all blotchy and my eyes are red!'

'No,' said Nubia loyally. 'Red around eyes makes them look more blue.'

'Are you girls getting ready?' called a voice from downstairs.

'Yes!' Flavia lied, and pushed the covers back.

Nubia held up Flavia's sky-blue tunic. 'I will do your hair but you must put this on quickly.'

'Oh, Nubia,' said Flavia, as she tried to put some kohl round her puffy eyes, 'this has got to be the worst day of my life.'

SCROLL V

Flavia almost forgot her troubles when she stepped into Jonathan's atrium.

She had never seen it so full of people. And she didn't recognise any of them, not even the person who opened the door. The girl was about her age, perhaps a bit younger. She had mousy brown hair and sharp features.

'Shalom,' said the girl, and then uttered a stream of words Flavia didn't understand.

Captain Geminus smiled down at the girl. 'Sorry,' he said. 'We don't speak Jewish.' Then he said very slowly. 'Do . . . you . . . speak . . . Latin?'

'Of course,' said the girl and rolled her eyes. Flavia noticed that one of her eyes was green and the other blue. 'I'm Miriam's cousin,' said the girl. 'My name is Chamat.'

'Hello, Chamat,' boomed Flavia's father. 'I'm Marcus. The groom is my brother. This is my daughter Flavia, her . . . friend Nubia and her tutor Aristo.'

'Captain Geminus!' Jonathan shouldered Chamat aside as he stepped forward. 'Shalom.' He bowed. 'Please come in and enjoy the festivities.'

Flavia stared at Jonathan. He was wearing a green

454

silk turban and a cinnamon-coloured kaftan. His eyes were lightly rimmed with kohl, which made them look very dark and mysterious.

Jonathan stepped back and extended his arm, solemnly inviting his guests to enter. As they filed past him into the atrium he winked at Flavia and Nubia.

Flavia looked around the atrium in wonder. Green garlands had been draped between the white columns around the impluvium. Small round tables were set out with honeyed sesame balls, stuffed dates and pastries. There were also dice-sized cubes of what looked like marbled flour.

'Halva,' said Jonathan, seeing the direction of Flavia's gaze. 'Try one.'

Flavia did. It was very dense and not too sweet.

'It's made of pressed pistachio and sesame flour,' he explained. 'My aunt makes the best halva in Italia. She organised the caterers.'

Another knock came at the door and Jonathan smiled apologetically. 'Excuse me,' he said with a little bow to Captain Geminus, then hurried to reach the door before Chamat, who was already undoing the bolt.

Flavia followed her father and Aristo through groups of chatting people. Most of them were dark-haired, with olive skin and black eyes. Although one or two of the men wore turbans and kaftans, most were dressed in Roman tunics and capes. They were speaking Latin, Greek and the language Flavia knew was

Hebrew. The women wore stolas or shifts in jewelled colours and some had filmy headscarves.

On the upstairs balcony hired musicians were playing double flute and castanets.

As they passed through a corridor into the columned peristyle that ringed the inner garden, Flavia's eyes opened wide. Two awnings of red canvas had been stretched across either end of the open courtyard, offering additional protection against the fine drizzle that had been falling since noon. These awnings cast a ruby light onto the garden below and made the glossy green shrubs look very dark. Although it was still daytime, oil-lamps hung all round the peristyle, burning like stars. As usual, the house smelled of exotic spices: cinnamon, cardamom, mint and sandalwood.

Aristo stopped abruptly and Flavia bumped into his back.

'Dear Apollo!' she heard him whisper. Flavia peered round him. A crowd of women had parted to reveal Miriam, dressed in her betrothal gown.

Flavia's jaw dropped.

Miriam wore a robe of violet silk embroidered with scarlet and gold thread. Over her head was an embroidered purple scarf hung with dozens of thin gold coins. Miriam's beautiful violet eyes – smoky and kohl-rimmed – smouldered beneath her straight black eyebrows. A tiny sapphire nose-stud above her left nostril emphasised the flawless texture of her creamy skin.

'Dear Apollo! She's the most beautiful thing I've ever seen,' breathed Aristo.

Miriam smiled when she saw them and stepped forward to greet them.

'Captain Geminus: welcome. And Flavia and Nubia. And Aristo.' She lifted her gaze to meet Aristo's and Flavia saw something flicker in Miriam's eyes. Sympathy? Regret?

Miriam was wearing silver bracelets that tinkled as she extended her hand to each of them in turn. As she squeezed Flavia's hand, Flavia saw that her fingers were covered with silver rings.

Flavia suddenly felt shy in the presence of such dazzling beauty. Miriam seemed like a stranger, and far older than her fourteen years.

At that moment Miriam's father approached them.

Doctor Mordecai ben Ezra wore his blue silk kaftan and best white turban. He had a sharp nose and a short grizzled beard. His heavy-lidded eyes always reminded Flavia of a turtle's.

'Marcus!' he said in his slightly accented voice. 'Welcome! You, too, Aristo. Shalom, Flavia and Nubia. It is good to see you all.' Mordecai gestured towards the study. 'Come and have some refreshments.' He guided them into the tablinum where they found more groups of chatting guests and more exotic delicacies on trays. There were sesame rings filled with fig paste, candied almonds, and star-shaped aniseed cakes.

Flavia was sucking a honeyed almond and gazing at

Miriam when a boy appeared at her elbow with drinks on a tray.

'Thank you,' she said, absently taking a cup of hot pomegranate juice.

'Thank you, Lupus,' said Nubia beside her, and Flavia turned to stare at the cupbearer.

Lupus was dressed like Jonathan, but his turban was dark blue silk and his kaftan pale green. Like Jonathan, he'd lined his eyes with kohl. He gave a mock solemn bow and grinned at them.

'Lupus!' breathed Flavia. 'You look so . . . exotic.'

The mute boy nodded, wiggled his shoulders, and swayed off exotically into the crowd, still carrying the tray of drinks.

Flavia heard a burst of laughter and her father's voice above the crowd. He sounded cheerful. She turned to see that he'd been joined by his patron Cordius and the woman called Cartilia Poplicola.

Flavia glared at Cartilia. 'Who invited her?' she muttered.

At that moment the voices and laughter died away. All eyes turned to the corridor.

Miriam's betrothed had arrived.

Fresh from the baths, Flavia's uncle Gaius wore a pure white toga over his best blue tunic. Tall and tanned, with light brown hair and clear grey eyes, he looked exactly as a Roman should. Even though his nose was broken he was very handsome. Flavia felt a surge of pride, then a pang as her father turned to greet him and the two brothers stood face to face.

Although they were identical twins, her father Marcus looked ten years older than his brother. She knew this was partly due to the happiness which lit Gaius's face, but Flavia suddenly saw how much her father had aged in the past few months. He looked like an old man of forty.

Suddenly Flavia's uncle Gaius caught sight of Miriam.

When he saw her his smile faded and his eyes opened wide. The chatter had subsided and the crowd was so quiet that Flavia could hear Miriam jingle as she moved towards Gaius. Miriam stopped shyly before her future husband. They stood for a moment, in the diffused red glow of the awning, gazing into one another's eyes.

'Miriam,' began Flavia's uncle, but his voice faltered and he began again. 'Miriam daughter of Mordecai, in the presence of all these witnesses, will you be my betrothed?'

Flavia couldn't see Miriam's expression because the embroidered headscarf covered her face. But her low, clear voice said it all.

'Yes, Gaius. In front of all these witnesses I will be your betrothed.'

He smiled and took Miriam's extended hand. Solemnly, he slipped a ring onto the fourth finger of her left hand.

Then, still holding her hand in his, Gaius turned so that everyone could see.

Flavia put her mouth close to Nubia's ear, 'Once

you hold hands in public, it means you are be-trothed.'

'Kiss her!' cried a woman.

And then a man's voice behind them, 'Yes, give her a kiss!'

Miriam lifted her face and as Gaius bent to kiss her, the crowd erupted in rowdy cheers.

Flavia heard a woman behind her tut: 'These young people are shameless! In my day a man would not even kiss his wife in public!'

'I know,' said the other one. 'It's scandalous!' She added with distaste: 'And it's obvious they're *in love*.'

Flavia glanced behind her to see two dark-haired women. One was short and stout, the other taller, with eyes as green and hard as unripe olives.

They didn't notice her glance and Flavia heard the green-eyed one remark grimly, 'It is never a good idea to marry for love.'

'Hmmph!' snorted the other woman. 'It looks as if the pagan's brother is about to make the same mistake.'

Flavia's head jerked round and she stared at her father.

Everyone was crowding round Gaius and Miriam to congratulate them, but her father and Cartilia were oblivious. They stood very close together, smiling and looking into one another's eyes.

And, to her horror, Flavia saw that they were holding hands.

SCROLL VI

Nubia saw that Flavia's face was as white as chalk.

'I feel sick,' said Flavia. 'Pater's holding hands with that witch.'

Nubia nodded sympathetically.

'No,' said Flavia in a strange voice. 'I'm really going to be sick . . .'

Nubia took Flavia's arm and gently pulled her towards the latrine. But the door was shut.

'Nubia!' Flavia covered her mouth with her hand.

Thinking quickly, Nubia pulled Flavia through Jonathan's back door. Someone had wedged it partially open. They were just in time.

Flavia bent over and vomited onto the wet grasses. Nubia gently held her friend's head and whispered soothing words in her own language. When Flavia had finished, she began to shiver, so Nubia put her arms around her.

'Pater was holding her hand,' Flavia said to Nubia in a small voice. 'That means he's going to ask her to marry him . . . if he hasn't already.'

Nubia nodded. 'Be happy for him,' she said.

'How can I be happy,' whispered Flavia. 'I don't even know who she is.'

'Come,' said Nubia. 'I am taking you home.'

It was only as she turned to guide Flavia back into the house that Nubia saw Aristo further along the wall. He was leaning against the rough, damp bricks of the town wall.

Aristo's eyes were closed and his face lifted to the sky. Like Flavia, he had wet cheeks, but Nubia could not tell whether from rain or from tears.

The sounds of revelry and music from next door kept Flavia awake well into the night. Presently her tears dried and she began to think. She rolled onto her back and stared up at the slanting timbers of her roof, dim in the light of a single oil-lamp.

Someone had been criticising her father for giving her too much freedom. And as far as she knew there was only one new person in his life: Cartilia.

It must be Cartilia's fault that she was now to be kept like a prisoner in her own home. It was Cartilia who had put an end to her detective work. Cartilia who wanted her to be a dutiful Roman daughter.

Suddenly Flavia had a thought which made her gasp. Her father wanted her to marry a senator's son from Rome. How did he know a senator? He hardly ever went up to Rome. But Cartilia had been living in Rome. The marriage was probably her idea to get Flavia out of the way.

'That witch wants pater all to herself,' Flavia murmured.

At the foot of her bed Scuto raised his head and looked at her.

'But why?' whispered Flavia.

Scuto thumped his tail.

'I've got to find out.' Flavia rolled over on her side and looked at her Felix doll. 'If I can prove to pater that she's evil, then maybe he'll let me keep solving mysteries. And maybe he won't make me marry someone else. Then things can stay just the way they are.'

The doll's dark eyes seemed to gaze back at her.

'This is a mystery,' she told the doll, 'and I've got to solve it. If pater won't allow me to go out without his permission, then I'll just have to get it.'

'Is it safe to come in?' whispered Jonathan, pushing his head through the wall.

Flavia nodded. 'Pater and Uncle Gaius and Caudex have gone to Laurentum to finish getting the Lodge ready.'

Jonathan crawled through the breech in the wall, greeted Scuto and Nipur and helped Lupus come through. 'We've been helping father clean up after the party,' he explained as he flopped onto Flavia's bed. 'And he said we could take a break.' He sighed. 'Sometimes I wish we had slaves like everybody else.'

Lupus nodded his agreement and sat beside Nubia on her bed. She was wearing five tunics and had a blanket wrapped round her shoulders. It was noon: damp, grey and cold.

'Isn't Miriam helping you?' asked Flavia. 'After all, it was her party.'

'No,' said Jonathan mildly, 'Miriam's gone to stay with my two aunts. They're going to help her get ready for the wedding.'

'Is one of them a woman with eyes like olives?' asked Flavia, pulling her blue palla tighter around her shoulders.

Jonathan nodded. 'That's Keturah. Father's eldest sister. He's a bit frightened of her.'

'I don't blame him,' muttered Flavia. 'Anyway,' she added, 'Nubia and I will help you clean up. Pater said we could go to your house today. That's the *only* place we're allowed to go. Plus the baths.' She rested her chin in her hands and stared glumly at the wall. 'At least he's not spending the day with *Cartilia*.' She sneered as she pronounced the name.

'Who is Cartilia, anyway?' asked Jonathan.

'She's the one who's convinced pater I'm running wild. It's her fault I'm trapped in this house like a bird in a cage.'

'How do you know it's her fault?' asked Jonathan.

'It's obvious. Pater tells me someone's been criticising him for the way he's raising me and a few hours later he introduces me to that woman. I'm sure it's her idea to marry me off, as well.'

'Who are you supposed to marry?' Jonathan scratched Scuto behind the ear.

Flavia snorted. 'Some boy my age who lives in Rome. Apparently we'll get on because we both like reading.' Flavia hugged her knees and grumbled: 'She probably doesn't even love him. She's probably after the money we don't have.'

'Who?'

'Cartilia, of course. If only I could do some investigating. I'm sure I could expose Cartilia for what she really is.'

Lupus uttered a bark of laughter.

Flavia looked at him. 'What?'

He scribbled on his wax tablet and held it up:

SATURNALIA!!

'Everybody is talking Saturnalia,' said Nubia. 'But I am still not knowing who she is.'

Jonathan grinned. 'The Saturnalia,' he said, 'is the Roman festival where everybody worships the god Saturn and asks him to make the days longer again.'

Flavia nodded. 'People give each other gifts and gambling is allowed and we don't have lessons—'

'I like lessons,' said Nubia.

'—and,' continued Flavia, 'slaves trade places with their masters and everything is upside down and back to front.'

Lupus had been writing throughout this exchange:

DON'T YOU CHOOSE KING OF
THE SATURNALIA TONIGHT?

'Lupus,' cried Flavia. 'You're brilliant!'

'What?' asked Nubia.

Flavia turned to her. 'On the night before the Saturnalia each household chooses a king of the Saturnalia. It can be anybody from the lowest slave to the master. Then, for the five days of the Saturnalia everyone *has to do what the king says!*'

Lupus was nodding vigorously.

'If I were chosen,' said Flavia. 'I could do as I liked! Within reason . . .' Then her face fell. 'But I might not be chosen.'

'A girl can be king?' asked Nubia, her amber eyes wide.

'Yes,' said Flavia. 'Anybody can be chosen. Then they're king for the remaining five days of the festival.'

'Sounds crazy to me,' said Jonathan.

Flavia nodded. 'Once, when Nero was Emperor, he fixed it so that he was elected king of the Saturnalia. Then he made everyone do the things they hated most, like singing in public or eating their worst food . . .'

'He was already Emperor and he had to be king of the Saturnalia, too?' Jonathan raised his eyebrows. 'What a big bully.'

'How are they choosing the king of the Saturnalia?' asked Nubia.

'By a throw of the dice,' said Flavia.

'So how did Nero get himself chosen?' asked Jonathan.

'Oh, he cheated,' said Flavia. 'He found a loaded dice, and . . .' Her eyes opened wide. 'If only we had a loaded dice,' she breathed.

'What is low dead dies?' asked Nubia, with a look of concern.

NOT LOADED, SHAVED

wrote Lupus. Then, with a mischievous grin, he reached into the pouch at his belt and held up a small ivory cube with black dots painted on each face.

Flavia's eyes grew wide as he blew on it and tossed it onto the bedroom floor. Then she squealed and gave Lupus a hug.

The dice had come up six.

SCROLL VII

'Sex!' cried Flavia Gemina.

'Tres!' said her father with a smile, relieved to see his daughter in good spirits again.

'Quattuor,' mumbled Caudex, standing in the wide doorway of the dining room.

'Quinque,' said Alma and nodded at the others. 'It's my lucky number.'

'Duo,' said Nubia, and looked expectantly at Aristo.

'Your turn, Aristo,' said Flavia.

'What?' He frowned absently and looked at them.

'We're throwing dice to choose the king of the Saturnalia,' said Flavia patiently. 'Choose a number.'

Aristo adjusted his ivy garland. 'Sex.'

'I've already chosen that number. The only number left is unus.'

'Then I must be unus.' He sighed.

'Now where did I put those dice?' muttered Captain Geminus. 'They were here a moment ago . . .'

Lupus tried to look innocent.

'Great Neptune's beard! I put them right on this table. Have you seen them, Caudex?'

'No, master.' Caudex looked confused.

Lupus fished in his belt pouch, held up his dice, and raised his eyebrows at Flavia's father.

'Thank goodness someone has their wits about them,' said Captain Geminus. 'Lupus, would you do us the honour of throwing the dice?'

Lupus nodded, blew on the dice and threw it onto the marble-topped table. It came up six.

'*Euge!*' squealed Flavia. 'I'm the king of the Saturnalia!'

'Congratulations, Flavia!' cried Jonathan, and Lupus clapped loudly.

Flavia's father gave her a long look, then sighed deeply. 'I don't know how you did it, Flavia. But you managed to buy yourself five more days of freedom. I suggest you act wisely. I am still your father and the head of this household.'

'Don't worry, pater,' said Flavia, lifting her chin. 'I won't be a tyrant. I promise I'll use my powers for good.'

Lupus was glad to be wearing his new fur-lined boots. The first day of the Saturnalia had dawned clear and bright, but very cold.

Although Jonathan's family didn't observe the other traditions of the Saturnalia, Mordecai had given each of Jonathan's three friends a seasonal gift of soft leather boots lined with fox fur.

The four friends stood on Flavia's front porch. They wore their warmest clothes. Nubia had on all the tunics she owned, plus a pair of Captain Geminus's woollen leggings which had shrunk at the fullers. She also had one of the captain's old woollen cloaks wrapped round her.

'Before we start investigating Cartilia,' said Flavia, 'we're going to watch the ceremony at the Temple of Saturn. Pater gave me permission to go.'

Flavia stepped off the porch and started along the cold pavement towards the fountain. Lupus and the others fell into step beside her. Up and down the street, other people were emerging from their houses, their breath coming in white puffs as they called out the traditional greeting: 'Yo, Saturnalia!'

'Pater told me that Cartilia is a widow,' said Flavia. 'She grew up here in Ostia but then she married a lawyer and they moved to Rome. Pater said her husband died a few years ago and they never had any children, so she moved back here.'

Three men wearing colourful cloaks and soft conical hats were staggering towards them, going against the flow. 'Yo, Saturnalia!' they cried happily and Lupus could smell the wine on their breath.

'Yo, Saturnalia!' replied Flavia and Nubia.

'They've started celebrating early!' muttered Jonathan.

'Pater told me Cartilia is staying with her parents here in Ostia,' continued Flavia. 'But when I asked him where they lived he gave me one of his looks. I think he was beginning to get suspicious. That's the first thing we need to find out: where Cartilia's parents' house is.'

'Did you ask Alma?' said Jonathan.

'She doesn't know anything.' Flavia frowned. 'Or she's not telling. Even though I made her breakfast today.'

'I helped,' said Nubia. 'We made the poculum.'

'Pater's gone to Laurentum again, but before he left I suggested he invite Cartilia to dinner this afternoon. He seemed pleased about that, and when I asked if we could go and watch the sacrifice this morning he said yes. He said we didn't even have to take a bodyguard. Since Venalicius died there hasn't been a single kidnapping!'

As they turned into Bakers Street, two pretty young women danced out of a tavern.

'Yo, Saturnalia!' they giggled. One of them darted forward to kiss Jonathan on the cheek.

'Yo!' He jumped back surprised, and then blushed as she smiled at him.

The other woman patted Lupus's head. 'Sweet little boy!'

Lupus snarled at her and the two of them ran giggling towards Ostia's main street.

'I've decided I like the Saturnalia,' remarked Jonathan. Lupus scowled.

'Great Neptune's beard!' exclaimed Flavia.

They had come out onto the Decumanus Maximus. It was full of people, all making their way towards the temple. The people of Ostia – both slaves and free – were dressed in their best winter clothes: long tunics, soft leather shoes, and thick woollen cloaks. Many of them wore the conical felt hats which slaves wore after they had been set free. The hats were red, blue, green and yellow.

'Yo, Saturnalia!' came the cry on all sides.

As the friends approached the theatre, Lupus heard the sound of drums, flutes and bells. Soon they caught up with a troupe of musicians playing a discordant tune with a strong beat. There were four men and a woman, all dressed in green tunics with matching leather boots. The woman wore an anklet of bells which jingled rhythmically as she danced. Lupus stopped to watch her for a moment before the crowd swept the four friends along with it.

Presently they found themselves in a sacred precinct just past the theatre. Before them were four small temples.

Lupus snarled again as a man stepped on his new boot. Lupus hated crowds. Looking around, he caught sight of a covered fountain built against a wall. In a moment he had clambered up onto its vaulted roof.

That was better. Now he had a perfect view of the little Temple of Saturn with its black marble columns and the cult statue.

'Hey, Lupus!' cried Jonathan. 'Give me a hand up.'

A moment later the four friends all sat on the fountain's roof, looking over the heads of the crowd as the priest of Saturn appeared beside the cult statue.

The priest was intoning something. Lupus caught a phrase above the excited babble of the crowd: '. . . today when the old order is restored so that the sun may return and the days grow longer . . .' Most people ignored the priest to catch up on gossip. But the happy buzz of the crowd grew quieter as the priest's assistants brought a dozen sacred piglets forward. This was of interest to them: after the piglets had been sacrificed their flesh would be roasted for a public feast.

Lupus knew that sacrificial animals were usually drugged to make them sleepy, but the small pink creatures seemed unusually nervous. As the piglets were carried up the steps, Lupus caught a glimpse of their rolling eyes and twitching noses. Suddenly one of them uttered a high-pitched squeal and writhed free.

There were screams of laughter as the rogue piglet charged the crowd.

'Come back, you!' shouted the attendant. 'We want to read your entrails!' He plunged into the crowd after the piglet. Lupus could see the crowd parting before the fugitive.

'Dignity!' bellowed the priest of Saturn from the top of the temple steps. 'Dignity and decorum. Nothing must spoil the sanctity of the sacrifice!'

Ignoring him, two other piglets also squirmed out of the arms locked round them.

One disappeared down a side street and the other set off back towards the theatre, his little trotters twinkling as he ran.

'He's off to Rome!' quipped a woman.

'You're too late for the races!' a man called after the piglet.

The crowd laughed.

Then a woman screamed. Below Lupus a man uttered an oath and pointed towards the temple steps. A tawny beast had appeared from behind a black column.

'Lion!' came a woman's hysterical voice. 'It's the escaped lion!'

SCROLL VIII

'Lion!' screamed a voice in the crowd. 'Run for your lives.'

As the people below them started to run, Nubia turned to her friends.

'Don't go down!' she cried. 'We will be squashed!'

Lupus was halfway off the fountain, about to drop to the ground. He stared wildly up at Nubia, then nodded. They helped him back up.

Within moments the square before the temple was deserted, apart from half a dozen people who'd been trampled in the stampede. One of them was a little boy, no more than four years old. He lay on the cold paving stones, whimpering for his mother.

Nubia kept her eyes on the lion. He was padding slowly down the temple steps. The priest had disappeared. His attendants, too.

'Look at his stomach,' Nubia said to the others. 'He is very fulled.'

'She's right,' gulped Jonathan. 'Either that or she's pregnant!'

'Not she,' said Nubia. 'He. Behold the . . . hair?' Nubia didn't know the Latin word.

'The mane?' Flavia was trembling. 'That means it's a boy lion?'

Nubia nodded.

'Can lions jump up?' asked Jonathan nervously.

Nubia shook her head. 'Lions are not so good climbers.'

The lion had reached the bottom step of the temple. Even from across the square Nubia could smell his strong musky scent. He lifted his nose and tested the air, just as her puppy Nipur sometimes did.

The boy's crying was louder now. The lion turned his head, then began to move towards the child.

Nubia's heart was pounding. She knew she had to act now. The lion had obviously eaten recently, so he was probably not hungry. But a wounded creature was always of interest to a meat-eater. She hoped her father's advice for stopping a lion was correct.

Nubia slipped off the fountain and landed lightly on her feet. The lion stopped and slowly turned his big head. For a moment his golden eyes locked with Nubia's, but they betrayed no flicker of interest in her. He turned his head again and padded slowly towards the little boy.

'Nubia!' hissed Flavia. 'What are you doing?'

Slowly and without taking her eyes from the lion, Nubia unwrapped the nutmeg-coloured cloak from her shoulders. Then she walked cautiously towards the boy on the ground. He had stopped crying but was shaking in terror. The lion glanced at her but did not stop moving forward.

Nubia and the lion converged, and when she and the lion were no more than two yards from the shivering child, Nubia tossed her cloak. The lion froze as the cloak fell over his head and shoulders. For a moment he remained motionless. Then he slowly lifted one great paw and tried to pull off the cloak.

'Get him, boys! Now!' The voice came from behind Nubia, along with the sound of running footsteps and the grating of wheels on paving stones. She turned to see a squad of six soldiers run forward. They were pulling a large wooden box on wheels. A brown-skinned man with a whip ran after them.

'Stop there, boys!' he cried. 'Wait for my order!'

The soldiers stopped and the man – he looked Syrian – cracked his whip. 'Stay, Monobaz!' he cried. 'Stay!'

The lion stopped trying to paw the cloak from its head and waited obediently.

'Put the cage right in front of him,' commanded the Syrian, 'and raise the door.'

The soldiers obeyed. Then one of them fainted.

'Good boy,' murmured the Syrian, while the soldiers attended to their fallen comrade.

The tamer moved towards the lion. 'Good Monobaz.'

Slowly he pulled Nubia's cloak from the lion's massive head. 'Good boy. Into your cage, Monobaz. Nice piece of calf's liver in there for you.'

The lion looked up at him with yellow eyes, blinked, and disappeared into the box. Now only his tail was visible, writhing and twitching like a tawny snake. The tamer pushed the lion's curling tail in and slid the door shut. Then he turned to Nubia and held out her cloak.

'My dear girl,' he said, 'I don't know who you are or where you come from, but you deserve a golden victor's wreath. That was the wisest thing you could have done. And the bravest!'

Flavia hugged Nubia. 'You're a hero,' she said. 'You saved us all!'

The little boy's hysterical mother had carried her child away without even thanking Nubia, but the lion tamer stayed to express his gratitude.

'You saved my skin,' he said. 'My name's Mnason. I'm Monobaz's owner.'

Flavia looked him up and down. He had light brown skin, dark hair slick with oil, and a neat pointed beard.

'I'm Flavia Gemina,' she said, 'daughter of Marcus Flavius Geminus, sea captain. This is Jonathan, Lupus and Nubia the heroine.'

'Delighted to meet you all. Especially you, Nubia. May I ask how you knew to throw a cloak over his head?'

'My father told me,' said Nubia solemnly.

'I'd like to congratulate him on the bravery of his daughter!'

Nubia dropped her head and Flavia whispered, 'You can't. Her father's dead.'

'Oh, I'm sorry,' said Mnason. He tugged his ear and Flavia noticed he wore three gold earrings in it.

The people were beginning to return. Vigiles were putting the injured people on stretchers, and the head priest had poked his head cautiously round the side of the temple.

'Listen,' said Mnason to Nubia. 'I'd like to reward you. But I see the magistrate is coming my way. Can you meet me at noon in the Forum of the Corporations? At the corporation of beast importers?'

Nubia looked at Flavia.

'Of course!' said Flavia.

'Good. Now, before he gets here, tell me. You four haven't seen a camelopard anywhere around here, have you?'

Lupus knew that the Forum of Corporations was behind the theatre near the river. He led his friends through the arched entrance. A porter appeared and Flavia stepped forward.

'We've come to see Mnason,' she said politely. 'He's expecting us.'

'At the Corpse of the Beast Importers,' added Nubia.

'Hey! You're the brave girl who caught the lion! Everyone's talking about it!' said the porter. 'Mnason and his lion are just over there. Near the temple.'

He gestured towards a pretty temple in the middle of a grassy rectangle. Lupus knew it was the Temple of Ceres, the goddess of grain. Grain was Ostia's

lifeblood, and the main reason for the town's exist-
ence. Without a port to receive the grain ships
from Egypt, docks to unload it and warehouses to
store it, Rome's million inhabitants would go without
bread.

Around the grassy precinct of the temple was a
three-storey colonnade which housed Ostia's various
corporations. Flavia's father had once told Lupus that
'corporation' meant a group of people. There were the
shipbuilders and owners; the tanners, rope-makers and
sailors; the measurers and importers of grain; and the
importers of other useful products: olive oil, wine,
honey, marble and exotic beasts.

Lupus liked the Forum of the Corporations because
of the black and white mosaics beneath the covered
colonnade at ground level. He often copied the pic-
tures of animals, ships, and buildings onto his wax
tablet. There were mosaics of tigers, lions, hunting
dogs, and his favourite, the elephant. To his delight,
he saw that was where Mnason sat: at the corporation
of beast importers. The tamer sat just outside the
colonnade on a folding leather chair, his eyes half
closed in the thin winter sunshine. He had a cup of
steaming wine in one hand and a wax tablet in the
other. Monobaz the lion paced up and down in his
wooden cage nearby.

When Mnason saw them approaching his dark eyes
widened and he leapt out of his chair.

'Welcome, young friends,' he greeted them. 'A cup
of hot wine? It is the Saturnalia, after all!'

Flavia shook her head. 'I need a clear head,' she said. 'But thank you.'

Lupus stepped closer to the lion's cage and the others followed.

'Nubia,' said the lion tamer. 'Thank you again for your bravery. Monobaz is gentle as a lamb, but people don't know that. Someone might have killed him. How can I reward you?'

Nubia looked at him shyly. 'May I stroke him?'

'Of course. Is that all you want?'

Nubia nodded and shivered. ·

'You're not afraid of him, are you?' asked Mnason.

'No,' whispered Nubia. 'I am just cold.'

'Come here, Monobaz. Look! Just scratch him behind the ear. He's like a big kitten.'

'Oh,' giggled Nubia. 'He is making a big purring.'

Mnason grinned. 'I told you. Lions are just big cats.'

'Except cats don't bite your arm off at the elbow,' said Jonathan.

'May I ask a question?' said Flavia.

'Anything for a friend of Nubia's,' said Mnason.

'Do you know of a woman named Cartilia Popli-cola?' asked Flavia.

'That's an unusual question!' said Mnason. 'Most people ask me if Monobaz is a man-eater!'

'It's for an investigation. I'm—' Flavia's eyes widened: 'Is Monobaz a man-eater?'

Mnason laughed. 'Of course not.'

Jonathan turned to look at the trainer. 'Then what's in his stomach?'

'A sheep,' said Mnason, his expression becoming serious. 'They found its remains yesterday. I'll have to compensate the owner. But Monobaz would never eat a person. He's as tame as a big kitten. In fact, I'm teaching him to hold a live rabbit in his mouth.' He saw Flavia looking at him and raised his eyebrows.

'Cartilia,' she said patiently. 'Cartilia Poplicola?'

'I'm not a native of Ostia,' he said, 'but everyone knows the Poplicola family. They've been here for generations. The harbour master is called Lucius Cartilius Poplicola.'

'I know,' said Flavia. 'But he's not married.'

'Well,' said Mnason, 'his brother Quintus is a chief grain measurer. He might be Cartilia's father, or husband, if she took his name . . .'

'Her husband's dead,' said Flavia.

'Then it must be her father,' said Mnason. 'I don't know much about him. But I do believe his corporation is that one there, right across the square. You'll recognise it by the mosaic of a man measuring grain.'

'Thank you, sir,' said Flavia and started across the grass. Lupus tapped her on the shoulder and showed her his wax tablet. Flavia read the question he had written there and turned back to the Syrian. 'Just one more question,' she said politely.

'Yes?'

'What does a camelopard look like?'

'Cartilia Poplicola?' The dark-skinned African frowned and scratched his head. Behind him and the column he leaned against, a group of men were drinking and laughing. Flavia could hear the rattle of dice and the clink of coins. She knew the Saturnalia was the only time when gambling was legally permitted.

Flavia studied the African. He had a bald head with two alarming bumps in it: one over his left ear and one over his right eye. 'Which Cartilia Poplicola?' he said.

'There are more than one?' Flavia tried not to stare at the lump on his forehead; it was the size of a chestnut.

'My master has three daughters. All called Cartilia Poplicola. Is she the youngest?'

'Maybe.'

Bumpy-head glanced round, then leaned forward. 'He's always moaning about one of them.' Flavia could smell the wine on his breath. 'He says she's a bit demented.'

'Demented like insane?'

He shrugged, then nodded.

'Which one is that?' asked Flavia.

'I'm not positive, but I think her nickname is Paula.'

SCROLL IX

'Nubia! Look out!' screamed Flavia Gemina. She pressed a hand to her heart. 'You almost dropped some eggshell in the bowl.'

'No,' said Nubia patiently. 'There is no eggshell.' She sighed. She wasn't enjoying herself. They were supposed to be making omelettes for the first course of the feast. Flavia might be a good detective, but she was not a very good cook.

Nubia shivered. Even though she had all her tunics on, she was still cold. And damp. Nothing ever seemed to get really dry. The only good thing about preparing dinner was that she could stand near the glowing coals of the kitchen hearth.

Alma was in the garden, loitering near the quince bush, pretending to look for any remaining fruit. Nubia knew she missed being in her kitchen.

'It's all right, Alma,' said Flavia, without looking up. 'I'm not going to break anything. Oh look! Saffron. Can we use some in the stew?'

'Be careful, dear.' Alma abandoned the quince bush and hurried to the doorway of the kitchen. Nubia glanced up from beating the eggs in time to see the look of dismay on Alma's face as Flavia dropped six thin red filaments of saffron in the stew.

'Saffron is terribly expensive . . .' Alma's voice trailed off.

'Don't worry!' said Flavia brightly. 'You only have a Saturnalia feast once a year . . . er, well, five afternoons a year.'

'You're going to cook again tomorrow?' said Alma in a small voice.

'Of course! We'll cook every day this week. We want you and Caudex to have a nice rest. Don't we Nubia? Nubia!' Flavia turned away from her stew and wrenched the ceramic bowl from Nubia's hands. 'Don't beat the eggs like *that*. Beat them like *this*.'

The dogs sped joyfully across the cold ground, barking as they went.

Nubia breathed a sigh of relief. Dogs were so simple and uncomplicated. They never told you what to do. They just loved you.

She was glad she could go into the woods again. Monobaz the lion was safely in his cage, everyone said the ostrich was not dangerous, and the camelopard had not been sighted since it loped off down the beach.

Nubia looked up at the sky. It was a sky unlike any she had ever seen before: very low, with swollen layers of bruised pink clouds all moving at different speeds. It was not long after noon, but already the light was fading. And it was cold. Always cold. She pulled her cloak tighter around her shoulders.

As Nubia followed the dogs into the woods, she inhaled. She loved the spicy fresh scent of the umbrella pines, and she knew she would always associate that smell with Ostia.

'Ostia.' She whispered the name to herself. It was a bittersweet word. It was her new home and she loved it, but sometimes she missed the clean hot sands of the desert and its infinite sky full of burning stars.

Suddenly Nubia stopped.

She had heard the snap of a twig. And a low moan.

It was not the dogs, they were off to her left, urgently sniffing the base of an acacia tree.

Was it the ostrich again? The camelopard?

Nubia heard the distant moan again.

Silently she stepped forward, then put out a hand to steady herself against an umbrella pine.

The couple were quite a distance away. A man and a woman, locked in a passionate embrace. Nubia felt the hot rush of blood to her face. She moved closer to the tree. The rough, wet bark of its trunk was cool against her cheek. She couldn't see the face of the woman in the dark hooded cloak, but when the man moved a little she saw his curly hair and short red hunting cape.

It was Aristo.

'So, Cartilia,' said Flavia Gemina, setting a platter of omelettes on the table in front of the central couch. 'Tell us about yourself. Tell us everything.' Flavia and Nubia had prepared the first feast of the Saturnalia all by themselves. Nubia was in the kitchen garnishing the main course while Flavia served the starter.

As she stepped back, Flavia saw her father frown.

He was reclining next to Cartilia. Aristo occupied the right-hand couch and Alma and Caudex reclined rather stiffly on the left-hand couch.

Jonathan and Lupus were not with them; they were at home, observing the start of the Sabbath with Mordecai.

'Do you have a big family?' Flavia asked Cartilia sweetly, ignoring her father's warning look.

Cartilia swallowed a bite of omelette. 'Yes. There are five of us. My father and mother, me, and my two sisters. My poor father is surrounded by women.'

Flavia laughed heartily, then stopped. 'And what does your father do?' she asked.

'He's one of Ostia's main agents for the grain business.' Cartilia took another bite of her omelette. Flavia glanced round at the others.

'Hey!' she said. 'Why aren't the rest of you eating your omelettes?'

'It's a little too salty for me,' said Aristo. He put down his spoon.

'And terribly fishy, Flavia,' said her father.

'And a bit slimy,' mumbled Caudex. 'Don't like slimy egg. Makes my throat close up.'

Alma sighed and pressed her lips together.

'Well,' said Flavia defensively, 'the recipe called for lots of garum. And I had a little accident with the salt pot. Watch out for shards of clay.'

Flavia turned back to Cartilia and nodded with approval as the woman dug in.

'So' she prompted. 'You have two sisters.'

'Yes,' said Cartilia. 'I'm the eldest. My middle sister is married. She lives in Bononia, up in the north. And my younger sister Diana lives here in Ostia. She's not married yet, even though she's almost eighteen. She still lives with my parents.'

Nubia came into the room with the next course, lentil and chicken stew.

'Where do your parents live? Do you live there too?' asked Flavia.

Cartilia nodded. 'We own one of the old houses behind the Temple of Rome and Augustus.'

Suddenly Flavia frowned. 'Your sister's name is Diana? I thought you were all called Cartilia.'

'We are,' said Cartilia with a smile, mopping up the last of her runny omelette with a piece of charred bread. 'Diana is just her nickname.'

'And do you have a nickname?'

'Yes,' said Cartilia brightly. 'My parents call me Paula.'

With a sharp intake of breath, Flavia glanced over at Nubia, who was serving the stew.

'And what was your husband's name again?' she asked.

Cartilia's smile faded. 'Postumus,' she said quietly. 'Postumus Sergius Caldus.'

'Was his death sudden?'

'Flavia!'

'Sorry, pater,' said Flavia.

But she had seen the blood drain from Cartilia's cheeks and she was not sorry at all.

'There's something fishy about her and it's not from my omelette,' whispered Flavia to her Felix doll. 'She smiles too much.'

It was dark and Nubia's breathing came steadily from the bed nearby. The dogs were asleep, too, curled up at the foot of the beds. But Flavia's mind was still too active for her to sleep.

'And she seemed very nervous when I mentioned her dead husband.'

In the flickering light of a close-trimmed oil-lamp, the doll's eyes seemed to gaze back at her. 'If I can prove to pater that she's not what she seems, then maybe he'll let me keep solving mysteries. And maybe he won't make me marry someone else. Then things can stay just the way they are.'

Flavia snuggled down under her woollen blanket and looked at the doll's little face for a moment. It really was a remarkable likeness. 'Goodnight, Felix,' she whispered. 'I hope I dream about you tonight.'

That night Flavia did dream. But it was not about Felix.

It was her old nightmare. Dogs were pursuing her through the woods on a steep mountainside. She ran and ran. At last she emerged into a clearing and skidded to a halt at the cliff edge. Below her the sea crashed onto jagged rocks. No escape that way.

She turned just in time to see a black-maned lion explode from the woods and launch himself at her. As

Flavia tried to scream, a muscular man in a loincloth tackled the lion and wrestled it to the ground. Helplessly, Flavia watched them struggle, gripping one another with straining muscles and bared teeth. At last the lion lay limp on the ground, and the hero turned to face her. He had grey-blue eyes and hair the same colour as the lion's tawny pelt. His bulging muscles gleamed with sweat and his brave chest rose and fell as he caught his breath. She knew it was Hercules.

'Flavia Gemina,' he said. 'With my help, you have accomplished the first task. But you must complete eleven more, just as I did.'

'What?'

'You must complete twelve tasks. Thus will you atone for your offence.'

'What offence?' cried Flavia in her dream. 'What have I done wrong?'

Hercules looked at her and shook his head sadly. 'Your crime and mine are the same,' he said.

And then he flew away.

SCROLL X

'And then he flew away?' said Jonathan.

Flavia nodded solemnly. It was the second day of the Saturnalia and the four friends were sitting on a dining couch in her triclinium watching the wall-painter work. He had whitewashed the first wall the day before and now he was making sketches with a twig of willow charcoal.

Jonathan frowned: 'And you think the dream was sent by the gods?'

'Definitely.'

'And in your dream Hercules said you had to atone for some offence? Like a sin?'

Flavia nodded again and Jonathan noticed she held the Felix doll in her lap.

WHAT OFFENCE? Lupus scrawled on his wax tablet.

'I've been thinking about it,' said Flavia. 'I think my crime is the same one that Hercules committed.'

'But Aristo is telling us that Hercules killed his family,' said Nubia.

'And you obviously haven't killed your family,'

chuckled Jonathan. His smile faded as Flavia nodded.

'That's exactly what I've done.'

Her three friends looked at her wide-eyed.

'I told pater I would never marry and he said that I was killing my descendants. Don't you see?' She looked round at her friends' puzzled faces. 'I'm pater's last burning coal and if I don't marry then I've killed my future family!'

'You're never getting married?' said Jonathan. 'Not ever?'

Flavia looked down at the Felix doll. 'No,' she whispered. 'I love someone I can never have.'

'So Hercules came to you in a dream and said you have to complete twelve tasks. What tasks?'

Flavia lowered her voice. 'I think I know what I have to do. That woman Cartilia has bewitched pater. She wants to marry him and get me out of the way. I need to find out why, and I need to stop her. Then everything will be the way it was and pater will be happy again. I think the twelve tasks will provide the clues I need to stop her.'

'What are the tasks Hercules had to do?' asked Nubia.

'His first task was to kill a huge lion with his bare hands. I haven't killed a lion, but you overpowered one, Nubia, and that led us to some clues: Cartilia's nickname is Paula and she's a bit demented. Now let me see if I can remember the other tasks. Aristo was teaching us a special way to remember them in order . . .'

Lupus raised his hand and eagerly began writing on his wax tablet.

LION
HYDRA
DEER
BOAR
STABLES
MAN-EATING BIRDS

'That's right!' said Flavia. 'Hercules' second task was to kill a monster called the hydra, his third was to capture a deer sacred to Diana, his fourth was to capture a fierce boar, his fifth was to clean the stables and his sixth was to kill the man-eating Stymphalian birds.' Flavia paused and frowned.

'Impressive!' said Jonathan, looking at Lupus's wax tablet. 'Are you using Aristo's method?'

Lupus nodded and gave them a smug grin. He had completed the list.

CRETAN BULL
MAN-EATING HORSES
AMAZON'S BELT
RED CATTLE
GOLDEN APPLES
CERBERUS

Flavia nodded. 'That's right, Lupus! Task seven was to capture the Cretan bull, task eight to capture some man-eating horses, task nine to get the Amazon's belt, ten was to capture the red cattle – they were sacred to Juno. His last two tasks were to get the golden apples of the Hesperides at the end of the world and to bring Cerberus the three-headed dog up from Hades.'

Jonathan frowned. 'So does that mean you have to kill a hydra and capture a deer and go to the ends of the world to fetch some apples?'

'I don't think I have to actually DO the tasks,' said Flavia. 'Hercules has done them already. But each task will give me a clue to help me find the truth about Cartilia.'

'It sounds a bit crazy to me.'

'Maybe,' said Flavia, 'but when I came downstairs this morning the gods gave me another sign as a confirmation.' She pointed to the wall-painter. 'Him. Hercules the wall-painter.'

'He's called Hercules?' Jonathan raised his eyebrows and grinned. Hercules the wall-painter was a small man with round shoulders, a bald head and a weak chin.

Flavia nodded.

'When I came downstairs, I found him making these sketches and when I asked him what he was going to paint he said . . . well, see for yourself.'

Jonathan looked at the scenes sketched on the white wall.

'The first one shows a naked man wrestling a lion,' said Jonathan, 'and in the next one the naked man has obviously won because now he's wearing the lion skin and . . . Great Jupiter's eyebrows! It's Her-cules!'

Flavia nodded. 'Hercules the wall-painter is painting the twelve tasks of Hercules the hero. As signs go, it couldn't be much clearer.'

Lupus nodded.

'Flavia,' said Nubia. 'If you are never having babies, maybe your father should be having babies.'

'But not with Cartilia.'

Lupus shrugged at her, as if to ask: Why not?

'I just have a feeling.' She looked round at them. 'Anyway, I think that each task I complete will give me a clue and so by the end of my quest I'll know the truth. Yesterday – with Nubia's help – we beat the lion. Our next clue will be something to do with a hydra.'

'But hydra is snake-headed dog,' said Nubia.

'Where will we find one of those?' asked Jonathan.

Lupus held up his wax-tablet:

HYDRA FOUNTAIN

'Of course!' cried Jonathan. 'In the part of town where we used to live, near the Marina Gate, there's a fountain called the hydra fountain. And there's an old lady who sits and spins wool nearby. They call her the Wise Woman of Ostia. Is that any good?'

'Perfect!' said Flavia. 'Absolutely perfect.'

Seven spouts of water gushed from seven serpents'

heads at the hydra fountain. They found the old woman sitting nearby, on the porch of her house.

She was a tiny creature in black with a humped back and hands like claws. Her head was down, and patches of pink scalp showed through her thin white hair. A mass of grey wool was piled on a stool beside her and sleeping on top of it was a cat of the same colour. The old woman was spinning the wool, and Nubia was fascinated to see the twist of grey yarn emerge from between her gnarled fingers.

'Hello,' said Flavia politely. 'Are you the Wise Woman of Ostia?'

The woman looked up at them sharply.

Nubia stifled a gasp. The old woman had one filmy grey eye and where the other should have been only an empty socket.

'No one is wise.' Her voice was high and clear, like a child's. 'But to some the gods give insight.' She chuckled. 'And others of us have just been around for a very long time.'

'But are you the one they call the Wise Woman?'

'Some call me Lusca, because I have only one eye. Others call me Anus, because I was born the year Octavian was proclaimed Augustus.'

Flavia gasped. 'But that would make you . . .'

'More than a hundred years old,' exclaimed Jonathan.

'Impossible!' snorted Flavia.

Nubia caught her breath. It was unimaginably rude to contradict a grey-hair. In Nubia's clan, the children

496

were always taught to honour the old. So she stepped forward and clapped her hands together softly, letting her knees bend as she did so.

'Thank you, Nubia, for showing me respect.'

'How did you know her name was Nubia?' gasped Flavia.

'I listen. People talk when they come to the hydra fountain here.'

'Please,' said Flavia. 'May we ask you a question?'

'You may ask. But I may not answer.'

Flavia reached for her coin purse. Nubia put a restraining hand on her arm, but Flavia shook it off. 'I can pay you,' she said. 'One denarius.'

With a sharp intake of breath, the old woman fixed her single eye on Flavia. 'You think you can buy wisdom, Flavia Gemina? No! But because Nubia showed respect, I will answer one question.'

'Thank you,' said Flavia. 'Can you please tell us where Cartilia—'

'A question of my own choosing!' said the Wise Woman.

Chastened, Flavia fell silent. Nubia held her breath and waited for a word of great wisdom.

'Cartilia Poplicola lives on Orchard Street,' said the Wise Woman. 'The house with the sky-blue door. You can't miss it: the knocker is in the shape of a club, like the one Hercules used to carry.' The old woman held out a claw-like hand. 'I'll have that bit of silver now.'

'The third task of Hercules,' said Flavia to the others,

when they were out of the old woman's earshot, 'was to capture the deer sacred to Diana. And I think we know who Diana is, don't we?'

Jonathan nodded. 'Cartilia's sister.'

'We know where she lives,' said Flavia, stopping in front of the house with the club knocker. 'But we can't just bang on the door and barge in. We need an excuse to visit. Luckily it's the Saturnalia. We can take Cartilia a gift and then they'll invite us in!'

'What are we giving her?' asked Nubia.

'I'm not sure. Traditionally on the Saturnalia you give a sigillum – one of those dolls – or silver or candles or food . . . That's it! We'll raid the store-room.'

'While you're doing that,' suggested Jonathan, 'should Lupus and I attempt the fourth task?'

'Good idea,' said Flavia. 'Hercules' fourth task was to capture the Erymanthean Boar. Now where will we find a boar in Ostia?'

'Maybe we could go hunting?' said Jonathan hopefully.

Flavia gave him a sharp look. 'You're not trying to get out of this, are you, Jonathan?'

'Of course not!'

Lupus snapped his fingers and wrote on his wax tablet:

BRUTUS

'That's right,' said Jonathan, 'Lupus and I saw a

huge boar outside the butcher's shop two days ago. They say he caught it himself.'

'That sounds promising,' said Flavia. 'Brutus always has the latest gossip. You boys go there while Nubia and I take a jar of prunes to Cartilia. We'll meet back at my house at noon. All right?'

'Great,' said Jonathan dryly. 'A visit to the pork butcher's on the Sabbath. Father will be *so* pleased.'

As Flavia banged the knocker on the sky-blue door, Nubia looked around. The shutters of the shops either side of Cartilia's house were pulled down, but music was coming from a tavern further down the road, and groups of rowdy people were spilling onto the street outside it.

'These houses are the oldest in Ostia,' Flavia said to her. 'Pater told me they were here even before the town wall was built.'

It was beginning to rain. Nubia shivered and pulled Captain Geminus's old nutmeg-coloured cloak tighter. Flavia banged the knocker again and glanced at Nubia.

'We'll just wait a little longer. The household slaves are probably down the road there at the Peacock Tavern.'

Sure enough, a moment later they heard the scraping of the bolt and the door swung open. A tall woman with an elaborate hairstyle opened the door. Although there was no grey in her hair, Nubia guessed she was over forty.

'Hello, girls, may I help you?' she asked.

'Is this the house of Quintus Cartilius Poplicola?' asked Flavia politely, and held out the ceramic jar of prunes. 'We've come to bring a Saturnalia gift for his daughter Cartilia.'

The woman's face lit up. 'How kind!' she said. 'Which of my Cartilias do you mean: Diana or Paula?'

Nubia and Flavia exchanged a quick glance. 'Paula,' said Flavia.

'She's not here at the moment . . .' The woman tipped her head to one side. 'Am I correct in thinking you're Captain Geminus's daughter?'

'Yes.' Flavia nodded. 'My name is Flavia Gemina, and this is my friend Nubia.'

'Then come in! I'm Paula's mother, Vibia.'

She stood aside with a smile and beckoned the girls in. Nubia smiled back at Cartilia's mother as they moved through the vestibule. The woman's eyes were warm and kind, and although her complicated hair style was out of fashion it was still very impressive.

'My husband's not here right now,' said Vibia. 'He's entertaining his clients at the Forum of the Corporations. Both my daughters are out, and of course the slaves are out too, celebrating the festival.'

She led them through a bright, chilly atrium into a red-walled tablinum which smelled of cloves and parchment. Nubia went straight to the bronze tripod full of glowing coals and warmed her hands over it.

'Yes,' said Vibia. 'I feel the cold too. This is my husband's study, but he won't mind us sitting here.'

'Oh,' said Flavia, going to an open scroll on the table. 'He's been reading Apollodorus.'

'No,' said Vibia with a smile. 'I have.'

'The story of Diana?' asked Flavia, scanning the scroll.

'Yes. Hot spiced wine?' Vibia gestured towards a silver jug.

Nubia nodded.

'Well-watered, thank you,' said Flavia, and added, 'I'm studying the myth of Hercules at the moment.'

Vibia's face lit up as she poured the steaming wine into glossy black cups.

'My father claims Hercules as his ancestor,' said Vibia. 'Do please sit.' She handed them their cups and added, 'I find Hercules a very complex hero, and not always likeable.'

Nubia sniffed the spicy wine and took a sip. It was nice: not too sweet and not too strong.

'I'm especially interested in the twelve tasks of Hercules,' said Flavia.

Vibia nodded. 'They say he had twelve but when you count up all his exploits, there were many more.'

'Were there?' said Flavia with a look of dismay.

'Roast chestnuts!' cried Vibia.

'Hercules had to roast some chestnuts?'

'No, no. Let me roast you some chestnuts. My middle daughter used to love them but the rest of the family doesn't share my passion for them. I bought a basket of them last week and I've been waiting for someone to share them with.' She put down her cup. 'I'll only be a moment.'

Vibia went out of the room. As soon as she was gone Flavia stood and wandered round the study, cup in hand, lightly touching the objects on the desk and reading the labels on the scrolls in their niches. Nubia looked around, too, but she remained in her chair, sipping her wine. The study, like so many in Ostia, had cinnabar red walls and a few elegant pieces of furniture. A black and white mosaic floor was mostly hidden by a threadbare eastern carpet. It occurred to Nubia that this was the home of someone who had once been wealthy but could not afford to replace expensive items.

Vibia returned with a bowl of chestnuts and a sharp little kitchen knife.

Flavia glanced over from beside the scroll shelves and said, 'I see you've got Euripides' play about Hercules.'

'Yes,' said Vibia, making an incision in one of the chestnuts and tossing it on the coals. 'I love plays, and that's a particularly good one.' She tossed another chestnut on the embers and smiled. 'It does please me to meet a girl who is literate,' she said. 'I've tried to teach my three daughters the classics.'

'Hello, mater!'

Nubia turned her head to see a slim boy of about sixteen enter the study. He wore a short red tunic. In one hand he held a bow and in the other a brace of long-beaked woodcock.

'Hello, dear,' said Vibia guardedly.

The boy slung the dead birds onto the desk and

turned his long-lashed eyes on the girls. Nubia stared. She had never seen such a pretty boy. He had full lips and his tanned cheeks were smooth as marble. His short hair was brown and feathery, the same colour as the birds' breasts.

Flavia was staring too, at the boy's chest, and suddenly Nubia realised why.

'Girls,' said Vibia, with a sigh, 'I'd like you to meet my youngest daughter Cartilia, whom we call Diana.'

SCROLL XI

'Great Neptune's beard!' breathed Flavia. 'You have *short hair!*'

She had never seen short hair on a freeborn girl before. She had read about it, knew that women often shaved their heads in extreme cases of grief or mourning, but to see a highborn girl with her head uncovered and a slave's haircut was shocking.

'Who did it to you?' she blurted out.

Diana turned her large brown eyes on Flavia and lifted her chin a fraction. 'I did it to myself last month,' she said. 'I hate men and I never want to marry. I want to be like Diana, the virgin huntress.'

Vibia smiled apologetically. 'My daughter has radical beliefs,' she said. 'Spiced wine, dear?'

'No, thank you mater, I'm just off to the tavern to meet my friends. Then I'm going hunting again.'

'Dressed in that short little tunic?' said Vibia.

'Yes, mater,' said Diana coolly. 'Dressed in this short little tunic.'

'Any luck?' asked Flavia as she tipped the roast chestnuts out of their papyrus cone onto the couch.

Jonathan took a chestnut and shook his head.

'Sorry,' he said. 'We just stood around for an hour listening to all the men tell their wild boar stories.'

Flavia peeled a chestnut. 'I guess we need to find another boar.'

It was noon and once again the four friends were sitting on one of the couches of her triclinium watching Hercules the wall-painter. A brazier glowing in the centre of the room did little to warm the cold air.

'He's very good,' whispered Jonathan, nodding at the little man, who had his back to them.

Lupus nodded enthusiastically.

Hercules was dabbing his brush rapidly on the damp wall, applying the colour before the plaster dried. He was painting the fourth task of Hercules. In this task, the hero was shown carrying a boar over his shoulders.

'Why is Hercules having no clothes?' asked Nubia. 'Isn't he cold?'

'That shows he's a hero,' explained Flavia. 'A hero is someone who is half mortal and half divine. Remember? Hercules was the son of Jupiter.'

'Yum,' said Jonathan. 'These chestnuts are delicious! Did you have any luck this morning?'

Flavia nodded. 'We met Cartilia's younger sister Diana. She dresses like a boy and she has short hair!'

Lupus pointed at Nubia's head and raised his eyebrows.

'Yes, I know Nubia has short hair, but she used to be a slave and anyway it looks right on Nubia. Diana looked very strange.'

Jonathan shelled another chestnut. 'Does she look like a really pretty boy?'

'Exactly.'

'Then I think I've seen her hunting in the woods once or twice. In Diana's Grove.'

'That'll be her,' said Flavia. 'I'd love to know her story!'

Nubia sighed with pleasure.

She and Flavia had lingered in the pink marble sudatorium of the Baths of Atalanta for nearly an hour. Now she was standing over a drain with three leaf-shaped holes and scraping her skin with a bronze strigil.

At first she had found it strange – almost uncomfortable – scraping the oil-softened dead skin from her body, but now she hated to go more than a day or two without scraping down. With satisfaction, she watched the grey sludge drip from the strigil into the drain. In a minute she and Flavia would visit the cold plunge to wash off the residue, followed by a brisk rubdown with a towel. But first they always scraped each other's backs.

'Ready, Nubia?'

Nubia nodded and handed Flavia her strigil. Then she turned her back. Flavia had always done Nubia first, since the first day she had demonstrated how to use the strigil. In a moment, Nubia would return the favour. But for now she closed her eyes and enjoyed the sensation of having her back gently scraped.

Once again, Nubia sighed with pleasure.

Behind her Flavia laughed. 'They say Romans love wine, the pleasure of Venus, and the baths, but you just love the baths!'

Nubia nodded happily. In the last month, she had learned the names of each of Ostia's twelve public baths. And over lunch she had remembered that one of them was called after the heroine who killed a foaming boar.

'This was a brilliant idea of yours to come to the Baths of Atalanta,' said Flavia. 'I've never been here before. They're so luxurious . . .'

Located near the Marina Gate, the Baths of Atalanta were exclusively for women. All the frescoes and mosaics showed Atalanta beating men at various tasks. On the wall of the frigidarium, a frescoed Atalanta ran a race far ahead of her gasping male competitors. On the domed ceiling of the caldarium she smugly watched her father execute the suitors who had failed to win her hand in marriage And here in the tepidarium – right at Nubia's feet – a black and white mosaic Atalanta speared a big, hairy boar while her male companions lay impotently around her.

Not only were the baths beautiful but so were the women who frequented them. Two exceptionally pretty women were oiling each other nearby. On the wall behind them was a fresco of Atalanta kissing Hippomenes, the youth who'd finally won her heart. It reminded Nubia of what she'd seen in the woods and she wondered again whether she should tell Flavia she had seen Aristo kissing a mysterious woman. But she found the words wouldn't come.

Behind her, Flavia stopped scraping.

'What?' Nubia turned her head.

'Shhh!' hissed Flavia, and put her mouth right in Nubia's ear. 'Listen to them.'

'Glycera only married him for his money,' the redhead was saying. 'She's already buried three husbands.'

'I don't know how she does it,' said the blonde. 'Glycera's not half as pretty as you are. I simply don't see the attraction.'

'They say,' murmured the first woman, and Nubia had to strain to hear her words, 'they say she's a witch, that she enchanted him.'

'That would explain a lot,' said the blonde in a less cautious tone of voice. 'She uses one potion to win them and another to kill them off!'

'And then,' said her friend, 'she collects the legacy!'

SCROLL XII

'And then,' said Jonathan, 'after he stopped scream-ing, he burst into tears. Imagine: a big old gladiator crying like a baby.'

The four friends were having a conference at Jonathan's house before resuming their investigations.

'What was your father doing to him?' Flavia asked Jonathan. 'Amputating a limb?'

He shook his head. 'Just burning off a little mole. The gladiator said it spoiled his looks.' Jonathan snorted as he spread some soft cheese on the flat bread. 'And I'm telling you: that brute is not pretty.'

Flavia's eyes opened wide. 'Is he a famous gladiator? It wasn't Rodan, was it?'

'Taurus,' said Jonathan. 'He's called Taurus. He's here in Ostia, visiting his mother for the holidays.'

'Wait!' cried Flavia. 'His name isn't Taurus, is it?'

'That's what I just said.'

'He's the one they call the Cretan Bull!'

Jonathan stared at her. 'That's a coincidence.'

'What coincidence?' asked Nubia.

'Hercules' seventh labour was to capture the Cretan bull,' said Flavia, her grey eyes bright. 'And Jonathan's father just treated a famous gladiator called the Cretan Bull!'

Lupus whistled softly.

Jonathan scratched his curly head. 'Did you find out anything this afternoon?'

'Yes. Nubia had the brilliant idea of going to the Baths of Atalanta and we overheard someone talking about a woman who marries men and then poisons them to inherit their wealth.'

'You don't think they were talking about Cartilia, do you?' asked Jonathan.

'No. The woman they were talking about was called Glycera and she was on her fourth husband. But apparently it's quite common. Women marry rich men, then kill them off. Or vice versa.'

Lupus wrote something on his wax tablet.

BUT YOUR FATHER ISN'T RICH

'I know,' said Flavia. 'But just between us, he's trying to give the *impression* we are. Maybe Cartilia thinks he's rich and wants to marry him for his money and then kill him off.'

'Whoa!' said Jonathan. 'You think Cartilia's only after your father's money? And that she's going to murder him for his inheritance?'

Flavia nodded. 'But I admit we need more proof. We've got to continue our investigations. We've completed the first four tasks: the lion, the hydra, the deer, and the boar. Hercules' fifth labour was to clean the stables.'

'Stables?' said Nubia, her eyes lighting up.

'Yes,' said Flavia, 'King Augeus had some stables. The fifth task of Hercules was to clean them out, because nobody had bothered for ten years.'

Lupus grimaced and held his nose.

Flavia giggled. 'Exactly. The poor horses were up to their noses in it.'

Jonathan grinned. 'Can I tell Nubia how he completed the task?'

'Of course.'

'Hercules wasn't just strong,' said Jonathan, turning to Nubia. 'He was clever, too. In the hills above the stables was a stream. Hercules put a huge boulder in the stream and diverted the water down the hillside. Then he opened the front doors and the back doors of the stables. The water swept through and washed all the dung away!'

'Clever,' said Nubia.

'Shouldn't we investigate Taurus the Cretan Bull before we go round the stables?' asked Jonathan.

'No,' said Flavia. 'I think we should complete the tasks in order. Capturing the Cretan bull was Hercules' seventh task. We still haven't completed five and six.'

'So we have to go and clean some stables this afternoon?' Jonathan raised an eyebrow.

'Hopefully we won't have to clean them, just visit them,' said Flavia. She sucked a strand of her light brown hair thoughtfully. 'There are two stables in Ostia. Any idea which one has the most dung?'

They all looked at Lupus.

He gave them his bug-eyed 'What?' expression, then snapped his fingers and nodded.

'I knew Lupus would have the answer,' laughed Flavia. They leaned in to watch him write:

HEAD SLAVE AT
LAURENTUM GATE STABLES
IS CALLED FIMUS

Flavia laughed again. 'That's it then. Shall we go?'

'Wait,' said Jonathan. 'The sixth task of Hercules was to kill the Stymphalian birds, wasn't it?'

'Correct,' said Flavia.

'Well,' said Jonathan, nudging Lupus, 'Apparently the ostrich was spotted in the woods this morning. Aristo invited Lupus and me to go hunting with him this afternoon. The magistrate declared all the escaped animals fair game, so Aristo and some friends are going to try to catch it.'

'Perfect! That's my Stymphalian bird! You two don't mind going, do you?'

'Do we mind hunting instead of trailing around the stables after you?'

Jonathan and Lupus glanced at each other.

'Not at all,' said Jonathan with a grin.

'There's definitely something strange about those Poplicola girls,' said Fimus the stable-slave. He was a pot-bellied man with a blotched face and infected eyes.

Nubia averted her eyes from his unpleasant face and

inhaled. The Laurentum Gate stables smelled nice – a mixture of hay and horses and dung. It was warm, here, too. Nubia knew that whenever Flavia's father or uncle needed to hire a horse, this was where they came.

'What's strange about the Poplicola girls?' asked Flavia.

A chestnut-coloured mare put her head over one of the stall doors and nickered softly. Nubia moved over to the stall and let the mare sniff her hand.

'The Poplicola women all ride,' Fimus said. 'It's not often you see a woman on horseback. Barbaric, if you ask me.'

Nubia stroked the mare's nose. She didn't think there was anything strange about a woman riding a horse. All the women in her clan could ride a horse as well as a camel.

'Also,' said Fimus, 'one of them's just gone and cut off all her hair.'

'Diana,' said Flavia.

'Is that her name?' Fimus frowned. 'I thought it was something else.'

'Diana's just her nickname,' said Flavia. 'She and her sisters are all called Cartilia.'

'Oh,' said the slave. 'Well, anyway, the women in that family aren't quite right, if you ask me. Their mother rides too.'

'Vibia?' said Flavia.

'That's her.'

'Can you tell us anything else about that family?'

'Paula! That's her name. She's the strange one. She came in here last week, asking about that gladiator.'

'Who? Taurus the Cretan Bull?'

'That's him. He's spending the holidays here in Ostia.'

'I know. And Paula asked where he lived?'

'No,' said Fimus, scratching his belly. 'That's the strange thing. She asked which baths he usually went to.'

Aristo's friend Lysander was a short dark Greek employed by the corporation of grain measurers as a scribe and accountant. But today he had put aside his abacus and wax tablets to enjoy a day of hunting.

'Can you boys make a lot of noise?' he asked Jonathan and Lupus. 'All the slaves are on holiday and we need some beaters.'

'Of course,' said Jonathan. Lupus nodded vigorously and started howling.

'Not yet!' Lysander rolled his eyes. 'We have to set up the net first.'

They were standing near the tomb of Avita Procula near the Grove of Diana. The afternoon was cold but the wind had died and a high cloud cover gave the world an unreal, pearly glow.

'Let's go then,' said Aristo.

'We're just waiting for one more person,' said Lysander, flushing.

Aristo gave Lysander a sharp look. 'Don't tell me you've invited her!'

'I'm sorry, Aristo. But she asked to come. And you know how I feel about her . . .'

'By the gods, Lysander! Now she's going to think I—'

'Shhh!' Lysander hissed. 'Here she comes.'

Lupus heard Aristo curse under his breath and he saw Jonathan's eyes open wide. He turned to see a boy striding confidently towards them from the direction of the Laurentum Gate. He wore a red tunic and red leather boots. A short cloak of moss-green wool was slung over his shoulders and in his right hand he carried a hunting javelin.

Lupus frowned and as the boy drew nearer he saw it was not a boy at all, but a girl with unnaturally short hair.

Jonathan bent his head and whispered in Lupus's ear, 'Diana.'

Lupus nodded. And stared. Jonathan had called her pretty. Nobody had said she was beautiful.

SCROLL XIII

'I'm afraid I can't let you girls in,' said Oleosus, the door-slave at the Forum Baths. 'Men only today . . .' He was a loose-limbed youth with floppy black hair and heavy-lidded brown eyes.

'But we just saw two women come in,' protested Flavia. 'One of them was wearing a pink mantle and the other was holding a waxed parasol.'

'Oh, them.' Oleosus gave them a lazy smile. 'The senator's daughters. They've just come to watch Taurus training. And for some of his scrapings.'

'For some *what*?'

'Some of his scrapings. After he's worked up a sweat, his slave scrapes him down. Then he puts the . . . er . . . mixture in cheap little bottles and sells it to the ladies. They pay a gold coin per bottle.'

'*What?*' Flavia's jaw dropped. '*Why?*'

He winked. 'They say if you mix a little in someone's food—'

'In their *food*?'

He nodded. 'Mix a little in someone's food and he'll become very passionate and desire you.'

'A love potion!' Flavia breathed.

She and Nubia glanced at each other.

'Does it work?' Flavia asked him.

Oleosus shrugged. 'It works for Taurus. They say he just bought his mother a nice little farm with the money he's made from his scrapings.'

'And respectable women buy the scrapings?'

'All sorts of women buy it.'

'I don't suppose you remember any of their names?' Flavia toyed with the pouch tied to her belt, so that the coins clinked softly. 'A woman named Cartilia Poplicola, for example?'

He frowned.

'A little taller than me?' prompted Flavia. 'About twenty-five? Pretty in a cold sort of way? Calls herself Paula?'

His face relaxed into a smile. 'Oh, Paula!' he said. 'She came round as soon as he arrived in town. Bought a jar last week and another one yesterday!'

As they set up the net, Lupus couldn't stop looking at Diana.

He noticed that Lysander was watching her, too, and saw a wounded look in his eyes. Glancing back at Diana, Lupus saw the reason. She had bent down to whisper something in Aristo's ear. Her fingers, resting lightly on the back of his neck, toyed with his curls in a gesture of startling intimacy.

Aristo, intent on anchoring the net to the ground, did not even raise his eyes to look at her. Lupus saw his jaw clench and suddenly he realised what was happening.

Lysander loved Diana, but she loved Aristo. And it was obvious that Aristo despised her. Lupus snorted as he tied one of the red feathers to the edge of the net: Cupid the love god was such a mischief-maker.

'So, Diana,' said Jonathan, 'you're Paula's sister.'

'What?' Diana scowled at him, then stood up.

'Cartilia Paula is your sister,' repeated Jonathan.

Diana nodded curtly and moved forward to inspect one of the fastenings on the net.

'Is she nice?'

Diana pouted. 'No. She's a greedy old witch.'

'Oh. Sorry to upset you.'

'Don't mention her and I won't be upset.'

'Right then.' Jonathan whistled a little tune, then gave Lupus a significant look.

When the net was securely fixed between some trees, and its edge marked with red feathers, the five of them moved quietly back through the grove, scanning the soft ground for any sign of their prey.

Lupus pretended to look for ostrich tracks, too, but he was really watching Diana out of the corner of his eye. His alertness paid off. When they were almost out of the grove, Lysander knelt to examine something near a tiny stream.

'Here,' said Lysander, pointing at the mud. 'That's the footprint of an ostrich.'

As they all gathered round to look, Lupus saw Diana slip something into Aristo's belt. A piece of papyrus.

'It's fresh!' said Jonathan.

As they all peered down at it, Lupus saw Aristo's hand close over the note.

'This must be where the creature comes to drink,' said Lysander, standing up again and looking round. 'I think the bird was here this morning and he may well return tomorrow.' He glanced up at the sky. 'It's getting late. I suggest we make an early start tomorrow – maybe bring some dogs. We'll start over there at the edge of the grove and beat towards the net. Agreed?'

The others nodded.

'Can you boys bring something noisy? Castanets, rattles, tambourines? There are only a few of us so we'll have to make a lot of noise.'

As they walked back towards the town walls, Lupus saw Aristo unfold the scrap of papyrus that Diana had slipped him. Aristo scanned the note, then crushed it into a ball and let it drop to the muddy ground.

'So we'll meet tomorrow just past dawn?' said Diana a few minutes later. They stood at the fork in the road. Diana was looking at Aristo but it was Lysander who replied.

'That's right,' he said. 'At the tomb of Avita Procula. Same place we met today.' Lysander nodded towards the Laurentum Gate, 'Are you going home now, Diana? Shall I walk with you?'

'No,' said Diana over her shoulder. 'I'm going to make an offering to the goddess and ask her to give me success in the hunt.'

I think I know what you're hunting, thought Lupus.

And later, back in his room, when he smoothed out her papyrus note, he saw that his suspicion had been correct.

'Scrapings,' said Flavia to Jonathan. 'The door-slave at the Forum Baths told us that if you mix some of a gladiator's sweaty scrapings in someone's food then that person will fall in love with you.'

'Ewww,' said Jonathan and then frowned. 'But how can you be sure the person falls in love with *you*? I mean, wouldn't he fall in love with the gladiator? Or the first person he sees? Because *that* never works. At least not in the plays . . .'

'No,' said Flavia. 'Before you put it in their food you say a kind of prayer over the mixture. To Venus. And then – here's the really disgusting bit – you spit in it. Or put some of your other bodily fluids in.'

'And again I say: ewww.' Jonathan shuddered. He was at Flavia's house, leaning against the warm kitchen wall and watching the girls prepare dinner. Nubia was stirring a pot of stew and Flavia was cutting up some firm white mushrooms. When she reached for another handful Jonathan grabbed some slices from the chopping board. They were delicious.

'Apparently,' said Flavia, 'when the person eats the food with the potion in it, they have a gladiator's passion for whoever spat in the potion. And that's why Cartilia wanted the gladiator's scrapings. She has obviously bewitched pater! I told Nubia the first day I saw her. I said: "I'll bet she's bewitched pater." Didn't I, Nubia?'

'Yes,' said Nubia and continued to stir the stew.

Jonathan popped a slice of mushroom in his mouth. 'And the slave at the baths said she bought some of Taurus's scrapings?'

Flavia nodded. 'Twice. About a week ago and yesterday.'

She slapped Jonathan's hand as it crept forward to take another mushroom.

'So you think she's already put some of this disgusting love potion in your father's food?' he asked.

'Yes. They saw each other a few days ago at Cordius's house. I think she must have done it then. Maybe mixed it in his spiced wine or something. Remember I told you he seemed different? That morning we ran away from the ostrich?'

'Yes,' said Jonathan.

Flavia pushed the mushroom slices to one side of the chopping board and removed some leeks from the bowl of salted water.

'Speaking of ostriches,' she said, as she began to slice the leeks, 'how did you get on today? Any luck?'

'No,' said Jonathan. 'The ostrich wasn't in the woods. But we saw a fresh footprint and we've set a trap for it. A big net with red feathers at the edges. Lysander says the animals avoid the feathers and run straight into the centre of the net. Tomorrow we'll beat the woods and drive the ostrich into it. If he's there, that is.'

'I meant did you get any more information about Cartilia?'

'Actually we did. Cartilia's sister was helping us set up the net.'

Flavia stopped slicing. 'Diana was hunting with you?'

Jonathan nodded. 'And she called Cartilia a greedy old witch.'

'I knew it!' said Flavia, putting down her knife. 'What else did she say?'

'Nothing. She went all pouty when I mentioned Cartilia.'

'Do you think you can milk her for more information?'

'I don't know,' said Jonathan. 'She doesn't like talking about her sister.' Seeing the expression on Flavia's face, he added: 'Lupus and I are going hunting with them tomorrow at dawn. We'll try to get more information then.'

'Good!' Flavia resumed her chopping. 'Where did you say Lupus was?'

'Running an errand for father. He volunteered to go into town and deliver some ointment to one of father's patients. He shouldn't be long.'

Lupus hid behind a column and waited until the group of drunken revellers had passed by on their way home from the tavern. Then he looked at the scrap of papyrus again. He was glad he had learned how to read. Only a few months ago the black marks would have meant nothing to him. Now they made his heart pound with excitement.

MEET ME BEHIND THE SHRINE OF THE
CROSSROADS AT DUSK. WE MUST TALK.
FROM CARTILIA.

Lupus could barely see the letters in the fading light.
Soon it would be dark. He had delivered the doctor's
medicine and now he was waiting to see whether
Aristo would meet Diana at the shrine.

Ostia's main street was almost deserted now. Only
one or two drunken slaves wandered about, trying to
remember where they lived. Lupus pressed his back to
the column as a pair of vigiles strolled past. Both held
torches. One had a large water skin slung over his
back, the other carried a thick hemp mat rolled up on
his shoulders. Lupus knew their job was to patrol the
town to prevent crime and especially fire, a particular
danger during the winter when braziers, oil-lamps and
torches burned in every home.

The men passed by without seeing him and Lupus
felt a slow smile spread across his face. He had missed
the excitement of the hunt. Of becoming invisible. Of
watching people who thought they were alone.

After the vigiles turned the corner, Lupus ran silently along the murky colonnade until he reached the
end. Then, like a shadow, he quickly descended the
three steps and slipped through the forum. Crouching
low, he moved towards the shrine of the crossroads,
glad of his silent new boots.

The thickening purple gloom of dusk blanketed the
town now. He could see a single yellow lamp flicker-

ing somewhere inside the shrine and the black silhouettes of two cypress trees rising up behind it. Somewhere a blackbird uttered its warning cry in the cold air. He could smell the winter smell of wood smoke.

As he started to make his way to the back of the marble shrine, he tripped on something and fell onto the damp ground.

He could barely make out the dark form lying beside the shrine.

Tentatively, Lupus reached out and touched it.

It was the body of a man.

SCROLL XIV

His heart pounding, Lupus recoiled from the body. It was still warm.

The body groaned.

He was still alive!

Then Lupus caught the rancid odour of vomit and he turned away with mixed relief and disgust. It was only a reveller who had passed out after drinking too much spiced wine.

He stood up again and his fingertips on the cold marble wall guided him around the back of the shrine. He sensed rather than saw the two trees ahead of him.

Suddenly, in the darkness, he heard a woman's voice, low and urgent

'Aristo?' said the voice. 'Aristo, is that you?'

Lupus pressed himself against the trunk of one of the trees and held his breath.

'Aristo?' repeated the voice.

Lupus's heart was pounding so loudly he was sure she must be able to hear it. The crunch of her foot on a twig alerted him and he moved round the trunk, keeping it between them.

'Aristo? Stop playing games with me . . .'

Silence.

'I know you're there. I can hear you breathing.'

Lupus tipped his head back and closed his eyes, listening with all his might: ready to move one way if she moved the other.

'Why are you doing this to me? Why are you torturing me? Aristo, I love you. I love you so much . . .'

From the road a flicker of lamplight and the crunch of military boots on paving stones. Another pair of vigiles were approaching.

Lupus heard the woman curse softly and move away.

After a moment he heard a man's deep voice. 'Hey, miss. You shouldn't be out after dark. This is a favourite hiding place for robbers.'

'Can we escort you home?' said the other watchman.

'Yes . . . yes please!' Her voice was trembling.

It was easy to follow her after that. The flickering torches lit the three figures as they moved down the centre of the road: the woman between the two big watchmen.

Once she turned to look back, but Lupus quickly pressed himself into the inky black shadows of a shopfront.

Presently, as he had expected, they stopped in front of Cartilia's house. He heard the brass knocker resound and saw a path of light pour out from within as the door opened almost immediately. There were relieved voices and the woman stepped inside.

Lupus was almost certain the woman had been

Diana. But he was not positive: she had worn a long cloak, and a hood which covered her face.

Nubia held her hands over the glowing coals and rubbed them together. It was just before dawn on the third day of the Saturnalia. The dogs were snuffling in the dark garden, eager to be off for the hunt. The four friends stood in the kitchen, warming themselves by the hearth while Lupus and Jonathan waited for Aristo to come out of the latrine. Captain Geminus and the slaves were still asleep.

'You're sure Aristo was here yesterday at dusk?' Jonathan whispered.

Flavia nodded. 'He came in right after you left. He'd caught some rabbits and we put them in the stew. Why do you ask?'

Jonathan lowered his voice even more: 'Yesterday, while we were setting up the net, Lupus saw Diana slip Aristo a note. She wanted him to meet her at the shrine of the crossroads. *She* came to the shrine but *he* never appeared.'

'Why did she want to meet him in such a strange place at such a strange time?'

'We think she's in love with him,' said Jonathan.

Nubia felt a strange sensation in the pit of her stomach.

'Cartilia's sister loves Aristo?' Flavia's eyes opened wide.

Lupus nodded emphatically and wrote on his tablet.

LYSANDER LOVES DIANA.
DIANA LOVES ARISTO.
BUT ARISTO DOESN'T LIKE DIANA.

'Who is Lysander?' asked Nubia.

'He's Aristo's Greek friend,' said Jonathan. 'Short. Dark. They often hunt together.'

'It's the classic love triangle,' said Flavia, nodding wisely.

'Why triangle?' asked Jonathan.

'Well, A loves B and B loves C. It's a triangle.'

'No it's not,' said Jonathan. 'It's a V. If C loves A, *then* it's a triangle.'

'Good point.' Flavia turned to Lupus. 'How did you know what Diana's note said?' she asked him.

Lupus presented the scrap of papyrus with a flourish.

Flavia grabbed the note and held it close to the red hearth-coals so she could read it. Nubia peered over her shoulder.

'But it's signed Cartilia.' Flavia frowned and straightened up. 'Are you sure it was Diana who came to the shrine?'

Lupus looked at her. Then he shrugged.

SHE WAS WEARING LONG CLOAK he wrote on his tablet.

'Grey cloak with hood?' whispered Nubia.

Lupus nodded and gave her his bug-eyed look.

'How did you know what she was wearing?' asked Flavia.

They all looked at Nubia.

She took a breath. 'Two days after Miriam's betrothal . . .'

'The first day of the Saturnalia?' asked Flavia.

Nubia nodded. 'On that afternoon when I take the dogs in woods, behold! I see Aristo and woman in cloak.'

'What were they doing?' asked Jonathan.

Nubia felt her face grow hot. 'Kissing. Very kissing.'

'Great Juno's peacock,' whispered Flavia. 'Why didn't you tell us this before?'

Nubia hung her head. She herself wasn't sure why she hadn't mentioned it.

'It doesn't matter,' said Flavia. 'But who was she? Did you see her face?'

Nubia shook her head and looked up at Flavia. 'No. I did not see her face. She was wearing cloak. Grey cloak with hood.'

SCROLL XV

'Man-eating horses,' said Flavia. 'Where will we find man-eating horses in Ostia?'

'Stables?' suggested Nubia.

'I suppose we could try the Laurentum Gate stables again. Or the other ones: the Cart Drivers' stables . . .' Flavia's voice trailed off.

It was an hour past dawn. The boys and Aristo had gone off to hunt their ostrich and once again the two girls were sitting on a dust-sheet covered couch in the dining room. They were sipping milky spiced wine and watching Hercules prepare the last wall. He was using a wide brush to cover the old mustard-yellow plaster with a thin coat of lime mixed with plaster. When this dried it would make a brilliant base for the new images.

'We need to find mad horses,' said Flavia. 'Or maybe someone called Diomedes. That was the name of their master. He used to feed chopped-up people to his horses. That's what drove his horses mad. So Hercules completed the labour by killing Diomedes and feeding him to his own horses. Then they were so full and sleepy that Hercules was easily able to capture them.'

'In baths?' said Nubia hopefully. 'Maybe mosaics of man-eating horses in baths.'

'I don't know of any,' said Flavia.

'There's a retired legionary named Diomedes,' said Hercules the wall-painter. 'New in town. Belongs to one of those new religions.'

'What?' cried Flavia. 'What did you just say?' It was the first time she had heard him speak.

Hercules turned to look at them. His watery eyes twinkled and his rubbery mouth curved in a smile.

'Diomedes,' he said in a squeaky voice. 'He's a retired soldier and he's the priest of a new cult. They worship a young god who was born near the end of December. Once a week his followers gather to share bread and wine, in order to remember the last supper he ate before he ascended to a higher plane.'

'Oh,' said Flavia. 'Diomedes must be a Christian. They worship a shepherd named Jesus. They call him the Christ or Messiah.'

'No,' said Hercules, dipping his brush in the white-wash mixture, 'Diomedes certainly isn't a Christian; I would know. The name of his god is something else. Starts with M . . . Menecrates? Marsyas? Mithras? That's it. Diomedes is a priest of Mithras. He lives not far from here, in a house just off Fuller's Street. I often pass that way. I see them gathering to observe their special meal on Sunday mornings.'

'But it's Sunday morning now!'

'Yes it is,' said Hercules. 'If you hurry, you might catch them . . .'

'My dear boys,' said Lysander, 'What are you doing with bows and arrows? You know we're using the net today. And I've got my hunting-spear.'

'Oh leave them alone,' said Aristo. 'We may never catch this ostrich and at least they might bring home a rabbit or two.'

'Very well,' Lysander sighed. 'You boys need to move slowly towards the net. Let the dogs bark and make as much noise as you can. Can you count as high as three hundred?'

Lupus nodded. Nipur was tugging at his lead, but Lupus was strong enough to hold him. Jonathan was in charge of Tigris and Aristo held Scuto. The three dogs were wheezing with eagerness to be off.

'Good,' said Lysander. 'Don't start beating till you've reached three hundred. That will give me time to take up position by the net.'

'What?' said Jonathan. 'You're going to sit by the net while the rest of us do all the work?'

'That's the way it works,' said Lysander with a grin. 'Diana. Would you like to join me?'

'Why don't *you* stay with the boys?' Diana said to Lysander. 'Aristo and I can wait by the net.'

Lysander's grin faded and Aristo looked up sharply.

'Er . . . no,' he said. 'I'm the boys' tutor. It's my job to protect them. I'll stay with them. Diana, you wait by the net with Lysander.'

Diana turned wounded brown eyes on Aristo. For a

moment their gazes locked. Aristo looked away first, guiltily it seemed to Lupus.

Diana turned on her heel. 'Come on then, Lysander!' she snapped over her shoulder. 'Let's go.'

Diomedes, priest of Mithras, stood in his open doorway and gazed down at Flavia. Although he was quite an old man – in his early fifties – he was still lean and muscular.

'Cartilia Poplicola,' she repeated. The stench of urine from the nearby fullers was so strong that Flavia had to breathe through her mouth.

Diomedes snorted. 'Don't mention that woman to me! Her husband Caldus was one of our new initiates. But he's not with us any more.' Diomedes shook his head angrily. 'And it's her fault,' he muttered.

Flavia's eyes opened wide. 'It was her fault?'

'That's what I was told.' He frowned. 'I'm sorry,' he said. 'What did you say your name was?'

'Flavia Gemina, daughter of Marcus Flavius Geminus, sea captain.'

'I don't know the name. Is he one of our followers?'

'No, I just—'

'Young lady. I am very busy today. I thought you were bringing a message from one of our members. That's why I opened the door to you. May I ask you to come back later?'

'That's all right,' said Flavia politely. 'I won't bother you again. Thank you very much. You've just told me what I needed to know.'

Jonathan shook his tambourine with one hand and gripped Tigris's lead in the other. They were moving slowly through the pine grove making as much noise as possible. Over on his right, Lupus was beating his goatskin drum.

'Steady, Tigris!' called Jonathan, feeling the tug on the lead. 'We want to take it slowly. Give the big bird time to hear us coming . . .'

He glanced at Aristo, just visible through the trees on his left. Aristo held Scuto's taut lead and occasionally he clattered some castanets.

Jonathan looked up. It was morning now, with a high clear sky which would deepen to blue as the day progressed. He sucked in a lungful of air, as cold and intoxicating as the snow-chilled wine he had tasted once at a rich man's house. It was good to be out in the woods hunting with his friends and the dogs.

Hunting helped him forget the worries that were as constant as the throbbing of the brand on his left arm.

Worries about how he and his father would cope when Miriam was married and living in Laurentum. Worries about Lupus, who occasionally still disappeared without a word. Worries about Aristo, who seemed so distracted lately. Worries about Flavia, who was becoming exactly what she had sworn not to become: a tyrant.

And the biggest worry of all, the subject that was always there, drawing his thoughts towards Rome . . .

'Jonathan! Look out!'

Aristo's voice clear across the glade and a crashing from the thicket ahead and there was the ostrich. The bird seemed confused by the din and in spite of Tigris's hysterical barking it took a flapping step towards Jonathan.

Jonathan lifted his tambourine and gave it a shake. 'Go the other way, you stupid ostrich,' he muttered. 'The other way! Towards the net!'

But the ostrich didn't understand Latin.

It charged straight at him.

SCROLL XVI

Jonathan reacted by instinct. He dropped the tambourine and Tigris's lead. In one fluid motion he lifted the bow from across his body with his left hand and plucked an arrow from his quiver with the right. There was no need to take careful aim. The enormous flapping bird was almost upon him.

Jonathan fired straight into its chest and then threw himself out of the way.

The ostrich's forward momentum carried it past and Jonathan lifted himself – gasping – on one muddy elbow. He was just in time to see the creature swerve towards Aristo, who threw his javelin.

The bird flapped, staggered, then veered again to receive a second arrow – this one in the neck – from Lupus's bow. Now the dogs were upon it and Jonathan was almost sorry as he watched them bring the bird heavily to the ground.

'Get the dogs away,' cried Aristo. 'The feathers are worth a fortune!'

Jonathan had trained the puppies well; they obeyed his command immediately and quickly backed away. But Scuto wanted to play with the giant thrashing bird. Suddenly one of the ostrich's powerful legs caught Flavia's dog in the chest. With a yelp, Scuto went flying through the air and Jonathan heard the terrible thud as he fell.

Aristo ran forward, hunting knife in hand, and stamped hard on the bird's neck just below the head. Then, with one swift, slashing movement, he ended the creature's misery.

Jonathan ran to Scuto. Flavia's dog lay motionless in the mud and pine needles. Nipur and Tigris were sniffing him and whimpering, and Lupus already had his ear against Scuto's chest.

Jonathan stopped and looked down at Lupus. 'Is he . . . Is he dead?'

Doctor Mordecai lifted his head from the patient and smiled. 'He's going to be all right. He may possibly have cracked a rib or two, but there's not much we can do. He just needs to rest until it heals.' Scuto lay panting quietly on Flavia's bed.

'Oh, Doctor Mordecai!' Flavia threw her arms round Mordecai's waist and squeezed. 'Thank you! Did you hear that?' She turned to the others and the look on her face made them all smile, even Aristo.

'We have to celebrate tonight!' Flavia cried. 'Alma, I know it's the Saturnalia, and I'm supposed to be cooking but I want to nurse Scuto back to health and would you mind?'

'My dear, I'd like nothing better!' cried Alma. 'We'll chop up that big bird and eat him for weeks.'

'Wait!' said Jonathan. 'We can't just go chopping it up. Aren't we supposed to share it out with Lysander and Diana?'

'Dear Apollo!' cried Aristo. 'I'd forgotten all about them.' He glanced out through the lattice-work screen of the window. 'It's almost noon. I hope they haven't been sitting out there this whole time! I'd better go tell them. Lysander will be furious.'

Lupus snorted and Jonathan nodded his agreement: 'He's not the only one.'

Lupus loved oysters.

They were cool and slippery and he could easily swallow them whole. He often had good dreams after eating them, and he was always full of energy the following day.

And so he was delighted when Alma set a plate of oysters before his couch.

It was mid-afternoon on the third day of the Saturnalia. They were celebrating the capture of the ostrich and Scuto's survival. Lupus reclined next to Jonathan and Mordecai. On the couch opposite him were Aristo, Flavia and Nubia. Flavia's father and Cartilia Poplicola shared the central couch.

Flavia had been in a good mood when she handed them their garlands of ivy and mistletoe. She didn't even seem to mind Cartilia's presence. Lupus saw the reason at once: Scuto lay in his usual place under the central couch.

Flavia's father was in a good mood, too. He'd spent

the day with his twin brother Gaius a few miles down the coast at Laurentum. Gaius's landlord, a young man named Pliny, had sent a Saturnalia gift of three dozen fresh oysters in a cask of seawater.

OYSTERS ARE MY FAVOURITE Lupus wrote on his wax tablet and held it up for all to see.

'Oh! What a good idea!' cried Flavia. 'Let's all say what our favourite food is! As king of the Saturnalia, I command it! Mine is roast chicken. And salad. What about you, Jonathan?'

'Venison stew,' he said, 'especially if I caught the deer myself.'

'I love mushrooms,' said Aristo.

'Me, too,' said Jonathan.

'My favourite food is salted tuna,' said Flavia's father. He laughed. 'How about you, Cartilia?'

'I love salads,' she said. 'But I also adore oysters. The first time I—'

'Next!' cried Flavia. 'What about you, Doctor Mordecai?'

After a short hesitation and a glance at Cartilia, Mordecai said softly: 'I am very partial to lamb. Roast lamb in particular.'

Flavia turned to Nubia and laughed. 'And I think we all know Nubia's favourite food . . .'

'Dates!' they all cried together, and Nubia smiled.

'Yes,' she said. 'I am loving dates. But now I am loving them even more with almond inside.'

'And that brings us back to Lupus and the oysters!' said Flavia. 'Let's eat!'

Lupus reached for the tiny glass jug of vinegar. He dribbled a few drops onto the first of his oysters.

The oyster twitched.

Lupus grunted with approval. Using his spoon, he freed the oyster from its shell, tipped his head back and let it slip down his throat. Then he tossed the shell into the centre of the room. It fell with a clatter onto the marble floor. Nipur trotted forward, sniffed it, then sneezed. Scuto yawned and remained where he was. He knew oyster shells weren't edible.

Lupus grinned. And tested the next oyster.

'Why are you putting vinegar on him?' asked Nubia.

'To see if it's still alive,' said Cartilia. 'Right Lupus?'

Lupus gave her a thumbs-up. Then he tipped his head back and swallowed the second oyster.

'They're still alive?' Jonathan had been examining an oyster. Now he hastily put it back on the plate and stared at it suspiciously.

'Try it, Jonathan!' said Cartilia. 'Drop a little vinegar on the oyster. If it contracts, that means it's still alive. They're very good for you, aren't they doctor?'

Mordecai nodded. 'I always recommend them for pregnant mothers and invalids. The fresher the better.'

Lupus grinned as Jonathan dribbled some vinegar from the cruet onto his oyster.

'Ahh!' Jonathan started back. 'It moved! It *is* alive. I'm not eating that!'

'Come on, Jonathan!' cried Flavia. 'They're good for you.'

'I don't want something alive crawling around inside me!'

'They can't crawl,' laughed Cartilia. 'They have no feet.'

Lupus showed Jonathan his wax tablet.

CAN I HAVE YOUR SHARE THEN?

'Jonathan,' said Mordecai. 'It is extremely impolite to refuse a host's food.'

'All right,' sighed Jonathan. 'I'll try one.'

'Just free it from its shell,' said Cartilia.

'It's attached by a little sucker,' explained Aristo.

'And swallow it down whole!' said Flavia.

'Shouldn't I chew it?' asked Jonathan, not taking his eyes from the grey blob glistening in its shell.

'No!' they all cried.

'Don't think about what you're eating,' said Cartilia. 'Just do it.'

Jonathan hesitated.

'Jonathan!' said Flavia firmly, 'as king of the Saturnalia I command you to eat that oyster!'

Everyone laughed and Jonathan gave them a queasy smile. Finally he took a deep breath, tipped back his head and bravely swallowed it whole.

Everyone laughed again at the expression on Jonathan's face and Lupus inclined his head in thanks as his friend grimly slid the plate of oysters towards him.

Flavia was in the latrine when she heard the first chords of Aristo's lyre and the warble of Nubia's flute.

She smiled. It was a new song Nubia had written for Aristo. She called it 'The Storyteller'. Flavia heard the beat of Lupus's drum and thought how much he'd improved in the past month. Then Jonathan came in on his barbiton, a steady thrum so low you hardly heard it, but missed if it wasn't there.

Flavia quickly finished her business and put the sponge-stick back in the beaker of vinegar. They needed her. It wasn't right without the tambourine.

She opened the door of the latrine and stepped out. Then she froze.

The tambourine had just joined the other instruments, strong, steady, confident. And much better than she ever played it. Flavia took a step forward and looked through the ivy-twined columns towards the dining room.

It was late: dusk was approaching. Beyond the blue-green garden, the dining room looked like an illuminated treasure box. A dozen oil-lamps filled the room with golden light and the two freshly painted walls glowed red. Jonathan was wearing his cinnamon kaftan. Lupus wore his sea-green tunic and a Saturn-alia cap he had found somewhere; it was red felt, trimmed with white fur. Flavia could hear Nubia and Aristo; she didn't need to see them. But she needed to know who was playing her part. She took another step forward and swallowed hard as the central couch came into view and she saw who was banging her tambourine.

It was Cartilia. Cartilia had taken her place.

For several days a particular sequence of notes – with what Aristo called a key change – had been sounding over and over in Nubia's head. It was a passage where her flute and Aristo's lyre played the notes above a strong deep beat of drum and barbiton, and a jingle of tambourine. Nubia had been craving the sound of it as she sometimes craved the taste of salt on bread. Now they were playing the song and the sequence was coming up. She could barely contain her excitement.

She was here. Sitting cross-legged on the foot of the couch. In this red and gold room. About to hear and play the music she had been longing for. The anticipation was delicious.

It was coming . . . coming . . . coming . . . and now!

As she played the key change, the notes inside her head fused with the notes outside her, notes so real that she physically felt them. Her body gave an involuntary shudder as they played the passage. How could that happen? How could you crave a melody as you craved a type of food? It was as if her heart had been hungry for the song.

Nubia turned her head as she played, and looked at her friends. Lupus, his head tipped to one side as he drummed away. And Jonathan, smiling up at her from his deep barbiton. Cartilia was a revelation, her eyes were closed and there was a sweet smile on her face as she shook the tambourine.

And Aristo – the storyteller – lost in the music. Nubia hadn't told him that the song was about him; she had been too shy. His curly head was down but she could see his thick eyelashes and as she watched his fingers moving swiftly over the strings, a huge wave of affection washed over Nubia. The music which had arisen in her heart now flowed back to her from him. He and the music were one. And because she loved the music, she loved him, too.

Suddenly her fingers were trembling too much to play. The notes of her flute hesitated, faltered and failed. Her heart was pounding louder than Lupus's drum.

The others stopped playing, too, and the music died.

'Are you all right, Nubia?' Aristo looked concerned. Nubia nodded and dropped her flute and pressed her cool hands against her hot face.

Oh no, she thought. It can't be.

'Nubia?' It was Mordecai's voice. 'What's the matter?'

'I am just feeling . . .' She knew they were all staring at her – that *he* was staring at her – and she couldn't bear it. Without looking at any of them, she slipped off the couch and ran out of the dining room.

Jonathan watched Nubia run out and opened his mouth to say something. But he closed it again as

Flavia stalked in. Her face was pale as she went straight to the central couch and held out her hand.

'That's my tambourine,' Flavia said to Cartilia. 'Please give it to me.'

'Flavia!' Captain Geminus's voice was angry but Cartilia answered calmly.

'I'm so sorry, Flavia. I didn't mean to take what was yours. Shall I bring my own next time?'

Jonathan saw the fury flicker in Flavia's eyes and he knew she was about to say something they would all regret.

'Aaaaah!' he yelled, and clutched his stomach. 'Owwwwww!' He writhed realistically on the couch, careful not to knock his barbiton onto the floor.

'Jonathan!' cried his father. 'What's the matter?'

'My stomach!' cried Jonathan, and then. 'Aaaaah! Feels like I've swallowed shards of clay! Urrrrgh!'

'Great Neptune's beard,' exclaimed Flavia's father.

'Oh dear!' Cartilia said. 'Oh dear!'

Flavia's face had gone blank for a moment, but now there was a look of concern on it. 'Jonathan!' she cried. 'It must have been a bad oyster! Oh Jonathan! I'm so sorry I made you eat it!'

His ploy had worked. Her anger was forgotten.

'I forgive you.' Jonathan smiled, then remembered he was supposed to be in agony. 'Ahhhh!' He writhed again and curled up into a ball so they wouldn't see his expression. He had caught a glimpse of Lupus's narrowed eyes. One person, at least, had seen through his ruse.

Jonathan knew that if he looked at Lupus again he would burst out laughing. So he pressed his face into one of the cushions on the dining couch and bit it hard.

SCROLL XVII

The next morning Jonathan and Lupus found Flavia in the dining room. She was sitting in her usual place on one of the dining couches, sipping her poculum and watching Hercules. It was a lovely morning: bright and clear and almost mild.

'Are you feeling better today, Jonathan?' asked Flavia after she had greeted the boys. She patted the dust sheet beside her and Jonathan and Lupus hopped up onto it.

'Yes, I'm much better,' said Jonathan. The look of genuine concern on her face made him feel quite guilty. 'Father gave me an infusion of camomile mixed with syrup of figs. He said it probably wasn't the oyster, just indigestion from eating while reclining.'

'But everybody knows it's better for you to eat lying down. Anyway,' Flavia lowered her voice, 'I'm glad you had a stomach-ache when you did. I almost got myself locked up for the rest of the year, Saturnalia or no Saturnalia.'

'Why?' asked Jonathan innocently.

'I was about to tell Cartilia where she could put her tambourine.'

Lupus held up his wax tablet:

WHERE IS NUBIA?

'Yes,' said Jonathan. 'Is she all right? Yesterday evening, she ran out of the room in the middle of a song.'

Flavia frowned. 'She's still in bed. She said she wasn't feeling well. Maybe it was something we ate.' Then her eyes widened. 'Maybe Cartilia is trying to poison us!' Flavia pressed her hand experimentally against her stomach and frowned. 'Do I feel sick?'

'I don't think she's trying to poison us,' said Jonathan. 'You know, Flavia . . .'

'Yes?' Flavia turned her head to look at him. 'What?'

'I don't think Cartilia is evil. I think she's quite nice. In fact . . .' his voice trailed off.

'What?' Flavia narrowed her eyes. 'What in fact?'

Jonathan took a deep breath. 'She reminds me a bit of you.'

Flavia opened her mouth to reply, but at that moment Nubia came into the room.

Jonathan breathed a sigh of relief.

'I'll ignore Jonathan's last remark,' said Flavia coolly. 'Now that Nubia's here, let's review the facts. In my dream, Hercules told me I must complete twelve tasks. I believe the tasks are clues to solving a mystery which will save my father from Cartilia's evil clutches.'

The four friends were still in the dining room,

548

watching the wall-painter work on the last wall. Now Flavia twisted to look at the wall behind them and gestured towards the fresco of Hercules wrestling a lion. 'After we captured the lion,' she said, 'we learned that Cartilia was one of three daughters, and that the one nicknamed Paula was a bit strange.'

Flavia pointed to the next painting. It showed Hercules cutting snaky heads off a dog-like creature.

'Then we visited the Wise Woman of Ostia near the hydra fountain. She directed us to Cartilia's house. So that was the second task completed. The third task of Hercules was to capture the deer sacred to Diana. We found Diana, rather than the deer, but we discovered that Cartilia's nickname is Paula.'

'And that her sister Diana is a bit strange, too,' said Jonathan.

I DON'T THINK SHE'S STRANGE wrote Lupus.

Jonathan grinned.

Flavia gestured at the last scene painted on the wall behind them. 'Hercules' fourth task was the boar,' she continued. 'At the Baths of Atalanta, near a boar mosaic, Nubia and I overheard a conversation and discovered a possible motive. Cartilia might be planning to marry my father and then kill him off to get her hands on his supposed wealth.'

Jonathan folded his arms, 'So far,' he said, 'all this is theory. And some of your informants were drunk as weasels.'

'*In vino veritas*,' quoted Flavia. 'In wine there is truth.'

Lupus nodded his agreement and Flavia pointed to the central wall. 'Hercules' fifth task led us to the stables, where we found out that Cartilia had been asking which baths Taurus the gladiator used!'

'I do have to admit that's strange,' said Jonathan, unfolding his arms.

'And while you were hunting the Stymphalian bird – task number six – you discovered that Cartilia is a greedy old witch.'

'According to her sister,' said Jonathan.

'Meanwhile, at the Forum Baths, we discovered that Taurus the Cretan Bull – obviously our seventh task – was selling his bath scrapings. And that Cartilia bought not one, but *two* bottles.'

Jonathan shuddered. 'And again I say: ewww.'

'Task number eight,' said Flavia, 'led us to Diomedes the priest of Mithras. He gave us our most crucial piece of evidence. "It was her fault," he said. And he clearly meant the death of Cartilia's first husband, because he mentioned Caldus.'

'That is a pretty serious accusation,' said Jonathan. 'Was he drunk?'

Flavia shook her head. 'Sober as a Vestal.'

Jonathan sighed.

'So we have four tasks left,' said Flavia, opening her wax tablet and leaning back against the red wall. 'The Amazon's belt, the Red Cattle, the Golden Apples and Cerberus the Hound of Hades. Before we investigate them, I want to know what you think.'

Lupus started writing on his wax tablet.

SOMETHING NOT RIGHT ABOUT CARTILIA
SHE IS NICE EVEN WHEN FLAVIA IS RUDE

'I'm not *that* rude to her,' protested Flavia.

'Yes you are,' said Jonathan. He ignored her glare. 'I like Cartilia. I think she really loves your father, and the fact that she's being so nice to you is proof of that.'

'That's your opinion,' said Flavia briskly. 'What about you, Nubia? You're good at sensing when people are hiding things.'

Nubia was quiet for a moment. 'Cartilia is being very nice to me. But when you were asking about her dead husband on first night, her face is pale. As if guilty.'

Flavia nodded. 'And there's something else we're forgetting,' she said.

They all looked at her.

'The note. Diana gave Aristo a note asking him to meet her at the shrine.'

Lupus wrote on his tablet:

THAT'S NOT STRANGE
DIANA LOVES ARISTO

'And yet the note was signed Cartilia. Doesn't it seem odd that Diana signed her note Cartilia?'

'Her name is Cartilia, too,' said Jonathan.

'I know. But why sign it Cartilia instead of Diana?'

Flavia lowered her voice. 'I have a theory. What if Diana was only the messenger, even if she loves Aristo? Lupus says Aristo doesn't even like Diana. So what if the note was really from Cartilia? Cartilia Paula, I mean.'

They stared at her.

'But Cartilia loves your father,' said Jonathan.

'Does she?' Flavia thoughtfully sucked a strand of hair. 'Lupus, could the woman at the shrine have been Cartilia?'

Lupus shrugged and then nodded. He wrote on his wax tablet.

THEIR VOICES ARE VERY SIMILAR

'But why?' said Jonathan. 'Why would Cartilia want to meet Aristo?'

'That's what I'm trying to discover,' said Flavia. 'Nubia. The woman in the woods. The one kissing Aristo. Is there any chance she could have been Cartilia?'

'Yes, there is any chance,' said Nubia. 'It could be any woman, if slim and not so tall.'

For a moment they were all silent, watching Hercules spread fresh plaster on the last wall of the dining room.

Then Lupus held up his wax tablet apologetically:

EVEN MIRIAM?

'Lupus!' cried Flavia and Jonathan at the same time.

'Don't be yelling at Lupus,' said Nubia quietly. 'Everybody knows Aristo is loving Miriam.'

'It couldn't have been Miriam,' said Jonathan. 'She's been at my aunt's house since the morning after the betrothal ceremony. And Nubia saw Aristo kissing the woman the following afternoon.'

'Besides,' said Flavia, 'Miriam loves my uncle and I'm sure she's faithful to him.'

They all nodded.

Jonathan raised his hand. 'Um, Flavia? Why don't we just ask Aristo who he was kissing?'

'We can't ask him,' whispered Flavia. 'What if Cartilia is using her love potion to enchant him, too!'

Nubia gasped. 'Why?' she asked.

'So that he'll be under her spell and help her accomplish her evil scheme!'

SCROLL XVIII

The Wise Woman sat in the weak winter sunshine and spun her grey wool. As Nubia's shadow fell across her lap the old woman squinted up at her. Nubia clapped her hands softly and let her knees bend.

'Ah, the lovely Nubia!' Lusca showed her single tooth in a smile. 'Come, sit beside me. Shoo there!' She put the mass of soft wool on her lap and pushed the grey cat off the stool. The cat landed on the cold paving stones, blinked up at them with green eyes, then nonchalantly began to clean itself.

Nubia sat on the stool and extended a small papyrus parcel.

'Halva!' The papyrus crinkled as the old woman undid the folds. 'Very tasty and easy on my gums. Thank you my dear.'

The Wise Woman peered about. 'Where's your bossy young mistress?'

'She is not my mistress,' said Nubia quietly. 'She set me free three months ago.'

'Loyalty.' The old woman nodded. 'I like that. But I think she is still your mistress in many ways.'

Nubia was silent. The grey cat rubbed itself against her leg and purred.

'Your friend is a truth seeker,' said the old woman, 'and she has a warm heart. But she has not yet learned that the truth can be dangerous. And sometimes painful. Also she tries to control people. This is never good. She must learn to trust the gods.'

'I want to help her,' said Nubia. 'To help her find the truth.'

'Then tell her this. Most of the evil in the world arises from two sources: greed and passion. She has been looking for actions motivated by greed. But in this particular case the troublemaker is Cupid, not Divitiae.'

'Who is Divity Eye?'

'Not who. What.' The old woman closed her eyes and sighed. 'Though it should be a god. "Divitiae" means wealth and only one deity has more power in the hearts of Romans: Cupid, the god of desire. Sometimes called Amor. Or Eros. Your friend Flavia should look to him.'

'Thank you,' said Nubia. 'I think I understand. Thank you.'

The old woman's eyes were still closed and her face turned up to the mild winter sun. In its light her skin was as translucent as parchment. The spindle lay among the wool in her lap.

Nubia reached down and stroked the purring cat. Presently she rose to go, then gasped as the old woman clutched her wrist.

'How old are you?' said the Wise Woman, opening her one good eye.

Nubia was too surprised to speak for a moment. 'Eleven,' she finally said. 'I'm becoming twelve in summer.'

The old woman nodded. 'You also must beware of Cupid. You and your mistress. Neither of you are old enough yet. If you see him aim his bow, you must run. If by chance his arrow strikes, you must pluck it out, throw it far away and take whatever cure you can find.'

'Bossy young mistress,' sighed Flavia. 'Is that how people see me?' She had been hiding round the corner and had heard everything.

'Little bit,' said Nubia. Then, seeing Flavia's expression, she quickly added: 'Not so much.'

'No.' Flavia took Nubia's arm as they turned onto Mulberry Street. 'The old woman is right. I am bossy. But I'm glad I listened to you and let you question her your own way. I must try that some time.'

'What?'

'Just sitting there and not saying anything.'

'Silence is making people talk,' said Nubia.

Flavia nodded. She could hear the faint sound of pipes and cymbals.

'I wonder if she's right about the motive,' said Flavia presently. 'Not greed, but passion. I need to think about that.'

The music was louder and as they turned onto Orchard Street they converged with a funeral procession making for the Laurentum Gate. The girls moved up onto the pavement. They stood, their pallas wrapped around them, resting against the red brick wall between shuttered shopfronts.

Weeping men and women led the procession and finally came the bier, a litter with the body of a girl whose profile looked very solemn and sad.

'Oh, Nubia!' whispered Flavia. 'It's Bruta, the daughter of Brutus the pork butcher. She was to be married next month.'

Marriage made Flavia think of Felix, as she did so many times each day, and she sighed. She closed her eyes and his face was there, as it always was. If you see Cupid aim his bow, the old woman had said . . . No use running now. Cupid's arrow had struck her months ago and there seemed to be no cure. If anything, the sickness was getting worse. She could not even begin to think of marrying anyone else.

Flavia opened her eyes and shook her head.

'Come on,' she said, taking Nubia's arm. 'Hercules' ninth task was to get the belt of the Amazon. I've just remembered something. In the Temple of Rome and Augustus, Rome is shown as a beautiful Amazon resting her foot on the world. Let's go see if we can find our next clue there.'

Nubia looked up into the vast space of the temple. Green marble columns rose up as high as the tallest palm trees in the oasis. High above her, a dove fluttered from the top of one column to the next.

Two priests, their heads draped with togas, were

placing incense balls on braziers before the statue of Rome and Augustus. Pale gold beams of winter sunshine pierced the smoke that rose above them.

'There,' whispered Flavia. 'That's Augustus. He used to be an Emperor but now he's a god.'

'Augustus who is wearing five tunics because of the cold? He is now a god?'

'That's right. And the woman beside him is Rome as an Amazon.'

'Rome is a girl with one breast not being covered?'

'Yes. That shows she's an Amazon. A brave female warrior. Sometimes Rome is depicted as an Amazon. And see? She has her foot on the world.'

'That ball? That ball is being the world?' Nubia didn't understand. The sickly-sweet smell made her head spin and she reached for Flavia's hand.

'Yes,' said Flavia. 'And her foot shows that Rome has conquered it.'

Nubia squinted through the incense smoke at the statue's lovely face. Then she turned to Flavia. 'Rome-the-Amazon is looking familiar,' she said.

'I was just thinking that.' Flavia lowered her voice to a whisper, because one of the priests had turned to glare at her. 'Now who does she remind me of?'

Suddenly Nubia knew.

She turned to Flavia. 'The Amazon is looking just like Cartilia's sister, Diana.'

SCROLL XIX

Flavia took a deep breath and rapped the door-knocker shaped like the club of Hercules. Nubia had been right. There was only one man-hating female warrior in the town. She knew the secret of the ninth clue – the clue of the Amazon's belt – had to lie with Cartilia's sister Diana.

Now Flavia's heart was pounding. What if Cartilia answered the door? Flavia knew she had been very rude to her the night before. She should never have revealed her true feelings like that. Now she must pretend to be sorry.

Perhaps nobody was home. That would almost be a relief.

The door swung open and a woman in a fine mesh hair-net stood looking at them. It took Flavia a moment to recognise Cartilia's mother, Vibia. Without a wig, her natural hair was straight and grey.

'Oh. Hello, Flavia.' Vibia's voice was flat. 'Nubia. Please come in.'

'Thank you,' said Flavia, and took a deep breath. 'Is Cartilia here. I mean Cartilia Paula?'

'No. My eldest daughter is at the baths.' She led them through the atrium and into the study. There were no scrolls open on the desk and no pitcher of spiced wine.

'Do have a seat.'

'Thank you.' Flavia and Nubia sat in the same chairs they had sat in on their previous visit. This time Vibia did not offer them any refreshments. She sat stiffly in her chair and looked at the girls. Flavia thought she looked vulnerable without her elegant wig.

'Um . . . Does Cartilia Paula go to the Baths of Atalanta?' said Flavia, twisting the hem of her palla.

'Why do you suppose that?' replied Vibia, almost sharply. She shook her head. 'No, both my daughters frequent the Baths of Minerva, a *respectable* establishment.'

'Oh. Well, I wanted to see Cartilia because . . . I want to apologise to her. I was rude last night.'

Vibia let out a breath. 'I'm glad to hear it. You hurt my daughter deeply. She was weeping last night.'

'What? Cartilia was crying?'

Vibia nodded. There were tears in her own eyes. 'She has tried so hard to win your affection. Your approval.'

'I made her cry?'

'Does it surprise you that a grown woman can cry?' Vibia's voice faltered. 'You should have seen her when she got home, after your father said goodbye. She told me how angry you were about the tambourine. She thought you were just beginning to warm to her—' Vibia patted her hair and stood. 'Oh dear. I shouldn't be telling you all this. But when she hurts, I hurt. She's still my little girl, you know.'

'I'm sorry,' said Flavia. She felt sick. 'I really didn't know . . . I'm sorry.'

Vibia looked down at Flavia. 'Paula desperately wants your approval, Flavia. She loves your father so very much. The day she met him – a few weeks ago – she came back here and I saw that for the first time in years the sparkle had returned to her eyes. Since then she's seemed to grow younger and happier. Until last week. I asked her what was wrong. At first she wouldn't say. Finally she said: "His daughter hates me and I don't know why."'

'I think,' said Flavia, rising to her feet, 'I think we have to go now.'

'Wait.' Vibia stepped forward and took Flavia's cold hands in her warm ones. 'Thank you so much for coming to apologise. I can't tell you how much it will mean to Cartilia Paula. And how much it means to me.'

'Yes. Well. We must go now. Come on, Nubia.'

She was almost out of the front door when she felt Nubia catch her hand to stop her. Flavia turned, a rebuke on her lips, but she was silenced by Nubia's discovery: several cloaks hanging in the vestibule.

'That is a very nice cloak,' Nubia said, pointing towards one in particular. 'Is it Diana's?'

Vibia glanced at the cloaks hanging by the door. 'What? The grey one with the hood?'

Nubia nodded.

'No,' said Vibia with a smile. 'That cloak belongs to

me. Isn't it lovely? It's made of special wool from the goat's stomach and it's very warm. It was a gift to me from my husband.'

SCROLL XX

'Behold, Flavia! Mushrooms!' Nubia bent and lifted the basket from the front porch. A red ribbon was tied round the basket's handle and a papyrus label attached to it.

'Oh Pollux,' said Flavia. 'They're from *her*. Now I really do feel bad.'

Nubia looked at the papyrus label as Flavia read it out:

MUSHROOMS WILL MAKE YOU A GOOD
SATURNALIA
THEY ARE STUFFED BY MY OWN HAND
WITH LOVE
FROM PAULA

'They look tasty,' said Nubia.

'Pater's not here tonight,' said Flavia. 'He's dining at Cartilia's. But Jonathan and Aristo like mushrooms. Why don't we invite the boys and Doctor Mordecai round? Our storeroom is getting bare. They can bring the meat.'

★

'Any luck with task number ten at the Red Cow Dairy?' asked Flavia.

Jonathan shook his head but Lupus nodded.

'Oh yes,' said Jonathan with a grin. 'Lupus won at dice.'

'How much?' asked Flavia, arranging the stuffed mushrooms on a platter.

Lupus emptied a papyrus cone of almonds onto the wooden cutting board.

'*Euge!*' said Nubia. 'I can prepare almond dates for dessert.'

'Any luck finding clues about Cartilia?'

'No,' said Jonathan. 'But did you know there's a new tavern up by the river called the Atlas Tavern?'

'And . . . ?' Flavia added some dried parsley to garnish the platter of mushrooms.

'Well. When Hercules performed his eleventh task, to find the golden apples, didn't he get some help from Atlas?'

'Yes,' said Flavia. 'He held the world on his shoulders while Atlas went to get the apples from the garden of the Hesperides.'

'So shouldn't we try the Atlas tavern? We could go now!'

Lupus shook his dice box and nodded enthusiastically.

'No,' sighed Flavia. 'I'm thinking of calling off the whole investigation. We talked to Cartilia's mother today. It seems Cartilia really does love my father. Oh, and apparently her mother is Aristo's secret lover.'

'What?'

'I don't know, Jonathan!' Flavia turned to look at him. 'I'm so depressed. Brutus's daughter died and I made Cartilia cry and everything's so confusing. Let's just have a nice feast tonight and play some music and forget about our woes. Can you all come?'

Jonathan nodded. 'Lupus and I can come but father said he wouldn't be home till late. He has lots of sick patients at the moment.'

'Can you bring some meat?'

Jonathan nodded again. 'One of father's patients paid him with a leg of wild boar. Father doesn't really like pork, so we'll bring that.'

Suddenly there was a clatter from the dining room, then a thud.

'What was that?' cried Jonathan.

Nipur skittered out of the kitchen and Scuto limped after him. The four friends followed them through the garden.

'In here!' Caudex the door-slave was bending over a body on the floor of the triclinium.

It was Hercules the wall-painter.

'Dear Lord, not another one.' Mordecai straightened from the dining couch upon which they had laid Hercules. 'I'm afraid he's got the fever, too. This is the sixth or seventh case this afternoon. He won't be going anywhere for at least two days. We need to get him home. Do any of you know where he lives?'

There was a pause. Lupus looked up from examining Hercules' paintbrush. Everyone was looking at him.

Lupus shrugged.

'We only know his name,' said Flavia, then added, 'Hercules.'

'I know where he lives,' said Caudex, scratching his armpit. 'I can carry him.'

'But who's going to finish painting the wall?' cried Flavia.

As they carried the wall-painter out of the room, Lupus looked down at the paintbrush in his hand. And smiled.

Jonathan took a mushroom from the platter and nodded at Scuto.

'He seems better now.'

It was late afternoon and they had all gathered in Flavia's triclinium for dinner.

'Yes,' said Flavia. 'He was resting earlier but Nubia and I took him for a short walk in the woods about an hour ago.'

'See anybody "very kissing"?' grinned Jonathan. Then he clapped his hand over his mouth and looked at Aristo.

Flavia glanced at Aristo, too, but he was staring wide-eyed at the wall behind her.

Flavia twisted to look over her shoulder.

Somehow, the fresco had been completed and the sketches of the last two tasks expertly filled in with colour. In the eleventh labour Hercules strained to hold the sky on his lion-covered shoulders while Atlas stood before him with three golden apples. In the final scene Hercules led a three-headed dog towards a man cowering in a huge jar.

'Hey!' said Jonathan, his mouth full. 'Those two Herculeses look a bit like you, Flavia! Apart from the beard and muscles, of course.'

'Very kissing?' said Aristo suddenly. 'What do you mean by that?'

Flavia ignored him. 'It *is* me!' she cried. 'But we took Hercules the wall-painter home! How did he manage to finish . . . ?' She stopped and slowly turned her head to look at Lupus.

Lupus was staring at the ceiling, whistling a little tune.

'Aha!' cried Jonathan, holding up Lupus's right hand. 'The proof! Paint on his fingers!'

'Lupus, did you finish those paintings?' said Flavia.

Lupus nodded and started writing on his tablet.

'They are wonderful,' said Nubia. 'Almost as good as wall-painter.'

Lupus held up his wax tablet:

I HAD TO FINISH IT
PLASTER DRIES FAST

'He's right,' said Aristo, leaning forward to take a mushroom. 'If you don't finish painting a fresco before the plaster dries you have to redo the whole wall. Or leave it unfinished.'

'Well, I like them,' said Jonathan, popping another mushroom into his mouth. 'I think a beard suits Flavia.'

'Who is man hiding in big jar?' asked Nubia.

'King Eurystheus,' said Flavia. 'He's the person Hercules had to serve for eight years while he did the tasks.'

'He is looking a bit like your pater,' said Nubia.

'Great Neptune's beard! Lupus! You've made him look like pater!'

Lupus grinned and nodded.

'These mushrooms taste a bit odd.' Aristo frowned.

Jonathan nodded. 'Did you make them, Flavia?'

'No.' Flavia turned away from the fresco. 'They're from Cartilia.' She reached for one. 'Her note said she stuffed them herself.'

'But what is the stuffing?' said Jonathan. 'It's something brown . . .'

'Olive paste?' suggested Aristo.

'Or thick fish sauce?' said Jonathan, chewing thoughtfully.

Suddenly Flavia's blood seemed to go cold.

'STOP!' she cried. 'Don't eat them! They're poisoned!'

SCROLL XXI

'What?' everyone cried. 'Poisoned?'

'Yes!' said Flavia. 'The mushrooms are poisoned! Cartilia is trying to kill us off because we're getting too close to the truth! She chose the one afternoon when pater was out to murder us! I was right about her after all.'

'What are you talking about?' said Aristo, sniffing a mushroom. 'This doesn't smell very nice but I don't think it's poison. It smells like oil, and cumin perhaps?' He paused and sniffed again. 'Cumin smells like sweat . . .'

'Great Juno's peacock!' cried Flavia. 'It's the love potion!'

'Love potion?' Aristo frowned.

Jonathan looked green. 'You don't mean?'

'Yes,' Flavia nodded grimly. 'You've been eating mushrooms stuffed with gladiator scrapings!'

'Argghhh!' cried Jonathan. 'Love mushrooms! I'd rather be poisoned!'

'By Apollo!' cried Aristo suddenly. 'I'm going to murder her!' He slid awkwardly off the couch, jostling the table and causing the plate of mushrooms to clatter to the floor. The damp note had stuck to the bottom of the platter and now it lay on the floor, still attached to its red ribbon.

Aristo bent, picked up the papyrus and read it. Breathing hard, he looked at the dogs gobbling up the love mushrooms at his feet. Then he crumpled up the note and threw it to the ground.

'I swear I'm going to murder her!' he repeated, and rushed out of the room.

Flavia Gemina sat up straight on her banqueting couch and turned to Lupus.

'Follow him!' she hissed. 'And don't let him see you.'

Eyes bright, Lupus nodded, then jumped down from the couch and slipped out of the room.

Flavia looked round at the others. 'Whoever Aristo goes to is the one behind all this,' she said. 'If Lupus doesn't lose him, we might finally solve this mystery.'

Lupus followed Aristo through the dusk as silently as a shadow. Once he lost him in a crowd of revellers but by then he suspected where Aristo was going, so he took a short cut. He was already hiding behind the column of a neighbour's porch when Aristo banged on the door with the club door-knocker.

Lupus listened with all his might, shutting out the sound of the wind in the trees and the singing from the Peacock Tavern.

He heard Aristo's voice, low and angry, then a woman's voice. The wind died for a moment and he faintly heard the woman call out, 'Mater, may I borrow your cloak?'

Lupus took a breath and slipped closer, to the porch of the nearest neighbour. The twilight around him was a vibrant blue. Nubia called it 'hour of blue'.

He listened, and suddenly heard the crunch of boots on the paving stone and Aristo's voice almost in his ear. They were just the other side of the column!

'It was you who sent those mushrooms, wasn't it? You stuffed them with your disgusting potion. Did you really think that would work?'

'No, Aristo . . . it wasn't me. Don't look at me like that!'

'Then take that ridiculous wig off.'

'But you don't like my short hair.'

'I don't like that wig either. And don't try to change the subject. You sent those mushrooms. You pretended they were from your sister. Admit it!'

'All right. But I'm only telling you because I love you, Aristo, I don't want anything to come between us.'

'Us? There is no "us" . . . I don't love you. Dear gods, I don't even like you.'

'But last week. In the woods. Didn't that mean anything to you? The way you held me, kissed me . . . You told me you loved me then . . .'

Lupus heard Aristo groan. 'Did I say I loved you? I was beside myself. Some god must have possessed me.'

'It wasn't a god. It was her, wasn't it? You were

thinking of her.' Her voice was quiet, almost calm. 'You called me something. What was it? Melania? Is that her name?'

'Diana, please. I'm sorry, but I don't love you.'

'No. You love her. Is that it, Aristo? You love Melania and she won't have you? I'm right, aren't I?' There was a note of wonder in her voice. 'So you closed your eyes and imagined I was her?'

There was a pause.

'Something like that.'

'You vile crawling thing.' Diana's voice was quiet. 'If she causes you half as much pain as you've caused me then I'll be glad.'

'Be glad,' Aristo said miserably.

Flavia's eyes grew wider and wider as Lupus wrote out the conversation he had just overheard. The four friends sat on the central dining couch near a brazier full of glowing coals. Outside in the garden, night had fallen.

'Diana!' breathed Flavia, as she watched Lupus write. 'Diana was the one Aristo was kissing!'

Lupus nodded.

'So she borrowed her mother's cloak? The one with the hood?'

Lupus nodded again and added three words to his tablet.

AND HER WIG

'I'm an idiot!' said Flavia pulling a blanket tighter

round her shoulders. 'I should have realised it was Diana. Look at this label, the one that came with the mushrooms. The handwriting is the same as the note Diana gave to Aristo. I don't know why I ever thought it was Cartilia.'

'You haven't been thinking very clearly,' said Jonathan.

'I know,' sighed Flavia. 'And I'm still confused.'

'Me, too,' said Jonathan, handing back the papyrus. 'I understand the bit about Diana loving Aristo. But why did Diana sign the label Paula?'

'Maybe because Aristo wouldn't have touched the mushrooms if he knew they were from Diana,' said Flavia.

'Ugh!' Jonathan shuddered. 'I can't believe I ate three of those things. I hope I don't fall in love with Diana!'

SHE'S NOT THAT BAD wrote Lupus.

'Oooh!' said Jonathan. 'Lupus loves Diana! Did you eat some tasty love mushrooms, Lupus? Ha!' Jonathan laughed as Lupus wrestled him to the couch. Nipur and Tigris barked with excitement.

'Be careful, you two!' cried Flavia. 'You'll knock over the brazier and set the whole house on fire!'

When the boys had calmed down Nubia said: 'I think Diana is being jealous of Cartilia. In my clan I was having a friend who always strives with her sister.'

'Nubia, you may be right,' said Flavia. 'Diana hasn't

even been married once and her sister is about to marry for a second time. That's probably why she said Cartilia was a greedy old witch. She meant greedy for husbands, not money.' Suddenly she gasped. 'Oh no!'

'What?' said Jonathan.

'I've just had a terrible thought. What if Diana didn't just sign Cartilia's name on notes. What if she actually *pretended* to be Cartilia?'

'But Diana has short hair.'

'Yes,' said Flavia. 'And her mother has a wig! I'll bet Diana's been telling everyone she's Paula: Fimus at the stables, Oleosus at the baths . . .'

Flavia looked at her friends. 'We haven't got much time to find the truth. Tomorrow is the last day of the Saturnalia. We have two labours left: the Golden Apples and Cerberus the Hound of Hades. Jonathan. You and Lupus check out the Atlas Tavern, the one you were telling me about. Find out whether Diana could have been impersonating her sister. And find out anything you can about Cartilia's dead husband. That's the one thing I still don't understand. Why she acts so strange whenever I mention him.'

'All right,' said Jonathan. 'How about you and Nubia? Are you going to pay a visit to the underworld?'

Nubia made the sign against evil but Flavia nodded slowly.

'In a way,' she said. 'Yes, in a way we are.'

SCROLL XXII

Flavia took Nubia's hand as they gazed down at the tomb of Avita Procula. In the grey light of an overcast morning the fresco of the little girl and her dog looked flat and dull.

Although she had never met the girl whose ashes lay there, Flavia felt she was looking at a friend's grave.

'Coming here makes me think of the first mystery we solved together. Do you remember, Nubia?'

Nubia nodded, not taking her eyes from the fresco of the little girl lying on her death couch. Scuto and Nipur had watered their favourite trees and came up to sniff the tomb.

'Can you believe it was only six months ago?' said Flavia. 'It seems like so much longer.'

'Her tomb is making me think of wild dogs,' said Nubia.

'And of the three-headed *thing* . . .' Flavia shivered. 'That's why we're here. The final task of Hercules was to bring Cerberus back from the land of the dead. This is the only place I could think of which is a bit like the underworld.'

'I hope we do not meet any wild dogs,' said Nubia.

'Me too.' Flavia ruffled Scuto's head and looked around. 'We've been here nearly half an hour. There's nobody here. I don't understand. The clues of Hercules haven't failed us yet.'

Nubia touched her arm. 'Listen. Do you hear that noise?'

Flavia listened, then nodded.

'Over there,' said Nubia suddenly, pointing towards some umbrella pines. 'There is someone sitting at bottom of tree.'

'You're right. It's a young hunter . . . no! It's Diana, and . . . and she's crying!'

'I guess this is the one,' said Jonathan, stopping in front of the tavern and peering up at the crude fresco over the wide doorway. 'Does that look like Atlas holding up the sky?'

I COULD PAINT A BETTER ATLAS wrote Lupus.

'You already did. At Flavia's.' Jonathan grinned and then shook his head. 'If father knew I was going into a tavern . . .' He went up the three steps, then moved to the bar and rested his forearms on the marble counter. Its smooth, cream-coloured surface was inlaid with a pattern of green and pink squares. Lupus leaned on the counter beside him.

'Good morning, boys!' said the innkeeper. 'What can I get you?'

'Two cups of hot spiced wine,' said Jonathan, with

as much confidence as he could muster. 'Well-watered please.'

'Certainly. Would you like extra pepper?'

Jonathan nodded.

The innkeeper dipped his ladle into a hole in the bar. Jonathan leaned over and looked in. The wine jar was actually sunk into the bar. Clever. The man filled two ceramic beakers half full of a wine so dark it was almost black, then topped up the mixture with hot water from a silver urn. Finally he sprinkled some pepper on top.

'There you are.'

'How much?'

'Three sestercii.'

Jonathan fished in his coin pouch for a denarius. He put the silver coin on the counter and sipped the wine.

The innkeeper took the denarius and slid a copper sestercius back across the marble surface. 'Tasty?'

'Very.' Jonathan took a breath and before the innkeeper could turn away he said, 'My friend Cartilia Poplicola hasn't been in today, has she?' It was a feeble question but Flavia had told them to try anything.

'No,' said the innkeeper, and jerked his thumb over his shoulder. 'But her husband's here.'

'Wh-ghak!' Jonathan nearly choked on his wine and Lupus coughed so hard he had to be patted on the back.

'Sorry,' said the innkeeper. 'Too much pepper?'

'Cartilia's *husband*? Her *dead* husband?'

577

The innkeeper chuckled. 'Caldus is a bit hung-over but I wouldn't call him dead. That's him right over there in the courtyard. Talking to his friends. He arrived from Rome last night. He's the big fellow in the brown cloak.'

SCROLL XXIII

'Hello, Diana.' Flavia sat cross-legged on the damp pine needles in front of the weeping girl. Nubia sat gracefully beside her. Scuto and Nipur greeted the huntress with cold noses and wagging tails.

Diana looked up at them with swollen eyes, then dropped her head. 'Go away.'

Flavia and Nubia exchanged glances.

Presently Diana lifted her head again. 'Why aren't you going away?'

'We want to comfort you,' lied Flavia.

'So he's told you? He's told you all about poor lovesick Diana?'

'No,' said Flavia. 'Aristo hasn't said anything. We guessed.'

'Oh.' Diana hugged her legs and pressed her forehead on her knees for a moment. She was wearing Vibia's grey, hooded cape over her short red tunic.

'You're so lucky,' Diana whispered at last. 'You can be with him every day.'

Flavia opened her mouth to say something, then remembered what Nubia had taught her and closed it again.

'I remember the first time I saw him,' whispered

Diana. 'Two years ago. I thought he was a god come down from Olympus. He was walking out of the woods with Lysander. He'd caught a deer. A beautiful dead doe. I longed to be that creature, draped over his shoulders.'

Diana's head was still down and her voice was muffled. 'That was when I decided to become a hunter. And about a year ago I finally met him. Sometimes we went hunting together, with Lysander. Then Aristo went away for the summer and when he came back he seemed distant. He barely looked at me.'

Diana shivered and pulled her cloak tighter around her.

'Last month I found him hunting in the woods alone. I went up to him and told him how I felt. It was the bravest thing I've ever done. And he . . . he looked at me as if I was demented. He told me he could never love me.'

In the tree above them, a bird trilled its sweet song.

'That was when I cut off my hair and dedicated it to Diana. I vowed I would never marry, that I'd be a virgin forever. Aristo didn't like my short hair. And he didn't like me calling myself Diana. But I didn't care. I felt new and strong. At first. Then, when the gladiator arrived and they said he was selling love potion, I couldn't resist. I bought a jar and put it in the quail pie.'

'Can I just ask . . .' said Flavia. 'You know you're supposed to put some of your bodily fluids in it . . .'

Diana looked up at them with liquid eyes. 'Tears,' she whispered. 'I added my tears.'

Flavia breathed a sigh of relief and waited.

'Last week I was hunting in the grove. It was afternoon. The first day of the Saturnalia. I heard a noise. It was him. Weeping. I thought that perhaps the potion had worked . . . So I went to him, took his face in my hands. He let me kiss away his tears and then he was kissing me back. And then . . . and then.' She hugged her knees tightly.

'But later he grew distant again. So I bought more potion. But yesterday he told me he didn't love me and I realised it had never been the potion. I was a fool. And now my sister is going to be married for the second time. It's not fair. I hate her! And I hate Melania, whoever she is. But most of all I hate Aristo!'

Scuto sensed Diana's distress and put a comforting paw on her arm. At this, she burst into tears.

'And I wish . . .' sobbed Diana. 'I wish I were dead!'

The courtyard of the Atlas Tavern was filled with the pearly light of a cloudy day and the smell of sizzling sausage. There was an ivy-covered trellis against one wall, a small bubbling fountain and a single wooden table with long benches on either side. Four men sat at this table, and although they were not wearing togas, Lupus could see immediately that they were highborn.

'How are we going to approach him?' whispered

Jonathan. 'We can't just march up to him and say: "Hello, why aren't you dead?"'

Lupus shrugged.

Then he grinned as he heard a sound he recognised. The rattle of dice in a wooden box.

He knew exactly how to break the ice.

Flavia ran to her front door, slid back the bolt and threw it open.

She and Jonathan stood face to face.

'You'll never believe what we found out!' they both cried at the same time. And laughed.

'You first,' said Jonathan. He and Lupus followed Flavia through the atrium into the study. Nubia was already there, warming her hands over the coal-filled brazier. It was still early in the afternoon but the red sun had already slipped behind the city wall and the inner garden was in cold shadow.

'We discovered,' said Flavia, 'that Diana has been in love with Aristo for nearly two years. She's angry at him because he got her hopes up last week only to dash them again. Also, she's furious that her sister is engaged for the second time.'

POOR DIANA wrote Lupus.

'I'd feel sorry for her, too, if she hadn't gone around town pretending to be Cartilia.'

'She admitted it?' said Jonathan.

Flavia nodded. 'She said she'd put on her mother's

wig and cloak and kept her head down. She told Oleosus the bath-slave that her name was Paula. And she's the one who asked Fimus where Taurus the gladiator bathed.'

Jonathan nodded. 'Because she didn't want anyone to know Diana the virgin huntress was out buying love potion!'

Flavia stared at the glowing embers and nodded. 'I hate to admit it, but it looks as if I was wrong about Cartilia. She's innocent. Her husband must have died of natural causes.'

'No,' said Jonathan, folding his arms. 'He didn't. That's our news.'

Flavia looked at him, wide-eyed. 'He was murdered? You have proof?'

'He wasn't murdered and he didn't die of natural causes,' said Jonathan. 'In fact he's not dead at all. He's alive and well and staying at the Atlas Tavern.'

Flavia opened her mouth but no sound came out. Finally she managed a squeaky, 'What?'

'He's down from Rome. Staying at the Atlas Tavern. We gamed with him. We won two dozen walnuts and we learned that he divorced Cartilia.'

Flavia gasped. 'He divorced her?'

Jonathan nodded.

'But that's wonderful!'

'I know,' said Jonathan. 'Now your father can marry her and he'll be happy and you'll have a mother again.'

'Cartilia will never be my mother,' said Flavia fiercely. 'She's the one trying to marry me off and keep me indoors. It's wonderful because it means she lied to pater. Now I'll be able to get rid of her and keep things just the way they are!'

Flavia had no time to waste. She put her plan into action immediately. Lupus delivered her carefully-worded message and returned before anybody missed him, just as they were all gathering for the last dinner of the Saturnalia.

Flavia was so nervous she could hardly eat her ostrich stew. When the knock came at the front door her heart started pounding, and her hands were shaking, so she put her spoon down.

'Man here to see you, master.'

'Caudex!' cried Captain Geminus, climbing off the couch. 'What are you doing here? It's the last day of the holiday! You should be down at the tavern enjoying yourself.'

'Feeling a little tired, master. Thought I'd come home, have a rest.'

'Well, show this fellow in and then go and have your rest . . . Who did you say he was?'

'Name's Caldus. He says he got your message.'

Flavia glanced up at Cartilia. And almost burst out laughing at the look of surprise on the woman's face. Flavia kept her head down and bit her lip.

'Caldus?' said Flavia's father. 'I don't know anyone named Caldus.'

'Says he got a message from you.'

'Well, I suppose you'd better show him in.'

'Marcus, no. Send him away.' Cartilia was trying to get off the couch but a table blocked her descent.

'Sweetheart! What's the matter?' Flavia's father pushed the table aside and lifted her down.

'I have to go! I can't stay here!' Cartilia turned and started for the doorway, then stopped as a figure in a brown cloak blocked her way. He was a red-faced man, as tall as Flavia's father but broader.

'Cartilia!' His eyes widened as he looked down at her. 'Cartilia, is this some kind of joke?'

'Postumus,' she stammered. 'Postumus, what are you doing here?'

'I got a message.' He frowned around at them all. 'Who are these people?'

'I'm Marcus Flavius Geminus, sea captain. This is my home. May I ask the nature of your business with Cartilia?' Flavia's father stood behind Cartilia with his hands protectively on her shoulders.

'Oh, so that's it!' Caldus snorted. 'Trying to make me jealous, Cartilia? Or do you just want to rub my nose in it?'

'Cartilia, who is this man?'

Flavia felt almost sorry for Cartilia as she said, 'Marcus, it's my husband. I'm sorry. I was going to tell you . . .'

'Your husband? But you said he was dead!'

Caldus gave a bark of laughter. 'What? Tried to kill me off, did you? Not a bad idea. Far better to be a grieving widow than a divorced woman.'

'You're divorced?' Marcus looked down at Cartilia. 'Why didn't you tell me?'

Cartilia was silent, so Caldus answered.

'Because if she told you she was divorced she'd have to tell you the reason why! Looks like the joke's on you, Cartilia. Why don't you tell Captain Square-jaw here why I divorced you? Go on!'

'No!' Cartilia covered her face with her hands.

Caldus folded his muscular arms and looked down at her, then up at Flavia's father. 'I divorced her,' he said, 'because she was incapable of giving me children. And because she was too damned independent!'

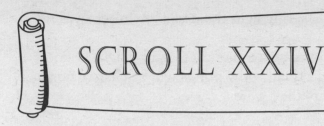

SCROLL XXIV

Flavia lay awake for a long time, going over the events of the evening.

After Caldus had left, her father and Cartilia had gone into the study.

In the dining room, while eating their dessert, they heard Flavia's father say 'How can I marry you now? You've broken our trust!'

A short time later the front door had closed and her father had gone heavily upstairs to his room.

The marriage was off. Cartilia was out of their lives. Flavia's plan had worked perfectly. She had won, but for some reason the victory seemed flat.

She rolled over on her side and gazed at her Felix doll, its face barely visible in the dim light of a night-lamp.

'I did the right thing, didn't I?' she asked him.

The doll did not reply.

'It was my task,' she whispered. 'Pater wants descendants and Cartilia wouldn't have been able to give him children. That must be why the gods wanted me to get rid of her.'

The Felix doll gazed back at her impassively.

'She lied to him! She broke his trust!'

In the flickering light the doll's tiny black eyes were steady.

'Don't look at me like that,' said Flavia. 'I know I did the right thing. Now things will be back to normal. Just the way they were.'

The next morning, it did seem as if things were back to normal. The Saturnalia was over. Alma made breakfast and Caudex unwrapped the ivy from the columns. Captain Geminus quietly made his offering at the lararium and went out early.

They resumed their lessons and after the boys went home Flavia and Nubia took the dogs for a walk among the tombs.

It was noon, and the sun was shining bravely.

As they approached a clearing, the dogs froze and Scuto growled.

'Behold!' breathed Nubia. 'The camelopard.'

'Great Neptune's beard,' gasped Flavia.

The camelopard stood in the pale sunshine. It had a body like a horse and a head like a camel, and its neck was immensely long. It was browsing among the branches of an acacia tree.

'Shhh, Scuto! Quiet!' commanded Flavia. 'Oh, Nubia, he's beautiful. Look at the pattern on his skin, and his long eyelashes. And his tongue is blue!'

They watched the camelopard until it moved slowly off into the woods.

The dogs looked up at the girls and Scuto gave a whining gulp.

'Good boy, Scuto!' said Flavia. 'You didn't chase it

away.' She turned to Nubia. 'One of us should go and tell Mnason. Shall I?'

'I will seek him,' said Nubia. 'Then I can greet Monobaz. I will run now swifter than the wind, before some hunters kill the giraffe.'

'What did you call it?'

'Giraffe. That is what we are calling him in my country.'

'I'll take the dogs back home then,' said Flavia and laughed as Nubia sprinted for the Fountain Gate.

Flavia followed the dogs slowly back. The day was almost warm. Birds were singing. The sky was blue. She wouldn't have to battle with a stepmother and there would be no more talk of marrying. Not yet.

And maybe one day – when she was sixteen and miraculously beautiful – Felix would carry her over the threshold in his arms. She didn't know how it might happen, but at least it was a possibility again.

Flavia felt a huge surge of euphoria as she pushed open the back door. Life was wonderful. It held the intoxicating promise of anything and everything.

Scuto and Nipur went straight to the kitchen and their water bowls. Flavia followed and hung their leads on the peg as they lapped thirstily.

'Pater?' she called happily. 'We saw the camelopard! Pater? Alma?'

Flavia bounced into the study, then stopped short. 'Pater, what's wrong?'

Her father was sitting at his desk with his head in his hands.

Flavia felt a cold sinking sensation, right down to her toes. 'Pater,' she said in a horrified whisper. 'Are you crying?'

He lifted his head and looked at her. His eyes were red and his cheeks wet.

'Oh, pater! Don't cry. Please don't cry.' Flavia ran to him and threw her arms round his neck.

'No!' He pushed her away. 'I just want to be alone. Please.'

'Shall I make you some mint tea? Would that cheer you up?'

'I don't want to see you right now, Flavia. Please go away.'

'What?'

'You sent that message, didn't you?' he said, then shook his head. 'It doesn't matter. Just go away.'

'But pater . . .' Her throat hurt and tears pricked her own eyes.

'GO AWAY!'

He rested his head on his arms and his shoulders shook.

Flavia looked down at him for a moment. Then she turned and ran out of the room.

'Oh, hello Flavia,' said Jonathan, standing in the open doorway. 'You just missed him.'

Tigris greeted Flavia with a wag of his tail and began sniffing her feet with great interest.

'What?' said Flavia, blinking back tears.

'You just missed him.'

'Who?'

'Felix. He left a few minutes ago.'

'What?' gasped Flavia. '*My* Felix?'

Jonathan nodded. 'He stopped by to pick up some more elixir.'

'Some more what?'

'Elixir. For his wife.'

Flavia stared at Jonathan. Nipur had moved on from sniffing her feet to sniffing the gutter.

'You remember his wife Polla wasn't well?'

'What do you mean, "Polla wasn't well"? She was barking mad.'

'Father says she was just depressed. He sent her some tonic last September and apparently it had an amazing effect. Felix was travelling back from Rome to Surrentum today, so he stopped by to pick up some more and discuss the dose with father.'

'He was here in your house? Just now?' Flavia felt as if someone had kicked her in the stomach.

Jonathan nodded. 'Don't you want to come in?'

'And you saw him?'

'Not for very long.'

'Did he . . .' Flavia felt sick. 'Did he mention me?'

'He said we must all come and stay with them again next summer.'

'He . . . What were his exact words?'

'Um . . . "You must all come and stay with us again next summer." Those were his exact words.'

'So he didn't mention me at all? Not even to ask how I was?'

'Tigris! Come here! Get away from that!' Jonathan focused on Flavia again. 'Sorry, Flavia. I think Felix was in a rush to get back. He was travelling light, on horseback with just two of his men.'

Flavia looked at Jonathan. His face seemed strange. Everything seemed strange. Why was she standing here in front of his open door on the bright pavement? Something was moaning. Just the wind. When had the wind started to blow?

Jonathan's face was sympathetic. 'Flavia,' he said gently. 'Come in and have some mint tea. It will – TIGRIS! I said get away from that! BAD DOG! Come here at once!'

'Excuse me,' said Flavia. 'I'm just . . .'

She turned towards her house, then remembered her weeping father and turned back to Jonathan. But he was bending over Tigris, struggling to drag the big puppy back into the house.

Flavia turned away and walked slowly past her front door, the blue one with the Castor and Pollux knocker. She walked past the brown door with its lion's head door-knocker, past the yellow door and the faded green one. Her step quickened. Faster and faster, until she was running. If she hurried she might just catch him.

She thought she heard Jonathan calling her but she kept her head down and ran. Past the green fountain. Out through the Fountain Gate. And down the tomb-lined road in the direction of Surrentum.

SCROLL XXV

'Flavia! Flavia, where are you?'

Nubia shut the back door and let the bolt fall. She bent to greet the wagging dogs, then stood and looked around.

'Flavia!' she called again. 'I am just now helping Mnason to catch the camelopard.'

No reply. The house was silent. Only the sound of the wind moaning in the eves.

'Alma? Caudex?' Nubia frowned. 'Captain Geminus?'

She went along the columned peristyle and through the corridor to the atrium. The door to Alma's cubicle was slightly ajar.

'Alma?'

As Nubia scratched on the door, it swung open.

Alma lay on the bed, a cloth draped across her forehead. She groaned and turned her head.

'Oh, Nubia,' she murmured. 'Not feeling too well. Bit hot. And my ears are buzzing. Just having a little rest. Caudex resting, too. Will you ask Doctor Mordecai . . . Will you ask . . . Will you . . . ?'

Doctor Mordecai shook his turbaned head. 'This is

bad,' he said to Nubia. 'Very bad. Lupus came down with a fever around noon and I've just put Jonathan to bed, too. And now both Alma and Caudex. How do you feel?' He pressed his hand to her forehead.

'I am fine,' said Nubia.

'And Flavia?' said Doctor Mordecai. 'How is she?'

'I don't know. She is not here. I think she is out with her father.'

Mordecai shook his head again. 'If I get many more cases it will be an epidemic. And I may not be able to attend everyone. Nubia?'

'Yes?'

'Can you make sure Alma and Caudex have plenty to drink? And keep them warm? They may want to kick off the covers, but they need to sweat out the fever. I'll have to treat them later. Do you understand?'

'Yes, Doctor Mordecai.'

'Can you make up a pot of broth? Chicken preferably. But anything clear and with some meat in it.'

'Yes, Doctor Mordecai.'

'You're a good girl,' said Mordecai. 'Bless you.' He rested his hand lightly on her head and she felt a sort of tingly warmth pass through her.

Nubia hoped it was not the fever.

Flavia waited for him under an acacia tree. Above her, the wind was moaning. In the space of an hour the temperature had plunged. The sun – exhausted from

594

trying to warm the world on one of his weakest days – was sinking towards the red horizon.

Flavia looked up at the rattling leaves. She wore only her tunic and she knew she should feel cold. But for some reason she felt curiously warm.

Presently her patience was rewarded. She heard him before she saw him. A strange buzzy pulsing tune filled her ears. It was unlike any she had ever heard. At last he came into view, gliding down the road between the tombs. He was riding a lion and he wore a garland of grape leaves. Strange creatures danced behind him. Mythical beasts who were partly man and partly goat. The satyrs played double flutes and shook tambourines. Behind them came a huge dog with three nodding heads: one white, one black, one red.

Flavia didn't care about the satyrs. She didn't care about Cerberus. She only cared about him. She struggled to her feet and called his name.

Felix turned his head and looked at her. Then he climbed down from the lion. Monobaz rolled at his feet, like Scuto when he wanted his stomach scratched. Felix took out a sharp knife, bent over and with one swift motion he cut the lion open.

'No!' Flavia cried. 'Not Monobaz!'

But it was too late. Felix smiled and walked towards her, holding the empty lion skin in his hands.

'It's all right,' said Monobaz's head. 'I don't mind.'

Felix put the lion's head on her, as if it were a hat, then he wrapped the empty paws around her shoulders. The fur was soft and warm. She looked up into his handsome face and he smiled down at her with his dangerous dark eyes. She didn't know if he was a man or a god.

'Felix?' she whispered.

He nodded, and placed a heavy shield gently on her head. Then he took first her right hand and then her left hand, lifting them up so that they supported the shield on either side.

Then he backed away.

'Felix!' she called after him. 'Come back! I love you!'

But now he was moving off down the road again, playing his lyre, his head back and his eyes closed. Behind him danced a crowd of people.

Jonathan and Miriam came first, and Mordecai too. Nubia danced behind them, playing her flute. Then came Lupus, banging his goatskin drum with a sponge-stick. Aristo followed, and then Diana, clutching the hem of his red cloak. Caudex and Alma skipped hand in hand. Pulchra was there, with her little sisters and her slave-girl Leda.

Then came Avita and her father Avitus. There was Captain Alga, old Pliny and young Pliny. And Phrixus. Vulcan rode his donkey. Rectina and Tascius and their nine daughters danced behind.

'No,' cried Flavia. 'You should have eleven now.'

The shield on her head was getting heavier and heavier.

'Why is it so heavy?' she asked Sisyphus.

'My dear,' he said, 'it's because you're carrying the

weight of the world.' And he jumped lightly up to join the others on the shield.

'Do you want me up there, too?' asked the Emperor Titus.

'No,' said Flavia. 'I can't hold you all.'

But he climbed up anyway.

'No, it's too heavy for me,' sobbed Flavia. 'I can't hold it. Pater? Where are you?'

'Right here.' Her father's voice came from up above. 'I can see the lighthouse.'

'Flavia,' said a woman's voice. 'Let go. You can't carry them all. You're only a girl.'

'Mater?' cried Flavia. 'Oh, mater, I've missed you so much.'

'Shhh!' Flavia felt a cool hand on her hot forehead. 'Let go, Flavia. The world will continue and the gods will have their way.'

'Won't everyone die if I let go?' said Flavia.

'Yes. Eventually. But you can't prevent it. Let go, Flavia.'

'I'm frightened.'

'Don't be frightened. Just let go. It will be all right.'

So Flavia let the shield fall and everyone tumbled onto the ground. Some of them were laughing and some of them were angry. But Flavia didn't care.

She felt lighter than she had ever felt before, and freer.

'Oh mater!' she sobbed. 'Promise you won't leave me again?'

'Shhh! I can't promise that. But I'm here now.'

Flavia felt her mother's arms around her – firm but soft – and she pressed her face against the smooth neck and wept.

And presently she slept.

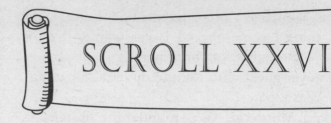

SCROLL XXVI

'Oh,' Flavia groaned. 'Where am I?'

'Father! She's awake!' It was Jonathan's voice.

'Ugh!' said Flavia. 'My mouth feels like something crawled in and died.'

'I know exactly what you mean,' said Jonathan. 'And I only had the fever for two days.' She felt his firm hand under her neck and tasted cool water on her tongue.

When she had drunk her fill, Flavia rested her head back on the pillow and looked around. She was in her bedroom. From the pattern of bright diamonds on her bedroom wall, she guessed it was mid-morning.

'What time is it?' She frowned.

'About the third hour,' said Jonathan. He was sitting on the side of her bed with a copper beaker of cool water. 'And in case you're interested, today's the Sabbath.'

'Saturn's day? But how can it be? Isn't today Mercury's day?'

Doctor Mordecai came into the room, drying his hands on a linen towel. His face looked thin and pale under the dark turban and there were shadows under his eyes.

'Doctor Mordecai, what happened?' said Flavia. 'The last thing I remembered I was waiting by the road for . . . How did I get back here?'

'You'll never guess who found you,' said Jonathan.

'Pater? Was it pater?'

'No,' said Mordecai. 'We found him upstairs in his bedroom. Everyone in your house has had the fever. All except for Nubia. You were lucky we found you.'

'Mater!' Flavia tried to sit up. Then she let her head fall back on the pillow. A hot tear trickled from the corner of her eye. 'I dreamt mater was alive. She was looking after me.'

Jonathan and his father exchanged glances.

'No,' said Jonathan. 'It was Cartilia. She stayed with you day and night for three days. She and Nubia tended you and your father and Aristo. Alma's better now. Caudex, too. Nubia's sleeping in the spare room, and Cartilia went home a few hours ago.'

'Oh,' said Flavia. 'I thought it was mater.' Her cheeks were wet and she turned to look at him. 'It was Cartilia? After all I've done to her?'

Jonathan nodded.

'It's thanks to her your father is alive,' said Mordecai. 'She called me out two nights ago when his fever was at its worst. If I hadn't treated him . . .'

'Is pater . . . ?'

'He'll be fine,' said Mordecai. 'I've just been with him. He's awake and he's having some broth. Alma's with him. I'm just about to check on Aristo.'

As Mordecai went out, Scuto tapped into the room and wandered over to Flavia.

'Oh, Scuto,' said Flavia, hugging his furry neck. 'I've missed you. Did you find me?'

'No,' said Jonathan with a grin. 'It was the last person you'd expect.'

Flavia looked at him. 'Was it Felix?' she whispered.

Jonathan sighed and rolled his eyes. 'No, Flavia. It wasn't Felix.'

'Give me a clue then.'

'Who practically lives out in the woods?'

Flavia thought for a moment. Then her eyes lit up: 'Diana?'

Jonathan nodded. 'Diana.'

Although the Saturnalia was officially over, Flavia's father had allowed them to recline for dinner on the pretext that they were still weak from the fever.

'Next week you're back at the table like proper Roman children,' he'd told them. 'But for the next few days I'll allow you to recline.'

'Those oysters were delicious!' said Flavia. 'Who sent them?'

'Pliny again,' laughed her father. 'He heard we were all at the Gates of Hades and he sent us four dozen, on ice if you can believe that! We still have a dozen if you want more.'

'No thanks,' said Flavia. 'I think my stomach shrank while I was ill. Lupus, do you want another one?'

Lupus shook his head, then uttered a deep, textured burp.

'Thank you for that compliment, Lupus,' said Captain Geminus and everyone laughed.

Jonathan tried his best to burp but could only manage a small one.

Flavia tried, too, without success, but Cartilia managed a rich yet ladylike belch.

Lupus clapped and Jonathan raised his eyebrows in admiration.

'Cartilia!' said Marcus, laughing, then he leant forward and kissed her quickly on the cheek.

'Marcus!' she said with a blush. 'Not in public.'

'It's not public. It's my home. I'm the paterfamilias and I'll do as I like. Any objections?' He looked around, his grey eyes bright.

'No, pater!' said Flavia with a smile. She was glad to see him happy again.

'I'm already feeling the effects of those oysters,' said Aristo. 'I feel like a new man. Nubia, shall we play some music?'

Nubia nodded.

'Oh yes,' said Flavia. 'I need to hear music so badly. Did you bring your barbiton, Jonathan?'

'Of course!' He smiled and pulled it out from beneath the couch.

Lupus already had his drums ready.

Flavia slipped off the couch and ran upstairs. A moment later she came back into the dining room. She went to Cartilia and solemnly held out her tambourine.

'Here, Cartilia,' she said. 'I'd like you to play it.'

'Thank you, Flavia!' Cartilia's eyes were moist. 'Thank you very much.'

Flavia sighed and looked at her father. He gave her the merest nod, and a smile. Flavia went back to the couch and stretched out beside Nubia. She still felt weak.

Aristo was tuning his lyre. He hadn't played it in several days.

Then he looked at Nubia and she looked back at him and they began to play together.

Presently Jonathan came in on his barbiton. Lupus was drumming but he'd found some ankle bells and wore them on his right wrist. They made a sparkling noise as he beat the drum. Cartilia's tambourine was perfect. It was as if she'd practised with the others for years.

Flavia smiled. They were playing 'Slave Song'.

As they played, she remembered another dining room in another time and place. And suddenly she felt his presence. As real as if he was reclining on the couch beside her.

He wasn't, of course, but when she closed her eyes she saw his face with its amused half-smile and beautiful dark eyes.

He hadn't come to save her. He probably hadn't even thought about her more than once or twice in the past few months. She knew it now with a terrible certainty. She knew the object of her passion was only a phantom.

The music and his image brought a surge of

emotion from her so strong that she had to bite her lip to stop the tears coming.

'No,' she whispered, digging her fingernails into her palms. 'No, no, NO!' And once again she slipped off the couch and ran upstairs.

'Flavia. Are you all right?'

Flavia lifted her head to see Cartilia standing at the door.

'Flavia,' said Cartilia. 'What's the matter? You look perfectly miserable.'

'You wouldn't understand . . .' Flavia dropped her head back onto the pillow.

The bed creaked a little as Cartilia sat on the edge of it. 'I might.'

Flavia buried her face in the damp pillow. After a moment she said in a muffled voice: 'I'm hopelessly in love.'

There was a pause.

'Tell me about him.'

Flavia slowly turned and looked up. Cartilia wasn't mocking; her expression was grave.

'He's married,' said Flavia. That should wipe the understanding look off Cartilia's face.

But it didn't.

'It's a shame he's married,' said Cartilia, 'but we can't always choose whom we fall in love with, can we?'

Flavia shook her head. 'And he's very old,' she added.

'How old?'

'As old as pater. Older maybe.'

'Lots of women marry older men. My sister in Bononia married a man twenty years her senior.'

'She did?' Flavia sniffed, then wiped her nose on her finger.

Cartilia nodded. 'And they have a very happy marriage.' She gently brushed a strand of hair away from Flavia's forehead. 'Tell me about this man,' she said. 'Why do you love him?'

Flavia had been longing to talk to someone about him. And Cartilia was listening. So she pushed her pillow against the wall and sat up in bed.

'I met him three months ago,' she said shyly. 'After the volcano exploded. He's not the most handsome man I've ever seen, but his eyes. The way he looks at you. And I love his voice and the way his hair smells and he's very important and everybody respects him but when he looks at me he really looks at me and I just melt inside. And I love him so much,' her chin began to tremble, 'but he doesn't even . . .' She was crying again.

'Good heavens,' said Cartilia. 'He sounds like an extraordinary man. May I ask his name?'

'Felix. He lives in Surrentum and he's—'

'What?' interrupted Cartilia. 'Not Publius Pollius Felix?'

Flavia's stomach flipped when Cartilia said his name. She nodded.

Cartilia burst out laughing.

Flavia felt fresh tears well up.

'I'm sorry,' said Cartilia. 'I shouldn't have laughed. But I suppose you know that half the women in Campania are in love with him.'

'They are?'

Cartilia nodded. 'I've never met him, but . . .' She smiled down at Flavia and then her eyes opened wide as Flavia shyly took her Felix doll out from under the pillow.

'Is this him?' said Cartilia, carefully taking the small wooden figure.

Flavia nodded. 'Jonathan and Lupus gave it to me for the Saturnalia. It looks just like him.'

'He's very handsome. I can see why you love him. But Flavia?'

'Yes?'

Cartilia held up the Felix doll. 'Isn't he a bit short for you?'

Flavia looked at Cartilia, whose eyes were wide and solemn. Then they both burst out laughing. They laughed for a long time and presently Cartilia said:

'Do you feel better now that you've told me and we've laughed about it?'

Flavia nodded and smiled.

'Will you still think about him all the time?'

'Maybe not . . .' But even as Flavia said it a lump rose in her throat and her heart felt too tight. She felt the tears well up again.

'Yes,' she whispered. 'I'm still going to think about him.'

'Flavia, you know the story of Pygmalion, don't you?'

'Of course. He was an artist and he made an ivory statue of the perfect woman. And then he fell in love with the statue and prayed to Venus and asked her to make the statue real.'

Cartilia took the Felix doll and gazed at its face. 'We are all a bit like Pygmalion,' she said. 'We create our perfect mate.'

'I don't understand.' Flavia hugged her legs and rested her chin on her blanketed knees.

'Pygmalion carved his ideal woman in his studio. We women carve the ideal man in our hearts.' Cartilia held up the Felix doll. 'We find someone whose appearance pleases us and then we create a man in their likeness and place him in our dreams. We build a whole life. One scene on another. And because we build them in our dreams, they're perfect. So we fall hopelessly in love. But we love a phantom. An image.'

'Yes,' said Flavia. 'That's exactly what I was thinking.'

'You don't really know anything about Felix, do you?'

'Not really,' said Flavia. 'But I still love him so much I could die.'

Cartilia sighed. 'You know what you have, don't you Flavia? You have the bite of the tarantula.'

'I don't think I've been bitten by one of those,' said Flavia. 'Unless it was at night while I was asleep.'

'No.' Cartilia smiled. 'The wise women of Calabria,

that's where my mother comes from . . . they believe that the awakening of first love is the most passionate love of our lives. This first love is so fierce that they call it the Tarantula's Bite.'

'Is it a bit like Cupid's arrow?' said Flavia.

'Exactly,' said Cartilia. 'That's exactly it. We just call it something else in Calabria.'

'Pater doesn't believe I'm in love. He says that I'm still just a child and it's only a "girlish infatuation".'

'I think he's wrong,' said Cartilia. 'Girls your age, on the cusp of womanhood, feel awakening love more acutely than at any other time in their lives. Your love is very strong. But Flavia,' she said, gently tipping Flavia's chin up and gazing into her eyes, 'you do know it can never be, don't you?'

Flavia nodded. 'But I love him so much. The longing won't go away. I've tried but I can't stop thinking about him.'

'If I told you I know a way to cure the Tarantula's Bite,' said Cartilia, 'would you be interested? Do you want to be cured of your longing for him?'

Flavia thought about it. Part of her loved being in love. But mostly it hurt too much. She looked up into Cartilia's warm brown eyes.

'Yes,' she said. 'I want to stop thinking about him all the time. I just want to be normal me again and think about puzzles and mysteries and stories. Is there a cure?'

'Yes,' said Cartilia. 'There is. It's a dance called the Little Tarantula. If you like, I will teach it to you.'

'Yes,' said Flavia. 'Please teach me.'

'Me too,' said Nubia, stepping shyly into the room. 'I would like to dance the Little Tarantula, too. I also have the spider bite.'

SCROLL XXVII

Nubia was trembling. At last she had told someone.

'You're in love, too?' cried Flavia.

Nubia nodded.

'Who is it?' said Flavia.

'I think I know,' said Cartilia softly. 'You love Aristo, don't you?'

Nubia dropped her head and nodded again.

'How did you know that?' Flavia stared at Cartilia. 'Even I didn't know.'

Cartilia beckoned Nubia, who came to sit beside her on Flavia's bed.

'I can tell by the way they play music together,' said Cartilia, putting her arm around Nubia's shoulder.

Presently she spoke.

'Usually we dance the Little Tarantula at the end of May, during the festival of Dionysus. But tomorrow night there is a full moon. We'll dance in the Grove of Diana.'

'Outside the city walls?' gasped Flavia. 'But what about the spirits of the dead?'

'They won't bother us,' said Cartilia. 'The god Dionysus will protect us.'

'It will be cold and dark,' Nubia shivered.

'Yes,' said Cartilia. 'At first. But as long as the weather stays dry, we'll be fine.' She squeezed Nubia's shoulder and laughed. 'You look at me reproachfully with those big golden eyes, but I promise you won't be cold. The dance will heat your blood.'

In the end there were ten of them.

Somehow, the young women of Ostia heard about the Little Tarantula and they slipped out of their homes and gathered at the house on Green Fountain Street. Alma let them in.

The men – Flavia's father, Aristo and Caudex – retreated to their rooms. If the sound of feminine chatter disturbed them, they gave no sign of it.

The young women drank hot spiced wine and gossiped and warmed their hands round the brazier in the triclinium. At last, when the moon's silver disc was at its zenith, they opened the back door and slipped out into the night.

Each one held a smoking torch and when they reached the grove they planted a circle of fire flowers.

Cartilia showed Flavia and Nubia how to hold the tambourine, not in the left hand, but in the right. She showed them how to keep the wrist and elbow moving but the forearm strong. She showed them how to let the emotion flow down the legs to the soles of the feet and through the arms to the fingertips.

'There will come a moment,' she said, 'when your feet will hurt, your forearms ache, your fingers might even bleed. You must keep playing; that is the point at which the god takes you and burns the passion from you.'

They nodded. Cartilia slowly started to beat her own tambourine and to sing. The women joined her and shook their tambourines, or castanets, or clapped their hands. Some were peasants and a few were high-born. Most were in their teens. Cartilia, at twenty-four, was the oldest.

Presently they settled into a rhythm and they began to dance.

At first Flavia felt foolish, self-conscious. What was she doing, dancing in the woods on a cold winter's night with strange women around her? But the beat was strong and soon the music filled her head.

Nubia was dancing the Little Tarantula as if she had known it from birth. Cartilia was lost in the music, too. Her beautiful dark hair – the colour of sesame oil – swung about her face. Flavia's forearms ached and her feet hurt, but the driving beat would not let her rest.

And then a figure appeared out of the darkness and joined them. It was Diana. She did not have a tambourine but she sang in a high, sweet voice and she begged the god to free her of her obsession.

It was then that the music took Flavia. Like a wave, it lifted her up and carried her and she was no longer tired. She closed her eyes and his face was there, so she danced out her yearning and her regret, her anger and her tenderness, her love and her hate.

Once, she opened her eyes and thought she saw him

standing in the deep shadows outside the torchlight. But she realised that if it was not her imagination, it must be the god Dionysus, watching his women with approval.

Flavia lost all sense of time. Above her the stars blazed in the cold black sky and it seemed to her that she saw their shining paths, like snail silver, arc across the sky. As she danced, his beautiful face faded and presently, when she closed her eyes, she saw only the red-brown flicker of the torches through her eyelids.

And by dawn, when the watery sun had diluted the dark wine of night, Flavia knew that at last she was free of love's poison.

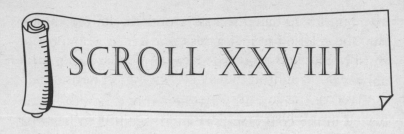

SCROLL XXVIII

Tired but happy, with dishevelled hair and blood-shot eyes, the group of women went chattering through the Laurentum Gate, laughing at the expression on the watchmen's faces. They had their arms round each other's waists. Flavia walked between Nubia and Cartilia, whose other arm encircled her sister Diana.

They went to the Baths of Minerva as the doors were opening and they paid their coin. They took off their sweat-stained clothes and sank gratefully into the myrtle-scented hot plunge. There, they let the steaming water soak away any remnants of passion, bitterness, jealousy and regret.

Back at Green Fountain Street, Flavia and Nubia slept all that day and through the following night. And when Flavia awoke from a sweet dreamless sleep, she rose and dressed and took her Felix doll to the Temple of Venus.

And there she laid his image down on the altar.

'Venus,' she prayed. 'I give you all my dreams of love and marriage and romance. I lay them on your altar.' Flavia bowed her head for a moment. The verse of a song Miriam often sang came into her head: 'By the gazelles, O daughters of Jerusalem, do not awaken or arouse love until it so desires.'

Flavia looked up at the statue of Venus. The marble goddess – caught in the act of slipping on her sandal – looked back at her in surprise.

'Venus,' whispered Flavia. 'Please do not arouse or awaken love in me until I'm ready.'

And it seemed to her, though it may have been a trick of the light, that the goddess smiled kindly.

That evening, after dinner, Cartilia came up to the girls' room to tuck them into bed.

After she had kissed Nubia's forehead she came and perched on Flavia's bed. Scuto thumped his tail and Cartilia scratched him behind the ear.

'I should have known you weren't evil,' said Flavia, 'because Scuto likes you.'

'Why did you think I was evil?' asked Cartilia, with a laugh.

'I thought you were the one who criticised pater for letting me be too independent,' said Flavia. 'I thought it was your idea to marry me off.'

'Not at all,' said Cartilia. 'That was your father's patron Cordius. He strongly disapproves of independence in women. That's why I told him my husband had died. If Cordius had found out that my husband divorced me for being too independent . . . Well, he never would have introduced me to your father. So my family all agreed to say I was a widow. It was foolish. I see that now. But I wanted to meet your father very badly.'

'Tell me again about the first time you saw him?'

'The very first time was over half a year ago. He was walking along the docks, talking to one of his sailors. The wind was in his hair and he was laughing and I remember thinking to myself: perhaps it's time I remarry. I asked my father to find out about him. Pater said he was a widower with one daughter and that his patron was Cordius, a very conservative man.'

'And then what?'

'He went away before I could meet him, but then he came back, as if from the dead. I thought I'd better seize the day.'

'*Carpe diem*!' laughed Flavia.

'Exactly. Pater invited Cordius to dinner and he invited us back. That was when I met your father.' She smiled. 'We got on very well. We laugh at the same things. He's kind and thoughtful. And he's honest.'

'So you weren't like Pygmalion. You didn't make him into your dream man. You didn't just fall in love with the way he looks.'

Cartilia flushed slightly. 'Well,' she said. 'I do have to admit I find him very attractive. Plus, he still has all his teeth.'

Flavia giggled and reached up to touch one of Cartilia's silver earrings; it was a pendant shaped like a tiny club of Hercules.

Then she remembered something: 'But someone said it was your fault your husband died.'

'Who?'

616

'Diomedes, the priest of Mithras. Actually I think his exact words were "He's not with us anymore and it's her fault." '

'Oh, that silly cult. I talked Postumus out of attending. All they wanted was his money.'

'But later he divorced you because you were too independent, and because you couldn't have children?'

Cartilia nodded. 'But he's just divorced his second wife for the same reason. So the fault may not be mine. As for my being too independent,' she dropped her voice to a whisper. 'I think your father likes independent women. The key is being subtle about it. And gracious. If you are those things I don't think he'll mind your independence.'

'Cartilia?' Flavia stopped toying with her earring.

'Yes?'

'Tomorrow is a special day in Miriam's wedding preparation. They call it the day of henna. Jonathan says all the women in her family go and they tell stories and play music while they put henna designs on Miriam's hands and feet. It's at her aunt's house and she's invited Nubia and me and . . . will you come with us? We're going about midday.'

'Oh, Flavia! I'd love to. Thank you so much for asking me.' Cartilia bent down and kissed Flavia's forehead and gave her a hug.

Presently she stood up and started out of the room. Then she stopped and turned and Flavia saw her slender silhouette against the pale rectangle of the doorway.

'Flavia. I know it's always hard to share a parent, especially if you're an only child. Thank you for sharing your father with me. I promise I'll make him very happy. And I'll try to make you happy, too.'

'I know,' said Flavia, and she smiled. 'Goodnight, Cartilia.'

Something was wrong.

Flavia's step quickened as she and Nubia approached Cartilia's house. The front door was wide open and Vibia stood weeping before a bald man in a toga. He was shaking his head and as they drew closer they saw that Vibia was not wearing her wig.

'Oh Flavia!' Vibia turned her tear-stained face towards the two girls. 'Tell your father to make an offering to the gods and come quickly. Cartilia and Diana, and my husband . . . They've all come down with fever and the doctor says it's very grave.'

SCROLL XXIX

Doctor Mordecai confirmed what the Greek doctor had said.

'This second wave of fever is worse than the first,' he said grimly. 'I've lost half a dozen patients in the last two days, four of them little children. I've treated Poplicola and his daughters. The best thing you can do now is make sure they drink plenty of broth and keep them covered. They need to sweat out the evil humours.'

Flavia and Nubia and Marcus stayed at Vibia's for three days. They helped her tend Cartilia and Diana, while she nursed her husband.

Presently Diana recovered and was able to sit up and take some solid food. But Cartilia's father died, and she herself slipped deeper into a fevered sleep. Now she could not even drink the broth. Her lips were blue and sometimes she fought for breath.

Once, when Flavia was sitting with her, she called out names in her delirium. First she cried out for her mother, then she called the name Marcus.

Flavia took Cartilia's hands and said, 'He'll be back, soon. Cartilia. He's just tired because he sat up with you all last night. He's having a little rest.' She felt the tears coming. 'Don't die, Cartilia,' she pleaded. 'Please get better. Pater loves you very much.'

Cartilia turned her head and though her eyes didn't open she seemed calmer.

Flavia pressed a cool cloth to her forehead and said, 'If you get better you can teach me more dances. And other things. Girl things.' Flavia tried to make her voice bright but the tears were spilling out now. 'Cartilia, I'm so sorry I was horrible to you. Please don't die. Pater needs you. And . . . I need you, too.'

Flavia had just finished dressing when she heard the front door close. She hurried downstairs to find her father in the atrium, standing before the lararium. He still wore his cloak and his boots were muddy. He turned as he heard her step, and the look of bleak despair on his face told her everything: Cartilia was dead.

'Oh, pater!' she cried, and ran to him. They held each other tightly and wept, standing there in the cold atrium before the household shrine.

Presently Flavia lifted her tear-streaked face.

'Pater, I know nothing will make it better but I promise I'll be good from now on. I'll never solve a mystery again and I'll stay inside and weave wool all day.'

'No.' He shook his head and looked at her through his tears. 'I loved Cartilia because she had spirit and intelligence.' He looked at the lararium. 'Your mother had it, too, Flavia. A passion for life and a deep curiosity about the world. That's what I loved most about her. And about Cartilia.' He looked at Flavia. 'And that's what I love about you. Don't ever lose your hunger for knowledge.'

'Then I can still be a detective?'

He nodded. 'Yes, my little owl. Just . . . be sensible.' He hugged her again and murmured into her hair. 'You're all I have left now.'

'I'll be sensible,' said Flavia. She felt the soft wool of his tunic brush her cheek as she turned to look at the household shrine. The ancestral masks were shut away but she could see the painted figures representing the genius of the Geminus household, and the lares on either side. And the good luck snake, coiling at the feet of Castor and Pollux and Vesta.

Flavia swallowed and stepped out of her father's arms so that she could look up into his face.

'Pater,' she said. 'Pater, I promise that I'll become a pious Roman matron and I'll have lots of children and then our family spirits won't be sad. And I promise . . .' Flavia took a deep breath: 'Pater, I promise I'll marry whoever you think best.'

The marriage took place seven days later.

The wedding procession was unlike any Ostia had ever seen before.

The young bride wore a white robe, a saffron yellow cloak and a veil of bright orange. On her head was a garland of myrtle and winter violets. The town of Ostia was clothed in white, too, for it had snowed the night before. And as the bride emerged from the house after the wedding feast, the orange sun came out from its gauzy veil of high cloud. The snow sparkled like marble and the lion-head drains wore icicle beards.

A black-maned lion named Monobaz led the procession and a long-lashed camelopard took up the rear. The beautiful Jewish bride and her handsome groom rode in a chariot pulled by two donkeys. Although dusk was still an hour away, Jonathan and Lupus held smoking torches, while Flavia and Nubia scattered nuts to the people lining the streets. Hired musicians played double flutes, lyre and tambourine, and the procession grew in number as they approached the Laurentum Gate.

Nubia wore her new fur cloak – a lion skin. It had been a gift from Mnason; the skin had belonged to one of his old lions. The combination of fur cloak and fur-lined boots meant that for the first time that winter Nubia felt warm outside the baths. When her nuts had all been scattered, she walked beside Monobaz and played her flute. The fresh clean scent of snow filled her head and she felt it scrunch under her leather boots.

As they passed under the arch of the Laurentum Gate, a new song came to her. It was a song about starting over, when everything is pure and fresh and clean. Nubia decided to call it 'Land of White'.

The wedding procession passed through the gate and made its way along the Laurentum Road.

The hired musicians had been playing a jolly, rather shrill air on their double flutes and lyre. But Nubia's flute was playing a new song now and the hired flutes wavered. Lupus handed his smoking torch to Chamat and started beating his drum. Jonathan gave away his torch, too, and swung his barbiton to the front of his body. Together, they made the beat harder and stronger. The flute-players struggled to keep up. Aristo hadn't brought his lyre, so he grabbed that of the lead musician who stared open-mouthed. Following his example, Flavia took the tambourine from another of the musicians.

It was a wonderful song that Flavia and her friends were playing now: a song of joyful hope with a driving beat.

As the procession moved on through the tombs, Flavia shook her tambourine and danced for Cartilia. She danced her regret for what would never be. For the laughter the two of them would never know. For the music Cartilia would never play. For the stories Cartilia would never hear. Or tell.

And when they left the tombs behind and moved between the woods and sea, towards the little house waiting in its snow-dusted vineyard, Flavia danced her joy of the family and friends who still remained. Her cheeks were wet but even as she wept, she smiled. Because although she grieved, she was alive. And that was a good thing.

Yes. It was very good to be alive.

FINIS

623

THE LAST SCROLL

Long before people celebrated Christmas, the Romans celebrated a festival called the Saturnalia. It began as a one-day holiday, but by Flavia's time it had been extended to five days. Much later, when Christianity became the official religion of the Roman Empire, church leaders decided to celebrate the birth of Jesus at this time, so that people wouldn't be tempted to celebrate the 'pagan' mid-winter festival. Therefore, many Christmas customs go back to the Saturnalia: decorating the house with green leaves, giving gifts, feasting and drinking. Even the riddles in Christmas crackers might go back to the practice of sending Saturnalia gifts with a short poem called an epigram.

The 'little tarantula' dance is real. Today it is called the Tarantella, and people still dance it in parts of Italy. Some believe it began as a cure for the first passion of adolescent girls. We are not sure of its origins, but we do know that as far back as Greek times groups of women sometimes used to go into the woods and dance themselves into a trance-line state.

Ostia was and is a real place. You can visit its ruins today. The characters in this story are made up, but who knows? People just like them might once have lived – and loved – in Ostia.

ARISTO'S SCROLL

Aeneas (uh-*nee*-uss)
> Trojan son of the goddess Venus, he escaped from conquered Troy to have many adventures and finally settle near the future site of Rome

Aeneid (uh-*nee*-id)
> Virgil's epic poem about Aeneas

alabastron (al-uh-*bas*-tron)
> a small ceramic perfume jar, designed to look as if it is made of alabaster

amphitheatre (*am*-fee-theatre)
> an oval-shaped stadium for watching gladiator shows, beast fights and mock sea-battles; the Colosseum in Rome is the most famous one

Amphitrite (am-fee-*try*-tee)
> beautiful sea nymph (minor goddess) loved by Neptune, god of the sea

Amphitryon (am-fee-*try*-on)
> mortal father of Hercules, (whose real father was supposedly Jupiter)

amphora (am-*for*-a)
> large clay storage jar for holding wine, oil or grain

Apollodorus (uh-pol-uh-*dor*-uss)
> Greek author who wrote an account of the Greek myths

Aramaic (air-uh-*may*-ik)

 closely related to Hebrew, it was the main language of first century Jews

Arion (*air*-ee-uhn)

 mythical musician from Corinth who rode on the back of a dolphin

Atalanta (at-uh-*lan*-ta)

 beautiful princess who preferred hunting to marriage and for this reason set impossible tasks for her suitors

atrium (*eh*-tree-um)

 the reception room in larger Roman homes, often with skylight and pool

Augeus (owg-*ee*-uss)

 a mythical Greek king who neglected to clean his stables

aulos (*owl*-oss)

 a wind instrument with double pipes; reeds probably gave it a buzzy sound

ballista (buh-*list*-uh)

 a type of Roman catapult used for hurling stones and other missiles

barbiton (*bar*-bi-ton)

 a kind of Greek bass lyre; NB: there is no evidence for a 'Syrian barbiton'

basilica (buh-*sill*-i-kuh)

 Roman building in the forum which housed law courts, offices and cells

Berenice (bare-uh-*neece*)

 a beautiful Jewish Queen, from the family of Herod, aged about fifty when *The Assassins of Rome* takes place

Bononia (bun-*own*-ee-uh)

 modern Bologna, a town in north-eastern Italy

Britannicus (bri-*tan*-ick-uss)
    son and heir of the Emperor Claudius, he was poisoned
    by Nero
Calabria (kuh-*la*-bree-uh)
    the region of the 'toe' of Italy
caldarium (call-*dar*-ee-um)
    the hot plunge in a Roman baths; usually with a deep
    round pool of hot water
Campania (kam-*pane*-yuh)
    the region around the Bay of Naples
Capua (*cap*-yoo-uh)
    a town south of Rome famed for its gladiator school
carruca (kuh-*roo*-kuh)
    a four-wheeled travelling coach, often covered
Castor
    one of the famous twins of Greek mythology (Pollux is
    the other)
Cerberus (*sur*-bur-uss)
    mythological three-headed dog who guards the gates of
    Hades
Ceres (*sear*-eez)
    known as Demeter in Greek: the goddess of grain, crops
    and food
Charybdis (kar-*ib*-diss)
    a mythical whirlpool near Sicily that could destroy
    entire ships
cicada (sick-*ah*-duh)
    an insect like a grasshopper that chirrs during the day
Circus Maximus (*sir*-kuss *max*-i-muss)
    long race-course in the centre of Rome, near the
    Palatine Hill

Corinth (*kor*-inth)
  Greek port town with a large Jewish population
cryptoporticus (krip-toe-*por*-tick-uss)
  means 'secret corridor' in Greek, usually a long inner
  corridor
Cupid (*kyoo*-pid)
  son of Venus and Vulcan, the winged boy god of love:
  those struck by his arrows fall in love
Cyclops (*sigh*-klops)
  a mythical monster with a single eye in the centre of his
  forehead
Decumanus Maximus (deck-yoo-*man*-uss *max*-ee-mus)
  literally 'the camp road', this was Ostia's main street
Delphinus (dell-*fee*-nuss)
  the Latin word for 'dolphin'; a constellation of the same
  name
denarii (den-*are*-ee)
  more than one denarius, a silver coin. A denarius equals
  four sestercii.
Dionysus (die-oh-*nye*-suss)
  Greek god of vineyards and wine
dithyramb (*dith*-i-ram)
  a kind of Greek hymn or poem, often passionate and wild
divitiae (div-*it*-ee-eye)
  the Latin word for 'wealth'
Domitian (duh-*mish*-an)
  the Emperor Titus's younger brother, twenty-nine when
  The Assassins of Rome takes place
duo
  Latin for 'two'

ecce! (*ek*-kay)

    Latin word meaning 'behold!' or 'look!'

equestrian (uh-kwes-tree-un)

    lit 'horseman', the social class of wealthy businessmen; to be a member of the equestrian class, you needed property worth at least 400,000 sesterces

Erymanthean (air-im-*anth*-ee-un)

    region of the Erymanthos River in Arcadia, a part of central Greece

euge! (*oh*-gay)

    Latin exclamation: 'hurray!'

Eurystheus (yur-*riss*-thoos)

    mythological king for whom Hercules had to perform his tasks

Feast of Trumpets

    the Jewish New Year (Rosh Hashanna) so called because the shofar is blown

Felix

    a wealthy patron and poet who lived in Surrentum in the late 1st century AD

Fortuna (for-*tew*-nuh)

    the goddess of good luck and success

forum (*for*-um)

    ancient marketplace and civic centre in Roman towns

freedman (*freed*-man)

    a slave who has been granted freedom. Also: freed-woman – a female slave who has been granted freedom

frigidarium (frig-id-*dar*-ee-um)

    the cold plunge in a Roman baths

fullers
   ancient laundry and clothmakers; they used human
   urine to bleach the wool
garum (*gar*-um)
   sauce made of fish entrails, extremely popular for
   seasoning foods
Hades (*hay*-deez)
   the Underworld where the spirits of the dead were
   believed to go
halva (*hal*-vuh)
   a sweet made of sesame flour, honey and tahina, often
   with added pistachio nuts
Hebrew (*hee*-brew)
   holy language of the Bible, spoken by (religious) Jews in
   the first century
Herculaneum (herk-you-*lane*-ee-um)
   town at the foot of Vesuvius, buried by the eruption in
   August AD 79
Hercules (*her*-kyoo-leez)
   mythological hero; he had to complete twelve tasks to
   atone for killing his family
Hesperides (hess-*pair*-id-eez)
   the daughters of Atlas, who lived in the remote west
   (modern Morocco)
Hippomenes (hip-*pa*-men-eez)
   mythological hero who beat Atalanta at a race by throwing golden apples
Ides (eyedz)
   The thirteenth day of most months in the Roman

calendar (including September); in March, July, October and May the Ides occur on the fifteenth of the month.

impluvium (im-*ploo*-vee-um)

a rainwater pool under a skylight in the atrium

insula (*in*-syu-luh)

a city block; literally: island

Jewish calendar

the Jewish calendar is a lunar one, based on the cycles of the moon, unlike the Roman calendar (and our modern one) based on cycles of the sun. Jewish months always begin on the day of the new moon. The fourteenth, therefore, always occurs on the full moon. Also, the new day starts in the evening.

Josephus (jo-*see*-fuss)

Jewish commander who surrendered to Vespasian, became Titus's freedman and wrote *The Jewish War*, an account of the Jewish revolt in seven volumes.

Judaea (*jew*-dee-ah)

ancient province of the Roman Empire; modern Israel

Juno (*jew*-no)

queen of the Roman gods and wife of the god Jupiter

Kalends

the Kalends mark the first day of the month in the Roman calendar

kohl (kole)

dark powder used to darken eyelids or outline eyes

krater (*kra*-tare)

big Greek ceramic bowl for mixing wine, often beautifully decorated

kylix (*kye*-licks)
 elegant Greek wine cup, especially for dinner parties
laconicum (luh-*cone*-i-kum)
 the hottest room in the Roman baths, the small
 laconicum had dry heat
lararium (lar-*ar*-ee-um)
 household shrine, often a chest with a miniature temple
 on top, sometimes a niche
lares (*la*-raise)
 household guardian spirits; it was the role of the
 paterfamilias to keep them happy
Laurentum (lore-*ent*-um)
 village on the coast of Italy a few miles south of Ostia
Livy (*liv*-ee)
 famous Roman historian, lived from 59 BC-AD 12
Ludi Romani (*loo*-dee ro-*mah*-nee)
 two-week Roman festival held in September and
 celebrated with chariot races
lustratio (lus-*tra*-tee-oh)
 a ritual for purification of houses, ships, etc.
Meditrinalia (med-i-trin-*all*-ya)
 Roman festival celebrating the wine harvest
Medusa (m-*dyoo*-suh)
 hideous female monster with snaky hair and a face so
 ugly it turned men to stone
Menelaus (men-uh-*lay*-uss)
 King of Sparta, younger brother of Agamemnon,
 husband of Helen
Messiah (mess-*eye*-uh)
 the Hebrew word for Christ; both words mean
 'anointed' or 'chosen' one

Minerva (min-*nerve*-uh)

    known as Athena in Greek: the virgin goddess of wisdom and war

Mithras (*mith*-rass)

    Persian god of light and truth, his cult – exclusively for men – spread throughout the Roman world after becoming popular with soldiers

Misenum (my-*see*-num)

    ancient Rome's chief naval harbour, near Naples

mortarium (more-*tar*-ee-um)

    rough flat pottery bowl, embedded with grit, for grinding spices, etc.

Neapolis (nee-*ap*-o-liss)

    a large city in the south of Italy near Vesuvius; modern Naples

Nero (*near*-oh)

    wicked Emperor; built the Golden House after the great fire of Rome in AD 64

Odysseus (oh-*diss*-ooss)

    Greek hero who fought against Troy, his journey home took ten years

Odyssey (*odd*-iss-ee)

    Homer's Greek epic poem about the adventures of Odysseus on his way home

Oppian Hill (*opp*-ee-an)

    part of the Esquiline Hill in Rome and site of Nero's Golden House

Ostia (*oss*-tee-ah)

    the port of ancient Rome and home town of Flavia Gemina

palaestra (pal-*eye*-struh)

the (usually open air) exercise area of public baths

Palatine (*pal*-uh-tine)

one of the seven hills of Rome; the greenest and most pleasant; the site of successive imperial palaces (the word 'palace' comes from 'Palatine')

palla (*pal*-uh)

a woman's cloak, could also be wrapped round the waist or worn over the head

papyrus (puh-*pie*-russ)

cheap writing material, made of Egyptian reeds

paterfamilias (*pa*-tare fa-*mill*-ee-us)

father of the household, with absolute control over his children and slaves

Pausilypon (pow-*sill*-ip-on)

modern Posillipo, a coastal town near Naples

Pella (*pell*-uh)

an ancient city across the Jordan river where the Jewish believers in Jesus (the first Christians) sought refuge during the Jewish Wars

Penelope (pen-*ell*-uh-pee)

faithful wife of Odysseus who waited twenty years for him to return from Troy

Periander (*pair*-ee-an-der)

mythological King of Corinth

pergola (*purr*-go-luh)

an arbour or walkway made of plants trained to grow over trellis-work

peristyle (*pair*-ee-style)

a columned walkway around an inner garden or courtyard

Perseus (*purr*-syooss)
    mythological son of Jupiter and Danae, his task was to get Medusa's head
Pliny (*plin*-ee)
    (the Elder) famous Roman author; died in the AD 79 eruption of Vesuvius
Pliny (*plin*-ee)
    (the Younger) nephew of Pliny the Elder; became famous for his letters
poculum (*pock*-you-lum)
    a cup or the drink in the cup; in this story a mixture of spiced wine and milk
Pollux
    one of the famous twins of Greek mythology (the other is Castor)
Polyphemus (polly-*fee*-muss)
    the Cyclops whom Odysseus blinded in order to escape being devoured
Pompeii (pom-*pay*)
    a prosperous coastal town buried by the eruption of Vesuvius in AD 79
psaltery (*salt*-ree)
    a kind of Jewish lyre or harp
Puteoli (poo-tee-*oh*-lee)
    modern Pozzuoli, Ancient Rome's great commercial port on the bay of Naples
quattor
    Latin for 'four'
quinque
    Latin for 'five'

Sabbath (*sab*-uth)
> the Jewish day of rest, counted from Friday evening to Saturday evening

sardonyx (*sar*-don-iks)
> semi-precious stone; usually orange or brown, sometimes streaked with white

Saturnalia (sat-ur-*nail*-yuh)
> Five-day festival of Saturn, celebrated by the giving of gifts and relaxation of restrictions about gambling, slaves and masters traditionally traded places.

scroll (skrole)
> a papyrus or parchment 'book', unrolled from side to side as it was read.

Scylla (*skill*-uh)
> a mythical sea-monster whose seven heads devoured passing sailors

sestercii (sess-*tur*-see)
> more than one sestercius, a silver coin

sex
> Latin for 'six'

Sextus Propertius (*sex*-tuss pro-*purr*-shuss)
> an elegant Roman poet who was a contemporary of Virgil and Ovid

shalom (shah-*lome*)
> the Hebrew word for 'peace'; can also mean 'hello' or 'goodbye'

shofar (*show*-far)
> a special trumpet made from a ram's horn, used to announce Jewish holy days

sica (*sick*-ah)
: small sickle-shaped dagger used by Jewish assassins (*si-carii*) in the 1st century AD

sigillum (*sig*-ill-um)
: a doll of clay or wood, traditional given on the Saturnalia; plural: sigilla

signet-ring (*sig*-net ring)
: ring with an image carved in it to be pressed into wax and used as a personal seal

Stabia (sta-*bee*-ah)
: modern Castellammare di Stabia; a town south of Pompeii

stola (*stole*-uh)
: a dress usually worn by Roman matrons (married women)

strigil (*strig*-ill)
: a blunt-edged, curved tool for scraping off dead skin, oil and dirt at the baths

stylus (*stile*-uss)
: a metal, wood or ivory tool for writing on wax tablets

Stymphalian bird (stim-*fay*-lee-an)
: fierce mythical bird with claws and beak of bronze

succah (*sook*-uh)
: a shelter woven of branches for the Feast of Tabernacles

Succot (sook-*ot*)
: another name for the Feast of Tabernacles, one of the great festivals of the Jewish year; for eight days Jews eat and sleep in shelters ('succot')

sudatorium (soo-da-*tor*-ee-um)
: the steam room in a Roman baths; often semi-circular with marble benches

Surrentum (sir-*wren*-tum)
    modern Sorrento, a pretty harbour town south of Vesuvius

Symi (*sim*-ee)
    Greek island near Rhodes, famous in antiquity for its sponge fishing industry

Tarantella (tare-an-*tell*-uh)
    literally: 'the little tarantula', a dance to rid the body of poison or passion

tablinum (ta-*blee*-num)
    the study in a Roman house

tepidarium (tep-id-*dar*-ee-um)
    the warm room in a Roman baths; usually for chatting and relaxing

Thetis (*thet*-iss)
    beautiful sea-nymph; mother of the Greek hero Achilles

Tishri (*tish*-ree)
    the month of the Jewish calendar roughly corresponding to September/October

Titus (*tie*-tuss)
    new Emperor of Rome and son of Vespasian, aged thirty-nine when *The Twelve Tasks of Flavia Gemina* takes place (full name: Titus Flavius Vespasianus)

toga (*toe*-ga)
    a blanket-like outer garment, worn by freeborn men and boys

Torah (*tor*-uh)
    Hebrew word meaning 'law' or 'instruction'. It can refer to the first five books of the Bible or to the entire Old Testament.

tres

Latin for 'three'

triclinium (tri-*clin*-ee-um)

ancient Roman dining-room, usually with three couches to recline on

trigon (*try*-gon)

ball game where three players stand at different points of an imaginary triangle and throw a ball to each other as fast and hard as they can; you lose if you drop it

tunic (*tew*-nic)

a piece of clothing like a big T-shirt; children often wore a long-sleeved one

Tyrrhenian (tur-*wren*-ee-un)

the name of the sea off the coast of Ostia and Laurentum

uno

Latin for 'one'

venefica (ven-eh-*fick*-uh)

a sorceress who uses drugs, potions and poisons

Vespasian (vess-*pay*-zhun)

Roman Emperor who died three months before *The Twelve Tasks of Flavia Gemina* begins; Titus's father

Vesta (*vest*-uh)

known as Hestia in Greek: goddess of the home and hearth (where the fire was)

Vesuvius (vuh-*soo*-vee-yus)

the volcano near Naples which erupted on 24 August AD 79

vigiles (*vig*-il-lays)

watchmen – usually soldiers – who guarded the town against robbery and fire

Virgil (*vur*-jill)

a famous Latin poet who died about sixty years before *The Twelve Tasks of Flavia Gemina* takes place; he wrote the *Aeneid*

wax tablet

a wax-covered rectangle of wood used for making notes

Yom Kippur (yom ki-*poor*)

The Day of Atonement, holiest and most solemn day in the Jewish calendar, when Jews fast for twenty-four hours to ask God's forgiveness for the sins of the past year. It ends the ten Days of Awe which began on the Jewish new year.